D1559879

TIM WAGGONER

Dark War

A MATT RICHTER NOVEL

ANGRY
ROBOT

ANGRY ROBOT
A member of the Osprey Group

Midland House, West Way
Botley, Oxford OX2 0PH
UK

www.angryrobotbooks.com
Off with his head

Originally published in the UK by Angry Robot 2011
First American paperback printing 2011

Cover by Vincent Chong
Set in Meridien by THL Design

Distributed in the United States by Random House, Inc., New York.

ISBN: 978-0-85766-112-8
eBook ISBN: 978-0-85766-113-5

Printed in the United States of America

9 8 7 6 5 4 3 2 1

DARK WAR

ONE

The air rippled like disturbed water, and the world folded in on itself, distorting this way and that, as if reality had been thrown into a vast cosmic Mixmaster and some deity had hit the on switch. When time and space finally decided to behave themselves once again, Devona and I found ourselves standing in exactly the same place as when we'd left. Except not.

"This is as close as I can get you," Darius said. "The wardspells on the *House* prevent me from materializing inside. Otherwise, I'd take you all the way in."

Darius had been holding onto our arms, but now that we'd reached our destination, he released his grip. The three of us – Darius, Devona, and I – stood in an alley across the street from a familiar white three-story building with green shutters and matching shingles. The *House of Dark Delights* was located on the southeast end of Sybarite Street within the Sprawl, the Dominion of the Demon Queen Varvara. At least, that's who rules the Sprawl in our Nekropolis, but I wasn't sure who was in charge in this one. Maybe no one, if the chaos raging in the street was any indication.

The Sprawl is a nightmarish combination of Vegas and rush-hour Manhattan, where predators of all kinds come to stalk their prey, and where, if the hunters aren't careful, they can all too easily become the hunted. The sidewalks of the Sprawl are choked with people in search of thrills – the darker and more decadent, the better – and the never-ending traffic roars by at speeds so appalling that even the most experienced Autobahn driver back on Earth would give serious thought to selling their car and converting to pedestrianism. And this wasn't just any street in the Sprawl – this was Sybarite Street, where the best (or worst, depending on your point of view) bars, clubs, restaurants, shops, and attractions in the city were located. So a certain amount of madness and mayhem was normal here. But the pandemonium currently raging in the street was shocking, even by Nekropolitan standards.

Bestial creatures of a type I'd never seen before filled the streets. They possessed similar features – pronounced brow ridges, sharp jagged teeth, bloodshot eyes, clawed hands, long shaggy hair – and misshapen bodies whose arms and legs didn't always match: some limbs were short and thickly muscled, while others were overlong and skeletally thin. Along with their twisted physiology, the creatures shared a similarly crazed temperament. They broke windows, tore doors off hinges, even bent street lamps and overturned cars with incredible strength. They gorged on food, swilled

booze, injected drugs, had sex – consensual or not – out
in the open, with no regard for modesty or shame. They
raced cars up and down the street, ramming into other
vehicles, mowing down pedestrians, or slamming into
buildings. Most of all, they fought each other with savage delight, sometimes using weapons, but more often
employing only their claws and fangs. Blood ran freely,
spraying the air, splattering onto the ground, and running through the gutters in crimson streams. Dead
bodies littered the sidewalks and streets, and more than
a few of the creatures took advantage of the carnage to
indulge in a bit of cannibalism or necrophilia, often at
the same time. And all the while the creatures laughed,
shouted, and roared with delight, even when their actions left them wounded, mutilated, or dying – or
perhaps especially then. Pleasure or pain, it was all the
same to them. The beasts appeared to live only for sensation, the more intense the better.

It only made sense, though, considering what the
creatures were: the physical incarnation of everything
cruel and selfish within a man or woman's soul, liber-
ated from all restraint and conscience and given free
rein to do whatever they pleased, and *to* whomever
they pleased.

They were Hydes.

The Sprawl is never quiet, but the chaotic din here
was so loud that we had to shout to hear each other. I
was grateful that my eardrums were as dead as the rest
of me, or else I might've found the noise level painful
instead of merely irritating.

"You told us it was bad here, but I never imagined it would be anything like this!" Devona said. "You should've brought an army instead of just the two of us!"

Darius shrugged. "It's hard enough traveling between dimensions on my own, let alone bringing people with me. Two is about all I can manage."

"Two is good," I said. "I've been getting sick of tagalongs, lately."

Devona looked out upon the mad riot taking place before us, her brow furrowing in concentration. Our goal was simply stated: we needed to enter the *House of Dark Delights* and put a stop to the madness that had gripped this Nekropolis – but in order to do that, we first had to cross the hellish war zone that was Sybarite Street. Devona was busy trying to figure out a way to make that happen, but she was an expert in security, not battle strategy. We share a telepathic link that enables us to know what the other is feeling most of the time, and I could sense her mounting anxiety. She felt as if she was in way over her head here, and I didn't blame her. I felt the same way. Devona and I had been in dangerous situations before, but nothing quite like this. I wasn't afraid of getting hurt or killed. I'm a zombie. I don't feel pain, and I'm just about as dead as I'm ever going to be. Don't get me wrong: I wasn't eager to step out into the street and be torn apart by those psychotic creatures, but only because it would be a real pain in the ass to put me back together. I was afraid for Devona. Normally she can handle herself in a fight just fine. She's smart as hell, and as a half-vampire, she's supernaturally strong and swift – but she was also several months pregnant.

She turned to look at me. "What do you think?"

"I think this is the last time I accept an invitation to travel to a parallel world."

A few hours earlier, Devona and I had been working at the Midnight Watch, the security business she owns and I sometimes help out with. Dr Moreau, the scientist who runs the *House of Pain*, was planning a big shindig to celebrate the unveiling of a whole new line of genetic mutations, kind of like the Nekropolis version of a fashion show. Devona had been building the business by leaps and bounds since she'd started it, and Dr M – impressed by the Midnight Watch's growing reputation – had come to her to handle the security for his event. It was a high-profile gig, and Devona was determined that everything would go off without a hitch. We were in her office, going over her security plans for the tenth time – well, she was going over them; I was doing my best to look like I was still paying attention – when Darius appeared out of nowhere. The Sideways Man explained to us that he'd just come from an alternate Nekropolis that was in desperate need of our help.

"Not to sound unsympathetic," I'd told him, "but I have a hard enough time trying to keep *this* Nekropolis in one piece. Don't they have anyone over there who can take care of the problem, whatever it is?"

"One man was working on it, but he got captured. He did manage to get a message to me, though. It was very simple: *Go get Matt.*"

"How do you know he meant me? Maybe he was referring to a different Matt."

Darius smiled. "I doubt it, considering the man who gave me the message was you."

I could hardly turn down a request for help from myself, could I?

Devona and I stopped worrying about Dr M's mutant extravaganza as Darius filled us in on what was happening in that other Nekropolis. When he finished, we left the Midnight Watch, made a stop to pick up supplies, and then Darius did his thing – I'm not sure how; he's pretty closemouthed about how his abilities work – and we found ourselves transported to this insane version of our city. Well… more insane than usual.

I'd had reservations about Devona coming along, given her current, ah, state of health, but she insisted, told me that she was made of sterner stuff than a fully human woman and added that I should stop being such a typical man. I'd pointed out to her that since I was a self-willed zombie – the only one that's ever existed, from what I've been told – I was hardly a typical anything, but she just said, "Dead or alive, a man's a man," and that was the end of that. But now that we were here and I could see just how bad the situation was in this Nekropolis, I wished I'd tried harder to talk her out of coming. But we were here now, for better or worse, and we had a job to do.

Devona was an attractive petite blonde who looked to be in her late twenties but was actually closer to eighty. The half-vampire blood flowing through her veins that gave her supernatural strength had the side benefit of keeping her looking young. When working, she usually wears a skin-tight black leather outfit which is something of a fetishist's dream – and which I appreciate looking at quite a bit. Hey, I may be dead, but I'm not *that* dead. Devona's outfit was a bit snug around her belly, but since she was only a few months along in her pregnancy, she could still fit into her gear, though I doubted she'd be able to for much longer.

Unlike Devona, my supernatural state of non-life doesn't do much for my appearance. I still look like I'm in my late thirties – and always will, I suppose – but unless I've had a recent application of preservative spells courtesy of Papa Chatha, my local houngan, my skin tends to be grayish green and flaky around the edges. Basically, I often look – and unfortunately smell – like something that's been left to mold in the refrigerator too long. This day I was halfway through the cycle of my current round of preservative spells, so while my flesh was a bit discolored and I smelled like trash that needed to be taken out, all things considered I wasn't too bad. When I was alive and living on Earth (in Cleveland, to be precise), I'd worked as a homicide detective, and I still dressed like I had then: white shirt, gray suit, black shoes, and tie. I tended to wear ties with cartoon characters on them – Looney Tunes are a particular favorite – and today I was sporting my Tasmanian Devil tie.

We needed to get across the street and enter the *House of Dark Delights*, and before we'd left our dimension, we'd worked out a plan for accomplishing this. The only problem was we hadn't realized just how many of the rampaging Hydes would be in our way. I was starting to regret my earlier comment about being glad Darius had brought only Devona and me. From the looks of things, we could've used some backup. Overkill would've come in handy right then, or maybe the Crimson Shadow. But the three of us would have to do.

I turned to Devona and started to speak, but I stopped myself before the first word came out. As a zombie, I'm not exactly the fastest creature in the supernatural kingdom. Even a normal living human is faster than I am. Devona can move far more swiftly than me – not to mention how much stronger she is – and when it came to carrying out an attack, it only made sense for her to take the lead. I wasn't sexist. As a cop, I'd worked with plenty of women who were just as good if not better at their jobs than men were, and Devona and I had worked enough cases together for me to fully respect her capabilities. But no matter how hard I tried, I couldn't put aside the fact that Devona was pregnant. It should've been impossible. After all, she's a half-vampire and I'm dead – meaning than I'm not functional in certain key biological areas, if you catch my drift. But not long ago, I'd helped recover a stolen artifact for Edrigu, the Darklord who rules the Dead, and he'd rewarded me with a magical coin that could grant me one day, and one day only, of mortal life again.

Once it became possible for Devona and me to have children, we discussed whether we wanted to. Devona was more than eager, me less so. After all, Nekropolis can be an insanely dangerous place – not exactly the best environment for raising children. But in the end I agreed and used the coin, and afterward, I was able to, er, get back in the game, so to speak. But things rarely go smoothly in Nekropolis. There were complications and we almost missed our opportunity, but that, as they say, is a story for another time. In the end, we managed to accomplish our goal and – with a bit of help from a fertility spell provided by Papa Chatha – Devona had conceived. So while I'm certain I'd have been hesitant for Devona to spring into action even if her pregnancy had been a normal one, the fact that it was literally a once-in-a-lifetime event made me even more reluctant to see her rush into a street full of homicidal monsters.

She recognized my hesitation for what it was, and she reached out to squeeze my arm in a familiar gesture of reassurance. I can't feel touch, but I can feel pressure, so she always makes sure to squeeze hard.

"Don't worry, Matt. I'll be OK." Her tone was confident, but I could see a trace of worry in her eyes, and I knew she was having similar thoughts, even if she'd never admit to it. But she didn't have to. Our telepathic link told me the truth.

I told myself that she was a fully capable adult who'd proven on numerous occasions that she could handle herself in dangerous situations. And we'd known this was going to be a risky mission when we'd agreed to accompany Darius. Still, it's not an easy thing to see the woman you love walk into battle – especially when she's carrying your child.

I was about to lie and tell her I knew she was going to be OK, when a rustling noise sounded behind us in the alley. The three of us turned to look and saw a hulking female Hyde like those rioting out in the street. The same bestial aspect and mismatched limbs, the same madness gleaming in her eyes, but there was one important difference: this creature had no skin.

"What do we have here?" she said in a guttural voice. Her red wet facial muscles pulled her mouth into a leering smile, the better to display her mouthful of sharp, jagged teeth. "You three need to join the party."

She leaned forward and I thought at first she was going to attack us, but instead she opened her mouth wide and breathed on us. Devona and Darius immediately started gagging, and I knew that the Hyde's breath must've been truly horrendous. Fortunately, the stench had no effect on me. Sometimes there are advantages to being dead, such as no functioning sense of smell.

The Hyde straightened and watched us for a moment, almost as if she were waiting for something to happen. When nothing did, she scowled.

"What's wrong? Why haven't you changed?"

"Well, Glassine, I'm a zombie, so I only breathe in order to take in enough air to speak. Since no air exchange occurs within my lungs, I can't be infected by the plague you're carrying. And as for my companions, they were each inoculated against your disease before we left home."

Glassine's scowl deepened. "How do you know my name?"

"We have a Glassine back where I come from. Her ancestor was a scientist who invented a formula for invisibility. Unfortunately, when she tried to use the formula on herself, it only made her skin transparent. Looks like the same thing happened to you in this dimension too."

Glassine leaned forward, her eyes narrowing as she got a better look at me.

"Do I know you?"

"One of me, maybe."

I reached inside one of jacket pockets and brought out a gun. It wasn't my 9mm – I carry that on a shoulder holster hidden by my jacket – and it wasn't my squirt gun, which I keep filled with a combination of holy water, garlic juice, liquid wolfsbane, and a few other special ingredients. This was a gleaming chrome device that looked more like a piece of medical equipment than a weapon. Fortunately for me, it was both. I squeezed the trigger and a burst of yellow gas struck Glassine in the face. She pulled back, coughing.

"What – the hell – was that?" she demanded between coughs.

"A cure for what ails you," I said.

Glassine's coughing gave way to harsh gagging, and she clawed at her throat, desperate to catch a breath. Her eyes bulged wildly, and for an instant I feared that the chemical I'd dosed her with had poisoned her – perhaps due to some unanticipated physiological differences between denizens of this Nekropolis and mine – but a moment later her breathing eased and a transformation began to sweep over her body. Her skin remained transparent, which was a natural state for her, but her body became symmetrical again – arms and legs properly proportioned and the same length – her claws became fingernails, and her teeth receded into her gums, becoming less sharp. Her wild tangle of hair smoothed out, her pronounced brow became less so, and best of all, the feral gleam in her eyes faded, to be replaced by confusion.

Glassine, normal once more – or at least looking *her* version of normal – took in the three of us, and while I saw recognition in her eyes, it didn't drive out the confusion.

"Matt? Devona? Is that you?" Her voice, though no longer guttural, was a bit raspy. The after-effect of all that coughing, I supposed. "You both look so different."

"I hate to do this, Glassine, but I really don't have a choice." I stepped forward, shifted my gas gun to my left hand, balled my right hand into a fist, and struck Glassine a solid blow to the jaw. Her eyes rolled white, her body went limp, and she started to collapse. Devona darted forward lightning-fast and caught the transparent woman before she could fall and lowered her gently to the ground.

Devona scowled at me as she straightened. "Did you have to hit her so hard?"

"I had to make sure she went down before she could be re-infected." As if to illustrate my words, Glassine's body convulsed and she began to change back to her bestial state. Thankfully, she remained unconscious once the transformation was complete. I had no idea how long she'd stay that way, though.

"Damn, that was fast!" Devona said. She turned to Darius. "You weren't exaggerating when you told us how contagious the Hyde plague was."

I scowled as a thought occurred to me. "If it's so contagious," I said to Darius, "how did you avoid getting infected the last time you were here?"

He smiled. "Who said I did? But I've picked up a lot of interesting… souvenirs during my travels between Nekropolises… Nekropoli? A universal antidote was one of them. Unfortunately, I used my final dose during my last trip here to counteract the transformation just as it started to take hold of me. If it wasn't for Bennie's inoculation, I'd look like her right now." He nodded to Glassine.

"At least she's out of action for the time being," I said. "With any luck, she'll stay unconscious until it's all over."

"We can't just leave her here," Devona said. "If one of the others finds her like this, she'll be easy prey."

"We don't have time to move her," I pointed out. "The longer we stand here talking, the greater the chance that another of the Hydes will discover us. And even if we did have time, where could we take her? The moment we leave the alley, we'll be spotted."

"I suppose you're right," Devona said, but she didn't sound happy about it. I didn't blame her. I didn't like the idea of leaving the unconscious Glassine behind either, even if she was currently a Hyde. But we really didn't have a choice, not if we wanted to do what we'd come here for – *and* survive long enough to go home. It was possible that Glassine might fall victim to one or more of the other Hydes before we could fix things, and after seeing the savage creatures rioting out in the street, I had a pretty good idea of the unpleasant things that would happen to her if she were discovered. But there was nothing we could do about that except work as fast as we could and hope it would be enough. Leaving Glassine like this would be hard, but I had a bad feeling it would only be the first of a number of tough choices we'd be forced to make before this was over.

I tucked away my gas gun and withdrew several plastic-coated yellow spheres the size of ping-pong balls from my jacket pocket. Devona and Darius also took out handfuls of spheres, though where Devona had been keeping hers, given how tight her leather outfit was, remained a mystery to me. The three of us walked to the mouth of the alley, a single sphere held in each of our right hands, ready to throw, the rest clasped tight in our left hands.

We then stepped onto the sidewalk and into Hell.

TWO

We tossed the first grenades underarm into the street, aiming at the Hydes closest to us. As soon as the spheres struck, they burst open, releasing yellow clouds of antidote gas, and every creature within range sucked in lungfuls of the stuff and began hacking. We didn't wait for the gas to take effect. As soon as the first wave of grenades detonated, we ran into the street and threw the next batch ahead of us to clear the way. We continued hurling grenades as we went, and within moments the homicidal chaos that had reigned in Sybarite Street gave way to mass confusion as clouds of yellow gas filled the air and dozens of the Hydes began to revert to their original forms. It wouldn't last – witness how long it had taken Glassine to become re-infected – but our goal wasn't to effect a permanent cure, at least not yet. Our goal was to create enough of a distraction so that we could cross the street and reach the *House of Dark Delights*, preferably without getting any limbs torn out of their sockets.

I've done a lot of difficult things during my time in Nekropolis, but crossing that dimension's version of Sybarite Street was one of the hardest. As soon as one of the Hydes reverted to his or her natural form, any unchanged creature close to them attacked, and the air was filled with the sounds of their screaming as they tried to escape and failed. It took everything I had to ignore their cries of agony and terror and force myself to keep running, and from the pained look on Devona's face, I knew she felt the same. I told myself that we were doing what we had to do, and maybe that was true, but it sure as hell didn't make it any easier.

We were two-thirds of the way across the street when a Hyde behind the wheel of an Agony DeLite aimed his vehicle at us and tromped on the accelerator. Agony DeLites are flesh-tech, formed from the bodies of a dozen sadomasochists. The vehicles run on pain, and the harder their drivers abuse them, the faster they go. I don't know what the Hyde inside the vehicle was doing to motivate his car, but it screamed in pleasure as it came toward us, hands and feet scrabbling for purchase on the asphalt. A glance showed me that the driver had the windows up, not that it mattered. Even if he got a dose of antidote and began to change back to normal, it wouldn't be in time for him to stop the car. I wasn't worried about Devona; I knew she could leap out of the way in time, but Darius and I were a good deal slower. Darius *might* be able to avoid being hit, but I'd end up zombie roadkill for sure. I'd survive the impact, but I'd sustain so many broken bones, I'd end up as little more than a rattling skin bag – zombie maracas. I figured I'd better do something to avoid that, seeing as how it would make saving this dimension's Nekropolis a bit harder.

I still had a couple gas grenades in my left hand, so I reached into my pants pocket with my right and pulled out an ancient coin. This was one of Charon's coins, paid to the ferryman as a fee for passage to the Land of the Dead. In my case, its magic had allowed me to purchase twenty-four hours as a living man. I'd used it, so its magic was gone, or at least that one aspect of its magic was gone. But that didn't mean the coin was without power. Magic items are funny. Some work like batteries: once their juice is used up, they're worthless. Others – especially objects of significant power – are more complicated. If you follow the instructions carefully and take the proper precautions, they'll work for you. But if you screw anything up, or if you get greedy and try to use them one more time than you should, they'll turn around and bite you on the ass in spectacularly awful ways. I was counting on the coin being the latter type of object. If I was wrong... well, I hoped Devona and Darius wouldn't mind carting around an undead bag of bone shards for a while.

I flipped the coin at the Agony DeLite. It spun end over end through the air, struck the vehicle on its fleshy hood, and bounced off. But that brief contact was enough for the coin's magic to take effect. The vehicle's nearly orgasmic shrieks became pained gasps, and its skin went from a healthy pink to a sickly gray-green. It lost speed and began wobbling back and forth, its discolored flesh growing hard and leathery, its windshield clouding over, as if it were a huge cyclopean eye covered by a thick, milky cataract. The car wheezed, veered off to the right, and stumbled by without hitting any of us. It struck a street lamp made from a large spinal column and curving rib bones, shattering it. The impact brought the vehicle to a sudden halt, and with a rattling cough the engine – hell, the whole damned car – died.

The driver's door flew open and the operator of the vehicle climbed out, looking mad as hell and no worse for the collision with the street lamp. The Hyde started toward us, fangs bared, claws outstretched, ready to inflict some serious damage on the person responsible for spoiling his fun. But he didn't get five steps from the dead Agony DeLite – which was suffering from an advanced state of decay, its flesh liquefying and beginning to slide off its skeletal chassis – when his own flesh began to take on a gray cast and his breathing became labored. He made it two more steps before his face contorted in a grimace and he clutched his chest. A second later he collapsed to the ground, as dead as his vehicle.

I'd hope that the coin's death energy would affect the vehicle, though I hadn't expected the effect to be quite so dramatic. But I hadn't realized the coin's magic might also affect the driver, whose bare hands had no doubt been gripping the steering wheel when the coin struck the Agony DeLite. As we watched, the creature returned to his natural form in death, revealing his true self to be a youthful-appearing vampire that I didn't recognize. I knew the vampire hadn't exactly been an innocent bystander – I'd lived in Nekropolis too long to believe any of its citizens are completely innocent – but he'd attacked us only because the Hyde plague had transformed him into a maniacally murderous beast. And without meaning to, I'd killed him. I half-expected him to open his eyes and sit up – after all, he *was* a vampire – but he remained motionless. I guess a coin imbued with powerful death magic is just as effective as a wooden stake for his kind.

I glanced at Devona to see if she recognized him, but she shook her head. Whoever I'd killed, it hadn't been someone either of us knew, but that didn't make me feel any better about it. I hoped he'd be the last casualty before this day was over, but somehow I doubted it.

The three of us continued on, throwing gas grenades and doing our best to avoid the slashing claws of the rioting Hydes. At one point, I ran out of grenades and switched to my gas gun.

I swiveled my weapon to the right, intending to fire a burst of antidote at a group of Hydes. But before I could squeeze the trigger, a Hyde lunged toward me from the side, a glowing blade clutched in his oversized paw. He wore the white uniform of a Bonegetter, one of Victor Baron's employees who scour Nekropolis in search of lost and discarded body parts, or better yet, entire bodies, of which there are quite an abundance, given the all-too-often violent nature of the Darkfolk. I recognized the instrument he held as a laser scalpel, a device that cuts through flesh and bone as if they were water – an exceptionally useful tool for performing vivisections on the go. Before I could react, the Bonegetter-Hyde slashed down with his laser scalpel and cut through my right wrist. My hand, still holding onto the gas gun, fell to the ground.

I felt no pain since my nerve-endings are as dead as the rest of me, and even if the laser scalpel hadn't automatically cauterized my wound, no blood would've spurted forth from my wrist stump. But that didn't mean I wasn't irritated to lose the hand, or more importantly right then, the gas gun that it held.

The Bonegetter-Hyde looked at me and grinned.

"So what are you going to do now, deader?" he growled.

"This," I said, and concentrated.

My hand flexed its muscles, managed to aim the gas gun's muzzle in the general direction of the Bonegetter-Hyde, and then pulled the trigger. A burst of yellowish gas shot up out of the Hyde's face, and he staggered back, coughing. He dropped the laser scalpel as he moved away from me, and I was half-tempted to retrieve the device and bury it in the Bonegetter's eye for what he'd done. But I didn't. For one thing, he was already in the process of changing back into his true form, and for another, I needed to get my right hand back ASAP.

I knelt down and held my wrist stump out toward my severed hand. Small tendrils of grayish-green flesh extended from both the stump and my hand, and within seconds my hand had reattached itself to my body. I stood up, and since my hand still held onto the gun, I tightened my grip on the weapon to test how successful the rejoining had been. The hand flexed just fine, and I turned and fired a fresh burst of gas at another group of Hydes that were determined to finish what their Bonegetter brother had started.

I was thrilled – and to be honest, more than a bit surprised – that the spell had worked. Over the years I've developed an unfortunate habit of losing pieces of myself in the line of duty, and I'd always relied on Papa Chatha to put me back together. But not long ago I'd literally lost my head... well, technically it had been my *body* that I had lost, but you get the idea. That injury had been beyond Papa's ability to repair, and I had to go to Victor Baron, the original Frankenstein monster, to get my head put back on my body. Papa's professional pride had been wounded, and he'd devoted himself to developing a spell that would allow me to reattach body parts in the field, at least temporarily. And what was even cooler, I could still exert control over any part of my body, whether it was attached to me or not. This was the first time I'd had the opportunity to try out the spell, and I was impressed by the results. Papa had been quick to caution me that the spell didn't make permanent fixes, though. The severed parts didn't literally rejoin with my body. They were held in place with strips of flesh, almost like bandages, and they would still function since my will animated them, but if I didn't get a more permanent repair done within twenty-four hours, any severed parts would fall off and stay off, and I'd no longer be able to control them. Still, as a temporary fix, the spell was more than adequate, as demonstrated by the fact that it had just saved my undead ass from getting sliced and diced by a homicidal Hyde wielding a high-tech surgical tool.

Devona, Darius, and I continued fighting, and though we finally made it to the other side of the street, we didn't get there entirely intact. I had several deep slashes on my arms and chest, as did Devona. My wounds were nothing to worry about; they didn't bleed and none of them were serious enough to slow me down, but the sight of Devona's injuries made me feel sick. They bled a lot, and even though they were healing rapidly, I couldn't help fearing damage had been done to the baby inside her. Sensing my worry, Devona gave me a smile, but it didn't do much to re-assure me. Even though I knew rationally that she was all right, I also knew I wouldn't feel better until we'd done what we'd come to this dimension for and re-turned home safe and sound.

Though Darius had a few scratches, he'd fared better than either of us in the injury department, no doubt having picked up more than a few survival skills during the course of his interdimensional travels. While the three of us had made it across Sybarite Street relatively intact, there was no guarantee we'd remain that way. The clouds of yellow gas we'd released into the street were beginning to dissipate, and the Hydes who'd been returned to their true forms were rapidly becoming re-infected by the plague. We'd managed to create the confusion we'd needed, but I knew it wouldn't last much longer. A few more moments, and the Hydes in the street would begin turning their attention to us, and once that happened, they'd come for us *en masse*, and no amount of strategy or trickery would save us then. We needed to get inside the *House of Dark Delights*, and we needed to do it fast.

In my Nekropolis, the *House of Dark Delights* is flanked by two businesses, a soul-modification parlor called Spiritus Mutatio and a casino called You Bet Your Life (a name which patrons often learn to their dismay should be taken literally). In this world, it had a Flense-crafters on one side, and a talent agency called Pickman's Models on the other. Otherwise, it looked much the same: a simple three-story white building with green shingles and matching shutters, no fence around the property, no bars on the windows, no obvious signs of any security precautions at all. But I knew the *House* was almost as well protected a Darklord's stronghold. Testament to this was the fact that despite the wild, savage nature of the creatures that had taken over this Nekropolis, not one of the Hydes had set foot upon the property. The yard was intact, and the *House*'s façade unmarred. We needed to get into the *House,* but attempting a break-in would be a fast, unpleasant, and extremely messy way of committing suicide.

Good thing I had a key.

We hurried up the front walk and stepped onto the porch. Nothing happened: no wardspells activated, no alarm sounded, and the front door didn't fly open to dis-gorge someone intent on killing us. So far, so good. We were out of gas grenades by this point, so we'd drawn our gas guns. Devona and Darius watched our backs while I shifted my gas gun to my left hand and removed a key from my shirt pocket. There was nothing special about it – it looked like any ordinary house key – but when I inserted it into the front lock and turned, I was rewarded with a rapid series of clicking sounds. And while we could hear the physical locks deactivating, we couldn't hear the door's wardspells powering down, but I knew they were. Or at least, I hoped they were. When the clicking noises ended, I waited for a count of five, as I'd been instructed, then I withdrew the key from the lock and tucked it back into my shirt pocket. I returned my gas gun to my right hand, and then – even though I didn't need to breathe – I took a deep breath before grip-ping the door knob and turning it.

The key had been given to us by Bennie, the owner of the *House of Dark Delights* in our world. And though according to Darius this dimension had its own version of Bennie who owned this *House*, that didn't mean *our* Bennie's key would successfully open *this* Bennie's lock, if you know what I mean. So as I pushed the door open, I steeled myself for any number of nasty physical and mystical surprises to go off in our faces, but the door swung open easily and quietly, without blasting us into nonexistence.

I turned to tell Devona and Darius that everything was all right, only to see a mass of Hydes running across the lawn toward us. Evidently their fear of Bennie had been overridden by their desire to get their claws on some fresh meat. Devona saw the look on my face, and without turning to glance over her shoulder, she grabbed hold of Darius and me by the arm, shoved us inside, and then leaped in after us. I scrambled to slam the door shut, and flipped the deadbolt switch just as the first Hyde slammed into the door. The one switch activated all the locks, both physical and mystical, and despite the furious pounding on the other side of the door, there was no way the creatures could get inside now. We were safe, in an out-of-the-frying-pan, into-the-fire kind of way.

I looked around, but aside from the three of us, the foyer was empty. Bennie usually has at least one bouncer working the door, more when business is especially good, but we were alone. I wasn't sure if this was a good sign or not, but since it meant no one was currently trying to kill us, I decided to take it as a positive development.

The *House of Dark Delights* is the premier bordello in Nekropolis. Whatever your sexual proclivities, capabilities, desires, fantasies, or fetishes, the *House of Dark Delights* can provide what you're looking for – *if* you have the darkgems to pay for it, that is. The hallways and rooms are perfumed with a variety of exotic-smelling aphrodisiacs – not that I can smell any of them or that they'd have any effect on my dead flesh if I could. And it's noisy: conversation from customers waiting for their "appointments" to begin, background

music playing, laughter, sighs, moans, and cries of ec-
stasy or pain – often both at the same time – from
behind closed doors. It was noisy, all right, but all the
sound seemed to be coming from a single direction:
the lounge. And instead of the usual good-natured
buzz of conversation and laughter, the air was filled
with guttural animalistic noises more suited to a zoo.

I turned to Devona. "Remind me how much we're
getting paid for this job."

"Nothing," she said.

I sighed. "Right."

We headed slowly down the foyer and toward the
lounge, gas guns held at the ready. Devona and me in
front, Darius behind us, covering our rear. We did our
best to move silently, though given how much noise
was coming from the lounge, we really didn't need to
bother. We could've skipped down the hallway singing
"We're Off to See the Wizard," at the top of our lungs,
and I doubt anyone would've heard us. When we
reached the end of the hallway, we flattened our backs
against the wall and peered into the lounge.

This lounge – just like its counterpart back in my
Nekropolis – was decorated like a tasteful upscale Earth
tavern with black lacquer tables and chairs, and Mind's
Eye sets mounted on the walls. The centerpiece of the
lounge was a large circular bar in the middle of the room
where the bartenders on duty – witches and warlocks
who specialize in potion-making – mix any aphrodisiac
or performance-enhancing drink you desire. Normally
the lounge is pretty lively, but in the wake of the plague

TIM WAGGONER   33

that had swept through this Nekropolis, it had become
a scene of absolute and utter depravity that would've
made Caligula himself blush like the most cloistered of
nuns. The lounge was packed wall-to-wall with the
same savage creatures that infested the street outside,
and the Hydes were doing their best to cause just as
much havoc: fighting and screwing – often at the same
time – and roaring with dark laughter whenever one of
them received an especially nasty injury. The Hydes
were so numerous and they shared so many common
physical traits that it was almost impossible to tell them
apart, but I recognized a few. Two of the creatures had
holo implants where their eyes should've been, and I
guessed they were the vampires Halima and Resham, a
brother and sister who often came to the lounge merely
to find a place where they could sit and play holoshards
for hours on end without being interrupted. They were
playing games of an entirely different sort now, but not
with each other, at least. One of the creatures possessed
somewhat feline features, and I guessed she was Lourdes, a werecat waitress employed by Bennie, and the
particularly monstrous creature who was, ah, servicing
her appeared to be Lyra, a woman's spirit who'd taken
up residence in the body of the genetically altered
mixblood lyke who'd killed her. A *male* lyke. I thought
I recognized some others, but I forced myself to ignore
them. We hadn't come here to help them, at least not
directly. We'd come to help the Hyde sitting atop the bar
and surveying the bacchanalia taking placing place with
the self-satisfied air of a proud ruler.

This Hyde was larger and more massive than the others, nearly twice their size, and the chair that had been placed on the bar barely supported its weight. It was wearing the torn remnants of a black tuxedo, and while its profusion of body hair was just as wild and shaggy as that of the other creatures, where theirs was brown, this Hyde's was a bright reddish-orange. Given the creature's bestial features, it was difficult to tell its gender, but after a moment its facial features softened a bit and its chest swelled, and I knew that, while it had been male when we first got here, it had now become female. No doubt about it, then. It was Bennie. Sometimes Master Benedict, sometimes Madame Bendetta, but always owner and operator of the *House of Dark Delights*.

Darius leaned close and spoke in my ear, more so that I could hear him over the din than to avoid being overheard by the Hydes. "How do you want to play this? Direct assault? Sneak attack?"

"How about a little of both?" I said.

I checked the readout on my gas gun and saw that I had a little less than half my ammunition left. I popped a couple fresh ampoules into the chamber to reload, and Devona and Darius did the same. We then stepped into the lounge and started firing.

The guns had a range of about six feet; after that, the gas dissipated too much to be effective. But there were so many Hydes packed into the lounge that for every burst of gas we fired, a half dozen or so began to change back to their normal selves. We kept firing around us as we moved farther into the lounge, rapidly depleting our supply of gas, but we only made it halfway to the bar before the Hydes realized what was happening, abandoned their orgy of sex and violence, and attacked. A crowd of the creatures came toward us, shoving aside or in more than a few cases stomping on those caught in the throes of transformation in order to reach us. I knew that even if we managed to dose our attackers with antidote gas, at least some of them would reach us before the antidote could take hold. Time to switch tactics.

"You two keep hitting them with the antidote!" I said, and then flicked the selector switch on my gun. I picked out the fastest, meanest-looking Hydes coming toward us – the ones I judged had the best chance of reaching us before the antidote could affect them – took aim, and fired.

Our guns weren't loaded only with antidote to the Hyde plague. They also fired chemical weapons of an entirely different sort. A tiny dart shot out of my gun's muzzle and streaked through the air toward a particularly grotesque Hyde that appeared to be part reptilian. I guessed his true form was that of a demon, but luckily his flesh was only partially covered by green scales, and the dart struck him on a soft part of his neck. He took two more steps before his eyes went wide with shock, then he doubled over, howling with pain as he grabbed his crotch.

I couldn't help grinning. A cocktail of instant syphilis, herpes, and gonorrhea was a potent weapon indeed.

So we continued fighting our way across the lounge toward the bar, Devona and Darius dosing Hydes with antidote, me making life extremely uncomfortable for any of the creatures who came too near. I kept glancing at Bennie as we drew closer to him/her, but instead of seeming concerned at our approach, Bennie looked amused, as if we were no more of a threat than a trio of actors in a Mind's Eye program.

Lyra broke off from her enthusiastic coupling with Lourdes to attack us, and I had no choice but to hit her with a VD dart, and when that didn't do much more than slow her down a little, I hit her with a second and third. She collapsed to the floor and writhed in agony, and while I knew she wasn't exactly the same Lyra as the one who lived in my Nekropolis, she was close enough, and I felt awful for having to put her through so much pain. But as least she was still alive, and hopefully she'd stay that way – *if* we could reach Bennie and put a stop to this plague.

By the time we were within ten feet of the bar, Darius' forehead dripped with sweat, and he looked exhausted. Despite his ability to traverse dimensions, he was only human, but since Devona and I were more than that (or perhaps in my case, less) we didn't tire, and the two of us were still in fine fighting shape when we reached the bar. Now that we were in firing range of Bennie, I flipped the selector switch on my weapon back to antidote, and the three of us hit Bennie with a triple blast of gas. Bennie – who'd continued to switch between genders the entire time we fought to reach him/her – merely sat smiling as the yellow cloud enveloped him.

The rest of the Hydes in the lounge stopped what they were doing, and all of us watched and waited to see what would happen.

When the cloud dissipated, Bennie was still a he, but he was also still very much a Hyde.

"Nice try," he said in a bestial rumble. "But my ancestor invented the Hyde formula, and I take regular doses of it – or rather, a variation of the original recipe – to maintain my dual gender nature. Imbibing the potion over so many years has had a permanent effect on my physiology. Your pathetic antidote won't work on me."

It was strange to hear such intelligent words coming out of a Hyde's mouth. Not because of the way Bennie looked – I'd been in Nekropolis too long to judge any being's intelligence based on appearance – but because of the violently chaotic nature displayed by the Hydes we'd seen up to this point. I was impressed that Bennie was able to focus past his lust for mayhem long enough to form, let alone express, coherent thoughts.

I thought about hitting Bennie with a few dozen VD darts, but I knew it wouldn't do any good. The pain might lay him/her low, but the other Hydes would still tear us to pieces. Since at the moment the other creatures were watching and waiting to see what would happen next, I decided our best bet was to keep Bennie talking.

"Not *our* antidote," I said. "*You* made it. Or rather, another you made it, one who lives in a different dimension."

Bennie's features softened slightly as she became female again. She leaned forward, her eyes narrowing as
she inspected us more closely. "I recognized Darius right
away," she said. "When I saw you use your weapons, I
guessed that he'd enlisted the help of another Bennie to
try to stop me." She nodded at the weapons in our hands.
"Those are just the sort of thing I'd design – especially
the VD darts!" She grinned nastily. "But I didn't recognize you at first, Matt. Nor you, Devona. You both look
quite a bit different than your counterparts in this world."

She raised her hand and snapped her fingers. At her
command a pair of Hydes rose from behind the bar,
each of them lifting a prisoner into view, a man and a
woman, both bound in coils of red velvet rope. The
rope was no doubt normally used for bondage games
around here, but no one was playing right now.

The two prisoners were familiar, so much so that
looking at them was like looking into a mirror, albeit a
funhouse mirror. The male was dressed in gray suit and
tie similar to mine, but his skin was ivory white, and he
had overlong incisors which protruded down over his
lower lip. The woman wore a scuffed and torn black
leather outfit, and her flaking skin was greenish-gray.

"It's us!" Devona said. Then she frowned. "Sort of."

I looked closely at our other selves. "We're reversed.
You're a zombie, while I… I don't look half-vampire,
do I?"

"That's because you're not," the other me said.
"You're the whole undead enchilada."

"Interesting. Do you like it?"

He gave me a sour look. "Do you like being a zombie?"

"Good point."

"Took you long enough to get here," Vampire Matt said. He looked at Darius. "I was beginning to think you didn't get my message."

"I got it," the Sideways Man said, "and I did as you asked."

"For all the good it did," Zombie Devona muttered. "Our Bennie is still a Hyde, and you three are in just as much trouble as Matt and I are."

"Speaking of Hydes," my Devona said, "I understand why *you* haven't changed, but from what we've seen, the Hyde plague affects vampires. Why didn't your Matt change?"

Bennie was a woman again, and she answered before Zombie Devona could. "Because your Bennie isn't the only one who was able to whip up an antidote to the plague. I gave my Matt a dose – one a good deal stronger than what your guns can deliver – so he'd remain unchanged. He and his Devona tried to stop me, and I wanted them both to witness the results of their failure."

"Stop you from doing what?" I asked. "I'm not exactly sure what your master plan is." I wanted to keep Bennie talking as long as I could. I'd been watching him/her closely, observing the gender change and trying to mark the exact moment when he/she was perfectly poised between male and female. I thought I had a good feel for it, but I needed to be absolutely sure.

Bennie Hyde looked at me as if I'd just asked the stupidest question imaginable. "Why, having fun, of course! I had a client who asked for a very special potion: one that would split him into two separate beings, one male, one female, so that he – or rather they – could…" Bennie trailed off and grinned. "I'm sure your imaginations can fill in the rest. No one on my staff had the skill necessary to create such an elixir, so I decided to give it a go. Since I already used a variation of my ancestor's original formula to shift gender, I figured all I'd have to do was tinker with the recipe a bit. Initial tests on lab animals were encouraging, and so I decided to try it on myself." Bennie – male again – smiled. "What can I say? I was curious to see what it would be like to truly become two genders instead of simply switching back and forth between them. But instead of splitting me into two separate beings, the formula turned me into a Hyde. But not just any Hyde – a super Hyde who could spread the transformation to others. Inside me, the formula mutated into an extremely contagious airborne virus, and all I had to do in order to make more Hydes was keep breathing. And once a new Hyde was created, it could spread the virus as well. By now every living – or semi-living – creature in my Nekropolis has been transformed. Only the dead are immune, but that's no great loss. The dead aren't much fun anyway. Now the city has become a non-stop party, and I get to have the fun of watching my Hydes run rampant, indulging their every dark whim until none of them are left."

"What then?" my Devona asked. "You'll be left to rule over a dead city. That doesn't sound like much fun."

Bennie shifted from male to female, and this time I was sure I saw the point where he/she hovered precisely between genders. I held my gas gun at my side, and while Bennie's gaze was focused on Devona, I flicked the selector switch on my weapon to its third setting.

"When I've squeezed every last drop of fun out of this city, I'll make Darius take me to another Nekropolis, and I'll start all over again there." Bennie grinned. "And when that one's used up, I'll move on to the next. How many different dimensions do you think there are that have Nekropolises? Hundreds? Thousands? I'm going to have so much fun playing with them all!"

Time to draw Bennie's attention back to me. "That's why your Matt had Darius get Devona and me. He knew that we'd go to our Bennie for help. There's no one else who understands more about your ancestor's formula and how to counter it."

"A smart move," Bennie Hyde said, "except it seems that your Bennie isn't quite the chemist I am. The antidote that Bennie gave you doesn't do more than temporarily change my Hydes back to their normal selves, and they're easily re-infected." She gestured, but I didn't take my eyes off her. I knew that all the Hydes we'd dosed with antidote gas had changed back to their bestial aspects again. But Bennie began to shift genders again, and I raised my weapon.

"My Bennie's a lot sharper than you think. For instance, Bennie made a special antidote just for you. And

Bennie told us that shifting genders always places a strain on your system, weakening it, if only for a few seconds. But that should be long enough for this to do its job."

I aimed the gun at Bennie's neck and squeezed the trigger. My Bennie had only had time to make enough of the special antidote to fill a single dart, and I had to make this shot count. The dart whistled through the air and struck Bennie Hyde at the base of the throat.

Male again, Bennie Hyde roared with anger and tore the dart out of his neck. He threw the dart aside, rose to his feet, and glared at me. "I'm going to order my Hydes to tear the three of you into bite-sized pieces, and then I'm going to have you for an afternoon snack!"

"Why would they listen to you?" I said. "You're not one of them anymore."

Bennie Hyde frowned. "What are you—" He grimaced, convulsed violently, then slumped down onto the bar and lay on his side. A moment later he sat up shakily, face pale, skin slick with sweat, but fully human once more.

"What… happened?" he said, rubbing his temples as if he had a terrible headache.

"I'll tell you in a minute," I said. "But first do me a favor: take a deep breath and let it out."

Bennie frowned at me. "What are you talking about?" Then she – for the gender switch had occurred again – noted the lounge full of Hydes surrounding us, all of whom began to snarl and step forward. "Oh, right."

A couple exhalations was all it took to begin spreading the Hyde antidote – which like the Hyde plague had become an airborne virus inside Bennie's body –

and all around us Hydes began returning to normal, and in turn passed the cure on to any Hydes standing near them.

As waves of transformation rippled through the lounge, Vampire Matt grinned at me. It was more than a little disconcerting to see my mouth stretch into a wide smile and display a pair of very sharp-looking fangs.

"Not bad," he said. "Almost as good as I could've done."

"*I'm* not the one who managed to get himself caught and tied up in bondage rope," I pointed out.

Zombie Devona looked at both of us. "Play nice, you two."

The two Hydes who'd been guarding our counterparts had changed back to themselves – a pair of Bennie's Arcane bartenders – and they quickly began untying their former prisoners. A couple moments later, our others selves were free and had come around from behind the bar to join us.

Everyone on the lounge had been returned to normal by that point. Quite a few people had been wounded during their time as Hydes, and those who weren't wounded saw to their care. A number of the cured headed outside to begin spreading the anti-Hyde virus to the rest of the city. I had no idea how long it would take before this Nekropolis was entirely free of the Hyde plague, but given how rapidly the virus had spread, I figured it wouldn't take more than a day or two.

Bennie climbed down from the bar and joined the five of us – Darius, both Devonas, myself and my vampiric doppelgänger.

"Thank Mother Kali that Darius was able to reach you!" Bennie said before giving both Devona and me a hug. "And when you get home, tell my other self that they're every bit the chemist our ancestor was!"

"We'll do that," I said. "And speaking of your other self…" I reached into my jacket pocket, took out a flash drive, and handed it to Bennie. "This contains the formula for the antidote that my Bennie designed to work on you. Just in case you ever need it again."

"Thank you." Bennie took the flash drive and tucked it into his pants pocket. "But after this, I'll never mess with my ancestor's formula again. It's simply too dangerous."

Vampire Matt and I exchanged looks. That might be how Bennie felt now, but Bennie was nothing if not an unabashed hedonist, and he/she was all too willing to take a chance if it meant experiencing new realms of pleasure. I took another flash drive out of my pocket and handed it to my other self.

"Again," I said, "just in case."

Bennie scowled at me, but – now female – she didn't protest. Vampire Matt nodded and put it in his inner jacket pocket.

"I'd ask you and your Devona to stay and visit," he said, "but I'm afraid our Nekropolis won't be in much shape for sightseeing for a while. We're going to have a lot of cleaning up to do."

"Besides," Zombie Devona said, "you two have your own lives to get back to." She gave my Devona a knowing smile, and I had to wonder if she somehow knew her other self was pregnant. My Devona might be half-vampire and the other a zombie, but they were both still women, and it seemed they possessed that special brand of telepathy that members of their gender shared.

My Devona gave her other self a smile, but there was something strained about it, and I immediately feared something was wrong.

"We do need to go home," she said. She placed a hand on her abdomen as she turned to Darius. She suddenly looked paler than usual, and her voice quavered when she spoke. "If you could take us right now, I'd appreciate it. I…" She took in a hiss of air and her face scrunched up in pain. "I think I need to see a doctor. *Now.*"

THREE

"Quit pacing, Matt. You're making me nervous."

I stopped and turned to look at her. "*I'm* making *you* nervous? You're the one lying in a hospital bed hooked up to a bunch of machines."

Devona smiled and patted the edge of the bed. "Come sit with me."

If there's one thing I can't stand to do when something's wrong, it's nothing. And pacing, useless as it might be, was still something. But I didn't want to make things any worse for Devona than they already were, so I went over to the bed and sat. She took my hand and gave it a strong squeeze, and I squeezed back.

"Everything's going to be all right," she said.

I nodded noncommittally. Even before I died, I knew things didn't always work out for the best, and being a zombie working in a city full of monsters hadn't done anything to change my mind about that. But I wisely kept my mouth shut – for a change.

The hospital room was small and sterile: white walls

and ceiling, white-tiled floor, white curtains over the windows, white sheets on the bed. Devona wore a white hospital gown, and even the furniture – a stool on rolling casters and a couple uncomfortable-looking wooden chairs – was white. The medical scanners were encased in white plastic, and the wires that stretched between Devona and the machines were also white. The IV bag hanging on a metal stand next to the bed made a startling contrast to the room's color scheme. It contained a dark red liquid that flowed slowly through a tube into Devona's left wrist. If this had been a hospital back on Earth, I might've thought she was getting a transfusion, but for a vampire – even a half-vampire like Devona – blood was more effective than the usual intravenous fluids.

A Mind's Eye set was mounted in the corner of the ceiling, and it was one of the healthiest I'd ever seen, certainly in better condition than the old rheumy-eyed set in the apartment I shared with Devona. The skin wasn't discolored, the iris was light blue with tiny gold flecks, the lashes were long and clean, the white of the eye was pure ivory, and its capillaries few and unswollen. Mind's Eyes telepathically broadcast their programs directly into your mind when you gaze upon them, and this one was currently showing an image of a reporter who looked human but had tiny black spiders crawling over every inch of her exposed skin. She was standing on a Sprawl street corner in front of a large building I didn't recognize, a serious expression on her face, mouth moving silently.

Mind's Eyes don't come with remote controls; they're not necessary. All you need to do to change the channel or control the volume is think about it. And since the information is transferred directly into your brain, two people can look at the same set and "hear" different volumes, even view separate programs if they wish. So I concentrated, putting a little extra effort into it, since Mind's Eyes have trouble transmitting to my zombie brain, and after a moment I could hear the sound.

"... at *Magewrights' Manor* refuse to comment on the reports that magic-users have been disappearing throughout the city over the last several weeks. The Darklord Talaith has also declined to make a statement on the matter."

It was hard watching the woman talk as spiders scuttled in and out of her mouth every time she opened it. It looked damned uncomfortable to me – wouldn't those little spiderlegs tickle her tongue? But she didn't seem to notice, let alone care.

"The official word from the Nightspire on the situation came to us today from First Adjudicator Quillion."

The picture changed to display the sharp-featured face of a man in his seventies who was completely hairless – not only was he bald, he had no eyebrows or eyelashes. He wore a crimson robe as sign of his office and projected an aura of haughty disdain. He gave a cold, thin-lipped smile before speaking.

"While it is true that certain members of the thaumaturgical community have gone missing recently, there's no reason to suspect their disappearances are connected. As we all know, magic is a high-risk profession, and there are any number of ways its practitioners can come to unfortunate and untimely ends – ones that don't always leave physical evidence behind." His smile widened a touch at that. "And not to put too fine a point on it, there is no shortage of predators in the city. At this time, there is simply no evidence to link the disappearances. If such evidence ever does come to light, I assure you my office will conduct a complete and thorough investigation, but until then I consider the matter closed."

I scowled. To say I'm not Quillion's biggest fan would be a huge understatement, considering that not long ago the sonofabitch sentenced me to Tenebrus, Nekropolis' subterranean prison. I'd escaped and later been pardoned, but Quillion still had it in for me, and I felt just as much antipathy toward him.

The image switched back to the spider-covered reporter who continued talking, but I concentrated on tuning her out and both the picture and sound faded from my mind. I wondered if there was something to the rumors about magic-users disappearing. I dismissed Quillion's disavowal of the story. He might be an Adjudicator, but he was just as much a politician as he was a combination of judge and jury. Of course he'd say the disappearances weren't linked. I hadn't heard any rumors on the street about the disappearances, but then I'd been too busy lately to visit my usual – you'll pardon the expression – haunts. Between helping Devona with the Midnight Watch and looking for a new place to live (because Devona didn't want to raise our child in a squalid little apartment that, despite all her best efforts, still looked too much like a bachelor's home) I hadn't been making the rounds and touching base with my network of contacts and informants. There'd been a time when I'd have known about the disappearances long before the media did. Now I was finding out the news the same time as any other average citizen, and the realization disturbed me for reasons I couldn't quite put my finger on.

"Did you hear me, Matt?"

I turned to Devona, feeling bad for having taken my attention off her, even momentarily. "What is it? Is something wrong?"

"No. I said I'm feeling better, and I am." When she saw the doubtful look on my face, she added. "Really."

I restricted my comment to a muffled *hmpf*. What I wanted to say was that I'd known Devona shouldn't have come with me to that other Nekropolis, and that if anything happened to her or the baby, it would be my fault for not making her stay behind. But saying all that wouldn't make her feel any better, so there was no point in it. Keeping quiet twice in one day? It was a new personal record for me.

When Darius returned us to our Nekropolis, we appeared in Bennie's lounge. Bennie – our Bennie – had been waiting for us, eager to learn whether or not we'd been able to help his/her other-dimensional counterpart. When Bennie saw Devona was in pain, he/she made a hand vox call to the Fever House and ordered

an ambulance. I told Bennie to skip the ambulance but
to let them know we'd be coming. Then I helped Devona outside where Lazlo was waiting for us. I have no
idea how the demon cabbie always knows when I need
a ride, but he's never let me down. I helped Devona
into the backseat of Lazlo's nightmarish conglomera-
tion of a vehicle, and he rocketed through the streets
of the Sprawl toward Gothtown, where the Fever
House was located. Lazlo got us to the hospital so fast
that I suspected he may have broken a few laws of
space and time to do so. He was sitting in his cab in the
parking lot now, waiting for me to call him with news
of Devona's condition, not that I had any to give him
yet. Beyond a quick examination from the nurse
who'd hooked Devona up to the medical equipment
when we first got to the room, we hadn't seen anyone.

A soft knock sounded at the door then, and I
thought our wait was finally over.

"Come in," I said, feeling a strange mixture of relief
and tension. I wanted to get this show on the road, but
at the same time, I was afraid of what a doctor's examination might ultimately reveal. But I needn't have
worried. The person who opened the door and poked
his head into the room wasn't a doctor.

"Is it all right if I come in?"

He was medium height, thin, with long brown hair
tied in a pony tail and a neatly trimmed beard. A tie-dyed
T-shirt, jeans, and sandals completed his bohemian look,
and his pale skin and elongated canines marked him
a vampire. Most Bloodborn – especially the older ones

– tend to disdain technology, especially when it's used in body modification. Vampires are more than a little fanatical about maintaining the purity of their blood, and they view cybernetic enhancements as a corruption of the body. Not so the younger Bloodborn, though. Varney appeared to be in his mid-twenties, and while I had no idea how old he truly was, the fact that he possessed a pair of cybernetic implants told me he was relatively young as vampires went. Both his left eye and left ear had been removed and replaced with electronic devices: a camera lens and a miniature directional microphone, respectively.

I got off the bed and started walking toward Varney, making sure to keep myself between him and Devona.

"You'd better not be recording right now," I said in what I hoped was a threatening voice.

Not threatening enough, evidently, for Varney slid the rest of the way into the room, though he did raise his hands in a placating gesture. "It's cool, man. My camera's off. I totally respect you and your lady's privacy. Besides, this isn't the kind of footage my producer's looking for." He glanced at Devona. "No offense." He turned back to me. "Now if it was you *lying* injured in that bed, Matt…"

It took all the self-restraint I had not to let out a series of extremely offensive words. Not long ago, I'd had a run-in with a gorgon named Acantha, host of a live interview program called *On the Scene*. She'd tried to interview me while I was working and I was, shall we say, less than gracious about it. Since then Acantha had done her best to go out of her way to give me bad publicity whenever she could – and not just me: she made sure to include Devona and the Midnight Watch in her petty vendetta. So for Devona's sake, I'd gone to the Eidolon Building where the city's major media outlets – Mind's Eye Theatre, the *Tome*, Bedlam 66.6, and the *Daily Atrocity* – are housed and tried to make peace with Acantha. She responded to my overtures about as well as you might expect (gorgons can carry grudges for centuries), but her boss, a demon named Murdock, overheard our conversation and pulled me into his office.

You want Acantha to lay off you and your woman? he'd said. *I can arrange that.* And then he'd smiled that smile demons give you when they're about to make you an offer you know you really should refuse. And when I heard his proposal, I turned him down at first. Until I spoke with Devona later.

I think it's flattering that Murdock wants to make a documentary about you, she'd said. *You have to admit, you've become something of a celebrity over the last few months, and it's only natural people would want to know more about you. And if people get to know you – the city's only self-willed zombie – a little better, it might change their attitude toward the reanimated dead.* And then she'd added the kicker. *Besides, the publicity would be good for business.*

So I called Murdock and told him I'd be honored to let him make a documentary about me, which is how I got saddled with Varney, the one-man – or maybe I should say one-vampire – film crew. With his cybernetic enhancements, all he had to do was follow me around and anything he saw and heard would be recorded. Every night he transmitted the day's footage to the Mind's Eye studio via the Aethernet, where it was reviewed and edited by his producer. Varney had been tailing me for five days now, and my patience with him was wearing more than a little thin. Despite the fact that he'd told me when we met that he'd "be as invisible as Casper, man," while I worked, Varney had a tendency to get in the way, and I'd begun looking for opportunities to ditch him whenever I could.

Varney went on. "I don't mean to intrude, but I just wanted to check in with you guys and see how things went in the other Nekropolis."

Varney had been waiting for us in Bennie's lounge when Darius brought us back, but I'd rushed Devona out of there so fast that he hadn't had a chance to talk to us – or get in Lazlo's cab and ride along to the hospital – which is just the way I'd wanted it. I figured he'd catch up to us sooner or later. Unfortunately, it hadn't been later enough for me.

"This really isn't a good time," I told him. "How about you go back to the Eidolon Building, and I'll give you a call later?"

"Matt…" Devona said in that tone she uses when she thinks I'm being unreasonable. But the last thing I cared about right then was helping Varney with the stupid documentary. All that mattered to me was Devona and the baby's health.

Varney smiled. "Don't sweat it, man. I got it covered." He held out his hand and a small silver object about the size of a thumbnail crawled out from beneath my jacket lapel. It looked a little like a mechanical ant, except it had a miniature camera lens in place of a head. As I watched, wings slid out of tiny panels in the artificial insect's back, and the creature took wing. It buzzed over to Varney, and the vampire opened his mouth, and the bug flew inside. Varney then closed his mouth and grinned.

"That's icky," Devona said.

"When I couldn't go with you to the other Nekropolis, I snuck a portable camera onto you when you weren't looking. The quality of its recording isn't quite as good as what I can do, but it'll serve in a pinch. Just let me start downloading..." He paused and his expression went blank. "Yeah... yeah, that's some good stuff." He looked at me and grinned. "My producer is gonna love it!"

I sighed. It seemed I couldn't get away from Varney no matter what I did. "Do me a favor: don't put any more of those damned things on me without my permission, OK? We dead folk have a thing about bugs."

While that was true enough, the real reason I disliked carrying around an insect – even a machine that resembled an insect – was because of an experience I'd had several months back with a friend of mine named Gregor. At least, I thought he'd been a friend. As it turned out, he'd been something far different. He was gone now, but I still didn't like bugs, and I especially didn't like them riding around concealed on me.

"Sure thing," Varney said. "Whatever you say, Matt."

What I wanted to say next was less than polite and

would've earned me another disapproving *Matt* from Devona, but a second knock sounded at the door before I could speak, this one sharp and businesslike. The door opened and a woman wearing a white doctor's coat walked in. She was a tall, thin Bloodborn woman, with short black hair and porcelain-white skin. Her lips were full and red, and I knew that she'd recently dined. But considering this was a hospital, I figured the staff had ready access to fresh blood. She appeared young – barely out of her teens – but she moved with the preternatural stillness that only very old vampires were capable of.

She crossed to Devona's bed with brisk strides, ignoring Varney as she passed, but when she saw me her brow furrowed and her lips pursed in distaste.

"What is this thing doing here?" she demanded in an icy tone. "This is a hospital room, not the morgue."

Devona scowled. "This *thing* is my husband, and I want him here."

It didn't surprise me that Devona stuck up for me. It wasn't the first time she'd done so. While Nekropolitans could be quite liberal-minded about some things, the idea of anyone having a zombie for a romantic partner was, to put it mildly, out of the ordinary, and people tended to have varying reactions when they saw us together. What surprised me was hearing Devona refer to me as her husband. We weren't married, not in any legal sense of the word. Before relocating to Nekropolis to escape the always-increasing human population, the Darkfolk had tended to live in isolated pockets and out-of-the-way places. They hadn't really had anything like a centralized government, so there was no need for formal laws. If one Darkfolk wanted to have a long-term romantic relationship with another, they just did so without worrying about any kind of legally binding agreement. Besides, the concept of *holy* matrimony didn't sit well with the more diabolical members of the Darkfolk. And so there were no priests or justices of the peace to marry people in Nekropolis – at least as far as I knew – and the issue had never come up between Devona and me, despite the fact that we'd been living together for a while now and she was carrying my child.

I'd been married once before, back on Earth when I was alive, but it hadn't lasted long. I'd been a cliché – the cop who was more dedicated to his career than his marriage – and eventually my wife got tired of trying and gave up. And I don't blame her one bit. But that had been years ago, and I'd long since moved on. I wasn't averse to the idea of getting married again; it just didn't seem like something that was even possible in Nekropolis, let alone necessary.

So why did it bother me to hear Devona refer to me as her husband?

The doctor looked at me like I was something nasty she'd found in a patient's bedpan. "Be that as it may, we maintain the strictest standards of cleanliness at the Fever House, and it's unacceptable for there to be a... person present in the room who's experiencing active – if delayed – decay. The germs..."

"I was thoroughly, and rather humiliatingly, decon-taminated when we arrived," I said. "And a nurse gave me this." I removed a gem-encrusted amulet from my jacket pocket and showed it to the doctor. "She told me that as long as I kept it on my person, I wouldn't be in danger of germifying anyone."

The doctor frowned. "Such magic isn't one hundred percent efficacious – it's the main reason we prefer to use technology whenever possible in our treatment plans – but I suppose it'll be sufficient in this case." She turned one again to Devona. "Especially since you so strongly desire your… *husband* to remain. Though I will have to ask him to please step away from the bed so that I might conduct my examination without hindrance."

The doctor was long past the point of getting on my nerves, but I reminded myself that she was here to help Devona, and I kept my mouth shut as I stood and stepped away from the bed.

The doctor introduced herself as she checked the readouts on the various monitors.

"I'm Dr Servia, director of emergency medicine. I re-alize that your past appointments have been with one of my colleagues in obstetrics, but as of now, I'll be tak-ing charge of your care. Tell me what happened."

So Devona gave the doctor a condensed version of our adventure in the parallel dimension Darius had trans-ported us to, while Servia continued examining her.

Fever House was an old-fashioned name for hospi-tal, and the first time I'd heard the term, I'd imagined something like an asylum filled with shrieking

straitjacketed patients confined in cell-like rooms with
stone floors and walls. But vampires have been prac-
ticing the art of medicine since before humanity had
developed a written language, and there's nothing
primitive about the facilities at the Fever House.
They're easily as sophisticated as any Earth hospital, if
not more so. You might wonder why vampires bother
with medicine – after all, as long as they have access
to a steady diet of human blood, they're immortal and
rapidly heal all injuries (with the exception of wooden
stakes to the heart and severe sunburn). But the
Bloodborn's interest in medicine has nothing to do
with them. Rather, it's all about maintaining a healthy
food supply. The healthier humanity is, the purer their
blood. So throughout the centuries vampires developed and passed on their medical knowledge to human
physicians so that the health of the herd might be
maintained. Most human beings are unaware of this,
of course, and good thing. Who would want to know
that the cough syrup they'd just given their sick child
was developed by a predator species that views humans as a tasty snack?

Over the course of the four centuries since Nekropolis was founded, the physicians at the Fever House
have expanded the scope of their medical knowledge
to encompass treating Darkfolk of all kinds, and while
many Nekropolitans have healing powers equal to
those of vampires, there are still any number of ill-
nesses and injuries – mundane and magical – that they
need help recovering from, and the Fever House does

a brisk trade. I knew Devona was in good hands medically speaking, the best the city had to offer, but I was still nervous. Our situation wasn't exactly a common one, and I doubted they covered half-vampire/zombie matings in vampire medical school.

As I was thinking, I saw movement out of the corner of my eye – something small and dark scuttling across the floor. Without a functioning nervous system, I couldn't feel a physical chill, but I experienced the psychic equivalent. The last time I'd seen something like that… I turned to get a clearer look, and I saw a black shape the size of a large insect zip past my feet and disappear beneath Devona's bed. Or thought I did. It moved so fast, I couldn't tell if it was real or maybe just a trick of the light combined with my anxiety over Devona's condition. I may not be the most imaginative guy, but living in Nekropolis will make anyone a bit jumpy. Here, monsters under the bed aren't just a childhood fantasy.

I didn't want to say anything, not only because I wanted to avoid worrying Devona but I also to avoid looking like a fool in case the bug was nothing more than my imagination. So I concentrated, and the thin flesh tendrils keeping my right hand attached to my wrist released their grip. I allowed my hand to fall to the floor, and I followed up the soft plap of its dead meat hitting the tiled floor with a muttered, "Damn it!" Then I bent down to retrieve my hand and took the opportunity to sneak a quick peek under the bed. There was nothing there, not even dust. It seemed the

hospital staff's fanatical devotion to keeping their in-
stitution germ-free extended to the finer points of
housekeeping as well. Which made the likelihood that
there were insects scuttling around the rooms seem all
the more impossible.

I decided the bug had been nothing but my imagination after all. I held my wrist stump near my hand,
and it obligingly backed up like a tiny vehicle in reverse
and reattached itself. I flexed my fingers to make sure
everything was working, and then I stood once more.

"You really should have someone sew that back on
while we're here," Devona said.

"Sorry," Dr Servia said, sounding anything but, "we
don't perform medical procedures on *your kind*."

The subtle added stress on those last two words got
my hackles up, but I kept myself from responding –
one more step on my way to becoming a paragon of
self-restraint. Devona's scowl told me she was going to
say something, but I reached out to her through our
link and projected a wave of calm to let her know that
I didn't think the doctor's comment was worth com-
menting on. Devona gave me a look that said, *All right,
if you say so*, but I could feel that she wasn't happy
about it. As a half-vampire she'd spent her whole life
dealing with the racism and classism of full-blooded
vampires, and she had little tolerance for it.

Servia continued with her examination with brisk
professionalism. When she was finished, she stepped
back and regarded Devona with unblinking eyes. Vampires don't need to blink, but the younger ones still do,

either to appear more lifelike or simply out of habit. Older vampires like Servia didn't bother with such mundane trivialities – if they even remembered them at all.

"Everything appears…" Her full red lips parted in a cold approximation of a smile. "Well, I can't say normal. But it seems that neither you nor your baby suffered any permanent ill effects from your interdimensional trip. But I advise you to refrain from any unnecessary exposure to magic during the remainder of your pregnancy. Half-vampires like you are typically sterile, and zombies…" she trailed off. "As I understand it, a significant amount of magical assistance was required in order for the two of you to conceive. While the spells were no doubt powerful ones, such magic is, in its own way, quite delicate. Other magic – especially the kind required for a dimensional crossing – may have a deleterious effect on the spells associated with your pregnancy. My advice is that you avoid both magic use and exposure until after your baby is born."

Though the doctor had just given us good news, you couldn't have told it from Devona's crestfallen expression.

"But Doctor, I'm a specialist in wardspells! I use magic in my business all the time!"

"Yes, the Midnight Watch. I've seen your commercials on Mind's Eye. Given your current situation, I suggest you take a leave of absence from work," Servia said. "And if that's not possible, then I advise you at least take a step back and assume a more supervisory role." She paused, and then added in a businesslike tone, "That is, if you wish to carry your child to term. Please see the receptionist at Admitting on your way out to schedule a follow-up appointment for next week."

And then without waiting for more questions – and without giving me another glance – Servia started toward the door. Varney hadn't said a word the entire time the doctor had been present, but he watched her go, his camera eye tracking her progress, and I wondered if despite his earlier pledge not to do any filming in here he'd been recording the entire time. I was just about to say something to him when the door opened and a male Bloodborn stepped into the room.

Both Servia and Varney immediately dropped to one knee and bowed their heads.

The newcomer was a huge, well-muscled barbarian of a man, wearing only a loincloth, boots, and a black fur cape. His skin was bone white, and his flesh appeared hard as marble. He had long brown hair, and a thick full beard which spilled down to his chest. His eyes were cold as arctic ice, and they gazed upon the world with the merciless calculation of an apex predator. This was Galm, Darklord and ruler of the Bloodborn, one of the most powerful and fearsome monsters that had ever existed. And he was one thing more…

Devona's father.

FOUR

Like all the Darklords, Galm projected an aura of power, and his presence filled the room with a charged atmosphere like the air right before a thunderstorm. He moved with the liquid grace of a jungle predator, seemingly at ease but ready to strike at any moment.

Servia and Varney kept their heads bowed and didn't move a muscle as their lord and master glided past. Devona didn't react to Galm with the same sort of subservience as the other two – he was her father, after all – but she looked shocked to see him, which was understandable, since the last time they'd spoken Galm had cast her out of the Bloodborn, told her that she wasn't welcome in his home, and – most hurtful of all – that as far as he was concerned, she was no longer his daughter.

I wasn't a vampire – at least not in this dimension – but I still felt the psychic impact of Galm's presence. I refused to let myself be intimidated, though. I'd dealt with Darklords before, Galm included, and while I respected the fact they were on top of the supernatural food chain, I'd be damned if I'd allow any of them to think they cowed me.

"Hello, Galm. I'd say it's nice to see you again, but my mother taught me never to lie to bloodsucking monsters."

Galm looked at me, his eyes flashing a dangerous crimson, but all he said was, "Richter," before turning his attention to Devona. He crossed to her bed and stood beside it, on the opposite side from where I was. He didn't smile, didn't reach out to take her hand. His eyes – cold blue once more – looked at her without even a glimmer of affection.

"When you were admitted, the hospital staff contacted the Cathedral and told my people. I came as soon as I was informed." Galm's tone was reserved, each of his words precisely enunciated, almost as if it required extra concentration for him to speak. He was thousands of years old, and I wondered if he was so ancient and powerful that he sometimes had difficulty remembering simple things, like how to use language. As inhuman as vampires can be by their very nature, the older they get, the more alien they become – and no vampire is older than Lord Galm.

Devona's initial surprise gave way to anger, and she struggled to control her voice as she spoke. "I didn't know you cared, Father."

Galm opened his mouth to reply, then stopped as if re-considering his words. He looked at Servia and Varney, who remained kneeling, and said, "You two may rise."

Servia and Varney did as they were commanded.

Neither spoke and they stood very still, as if afraid to draw the vampire king's attention. Unfortunately for them, Galm did not take his gaze off them.

He pointed to Varney. "What is your purpose here?"

Varney quickly – and without stuttering too badly – told Galm about the documentary he was filming. Galm looked at him a moment, and then said, "You may wait in the hall."

Varney, looking very relieved to be dismissed, bowed his head once, and got the hell out of there. I half-expected him to leave one of his little bug-cameras behind, but I didn't see him launch one. As much as Varney wanted to get good footage for the documentary, it seemed he wanted to risk angering Galm even less. I can't say I was sorry to see Varney kicked out.

Galm then looked at Servia. "You are her doctor, I assume?"

"Yes, my lord," Servia answered in a docile tone that contained no hint of her former haughtiness.

"Tell me about my daughter's condition."

Servia did so, clearly and concisely, and then Galm dismissed her. She left with more dignity than Varney, but it was still obvious from her expression that she was just as relieved to go. When the doctor was gone, Galm turned back to Devona.

"I am glad to hear that you and your baby suffered no permanent ill effects from your journey."

"Let's skip the pleasantries, Father," Devona said. "Why are you here? It's not out of concern for me, so there must be something you want."

Galm's features were as composed as any statue's, but as I looked across Devona's bed at him, I thought I detected a slight softening of his gaze. If he had been human, I might have thought her comment had hurt him. But this was Galm; mere words could never harm a being like him. Could they?

"Devona… as you know, live births are rare events among our kind."

That was putting it mildly. Vampires' primary method of reproduction was to exchange blood with a human who they'd drained near to death, hence the term Bloodborn. Vampires considered these converts to be their true children, normally carefully chosen and groomed to enter the realm of the undead. Sometimes, however, vampires mated with humans because their crossbreed progeny often possessed powerful psychic abilities that fully undead vampires didn't. That was the reason Galm had impregnated Devona's human mother, who had died during childbirth, as is often the case when human women bear half-vampire children, even with the help of the doctors at the Fever House. Galm had never demonstrated any love for Devona. He'd viewed her as nothing more than a useful tool, and when she was old enough, he'd put her to work in the Cathedral. In time, she had demonstrated an aptitude for understanding magic, if not casting spells herself, and Galm had made her the caretaker of his collection of rare and powerful artifacts. It had been her task to maintain the wardspells protecting the collection, and she had done so successfully for over fifty years before one of the objects was stolen and she'd hired me to find it.

"Don't tell me you're becoming sentimental in your old age," Devona said. "You're not exactly the type to get all excited about being a grandfather."

Devona was being pretty harsh with Galm, and though the sonofabitch undoubtedly deserved it, I couldn't help but feel a bit sorry for him. But only a bit.

Galm continued as if she hadn't spoken. "And no half-vampire has ever become pregnant before. This is a unique occurrence in the history of the Bloodborn, so naturally I am interested in following its progress." He paused. "I have had some time to think about what I said to you when we last spoke, and I have come to the conclusion that I was too hard on you. You have twice saved the city from destruction…" He looked at me, and one side of his mouth curled in mild disgust. "With your help, of course, Richter."

"Nice to be included," I said.

"And you have gone on to create a successful business for yourself. In only a few short months, the Midnight Watch has become the most sought-after security firm in the city, with a reputation for providing protection equal to none. All most impressive accomplishments, befitting the daughter of a Darklord."

I could feel Devona's emotions through our link. On one hand she was deeply suspicious of her father's change of heart – he *was* a Darklord, after all, and none of them are to be entirely trusted – but she also couldn't help hoping that what he was telling her was true, that if he didn't exactly love his half-human daughter, he'd at least finally come to see some value in her. Me? I didn't know what to believe, but I figured remaining suspicious was the safest bet.

"Does this mean she's no longer outcast?" I asked.

Galm looked down at Devona and smiled, though the expression looked unnatural on him, as if it had been many years since he'd last attempted it and couldn't quite recall how.

"You are once again a full member of the Blood-born, my daughter, and you are welcome in my home whenever you wish to come." He glanced at me. "And as her... partner, you are also welcome in the Cathedral."

"Does this mean I get to call you Dad?" I asked.

His ice-blue eyes flashed red and a low growl escaped his throat. "As the saying goes, 'Don't push your luck.'" His eyes returned to normal and he looked at Devona once more.

"I... I don't know what to say."

Galm smiled once more, and this time it seemed more natural. "You could always try 'thank you.'"

Galm hadn't exactly apologized for how he'd treated Devona, but he'd come as close as a creature like him could. Evidently Devona thought the same thing because she returned his smile and said, "Thanks."

Galm nodded briskly, as if they'd just concluded a business deal. "Good! And now that the matter is settled, I urge you to consider moving into the Cathedral for the remainder of your pregnancy."

"What?" Devona looked shocked, and I couldn't blame her. For the last several months, she'd been an outcast among her people, and now not only had her father welcomed her back into the fold, he was asking her to move home.

"The doctor advised you to avoid exposure to magic until you deliver your baby. In the Cathedral, I can arrange for the construction of a completely magic-free chamber for you. Not only would you be protected from mystical energies there, you could avoid some of the more, ah, *hazardous* aspects of your profession. You could still manage your business from the Cathedral, of course. I'd make certain you had whatever technology you require for your work: voxes, Aethernet access…"

"That's… very generous of you, Father," Devona said. "But I assure you, I'll be fine. Won't I, Matt?"

When I didn't answer right away, Devona scowled. "Won't I?" she repeated in a tone that said I'd better hurry up and agree with her if I knew what was good for me.

"I can't believe I'm saying this, but maybe you should give some thought to Galm's proposal." I hurried on before she could interrupt. "I know you hate the idea of being shut away from the world like some too-delicate thing that can't take care of herself. And I know that Galm and I sound like a couple of sexist Neanderthals for suggesting it." I glanced at Galm. "Although as old as he is, he probably can't help acting like a caveman since he literally was one once."

Galm frowned at me but said nothing, so I went on.

"Back on Earth, when a woman has a high-risk pregnancy, doctors often advise her to avoid strenuous activity and remain at home on bed rest. Not because they're patronizing her, but because they truly believe that's what's best for her health and the health of her baby. I'll support whatever decision you make – you know that – but I think you should make your decision based on logic, not emotion."

Devona looked at me for a long moment. Not only was her expression unreadable, but I couldn't sense anything through our link, and I knew she was shutting me out, psychically speaking.

"That's good advice," she said to me at last, and then turned to her father. "That's how you always make decisions, isn't it? Logically. I'd almost started to believe that there might have been some scrap of emotion motivating your offer to have me stay in the Cathedral, but you never do anything unless it's in your best interest or that of the Bloodborn – and as far as you're concerned, they amount to the same thing, don't they? You created me because you hoped I'd possess psychic abilities you'd find useful. And while those abilities have grown and strengthened over the last few months, they aren't so powerful or irreplaceable that you'd rescind my exile just to get them back. No, there has to be another reason behind your offer, and since you don't want me or my powers, it must be my baby that you want."

I felt a surge of anger upon hearing Devona's words, and I felt like kicking myself for being dumb enough to think that Galm might've actually cared about his daughter's health.

For his part, Galm gave no response to Devona, but while his face remained as impassive and cold as an ice sculpture, there was something in his gaze that told me Devona had hit upon the truth.

"What makes my baby so special?" she asked.

Galm didn't answer right away, but Devona just glared at him, and eventually he let out a surprisingly human-sounding sigh.

"I don't know," he said. "But there has never been a child like it before in the history of the Darkfolk. It will be a blend of human, Bloodborn, and–" he glanced at me with obvious distaste, "zombie."

"But I was human when we conceived the child," I pointed out.

"True, but that was only a temporary condition, brought about by a powerful token of death magic given to you by Edrigu. In a sense, the spell's effect was primarily cosmetic, and thus didn't alter your fundamental nature. It's why the change could not be a permanent one for you. Your child shall belong to three realms: the living, the dead, and the in-between. It is impossible to predict what such a child will be like – and what sort of power, if any, it might wield."

"But if the baby does possess powerful magic, you want to be the one to control it," I said.

"Yes, and why not?" Galm said. "Edrigu may have given you the token that made conceiving the child possible, but I will be its grandfather. I have more right to the child than anyone."

"You seem to be forgetting about the two of us," Devona said. Her eyes glimmered with crimson light and her canine teeth had grown more pronounced. More, I could once again feel her through our link, and I could sense her anger building.

"You are my daughter and one of the Bloodborn," Galm said. "Your child's magic *must* be made to serve your people's needs. It is your duty."

"*I'm* not one of the Bloodborn," I said, "and my child isn't going to serve anyone. Ever." I reached into my jacket pocket and took hold of my squirt gun. The mixture of holy water, garlic, and other chemicals inside would prove little more than an irritant to a vampire of Galm's power, but right then I felt like giving the sonofabitch a face full of the stuff. But I didn't draw the gun, though I was sorely tempted.

"I want you to go, Father," Devona said. "Now."

Galm regarded her for a moment, and then inclined his head slightly. "As you wish. But regardless of what transpires between the two of us from this point forward, I pledge that I shall never again turn my back upon you. You will always remain a member of the Bloodborn, and you shall always be welcome in the Cathedral."

Then without saying goodbye, Galm's body burst into several dozen shadowy fragments shaped like bats. This was his travel form, and the shadow-bats darted and swirled around the room for a moment before flying toward the door and slipping through the cracks. Galm was gone.

I turned to Devona to ask her how she was doing, but before I could speak, she buried her face in her hands and began to cry. I put my arms around her and held her tight and regretted not blasting her father in the face with holy water when I'd had the chance.

"But why do we need to fill out more forms?" I asked. "We already filled out a bunch when we checked in!"

The vampire behind the registration desk gazed at me with a blank, lifeless expression that would've done the most burnt-out office worker back on Earth proud. In fact, the resemblance was so uncanny I wondered if most drone jobs back home were staffed by vampires. It would explain a lot.

"Standard procedure, sir," she said in monotone as she pushed a sheaf of papers on a clipboard across the desktop toward us. She wore a spotless white uniform with a stylized red FH over her left breast. She had the usual vampiric ivory complexion, and her short black hair was practically a buzz cut. With the exception of the doctors, all of the staff I'd seen at the Fever House wore their hair similarly short, and I wondered if it was a hospital regulation.

Devona sat in a wheelchair next to me, and Varney stood behind us, presumably recording the whole banal scene. Just like in hospitals back on Earth, Devona was required to ride in a wheelchair until she was outside the building, and she didn't like it one bit. She was still upset about the less-than-pleasant reunion with her father, and I could feel her mounting

frustration with having to jump one more bureau-
cratic hurdle before we could check out. If we didn't
get out of here soon, I was afraid she might leap out
of her chair, grab the registration clerk by the throat,
and show her precisely what she thought of her "standard procedure."

"You already have our information in your system,"
Devona said, nodding toward the computer terminal
on the woman's desk. "Can't you just copy it elec-
tronically?"

The woman looked at Devona as if her body had just
made a socially awkward noise. "Computers have their
place, of course, but electronic files are no substitute
for handwritten records."

The vampires who live in Gothtown tend to be centuries old, and while they aren't above using
technology when it suits their purpose, they tend to
view it with suspicion and keep it at arm's length.
Younger Bloodborn – those only a century or so old –
have an easier time adapting to technology, and they
usually end up living in the Sprawl where most of the
high-tech in Nekropolis is found. Varvara is the only
Darklord who openly embraces technology, but then
as the Demon Queen, she'll embrace anything and
everything – and anyone – as long as it amuses her.

Devona bared her fangs at the woman, and I quickly
snatched up the clipboard, tucked it under my arm,
and wheeled Devona over to a empty seat in the waiting room. I parked her next to the chair, then I handed
Varney the clipboard.

"Were you filming when we checked in?" I asked him.

"Yeah."

"Good. Then if you were paying attention, you should be able to fill these out." I handed the clipboard to him before sitting down next to Devona. He looked at me, and I added, "Consider it a chance to get some close-up action footage."

He looked less than thrilled, but he wandered off to find an open seat – by some astounding coincidence I'd chosen the only available one on this side of the waiting area – and I turned to Devona.

"That was mean," she said, though she smiled. "You should treat him more nicely. When the documentary's finished, it'll be a good publicity tool for us."

"I'll see what I can do."

The Emergency reception area was even more crowded than when we'd checked in, and I recognized some of the Darkfolk waiting for treatment. Legion is a human who regularly rents himself out to several dozen spirits who take turns controlling his body, and he was covered with cuts and contusions. It looked like one or more of his tenants had indulged in a little too much fun again. Unfortunately, such injuries are an occupational hazard for him, making him a regular at the Fever House. Antwerp the Psychotic Clown sat next to Legion, giggling softly to himself. At least, I think it was Antwerp. It was hard to tell since whoever it was had somehow managed to get turned inside out. I wasn't surprised at Antwerp's bizarre condition, nor was I surprised that he seemed to be in no apparent pain. I was, however, surprised that he'd come to the Fever House to seek treatment. I would've thought Antwerp liked having his insides on the outside. On the other side of Antwerp sat a were-thylacine named Jerboa. The poor thing was suffering from a nasty case of silver rot in her pouch, and from the way she was whining, I figured it must've hurt like a bitch.

I turned to Devona. "How are you doing?"

"I feel fine."

"I'm not talking physically. I mean emotionally. That wasn't exactly the most tender of reunions between you and Galm."

She reached out and squeezed my hand. "I'm all right. Angry at myself a little, I guess. I know he can't change, but I allowed myself to hope he had anyway. When someone becomes Bloodborn, they don't just stop aging. Their personalities freeze, and they stop developing mentally and emotionally. They become like living portraits that can move and talk but never change. I should've known that the only interest he'd have in our baby is in how it might increase his own power."

"I'm not denying that Galm wants to use our child for his own purposes, but – and I can't believe I'm sticking up for him – it seemed like his offer was motivated by more than self-interest. He seemed to genuinely care about your health too."

Devona scowled at me, and I could feel a flash of anger through our link. "Are you going to tell me you've changed your mind and think we should move into the Cathedral?"

"Nope. As far as I'm concerned, your father can take his offer and shove it where Umbriel doesn't shine. I'm just saying that maybe it's possible that even a being who's millennia old can change, if only a little."

Devona scrunched her face at me, but she didn't reply. A nurse summoned the patient sitting next to me – a squat little bald man in a shapeless black coat who seemed to have a glowing light bulb stuck in his mouth – and he got up and followed her to an examining room. The seat next to me didn't remain vacant for long. A tall male vampire with a pair of huge ebon wings sprouting from his shoulder blades took it. His wing feathers were made of lightweight metal, with razor-sharp edges, and I had no idea if they were technological, magical, or some combination. He wore no shirt so as not to constrain his wings, only a pair of black pants. His chest was covered with scars, but they were old and long healed – or at least as healed as they were ever going to get – and I knew they hadn't brought him to the Fever House. What had was obvious: one of his wings hung significantly lower than the other, and a good half of its feathers looked loose, as if they might fall out any moment, and they were blackened, as if they'd suffered fire damage.

"Hey, Matt. Hey, Devona. What are you guys doing here?"

"Hey, Ichorus," Devona said. "We just came for a routine check-up." She patted her slightly swollen belly and smiled at him. Ichorus was an acquaintance more than a friend, and I guess that Devona didn't feel comfortable telling him about what had really brought us here. Or maybe she just figured it was too complicated to bother going into. Either way suited me. I tend to be a private person, and I'd rather ask people questions than answer them.

"Let me guess: you had a flying accident," I said.

He grinned. "What else?"

Ichorus lived to violate the "no-flying" law in Nekropolis, which was why he carried so many scars. The Darklords defended their Dominions' airspace quite aggressively, and the fact that Ichorus' vampiric healing abilities hadn't been able to completely deal with all the injuries he'd received during his illegal flights was testament to how serious the Darklords were about the sanctity of their airspace.

"Still trying to see how close you can come to the Darklords' strongholds without getting killed?" I asked. "Or were you flying low over Phlegethon and dodging the Lesk again?"

"Neither," Ichorus said. "I have a new passion these days. I've been searching for Ulterion."

"Seriously? Don't tell me you fell for that fairy tale!"

Devona frowned. "What's Ulterion?"

Devona had lived most of her life sheltered in the Cathedral, rarely venturing outside its walls. Because of this, there were lots of things she didn't know about Nekropolis, things that I – a relative newcomer – often had to fill her in about.

"The moon," I said. "Umbriel is the Shadowsun, and Ulterion is the Hidden Moon." I glanced sideways at Ichorus. "Or so the stories go. I don't know anyone who takes them seriously."

Ichorus grinned again. "You do now! I've been looking for Ulterion for the last couple weeks, flying as high as I can, testing the upper limits of the city's atmosphere. I figure Ulterion has to be within Nekropolis' atmospheric bubble. After all, Umbriel is."

"Why would we need a moon?" Devona asked. "Umbriel provides the power that keeps the city stabilized in this dimension, as well as providing the energy for Phlegethon. What would Ulterion *do*?"

"That's the mystery," Ichorus said. "When I find it, I'll figure out what its purpose is."

"You can't find it because it doesn't exist," I said. "Dis and the Darklords created Nekropolis and Umbriel. Why would they create a moon only to hide it and conceal its existence?"

"I don't know," Ichorus said. "That's—"

"— the mystery," I finished for him. "I get that."

"Besides, I have proof that Ulterion exists." He paused. "Well, *maybe* it's proof. On this last flight, I went higher than I ever had before, and I thought I saw something in the sky. No, *saw* is the wrong word. Even vampire eyesight can't make out anything in the starless void over the city. But I sensed something… something *big*, and I headed toward it. I kept on flying, getting closer and closer, and then… Well, I don't know what happened next, but *something* happened, because

I woke up on the ground – specifically, in the middle of a fair-sized crater I made in one of the Wyldwood forests. My left wing had been damaged by some kind of blast attack, and the rest of me was extra crispy, as if I'd been severely burned. I lay there awhile, letting myself heal, until I heard a group of lykes approaching, no doubt coming to investigate what had crashed in their forest. I hadn't healed enough to fly, but I could move, so I climbed out of the crater and started running. I managed to heal the worst of the burns as I ran, but my wing didn't heal all the way. But it got good enough to allow me to leap into the air and glide for decent distances, which is how I avoided becoming lyke chow. Once I got out of the Wyldwood, I came straight here. The doctors should be able to help my wing heal the rest of the way. At least, I hope they can. The idea of being grounded…" He shuddered as he trailed off.

"So you have no memory of being attacked?" Devona asked.

"None whatsoever. I don't know if I blocked it out or if it just happened too fast. But I figure I got too close to Ulterion and triggered some sort of defense mechanism. A spell or some kind of tech. There's got to be a reason it's called the *Hidden* Moon, right? Maybe somebody wants to make sure it stays hidden."

"Or maybe you just ran into another of the Darklords' air defenses," I said. "A kind you've never encountered before."

Ichorus tried to shrug, but the shoulder with the damaged wing refused to move. "Maybe." He grinned once more. "When my wing is healed, I'll go back and find out for sure."

"You'll go back and get yourself incinerated if you're not careful," I muttered.

"Maybe," he said. "But you know my motto: 'Fly free or die.'"

Varney came over to us then. "I finished the forms and returned them to the registration desk. Can we go do something interesting now? Please? My producer will kill me if I don't keep delivering good footage." He paused as if reconsidering. "Actually, since my producer is a demon, killing me is probably the least of what he'll do to me."

"I suppose we can't have you suffering the tortures of the damned just because we're boring," I said. "Let's go." I stood and began pushing Devona's wheelchair toward the exit. "Good luck with the wing," I said to Ichorus as we left.

Ichorus grinned one last time and gave me a thumbs-up.

As we walked, I turned to Varney. "You know, if it's exciting footage you want, maybe you should forget about filming us and do a documentary on Ichorus. Think about it: an intrepid explorer, a rebel who defies authority, on a perilous quest to discover the truth about one of Nekropolis' oldest legends…"

Varney gave me a look.

I shrugged. "Can't blame a guy for trying."

FIVE

"Make sure to get my good side, OK?"

I wanted to point out to Lazlo that he didn't *have* a good side, but Varney was the cameraman, not me, and I decided to let him break the news. He decided, however, to duck the issue. "I'll, uh, do my best."

Lazlo's a demon, and to put it mildly, not a particularly attractive one. He's a mix of mammal and insect and looks as if a good portion of his insides are on the outside. Clothing might help – especially if he wore a full-body hazmat suit with a darkened visor – but Lazlo prefers to go au naturel, which is most unfortunate for everyone in Nekropolis with functioning eyesight. He exudes a horrendous stench that I thankfully can't smell, but I didn't like to think about how bad it was for Devona and Varney, considering their enhanced vampire senses. Devona at least had the advantage of having been around Lazlo enough times over the last few months to get somewhat used to his stink. Varney, who had been relegated to sitting up front with Lazlo,

hadn't had that dubious pleasure, and his face was
paler than usual and he kept swallowing, as if he were
fighting to keep from throwing up.

We'd left the Fever House and were driving through
Gothtown's major cultural district. We'd just passed the
theaters and concert halls on Mummer's Row and were
now heading down the Avenue of Dread Wonders.
Given their long lives, vampires have a strong appreci-
ation of history and the arts, and the Avenue of Dread
Wonders was where the greatest museums in the city
were located. We passed the Pavilion of Nightmares In-
carnate, the Great Library, and the Hemesphere, among
others. I was tempted to ask Lazlo to stop at the Great
Library, as it had been a while since I'd talked with
Waldemar, and I thought the ancient vampire might be
able to shed some light on Devona's condition. There
was no limit to Waldemar's knowledge, and he could
answer any question – for a price. It was a price I was
willing to pay and had before, but I knew Devona
wouldn't approve, and so I let Lazlo drive on by without
saying a word. I told myself that maybe I could come
back later, when Devona was otherwise occupied. I
didn't like the idea of sneaking around behind her back,
but I liked the idea of gambling with her health and the
health of our baby even less. As far as I was concerned,
the more knowledge we could get, the better. And if the
price I had to pay for that knowledge was a bit steep, so
what? It would be worth it to me.

Devona had been mostly quiet since we'd left the
Fever House, gazing out the back passenger window as

we traveled, and I knew that she was brooding over her less-than-warm reunion with her father. I wanted to talk to her about it, but it wasn't the sort of subject I felt comfortable bringing up in front of either Lazlo or Varney, and so I left Devona to her silence and contented myself with holding her hand. Eventually she spoke.

"Do you really think Papa Chatha will be able to give us any advice?" she asked. "He's not a doctor, and he's not even exactly a magician. He's a voodoo priest."

"True, but he has one thing that no other doctor or magic-user in the city has," I said. "My trust. Not only does he know enough about magic to keep me from rotting away to nothing, he's provided magical assistance to me on numerous cases over the years." I paused. "Besides that, he's my friend."

"I suppose it wouldn't hurt to get a second opinion," Devona said, managing to give me a smile. It wasn't very big and it didn't last very long, but I appreciated the effort.

And while we were there, I'd see if Papa could take a look at my right hand. It remained attached to my wrist and continued to work just fine, but that condition was merely temporary. I needed Papa's magic to effect a more permanent repair job. But what was foremost on my mind was the revelation Galm had given us about our child. Could it really be possible that our baby would be as powerful as Galm claimed? That he or she would possess a kind of magic unlike any that the Darkfolk had ever known before? The thought scared the hell out of me. I was already afraid of being a father – afraid that I wouldn't be smart enough, patient enough, loving enough – but to be a father to a being of immense power? There was no way I was up to that kind of challenge.

Varney turned around in his seat to look at me. "Sounds like Papa Chatha's been a real help to you over the years. Can you tell me how the two of you met?" His camera eye whirred softly as it focused on me, and I felt a now-familiar urge to draw my 9mm and smash the gun butt into the lens. Instead I sighed.

"I'm not sure it's that interesting a story, but all right. I'd only been in Nekropolis for a couple weeks when Baron Samedi got wind that there was a new kind of zombie in town – one who was not only intelligent but wasn't under the control of a sorcerer. Samedi decided he wanted to examine this undead novelty, and he sent one of his servants to collect me."

I continued relating the tale, only half paying attention to myself as I talked. I saw a greenish flickering light ahead, and I knew we were approaching the edge of Gothtown. Nekropolis is shaped like a gigantic pentagram and split into five separate Dominions, each ruled by a separate Darklord. At the center of the city is the Nightspire, home to Father Dis, the ultimate ruler of Nekropolis, and floating in the starless sky directly above the Nightspire is Umbriel the Shadowsun, the dark celestial orb which provides the city with the shadowy gloom that serves in place of light. A river of mystical green fire called Phlegethon forms the city's outer border and also the divisions between Dominions. Phlegethon's flames are deadly to all creatures living, dead, or undead, with the exception of the monstrous serpents called Lesk which swim its waters. While it's possible to fly over the flames – assuming one possesses the capability – it's illegal to do so. Not to mention dangerous as hell since the Lesk will try to leap out of the water and snatch you out of the air. The only legal and safe way to travel between the Dominions is across one of the five bridges that connect the Dominions, and we were nearing the Bridge of Nine Sorrows, the passage between Gothtown and the Sprawl.

Papa Chatha's place was located in the Sprawl not far from the bridge, and I knew we'd be there soon, which suited me just fine. I was more nervous about the complications with Devona's pregnancy than I wanted to admit, even to myself, and even though I knew Papa wasn't a physician, he had a calming way about him, and I figured I could use all the reassurance I could get.

The greenish glow increased in intensity as we drew closer to the bridge, its light standing out dramatically against the black void that serves in place of a sky in Nekropolis. When the Darkfolk decided to emigrate from Earth long ago, they chose to relocate to a distant uninhabited dimension called the Null Plains, a place of utter darkness and desolation. But the Null Plains aren't, as it turned out, entirely uninhabited, as I'd learned during the last Descension Day, and as I looked at the empty dark sky, I wondered if it too was truly empty or merely *seemed* that way.

By this time Lazlo had pulled onto the Obsidian Way, the glossy black road which passes through all five

Dominions, and joined the line of traffic leaving Goth-town and heading for the Sprawl. There was the usual mix of Earthly vehicles – limousines and high-performance sports cars being favorite choices – traveling alongside stranger conveyances: ghostly coaches, riders on hell-mounts, and Agony DeLites. There were also a fair amount of scuttling Carapacers, hollowed-out giant insect husks reanimated to serve as vehicles, and Meatrunners, leprous obscenities constructed (if that's the right word) from sinew, muscle and bone. Both of these vehicles had sprung from the diseased imagination of Victor Baron, the original Frankenstein monster and the city's leading inventor and industrialist. He's responsible for all the flesh-tech in Nekropolis. All the "repurposed dead," as they're called, bear his tattooed label: "Another Victor Baron creation." Baron had reattached my head to my body for me once, and though my left hand still didn't work quite right, he'd gotten most of the major connections hooked back up properly, so I figured I couldn't complain. I wouldn't let him slap a tattoo on me when he'd finished, though.

We pulled onto the bridge and were about a third of the way across when a bright light flashed overhead. Both Lazlo and Varney cried out in alarm – light in any form is at best frightening to Darkfolk and at worst deadly – and our demon cabbie slammed a misshapen foot onto the brake pedal. The vehicle swerved and sideswiped a were-panther motorcyclist. The catman veered off, struck the bridge railing, flew over his handlebars of his bike, and plummeted over the edge and

into the fiery river below. Lykes can heal almost any
injury, but I wasn't sure he could survive Phlegethon's
flames. Maybe if he managed to crawl out before one
of the Lesk got hold of him… I forgot all about the
were-panther then, for the light continued to shine
brightly onto the bridge, and the other drivers had either hit their brakes like Lazlo or jammed down on the
gas in hope of making an escape. The result was, as you
might imagine, a complete and total traffic clusterfuck,
and the air was filled with the sounds of crunching
metal and the howls of frustrated, terrified, and injured
drivers. Whatever was happening, one thing was clear:
none of us were going anywhere anytime soon.

"Is that sunlight?" Varney asked. He'd slumped
down onto the seat and curled into a ball. As scared as
he looked, I wouldn't have been surprised if he'd tried
to claw through the upholstery and climb inside the
seat to hide.

"I don't think so," Devona said. "It looks more like a
release of mystic energy to me."

"I'll go out and take a look," I said. Sunlight has no
effect on zombies, except maybe to dry out our rotting
skin a bit faster. As a half-vampire, Devona wasn't as
affected by sunlight as Varney, and I had no idea about
Lazlo. Some demons shun sunlight, some don't mind
it, and some few actually thrive on it. I didn't know
what kind he was. But if anyone was going to step outside and take a gander at the situation, I was the safest
bet. Besides, I was more than a wee bit curious. I knew
of only one object capable of projecting sunlight in this

dark dimension, and Dis had it safely locked away in the Nightspire – or so I believed. If someone had managed to get hold of it somehow, it would be a Very Bad Thing. I opened the rear passenger door and stepped out onto the bridge.

The first thing I noticed was that the sides of Lazlo's cab were expanding and contracting rapidly. The vehicle is, at least in some rudimentary sense, alive, and from its rapid breathing, I knew it was scared. I reached up and patted it on the roof.

"There, there," I murmured. "It'll be OK."

The cab whined like a frightened puppy and shivered under my touch. I doubted I'd done anything to reassure it, and I decided to leave that task to Lazlo. After all, he was its owner. Or sibling. Or lover. Or perhaps something else entirely. I didn't know, and I didn't *want* to know. I looked around and saw that a number of other motorists had gotten out of their vehicles and were gazing up into the sky. They were a mixture of Darkfolk – lykes, ghosts, demons, ghouls and some other less common types – but no Bloodborn. Presumably any vampires trapped on the bridge, like Varney, were remaining hidden inside their vehicles. I directed my gaze upward, touching a hand to my brow to shield my eyes.

The light shone above us bright white and cold, like starlight against the stark black sky, but by squinting I was able to make out a trio of figures floating in the air within the patch of illumination. The light began to fade, and once it was gone I could see the figures more clearly. They were human – or at least human-seeming – all female, and all using some sort of magical steed to remain aloft. One sat astride a giant raven, another rode a midnight-black horse whose mane and tail crackled with electric energy, and the last sat in a chair made from human bones with a pair of large flapping bat wings protruding from the back. The women were dressed in medieval-era clothing, making them look like refugees from a Renaissance fair, and they held wooden staves with glowing crystals affixed to the ends.

The witch on the raven's back spoke, her magically amplified voice booming forth like thunder.

"Tell Varvara that if she does not return our people to us within twenty-four hours, Talaith shall consider it a declaration of war between our two Dominions! This shall be her only warning!"

Before I could say anything – not that I had any idea what to say – the three Arcane women leveled their staves at the bridge and their already-glowing lux crystals blazed even brighter with power. As I watched, I became distantly aware of Lazlo shouting at me.

"Matt! Get back inside! Now!'"

The lux crystals grew so bright that it hurt even my dead eyes to look at them, and I wracked my brain to try to come up with something I could do to stop the Arcane. I usually carry a number of magical weapons and tricks with me, but I didn't have anything even close to powerful enough to deal with a trio of pissed-off sorceresses.

Lazlo yelled again, louder this time. "Matt!"

The demon's voice was drowned out by a deafening roar, and the reptilian head of a Lesk came into view. The great serpents were tasked by Father Dis with protecting the borders of the city, and this one looked more than ready to do its job. The behemoth's plate-sized eyes shone with anger, and green fire trailed down its scaly neck as the serpent stretched up toward the hovering witches, jaws open, teeth glinting in the light cast by their magic. The horse rider swiveled her staff toward the attacking beast and a beam of magic energy shot forth from the lux crystal to strike the massive serpent in the face. The Lesk shuddered once and then exploded into a cloud of butterflies which – as if realizing they were no longer quite as intimidating as they had been a moment ago – quickly scattered and flew off in separate directions.

I generally don't have much use for the Arcane, as they tend to think a little too highly of themselves, but I had to admit that was a nifty trick. I felt a hand grab my shoulder then, and out of reflex I drew my 9mm and jammed the muzzle into the soft flesh behind Lazlo's chin. Luckily, I had enough presence of mind not to fire… although as awful as the demon looked, he could probably stand to have his facial features re-arranged a bit.

"You need to get into the cab, Matt!" Lazlo shouted, seeming not at all intimidated by having a gun pressed against his throat. "We're leaving!"

"What the hell are you–" I heard a tearing sound then and looked down to see that Lazlo's cab was, for

lack of a better word, shedding its tires. Thick strips of
black rubber peeled away to reveal clawed lizard feet
instead of metal rims, and the vehicle's chassis began
to rise as scaled legs extended from the wheel wells.
Evidently, the cab had decided not to stick around for
a fleet of tow trucks to arrive and clear away the
wrecked and stalled vehicles clogging the bridge, which
– since it looked as if there wasn't going to be a bridge
in a few moments – was a very smart move.

I'd long ago given up questioning the bizarre nature
of Lazlo's cab and had decided to do my best to appreciate its quirky charms, especially when they saved my
undead ass. I holstered my gun, and Lazlo and I
hopped back into the cab. Before we slammed the
doors shut, the cab fully extended its legs and began
racing forward, scuttling between and, when necessary, crawling over the mass of unmoving vehicles as
it made a beeline – or in this case, a lizardline – for the
Sprawl side of the bridge. Lazlo's cab has no seatbelts
(he feels they only cause passengers to doubt their driver's capability), and so Devona and I held on to each
other as best we could as the cab surged forward. Varney, who up until this point hadn't had occasion to
experience the special surprises that Lazlo's cab served
up from time to time, looked about as bewildered as
you might imagine. Still, he was a professional cameraman, and he hurriedly rolled down his window,
crawled halfway out, and used all his vampiric strength
to hold onto the roof for support while he filmed what
was happening.

The cab had made it halfway across when all three
Arcane women released blasts of mystic energy from
their staves at different points of the bridge to devastat-
ing effect. First, they targeted the supports beneath the
bridge, then they fired again, this time shearing through
the bridge's surface, cutting it into separate pieces.
Cracks appeared in the glossy black substance of the
Obsidian Way, and the loud groaning of slowly twisting
metal filled the air. It was quickly followed by shouting
and screaming as terrified motorists abandoned their
vehicles and began running to get off the bridge before
it collapsed. Some of the fleeing drivers had the misfor-
tune to get in the way of Lazlo's cab, and they were
either knocked aside or trampled as the lizard-legged
vehicle raced pell-mell toward the Sprawl. Four more
Lesk rose from Phlegethon's fiery waters to attack the
Arcane, but they met with no more success than their
predecessor. A few blasts from the magic-users' staves
was all it took to deal with the serpents. One exploded
in a shower of what looked like dandelion fluff, one's
flesh ran off its skeleton like melting wax, one turned
into several thousand minnows, and the last shrank
down to the size of an earthworm before falling back
into the river.

The damaged bridge shuddered beneath us, and the
cab lurched as it fought to maintain its footing. The railing collapsed, the bridge listed to one side, and the
Obsidian Way – already cut into three pieces – shattered
into dozens of jagged fragments that then began to slide
toward the blazing green waters of Phlegethon. Vehicles

and fleeing drivers tumbled into the river, the Darkfolk screaming all the way down, though their screams ended abruptly once they were claimed by Phlegethon's fiery embrace. The cab's lizard claws scuttled frantically for purchase on what remained of the Obsidian Way, broken fragments of the road shifting beneath its feet as it ran. The cab slipped and slid, and more than once I thought we would fall into the river and be lost. But when the cab was within twenty feet of the Sprawl side, it hunkered down, coiled its leg muscles, and then sprang forward with a mighty leap just as what was left of the Bridge of Nine Sorrows collapsed completely. The cab soared through the air, and Varney pulled himself back inside with a panicked yelp as the bridge – and those unlucky enough not to get off it in time – plunged into the river, gouts of water splashing upward with accompanying bursts of green flame.

The cab landed on the broken edge of the Obsidian Way where the bridge had torn away from the road, and it scrabbled with its back legs to keep from falling into the water. It was close, but the cab managed to climb up onto the road, where it collapsed, exhausted.

"You OK?" Devona and I asked each other at the same time. We nodded in answer, then we climbed out of the cab, along with Varney and Lazlo, and surveyed the devastation that the Arcane had wrought. The bridge and its occupants were gone, swallowed by Phlegethon, and the river's roiling fiery surface was slowly becoming calm once more. The three witches remained hovering in the sky, and the raven rider spoke, her voice once again magically augmented so that it could carry for miles.

"Tell Varvara she has twenty-four hours, and not a moment more!"

And then light erupted around the three Arcane women, and when it was gone, so were they. A tele-portation spell, I assumed.

"What in the name of Oblivion was *that* all about?" Varney asked. While he gazed at the river's surface, continuing to film, he sounded quite shaken.

"I believe that is what's known as an attention-get-ter," I said. If Varvara wasn't already aware of the attack on the bridge, she soon would be, and I doubted the Demon Queen was going to take the news calmly.

"It's more than that," Devona said, sounding just as shaken as Varney. "It's an opening salvo."

I had a bad feeling she was right.

Devona stepped closer to the broken ledge and peered down at the river. She was six feet to the left of Varney and stood even closer to the edge than he did. I was still standing next to the cab, and I felt extremely uncomfortable seeing Devona so close to the edge. I wanted to call out and tell her that she should step back, that it wasn't safe, but I hesitated, mindful that the last thing she wanted was for me to babysit her. I decided I'd rather irritate her than risk her falling, and I opened my mouth to ask her – in as non-patronizing a manner as I could manage – not to stand too near the edge. But before I could say anything, a chunk of the Obsidian Way – already cracked from the bridge's collapse – beneath Devona's feet broke into several fragments, slid out from under her, and tumbled toward the river. Devona's feet slipped, she lost her balance, and started to pitch forward.

For a horrible instant, time seemed to stand still, and I saw Devona slide, arms flailing, in the process of following the stone fragments down into Phlegethon's deadly flames. I was too far away to reach her in time, even if I had normal reflexes, which as a zombie, I don't. Half-vampires don't possess the ability to assume travel forms, and her psychic powers were restricted to telepathy for the most part, so there was no way she could fly or use telekinesis to save herself. She was a dead woman, and there was nothing I could do about it.

But then Varney was standing next to her, gripping her upper arm to steady her as he pulled her back from the edge.

"Careful," he said, smiling. "You taking a nose-dive into Phlegethon might make for some spectacular footage, but it would be a real downer." His smile turned into a grin. "No pun intended."

"Thanks," Devona said, looking shaken, and then she and Varney returned to the cab.

I thanked Varney too, said something about him not being entirely useless after all, and we got inside the cab and Lazlo drove off. Or maybe I should say he lizard-legged off. I was quiet as we traveled. Full-blooded vampires can move hellaciously fast when they want to, but I hadn't seen Varney move at all – not even a blur. One moment he'd been nowhere near

Devona and the next he was right beside her, saving her life. The whole thing struck me as way too mysterious man-of-action for Varney, the airheaded hippy cameraman. Then again, I'd only known him a short time and I'd done my best to ignore him for most of it. Maybe there were other sides to him that I just hadn't experienced yet. I told myself just to be grateful that Varney had reacted swiftly enough to keep Devona from falling into Phlegethon. But something about the whole thing raised my suspicions – which, given what I do for a living, isn't all that hard to do, I'll admit – and I decided to keep a closer eye on Varney to see what other surprises he might have in store for us.

SIX

We continued on our way to Papa Chatha's house, the vehicle trotting down the cramped streets of the Sprawl on its lizard claws. The motion felt odd, but overall the ride was smoother than usual, and since I'd had enough of being shaken around during the bridge's collapse, I was grateful.

Lazlo turned the radio to Bedlam 66.6, and we listened to an announcer report the news of the destruction of the Bridge of Nine Sorrows as well as the Bridge of Forgotten Pleasures. It seemed that after the three witches had finished with the first bridge, they had teleported to the second – which connected the Sprawl to the Wyldwood – and destroyed that as well, once again delivering the message that Varvara should return the abducted magic-users. The Sprawl was now cut off from its neighboring Dominions, and I didn't want to think about how furious Varvara would be. There was a reason she was queen of the demons, and it had nothing to do with her having a sunny disposition. According to the report, Sentinels – Father Dis' police force – were on the scene to assist with the rescue efforts, and while I was confident the golems would prove immune to Phlegethon's fire, I doubted they'd find anyone alive to pull out of the river.

I felt as if we should do something to help, but I had no idea what. Open conflict between Darklords was rare – they usually preferred to conspire against one another in secret and strike through intermediaries – but if Talaith and Varvara were going to mix it up on the streets of Nekropolis, the best thing to do was to stay the hell out of their way and hope not to get caught in the cross-fire. Better to mind our own business and go visit Papa.

The Sprawl is a wild mishmash of architectural styles – ancient, medieval, Renaissance, colonial, Victorian, art deco, Bauhaus, modern, and post-modern, inter-spersed with bizarre structures that can only be classified as alien. You can find a sleek glass and steel office building sitting next to a lopsided lumpy mon-strosity that looks like a mound of suppurating tumors, and a quaint little antique shop nestled next to a busi-ness housed in a gigantic hollowed-out skull. Considering the Sprawl is the Dominion of the De-monkin, the mad disregard for even the basics of urban planning makes a kind of nightmarish sense, and it cer-tainly makes navigating by landmarks easier. In what other city can you tell someone to hang a left at the building made from intertwined spinal columns and continue north until you come to something that looks like a gigantic diseased pancreas?

Papa Chatha lives in a little shack that wouldn't be out of place in a bayou on Earth. The worn gray wood could use some paint, the black shingles on the bowed roof need replacing, and the windows could stand to be washed and the cracked panes swapped for new ones. But compared to some of the more surreal structures in the Sprawl, Papa's shack looks almost cheerfully normal. Besides, it's something of a second home for me, the place I come when I need a fresh application of preservative spells, a quick repair job, or – just as often – a good game of rattlebones, an understanding smile, and a sympathetic ear. After Devona, Papa is my best friend in Nekropolis, always there when I need him, and always understanding if it's going to take me a while to scrounge up enough darkgems to pay him for his services. And in a town where there are literal loan sharks who'll devour you if you're so much as a few minutes past your payment deadline, such understanding when it comes to settling a debt is indicative of the deepest levels of friendship indeed.

Papa's shack sits between an eye-scream parlor and a florist's that featured a half-off sale on Audrey II's. Lazlo pulled his cab up to the curb in front of Papa's, and the vehicle retracted its lizard legs and lowered itself to the ground.

"Here you go," Lazlo said. "Safe and sound, as usual."

"Safe I'll grant you," I said. "The jury's still out on sound, though."

Lazlo let out one of his raucous laughs that sound

like a cross between a donkey's bray and an explosive blast of flatulence.

"You never stop kidding, do you, Matt?"

Varney, Devona, and I climbed out of the cab, and I had to resist the urge to hold out my hand to help Devona out. She wasn't so far along in her pregnancy that she needed assistance, and I didn't want it to seem like I was patronizing her. When we were all out, I leaned inside the front passenger window.

"You going to wait for us or do you have somewhere to be?" I asked Lazlo.

"I should go home for a bit," Lazlo said. "My sweetie needs to eat so she can regenerate her tires, and she could probably use a nap to help her recover from all the excitement. Isn't that right, dear?" He patted the dash and a loud purring sound came from under the cab's hood.

I had no idea Lazlo had a home. Given the way he always appears whenever I need him, I'd just assumed that he lived in his cab. After all, from what Devona tells me, the cab certainly smells like he lives in it. And I didn't want to think about what the cab might eat.

I thanked Lazlo for the lift, he gave me a parting wave, and the cab stood once more on its lizard legs and trotted off down the street. Varney's gaze tracked the departing vehicle, his cyborg camera-eye no doubt recording its departure.

"You know" he said, "even for Nekropolis, that thing's weird."

I didn't know if he was referring to Lazlo or the cab, but either way, I couldn't help but agree. We walked up to the front door of Papa's shack and I knocked. He didn't answer right away, but that wasn't unusual. Like a lot of magic-users, Papa's often conducting one experiment or another, and sometimes he's so engrossed in what he's doing that he doesn't hear people knocking. Or if he does hear, he chooses to ignore them. So I knocked again, louder this time, and called out, "Papa, it's me – Matt!" A few more moments passed, but I still didn't worry. Papa tends to be something of a homebody – after all, he works out of his shack – but he regularly leaves to go shopping for supplies. Even the most skilled practitioner of voodoo magic has to run out to the store to pick up a bag of severed rooster claws now and again. And while Papa wasn't much for the Sprawl's party scene, I'd known him to hit a club or two in his time. So when he didn't answer, I merely chastised myself for not calling ahead first to see if he was home before we stopped by. I turned to Devona, about to ask her what she wanted to do now, when the door opened.

I expected to see Papa Chatha looking out at me: a dignified bald black man in his sixties with a blue butterfly tattoo spread across his smooth-shaven face. The person looking through the crack at me was black, but that's where the resemblance ended. She was a pretty girl of thirteen or so, medium height – which made her taller than Devona – with long straight hair that stretched almost down to her waist. She wore a purple pullover dress that reached to the ankles of her bare feet, and no makeup or jewelry. She gazed at me with startling eyes, the irises so dark blue they were almost black. They made her seem far older than her apparent years, which in Nekropolis is always a possibility.

"May I help you?" she said. Her voice held an almost musical quality, but her words were precisely enunciated and her tone formal, almost as if she were speaking a language foreign to her.

I almost said, *And you are?* but I remembered my manners. "We're here to see Papa Chatha."

She looked past me at Devona and Varney. She must've decided they didn't appear too suspicious because she then turned her attention back to me and asked, "Are you clients of his?"

"We're friends. At least, she and I are," I said, nodding toward Devona. "Is Papa home?"

Her expression grew solemn. "No," she said, "and that's the problem."

We were gathered in Papa's workroom. Whenever I visited Papa, whether professionally or personally, the two of us usually hung out here, and it was where I felt most comfortable. Besides, for some reason it seemed like an invasion of Papa's privacy to use his living quarters when he wasn't home.

Papa's workroom contained everything a self-respecting houngan needed: chemical-filled vials, jars filled with ground herbs and preserved bits of animals – raven wings, rooster claws, and lizard tails – all sizes and colors of candles, rope of varying lengths twisted into complex patterns of knots, voodoo dolls made of horsehair and corn shucks, tambourines and rattles lying on tabletops next to piles of books and scrolls. To the untrained eye, it looked like things were placed haphazardly about the room, but I knew better. Papa keeps everything just where he wants it, and just because his system of organization isn't immediately apparent doesn't mean he doesn't have one.

I leaned against a workbench, arms folded over my chest, Devona standing next to me. Varney stood on the other side of the room in the corner, the better to film the entire room, I supposed. The girl, who'd introduced herself as Shamika, sat on a high stool, bare feet dangling several inches from the wooden floor.

I looked at Shamika. "You're really Papa's niece?"

Devona elbowed me. "She already told you she was."

"Sorry. I don't mean to sound so skeptical, but Papa's never mentioned you before."

I wasn't sure what bothered me more. The fact that Papa had never spoken about his family to me or that I'd never asked him about them. Maybe we weren't as close as I thought we were, and I wondered how much of that was my fault.

"Most of our family lives on Earth," Shamika said. "Our ancestors were pure Arcane, but many of their descendants married humans over the years, and not all of their children could work magic. Those that could moved to Nekropolis. The rest stayed on Earth."

Unlike other Darkfolk, Arcane appear perfectly human, and this allows them to interbreed with humans, if for no other reason than humans don't find them automatically repulsive and run screaming in the

other direction. Because of this, Arcane bloodlines
have become greatly diluted over the centuries, resulting in fewer true Arcane being born, and those who
are born with the ability to work magic aren't always
very powerful. It's one of the reasons Talaith is fiercely
protective of her people: she fears the eventual extinc-
tion of the Arcane race. Among the five Darklords, she
was one of the strongest proponents for the creation of
Nekropolis. She hoped that relocating her people to another dimension would limit their opportunities to
breed with humans, forcing them to mate within their
own race. She couldn't outright forbid intermarriage –
that would go against the Blood Accords, the laws that
govern all Nekropolitans, Darklords included – but she
does everything she can to discourage it.

I glanced at Devona's slightly swollen belly. If what
Galm had told us was true, our interbreeding was going
to produce a truly special child. And while I suppose I
understood the rationale behind Talaith's medieval
mindset, I was glad neither Devona nor I shared it.
What a great adventure we'd have missed out on.

"How long has it been since you heard from Papa?"
Devona asked Shamika. Her tone was gentle, and
through our link I could feel her concern for the girl.

"Three days. I stopped by for a visit, but he wasn't
here, so I called his vox and left a message. He usually
calls back within a couple hours, but when he didn't, I
tried again. He didn't answer, so I left another message.
I kept calling and leaving messages, but he never called
me back. Finally, I got so worried that I came over here

and…" She looked suddenly sheepish. "I used my magic to let myself in." She brightened a bit. "I'm not as powerful as Uncle, but I can do a few tricks."

"Don't be so modest," Devona said. "The security spells Papa has placed on his shack are top-notch, if a little… idiosyncratic. You have to know more than a 'few tricks' to get past them."

Shamika looked suddenly uncomfortable. She gazed down at the floor and shrugged. "I suppose."

I pulled out my hand vox, flipped open the lid, and pressed Papa's number. I hated using the damned thing – the tiny ear you speak into is weird enough, but the small mouth you press your own ear against is just plain gross, especially when it gets a little sloppy with its tongue. I listened to Papa's phone ring several times, and then I got his voicemail. The vox-mouth spoke in a perfect imitation of Papa's voice, and the effect was eerie as always, like Papa was whispering in my ear.

"If you called my number, you know who I am, and you know what to do."

The vox-mouth made a tiny beep sound, and I started talking.

"Hey, Papa, it's Matt. Devona and I are at your place, sitting and talking with Shamika. She's worried about you and wonders why you haven't been returning her messages. Give her a call ASAP, and call me back too, while you're at it."

I disconnected and put my vox away.

"So Papa's been gone for three days, and he's not an-swering his vox or returning messages." I didn't like

the way this was looking. Like most magic-users, Papa
was highly disciplined – you need to be when working
with chaotic and potentially lethal forces – and he lived
by a regular routine. It simply wasn't like him to devi-
ate from it. I'd never known him to leave his home for
so long, and I had a hard time believing he would ignore his niece's messages. He was too considerate.

Devona looked at me, and though she didn't speak
aloud, I heard her voice in my mind.

*Do you think Papa's disappeared like those other magic-
users who've vanished?*

I understood why Devona was speaking telepathically. She didn't want to alarm Shamika unnecessarily.

It's possible, I answered. *It's also possible that any number of awful things have happened to him. This is Nekropolis,
you know. But Papa's a highly skilled magic-user and, more
importantly, a smart man. He can protect himself well enough
from the city's usual dangers.*

It's the unusual ones I'm worried about, Devona said.

*I agree. I think we should ask around a bit and see if we
can find out what Papa's gotten himself into. Don't you?*

I waited for Devona to respond, but all I heard in my
mind was silence. I looked at her, but she was staring
off into space, not moving, not even blinking.

"Devona? Honey?"

No response. I leaned over and nudged her, but she
didn't budge. She felt as solid and immobile as a statue.

I looked over at Varney and Shamika, and saw both
of them were similarly frozen. What the hell was going
on here? Had we accidentally activated one of the

magic objects lying around in Papa's workroom, and if so, why hadn't its power affected me?

"Because if I froze you too, it would be awfully difficult for us to hold a conversation, wouldn't it?"

The voice was a rich, mellow tenor, and it seemed to issue from the empty air. An instant later the shadows in the room all flowed toward a corner, merged and expanded, shaping themselves until they finally resolved into the form of a man. He appeared to be in his mid-thirties, stood over six feet, and wore a purple toga. He was movie-star handsome, with short curly black hair, a large but distinguished-looking nose, and the kind of smile that when you saw it made you want to smile back. But appearances are all too often deceiving in Nekropolis, and not only was he not a man, he was far, far older than he seemed. This was Father Dis, once worshipped as a god of death by the Romans, the absolute ruler of the Darkfolk and the single most powerful being in the city – which also made him the most dangerous.

He walked toward me with an easy, relaxed stride, but the aura of power that surrounded him put Galm's to shame. If being in Galm's presence was like sensing an oncoming thunderstorm, being close to Dis was like sensing the approach of a Category 5 hurricane, with an earthquake or two tossed in for good measure.

"Hello, Matthew."

Dis stopped when he reached me and held out his hand, but I hesitated to shake it. As far as I knew, Dis had no ill feelings toward me, but I still found him intimidating as hell. After all, he could reduce me to a pile of dust with a mere thought, and he could do far worse if he felt like exerting himself. But in the end I shook his hand, and it felt like any other. I didn't look too deeply into his eyes, though. I was afraid of what I might see there.

Dis frowned as we shook. "Had a little accident, did you?"

I was startled by a sudden warmth in my wrist. I don't experience physical sensation on a regular basis, and when I do, it usually means there's some serious magic at work.

"There," Dis said as he released my hand. "Good as new! Well... as new as a zombie can get, I suppose."

I flexed my fingers, then rotated my wrist. Everything felt solid and properly connected once more, and I realized Dis had reattached my hand to my body. I'm sure it was child's play for him, considering that he'd once reconstructed my entire undead body.

"Thanks," I said, because when a god does a favor for you – even when that god scares the crap out you – it's a good idea to be suitably grateful.

"You're welcome. You don't have to worry about Devona and the others. I'll return them to normal when we're finished talking, and they'll be none the worse for wear. And there will be no ill effects for Devona's pregnancy either. Congratulations on that, by the way."

"Thank you. I'm a little confused about why you felt a need to freeze them at all, though."

Dis walked around Papa's workroom as he talked, looking over the items on the tables and shelves, occasionally lifting one to examine it, before putting it back down and moving on to another. "The balance of power in Nekropolis is a tenuous thing at best. The laws that govern the city apply not just to its citizens, but also to the Darklords – and myself. But there is one law that applies to me alone: I may not directly interfere in a dispute between the Darklords."

"By 'dispute,' I assume you're talking about Talaith sending a strike force to destroy the bridges that link the Sprawl to its neighboring Dominions."

"Yes. The Weyward Sisters, often mistakenly referred to as the 'Weird Sisters.' A trio of sorceresses almost as powerful as Talaith herself. The ancient Greeks called them the three Fates, and the Vikings knew them as the three Norns. Dispatching them to destroy the bridges was Talaith's way of telling Varvara that she is deadly serious about her ultimatum."

"Talaith believes Varvara is responsible for the missing magic-users. Is she?" I asked.

Dis stood before Shamika now, and he paused to regard the girl, reaching out to gently brush her cheek with his fingers. He then turned to face me.

"If I knew, I couldn't tell you, as passing along such information would constitute interference."

"Not to point out the obvious, but you're Dis. You're more powerful than all five Darklords put together. If you really want to interfere, who can stop you?"

"I'm not as strong as you might imagine, Matthew, and as I've told you before, most of my strength goes toward maintaining both Phlegethon and the city's stability in this dimension. I don't have much power left over for settling arguments between squabbling Darklords. But even if I did, I wouldn't try. The cooperation of all six of us is needed to recharge Umbriel each year, and while I donate the lion's share of mystic energy to that process, I couldn't accomplish it without the others. When the Darkfolk first moved to Nekropolis, I tried to impose my will upon the Darklords in order to keep the peace, and not only did it not work out, it nearly resulted in the destruction of the city on more than one occasion. It took a while, but I finally learned my lesson. The less I interfere, the better. My Sentinels patrol the Dominions, and my Adjudicators deal with any criminal investigations or legal disputes that the Darklords either don't wish to or cannot handle on their own, but that's the extent of my interference."

"That's not completely true," I said. "You destroyed Gregor."

"Gregor was a threat from outside the city, and thus not specifically covered by our laws."

"What about this conversation? That's why you froze the others, isn't it? So they wouldn't hear it." I nodded toward Varney. "You froze his eye camera too, right? He's not recording us, is he?"

Dis gave me a look that said, *You know I'm a god, right?* "Varney's ocular device is paused, and I've made sure that when he plays back his footage of this visit, there will be no indication he missed recording anything. And to answer your original question, yes, I want to make sure this conversation is private between you and me." A hint of a smile played across his lips.

"I may not exactly be breaking any laws by talking to you, but I am bending them significantly."

"Then let me save you the trouble of having to bend them any further. If someone – say, for example, me – were to investigate the disappearances of the magic-users and discover who's behind them and why, the answers will hopefully settle the conflict between Talaith and Varvara, preventing all-out war between the two Dominions."

"Such a person would be doing the city a great service," Dis said noncommittally.

"Assuming this person manages to remain in one piece long enough to get the answers," I said. "I doubt if either Varvara or Talaith will be in a mood to cooperate with an investigation, especially one that doesn't have any official sanction. And when Darklords get cranky, they have a tendency to annihilate first and ask questions later." A thought occurred to me. "Speaking of official investigations, why not have the Adjudicators look into the disappearances?"

"They have been," Dis admitted, "but without much success. Like too many of the Darkfolk, they tend to believe most problems are better solved by the application of force – the more extreme the better – instead of brainpower."

I thought about my less-than-pleasant experience with First Adjudicator Quillion. "I know what you mean."

"But this situation requires someone who's not only a skilled investigator but also an insightful one. Someone who can see things as they are, not as they appear."

There was nothing special in the way Dis spoke these last words, but I nevertheless had the feeling that he was trying to tell me something important. Just because he couldn't come out and tell me clearly didn't mean that he couldn't hint, and I filed the comment away for later pondering.

"I don't suppose this job comes with a fee attached?" I said hopefully.

"Just my undying gratitude," Dis said, giving me that movie-star smile of his.

"That's what I was afraid of." I sighed. "All right, but tell me this: is Papa's disappearance linked to that of the other magic-users?"

Dis just looked at me, and for a moment I thought he wasn't going to answer, but then he simply said, "Yes."

I nodded. "Then I'll take the case. Is there anything else you can tell me before I get started?"

"Just good luck."

And then Dis turned, stepped back into a pool of shadows that had gathered in one corner of the room, and vanished.

"Thanks a lot," I muttered.

"Thanks for what?" Devona said, frowning.

She was moving again, as were Varney and Shamika.

"Nothing. Just thinking out loud." I wanted to tell Devona about the visit from Dis, but I didn't feel comfortable doing so in front of Varney and Shamika. I considered filling Devona in telepathically, but the others would see the two of us staring silently at one another and wonder what was going on. I decided I'd tell her later. I knew Dis wanted me to keep his visit secret, and I would, but not from Devona. She was my... well, my partner, and I wasn't going to keep any secrets from her, even if a god wanted me to.

Devona gave me a strange look, but she didn't press any further. Instead, she said, "So what's our next move?"

"I think we should head on over to the Midnight Watch. Maybe Bogdan will be able to cast some kind of tracking spell that will allow us to locate Papa Chatha." I knew it wouldn't be that simple, though. The Adjudicators had access to the best magic and technology available in the city, and if they hadn't been able to track down the missing magic-users, I doubted the Midnight Watch's resident warlock would be able to. But since Bogdan was Arcane, he might have some insight into why someone would want to abduct magic-users in the first place. If nothing else, it was a place to start. Too bad I could barely stand to look at the sonofabitch, let alone talk to him.

I turned to Shamika. "Why don't you come with us? Maybe you can help Bogdan." I had no idea how powerful or skilled a witch Shamika was, but I figured Papa was her uncle and she deserved to be included in the investigation – until it started to get dangerous anyway. And what could possibly be dangerous about going to the Midnight Watch?

SEVEN

"I'm going to tear your head off and use it for a bowling ball!"

"Not before I transform you into something small and extremely squishable!"

Devona, Varney, Shamika and I stood in the entrance to the great room of the Midnight Watch. Since Lazlo hadn't been available, we'd hired a skeletal rickshaw pulled by a long-limbed ghoul to get us here. Devona had renovated the great room not long ago, and it had all-new leather furniture, abstract holo art hanging on the walls, and an illusory fire flickering in a brazier set in the fireplace. The mystic fire produced light but no heat, which was great for me since I tend to get a little on the dry and flammable side when my preservative spells start to wear off.

Devona's three employees were there: Tavi stood next to the fireplace, keeping his distance from Bogdan and Scorch, who from the look of things were less than pleased with one another. The two faced each other in front of the large black leather couch, hands balled into fists, jaws jutting forward pugnaciously, looking for all the world like a pair of bickering children.

Despite the fact that it sounded as if Bogdan and Scorch might soon come to blows – or more likely, because of it – Devona strode into the room, looking pretty angry herself. I almost asked her to hang back just in case a fight really did break out, but I managed to keep quiet. I told myself no matter how upset Bogdan and Scorch were, they wouldn't hurt Devona, and I believed it. More or less.

"What the hell are you two doing?" she demanded.

Bogdan answered Devona without taking his eyes off Scorch. "She started it!" His right hand touched the golden medallion that hung from his neck, and I knew he was prepared to cast a spell – in all likelihood, an appallingly nasty one – on Scorch if she so much as made a move toward him.

Bogdan was an irritatingly handsome warlock in his late thirties, tall, broad-shouldered, with red hair and beard with just a hint of gray. A sharp dresser, he always wore a stylish outfit of one kind or another, and today he had on a suit made of spidermesh that hugged his fit body like spandex. I think spidermesh looks silly on most people, but I had to admit he made it work, damn him.

I should probably mention that he has a crush on Devona too. At least, that's what I – the trained detective – think. Devona says I'm a jealous idiot and it's just my imagination. I admit that Bogdan's never come out and hit on Devona, but I think he's just biding his time.

Devona turned to Scorch. "Well?" she demanded.

Scorch appeared to be a slender teenage girl with a long blonde ponytail that stretched down to the middle of her back. She usually dressed garishly, and today she wore a Black Flag concert T-shirt cut to expose her bare midriff, along with a mini-miniskirt over a pair of hot pink tights and ultra-high heels. If I hadn't already known she was a supernatural creature, the shoes would've given it away. There's no way a human woman could've successfully maintained her balance on such ridiculous footwear.

Scorch's skin is usually the typically light color of blondes, but at the moment it had a reddish cast to it, and though I couldn't feel it, I knew waves of heat were rolling off her. She was a fire demon, and when she got angry, she literally got hot under the collar, or in her case, under the cut-off T-shirt.

"We were talking about Talaith's unprovoked attack on the Sprawl–" Scorch began.

Bogdan cut in before she could finish. "Hardly un-provoked. Rumor has it that there's evidence Varvara is somehow involved in the recent disappearances of magic-users. While I admit that Talaith was a bit... overzealous in her response, I wouldn't say–"

"Overzealous!" Scorch's skin darkened a couple shades and patches of scale began to appear. Her girl-ishly thin limbs swelled a couple sizes, her neck thickened, and a pair of stubby horns protruded from her forehead. Scorch's other form was that of a classical fire demon – big, scaly, powerfully muscled, horned, fanged, clawed, with a long tail that ended in an arrow-tipped point. She only assumed her full demonic aspect when she intended to wreak some serious havoc, and the fact that her change was beginning was not a good sign that she was going to be calming down anytime soon. "Talaith had the Weyward Sisters destroy *both* bridges! And without so much as a warning! That sounds more than a 'bit overzealous' to me! It sounds like Talaith is looking to start a war, and if that's what the bitch-witch wants, that's what we Demonkin will give her!" Scorch paused ominously, her eyes turning a very disturbing crimson. "That's what we'll give all of you Arcane!"

Bogdan glared at her and clutched his mystic medallion tighter, but he didn't start slinging spells just yet.

Tavi looked at Devona. "I am so glad you're here!" he said. "The two of them have been going at it like this for twenty minutes now. I tried to settle them down, but they wouldn't listen to me."

Tavi was an East Indian man, lean and wiry, wearing a tan nehru jacket and matching pants. At least, that was his current form. Like Scorch he was a shapeshifter, but he wasn't a demon. He was a lyke, and as such he could assume a wildform whenever he wished, and given the way he was eyeing Bogdan and Scorch with increasing alarm, I figured he'd been on the verge of transforming in order to protect himself when we'd walked in.

I looked at Varney and Shamika. Varney was grinning like a kid on Descension Day, no doubt recording

every second of Bogdan and Scorch's fight for his documentary. Shamika looked at the two of them with
curiosity but no alarm. I didn't know if she'd spent all
her life in Nekropolis or if she was an immigrant like
me, but I chalked up her lack of fear to living in a city
where the denizens are just as likely to go at each
other's throats as they are to say hello. Nekropolitans
are used to sudden outbreaks of violence in the same
way that people who live in rainy climates come to expect periodic cloudbursts.

"They're not always like this," I assured her.

She looked at me skeptically, but didn't say anything.

"The two of you need to sit down, cool off, and discuss this like adults!" Devona said in a
you'll-listen-to-me-if-you-know-what's-good-for-you
voice. A tone that like would serve her in good stead
as a mother, I thought. Hell, *I* practically took a seat on
the couch, and she wasn't even yelling at me.

Bogdan smirked at Scorch, whose skin had turned
scaly and a deep crimson; her horns had become far
more pronounced, though she still appeared partially human.

He said, "I have a feeling I'll have an easier time
cooling down than she will."

An angry bellow burst from Scorch's throat, the
sound deep and savage, like something a jungle animal
might make. She raised her right hand palm upward
and materialized a ball of fire in it. I knew we had only
a split second before she hurled it at Bogdan, prompt-
ing him to defend himself magically, and then the

fighting would begin in earnest. I decided I'd stood by long enough.

"Rover!" I called out to the air.

A sudden gust of wind blew through the great room, extinguishing Scorch's fireball. But the wind didn't stop there. It increased in intensity, centering on Bogdan and Scorch, swirling around them like a mini cyclone. The wind whipped their hair around and tore at their clothes as it lifted them off the floor and held them suspended several feet in the air.

I shouted to make sure they could hear me over the roaring wind. "Are you two going to cut it the hell out, or should I tell Rover to start spinning you around?"

Both Bogdan and Scorch yelled various rude phrases at me, but eventually they acquiesced, and I commanded Rover to put them down. I should've been a bit more specific about how, I suppose, because the wind abruptly ceased, unceremoniously dumping both Bogdan and Scorch onto their backsides. Oh well. Maybe it would knock some sense into them, I thought.

A gentle breeze ruffled my hair, and I reached up to trail my fingers through the air as a way of petting Rover. "Good boy," I said.

Shamika looked up at the air with a frown. "What is that?"

"Rover is a sentient security spell created by the warlock who originally owned the Midnight Watch," I told her. "Devona inherited him when she bought the place. He's kind of like our pet, I suppose." A deadly pet who had killed everyone who'd tried to purchase the Midnight Watch for years until we came along, but I figured there was no point in telling Shamika that. Once Rover understood that we meant no harm to him or the business his creator had established, he'd curbed his murderous tendencies and had been well behaved ever since.

Shamika continued staring into the air as if she could see Rover. Who knows? I thought. Since she was a magic-user, maybe she could. "Interesting," was all she said.

Bogdan and Scorch – the latter looking once more like an ordinary teenage girl – both got up off the floor, took seats on the opposite ends of the couch, and pointedly avoided looking at one another.

"Sorry," Scorch muttered grudgingly.

"As am I," Bogdan said with stiff dignity.

"There," I said. "Was that so hard?"

In answer, they just glared at me.

Tavi looked relieved, Devona looked like she was trying very hard not to smile, and Varney looked as if I'd just pooped on his parade. I'm sure he was disappointed that I'd robbed him of some great hand-to-hand combat footage.

"Everyone, I'd like to introduce you to Shamika," I said. "She's Papa Chatha's niece, and it looks like Papa may be among the missing magic-users."

Despite the fact that Bogdan and Scorch had been ready to kill each other only a few moments ago, they were professionals, and they – along with Tavi – listened with full attention as I told them about our witnessing the attack on the Bridge of Nine Sorrows and our visit to Papa's home – omitting the visit by Dis, of course.

When I was finished, Scorch started to say something, but I held up a hand to stop her. "I'd rather not discuss the destruction of the bridge right now. I want to focus on Papa's disappearance."

Scorch scowled, but she nodded and kept whatever she'd been about to say to herself. While any citizen of Nekropolis is technically free to live in any of the five Dominions, the Darkfolk tend to stay in whichever one the Darklord of their species rules. Thus Bloodborn tend to live in Gothtown, the Arcane in Glamere, lykes in the Wyldwood, and the Dead in the Boneyard. Since Varvara rules the Sprawl, the Demonkin live there, but since the Demon Queen believes the bigger the party the better, she encourages anyone and everyone to come play in the Sprawl and, if they wish, to live there. And as a result, the Sprawl is by the far the most cosmopolitan and diverse Dominion in the city. But those of us who live here and aren't of the diabolic persuasion forget that the Demonkin view the Sprawl as their home and see the rest of us as guests. Scorch was angry because she saw the destruction of the two bridges as an insult to her people and their Darklord, and I had no doubt the rest of her demonic brothers and sisters felt the same way. I wondered how many more scenes like the one I'd just witnessed between Scorch and Bogdan were playing themselves out in the businesses and streets of the Sprawl right now. Angry demons confronting equally angry witches and warlocks, all of them far too eager to settle their disputes with blood. The Sprawl was dangerous enough at the best of times, but I had a bad feeling it was swiftly going to get a hell of a lot worse out there if someone didn't find out who was behind the disappearances of the magic-users – and soon. And unfortunately for me, I'd been elected to be that someone.

Thanks a lot, Dis, I thought to myself.

"But you don't have any actual evidence that Papa was abducted," Bogdan pointed out.

"As far as we know right now, there's no evidence that any of the missing magic-users were abducted," I said. "All we know is that they're gone."

Bogdan opened his mouth as if to contradict me, then he frowned. "I suppose you're right." He glanced at Scorch, she looked back at him, and I could see the last of their anger at each other drain away.

"That's not to say there isn't *any* evidence," Devona pointed out. "Presumably Talaith believes she has some, or else she wouldn't have attacked."

"Maybe," I said. "But Talaith's nuts. It wouldn't take much to prompt her to order an attack. A vague suspicion or whispered rumor could easily have been enough to set her off."

Again, Bogdan looked as if he might say something, but he didn't. The Arcane might be loyal to their Darklord, but I haven't met one yet who didn't understand that Talaith could be, as Bogdan himself had put it a while ago, *overzealous* at times. Instead, the warlock shifted back to professional mode.

"Since we don't have any evidence at our disposal, I suppose we should try to get some," he said. "I could attempt to cast a spell to locate Papa Chatha."

"Which is why we came here," I told him.

"And you've probably already come to the conclusion that if Papa has experienced the same fate as the other missing Arcane, I likely won't be able to find him. Because if it were that simple, someone else would've tracked down the missing people by now."

"Yes," Devona said, "but if Papa's missing for a different reason..."

Bogdan nodded. "Then with any luck, I'll be able to find out, and hopefully locate him in the bargain." He stood up, clapped his hands together, and rubbed them briskly. "I'll need something of Papa's to help me work the spell, or at least something related to him." He looked at Shamika. "Actually, you might work best since you're literally related to him. Would you be willing to help? I assure you, you'll be perfectly safe and suffer no ill effects."

A look of panic came into Shamika's eyes, but it vanished just as quickly as it appeared. "I'll be glad to help in any way I can, but I think Mr Richter would be a better choice. Uncle has cast many spells on him over the years, leaving traces of his personal aura behind. I would think you could use that to make a more effective connection."

Bogdan looked at her blankly for a moment, then grinned. "That's a brilliant idea! You might have a genetic link to Papa, but Matt has a mystical one, and magic is what we need most right now. I'm impressed. You don't usually find such a high level of thaumaturgical thinking in someone so young."

Shamika looked uncomfortable, and I figured Bogdan's comment had embarrassed her.

"What's wrong, Bogdan?" I said. "Surprised that you got outthought by a kid?"

He gave me a look that said I wasn't half as funny as I thought I was. "Let's go into another room. The spell will be more effective if the two of us are alone when I cast it." He glanced at Varney. "And before you ask, when I say just Matt and me, I mean it."

"Bummer," Varney muttered, but he stayed where he was.

"Come on, Matt," Bogdan said. "Let's go."

I turned to Shamika. "Hopefully, this won't take long, and with any luck, we'll get some information that will lead us to Papa."

"Maybe," she said, but didn't sound confident, and I didn't blame her. Still, I didn't want to discourage her, so I gave her a parting smile before turning to Devona.

Don't worry, she thought to me. *I'll look after her while you're gone*.

I nodded, and then followed Bogdan out of the great room.

Bogdan and I went into Devona's office, where it took him only ten minutes to cast his spell. He gripped his medallion, chanted words in a language I didn't recognize, and made a series of mystical gestures in the air

with his free hand. But in the end, the result came as
no surprise.

"Sorry, Matt," Bogdan said. "I'm unable to locate any
trace of Papa at all."

I'd had plenty of time to think while Bogdan had
been working his magic, and I asked him about one of
the things that had occurred to me. "Is it possible that
Papa is using his own magic to hide himself from tracking spells?" I knew he was capable of it, since he'd
done the same for me not long ago when Quillion had
put a price on my head and every bounty hunter in the
city had been hunting me.

"Normally, I'd say yes," Bogdan said. "But Shamika
was right. Papa's put a lot of work into you over the
years, and because of this the two of you have a strong
mystical connection to each other. That connection
should allow me to locate him even if he is attempting
to hide. Even if he were dead, I would be able to locate
his corpse. But as I said, I can detect no trace of him.
Something is preventing Papa from being tracked magically – something powerful."

I might not be Bogdan's biggest fan, but he's a highly
skilled warlock, and I took him at his word.

We left Devona's office and headed back to the great
room. Someone had brought in a portable Mind's Eye
set and put it on the floor in front of the couch. Everyone had gathered around it, and they were all grinning
and laughing.

"What are you watching?" I asked as Bogdan and
I entered.

Varney turned to me. "While you were gone, my producer transmitted some finished footage of the documentary to me, and I'm playing it for everyone."

"You can do that?" I'd had no idea Varney could receive information transmitted directly to him, and then turn around and transmit it to a nearby Mind's Eye set.

Devona had saved a seat for me on the couch, and she patted it, indicating I should join the group. From the amused way everyone was looking at me, I already had a bad feeling before I sat down, but once I did and mentally tuned into the Mind's Eye transmission, I realized things were far worse than I could've imagined.

I saw an image of a shadowy alley, and the silhouette of a man walking down it, away from the camera. A voiceover accompanied the footage – *my* voice, but they were words I'd never spoken.

"It was dark, even for Nekropolis. The shadows in the alley were as cold and unfeeling as my undead flesh, and though I moved among them like a creature born to darkness, they gave me no comfort. The shadows might be where I belonged now, but they'd never be home.

"I was searching for Argus of the Thousand Eyes, a small-time criminal who worked the streets of Ruination Row, one of the most squalid neighborhoods in the Sprawl. The sidewalks there are caked with filth, the gutters slick with blood, and the air heavy with despair and suffering. On Ruination Row, a visitor's life expectancy can be measured in mere moments, but that didn't scare me because I was already dead."

"Oh my God," I said, but everyone shushed me and the travesty continued.

"*Counterfeit darkgems had been appearing on the streets of the Sprawl over the last few weeks, and I'd been hired by the Dread Exchequer to discover the source of the faux darkgems. Argus had a thing for highlander ale – made with real Scotsmen – and rumor had it that he'd been paying his extensive bar tabs with the phony darkgems. I'd encountered him a few times before, and I knew he was the type to cave under pressure. All I had to do was find him and after a brief but painful conversation – painful for him, anyway – he'd tell me what I needed to know. Of course, by the time I was finished with him, he might have to change his name to Argus of the Rather Less Than a Thousand Eyes, but that was OK. It wasn't as if he couldn't spare a few dozen.*

"*I stepped out of the alley and nearly bumped into a human woman wearing a tight red dress with a bodice so low and a hemline so high she might as well have been walking around naked. She was a beautiful brunette with long hair that spilled over her shoulders and framed her more than ample breasts. No rail-thin model type she. She was luscious, just this side of Rubenesque, and I felt hunger begin to rise. My needs weren't sexual, though. My hunger was literal. I wanted nothing more than to sink my teeth into her succulent flesh and tear off sweet bloody chunks of meat. Without realizing it, I took a step toward her, my hands raised, ready to reach out and snatch hold of her. But though it took every ounce of self-control I possessed, I fought my hunger down and slowly lowered my hands.*

"*The woman gave me a knowing wink.*

"'*See something you like?*' *she said in voice seasoned by too many cigarettes and too much whisky.*

"'*Too much,' I said, my own voice husky with barely suppressed need, and for perhaps the thousandth time since I'd found myself condemned to the hellish nightmare that was Nekropolis, I cursed my undead existence, I cursed my undead desires. I loathe this city, but not nearly as much as I loathe the monstrous thing I've become.*"

I'd had enough. I rose from the couch and swiftly turned off the Mind's Eye set, eliciting disappointed groans from the others.

"C'mon, Matt!" Scorch said. "It was just getting good!"

Bogdan was grinning so wide I thought his face might break. "That was a fascinating glimpse of the master at work. I had no idea you were such a tortured soul, Matt."

Devona's grin was just as big. "And *I* never knew you had a thing for well-padded brunettes."

"But that's not how it happened! I mean, it *is* what happened, but that's not what I was thinking at the time. For godsakes, you all know I'm not a flesh-eater!"

"Maybe you've just been suppressing the urge," Tavi said, grinning like the rest of them. "No need to feel ashamed. I'm a lyke; I understand."

I scowled at him, then turned to look at Varney. The vampire didn't even have the good grace to at least pretend to be embarrassed.

"Nothing personal, but my producer thought the footage of you tracking down Argus was a bit on the, uh, dry side. So he decided to spice it up a bit with the voiceover. He used a speech synthesizer to make it sound like you. Turned out great, huh?"

"Look, I don't know what journalistic standards you Darkfolk practice – if any – but back on Earth, a documentary is supposed to be nonfiction. Heavy emphasis on the *non*!"

Varney shrugged. "Sure, but that doesn't mean it can't be entertaining too, right?"

I sensed Acantha's hand in this. She'd love nothing more than to get back at me for how I'd humiliated her during her live broadcast, and it looked like she'd finally found a way.

"Can we watch some more?" Shamika asked, almost shyly. "It was fun."

"No, we cannot," I told her, then I turned to look at the others. "We're supposed to be trying to find Papa Chatha, remember?" I told them of Bogdan's failed attempt to mystically trace Papa. I thought Shamika would be disappointed, but she displayed no reaction to the news. I told myself that she probably hadn't expected Bogdan's spell to work, but I still found her lack of expression odd.

"So what do we do next?" Scorch asked.

Tavi spoke up. "I can dash over to Papa's and see if I can pick up a scent trail to follow. I'll give you a call if I find anything." Before any of us could respond, Tavi started to change. Patches of fur and scales covered his flesh, and his limbs became long and flexible as if they were made of rubber. His mouth and nose elongated into a canine snout, his eyes became yellow and serpent-like, and a reptilian hood spread out from his head. Tavi was a mixblood, a lyke who'd used genetic engineering to alter his wildform. He was a combination of mongoose and cobra, and while I had no idea which had been his original wildform, the combination of the two made him most formidable. Speed, strength, cunning, agility – he had them in abundance.

When Tavi said he intended to dash over to Papa's, he'd meant it literally. He ran out of the room so fast he was little more than a blur of motion, and the wind kicked up by his swift exit was strong enough to rival any gust that Rover could produce.

When Tavi was gone, Bogdan stroked his beard in thought. "I'll make some discreet inquiries among my contacts in the Arcane community here in the Sprawl. Perhaps some of them can provide insight into the disappearances of the magic-users."

"Sounds good," I said. "And Devona and I will go straight to the top."

Devona frowned. "Why do I not like the sound of that? Are you suggesting we talk to–"

"Varvara," I finished for her. "Yep. After all, right now she's the chief suspect in the disappearances. The only suspect, really."

"Are you sure that's a good idea?" Devona asked. "Varvara likes you well enough, but her attention is going to be focused on preparing a retaliation against Talaith for destroying the bridges. Even if she's behind the disappearances and Talaith was justified in her attack, Varvara can't let her aggression go unanswered. I doubt the Demon Queen will be in the mood to receive visitors."

"Maybe not," I admitted. "But when have I ever let the fact that someone didn't want to talk with me ever stop *me* from talking with *them*?"

Devona smiled. "Good point."

"If you two are planning on going to Demon's Roost, then I should accompany you," Scorch said. I started to protest, but Scorch cut me off. "The Demonkin are going to be upset over the Weyward Sisters' attack. Neither of you are Arcane, so their anger won't necessarily be directed at you, but once my people get stirred up, they can be like a nest of angry hornets. They'll sting anyone unlucky enough to get in their way. Having a demon escort might make things go more smoothly for you."

I wanted to tell her that Devona and I could handle ourselves just fine without her help, but I had to admit the precaution she suggested was a sensible one.

"All right. And that leaves just one detail to attend to." I turned to Shamika. "We could drop you off at your home."

It was a given that Shamika wouldn't be accompanying us to Varvara. I wouldn't take a kid to Demon's Roost at the best of times, and I certainly had no intention of taking her there while Varvara might be preparing for war. But I didn't like the idea of the girl going home by herself, either. Traversing the streets of the Sprawl is always an iffy proposition safety-wise, and having a whole lot of pissed-off demons running around wasn't going to make them any safer – especially for a young Arcane woman.

Shamika looked at me for a moment, and I had the feeling that she was at loss for how to answer. But then she said, "I'm too worried about Uncle to go home. I need to know what happened to him."

Devona scooted closer to Shamika and put a sympathetic hand on the girl's arm. My better half may have been raised in a Darklord's stronghold, but she's one of the kindest souls I've ever met. She can also kick major ass when she wishes, making her the woman who has it all, as far as I'm concerned.

"I'd feel the same way if I were in your position," Devona said. "Why don't you stay here? The rest of us will be gone for a while, but the Midnight Watch is one of the most secure places in the city."

"And Rover will be here to watch you," I added.

"We'll make sure to call you as soon as we learn anything," Devona finished.

Shamika didn't even think about it. "I'd rather go with you." She hurried on before we could say anything. "I don't think I could stand to just sit around here by myself waiting. And it's not like I can't take care of myself. I *am* Arcane, you know."

But you're just a teenager, I thought, but I didn't say it. Regardless of appearances, everything and everyone in Nekropolis is dangerous in one way or another. You have to be in order to survive from one tick of the clock to the next. Just because Shamika looked sweet and innocent didn't mean she couldn't be lethal when she had to. Scorch's teenage girl guise was a perfect example.

I looked at Devona and she looked at me. This time I didn't have to access our telepathic link to know what she was thinking. Devona smiled at Shamika.

"OK, honey, but stick close to us," she said. "All right?"

Shamika smiled gratefully and nodded.

I hoped Shamika really could take care of herself and that Devona wasn't letting her burgeoning maternal instincts get the best of her.

"All right then," I said, turning to Scorch. "Take us to your leader."

EIGHT

We saw no sign of Lazlo when we stepped outside, so I figured he was still tending to his cab. Besides, the only times he's sure to show up is when I'm truly desperate for a ride, and as much as I wanted to get to Demon's Roost, our current situation wasn't exactly a dire one. Bogdan said farewell and headed off on foot to track down whatever Arcane sources he intended to consult, and I can't say I was sorry to see him go. After a few moments of discussion, the rest of us decided to follow suit and take shanks' mare, as some of the longer-lived Darkfolk put it, and we headed down the sidewalk, traveling east in the general direction of Demon's Roost.

Varney was thrilled. "Righteous! There's more chance of getting good footage if we hoof it!"

I didn't reply. I was still mad at him for the "improved" video he'd shown us earlier. And, truth to tell, I was a little depressed, too. Without realizing it, I'd kind of gotten used to being a celebrity in town, but seeing how Varney's producer had felt the need to noir-ify the footage Varney had shot of me made me realize that maybe my unvarnished life wasn't all that fascinating after all. Being brought back down to earth was probably a good thing, if sobering.

We hadn't gone far when my hand vox rang – actually, its mouth called out the words "Ring-ring, ring-ring!" – and I answered. It was Tavi.

"I'm at Papa Chatha's," he said. His voice was guttural and hard to understand, and I knew he was still in his wildform. "I can't get inside because of the security spells on the place, but I've sniffed around outside. It was hard to pick up Papa's scent, not because he hasn't been here for a while but because you've been here recently. Nothing personal, but the scent of ripe zombie tends to be a bit overpowering."

"But you found a scent trail."

"Yes. There's another scent mingled with it that I don't recognize, though it's similar to certain breeds of Demonkin. I don't know what it is, but I'm going to attempt to follow the trail and see what I can turn up."

"All right, but if you find him, call me before you do anything." I'd come to respect Tavi's skills, but Devona had hired him not because he was a fighter but because he was a reformed thief. He'd stolen something from the notorious demon Mammon who hired me to retrieve the object. I'd done so after a certain amount of highly skilled detecting, but in the process I learned that Tavi was a decent enough sort who stole primarily for the sport and challenge of it. It had taken some swift talking on my part to convince Mammon not to devour Tavi's soul for his crime. In the end, Mammon reluctantly agreed to spare Tavi, and Devona offered the lyke a job working for the Midnight Watch. His knowledge of thievery, coupled with his contacts among Nekropolis' criminal element, had proved invaluable to Devona's business, but as swift and clever as Tavi was, he wasn't a warrior, and if he did manage track down Papa and the other missing magic-users, I didn't want him to try to deal with the situation on his own. I'd already saved his mixblood ass once, and I didn't want to have to do it again.

Tavi promised he'd do as I asked, then hung up, and I imagined him racing away from Papa's shack, following the scent trail at top supernatural speed. I tucked my vox back in my pocket, relayed Tavi's report to the others, and we continued walking.

There were still plenty of people crowding the sidewalks, and traffic roared by in the street at suicidal speeds, but the atmosphere in the Sprawl was noticeably subdued. The pedestrians were quieter than usual, continuously casting furtive glances about and keeping their hands in their pockets, no doubt grasping a weapon or two. There were fewer vehicles than normal in the street, and those that passed by were more often than not armored – or encased in force fields of magical or technological origin. Hood, roof, and side-mounted weapons were prominent, everything from machine guns to rocket launchers, energy blasters to curse throwers. The threat of open warfare in the

Sprawl might not have been enough to keep the die-hard partiers indoors, but it had made them more cautious. The Sprawl was already a powder keg most of the time, and Talaith's destruction of the bridges had lit the fuse. The only question was how long it would take to burn down and ignite an explosion.

We'd gotten maybe halfway to Demon's Roost when that question was answered. There were two popular dance clubs on either side of the street here: *Overhexed*, which catered primarily to Arcane clientele, and *Disco Infernal*, a demonic hotspot. But the action wasn't confined to the clubs' interiors tonight. Revelers from both places had taken to the street, where they stood in two groups, facing each other. And from the way they were shouting and gesturing, I knew that they hadn't met for a civilized cross-cultural exchange. Traffic had been blocked off at one end of the street by a barrier of mystic flame, while a jagged line of sharp bonelike projections protruded from the asphalt at the other end. It seemed that neither the demons nor the magic-users wanted anyone to interrupt their little get-together.

The sidewalks on both sides of the street were deserted here. Evidently our fellow pedestrians possessed stronger survival instincts than us and had gotten the hell away at the first sign of trouble. I figured it would be wise of us to follow suit, and I motioned for everyone in our group to stop.

"I think we should quickly and quietly retrace our steps, then cut over a couple streets and take a nice wide detour around this block," I said.

"I like that idea," Devona said softly, never taking her eyes off the shouting demons and magic-users. "I like it very much."

The two groups were an eclectic mix of their kinds. Many of the Arcane were dressed in standard Nekropolitan street clothes, but some wore period costumes: medieval robes, stark Puritan outfits, Arabian finery, Native American deerskins, Aztec capes, stage magician tuxedos or sparkling gowns, and a good number of them carried wooden or metal staves with lux crystals affixed to the ends. The demons varied more in their physical forms. Some were the standard diabolic type, like Scorch's true shape, while others were bizarre amalgams of different animals: insects combined with fish, mammals with lizards, birds with crustaceans and so on... Some of the demons wore ethnic garb that indicated which human mythology they belonged to – Chinese, Japanese, Inuit, Persian, Egyptian, Hindu – while some appeared so alien that their shapes not only defied description, they defied perception. Creatures that appeared to be made of a series of floating transdimensional geometric shapes that seemed to warp in and out of existence, and others that were purely conceptual in nature. I saw one demon I recognized as Schadenfreude, and another that was Antidisestablishmentarianism.

But despite the two groups' striking differences, they had one important thing in common: they clearly loathed one another, and given the aggressive way they were acting, I knew it would only be a matter of moments until...

A heavily tattooed Arcane man wearing a dragon-skin jacket raised his hands and began chanting a spell in a language I didn't recognize. The words seemed to echo in the air, and despite the fact that I have no nerve endings in my ears, it hurt to hear those words spoken aloud. A few seconds later, a half-dozen other Arcane joined in, and soon all of the magic-users stood chanting, hands raised toward the sky.

The Demonkin's reaction to the spell was dramatic. They fell back several steps, roaring and hissing, shrinking in upon themselves and averting their gazes as if it was too painful to look upon the faces of the chanting Arcane.

"What's happening?" I turned to Scorch, hoping she might be able to tell me, but she didn't respond. She stood there with her hands pressed over her ears, eyes squinted closed, jaws clenched tight, as if she were trying to shut out the world – or perhaps just the Arcanes' chanting.

"The magic-users are attempting a binding spell!" Devona said.

I understood what was going on then, but I had a hard time believing it. The enmity between Demonkin and Arcane goes back centuries, back to before the Darkfolk left Earth and emigrated to Nekropolis, when witches, warlocks, and wizards would attempt to summon demons, bind them to their will, and enslave them. Having a powerful creature like a demon to command was an attractive prospect for a magic-user, but you can see how a demon would find the arrangement less than appealing. After the founding of Nekropolis, slavery of any sort was outlawed by Dis and the Darklords, more as a practical matter than for any other reason. It's hard enough to keep the peace in a city full of monsters without having to worry about them running around constantly trying to enslave one another. The prohibition against slavery included the summoning and binding of demons, but the fact that it was now a major crime didn't seem to deter these Arcane in the least, and I doubted any of them considered what they were doing as breaking the law. After all, war was in the offing between Glamere and the Sprawl, and people – Darkfolk or human – are only too willing to suspend the rule of law during wartime… especially when it gives them an excuse to indulge the darker side of their nature.

Devona put her arm around Scorch as if to lend the demon strength and turned to look at me. "We have to stop the spell, Matt! If we don't she'll become the Arcanes' slave, bound to them until they set her free!"

I sighed. "Of course we do. Shamika, you stay here and take care of Scorch. Devona and I will be right back."

Up to this point Shamika had been staring wide-eyed at the scene in the street, but she tore her gaze away and gave me a solemn nod.

"But if the Arcane finish the spell and Scorch becomes bound, get away from her as fast as you can," Devona added. "They'll be able to make her do what they want, and she won't be able to resist their commands."

Shamika nodded once again, and I turned to Varney, who was watching the action in the street, undoubtedly filming it all with his cyber-eye camera.

"As for you…" I trailed off. I wanted to tell him to stay put, but I knew there wasn't any point. "Just try not to get in the way."

"Will do," he said. "You know, Matt, you get into some of the strangest situations."

I sighed again. "It's a gift."

Devona gave Scorch's shoulder a last squeeze, and then the two of us starting walking into the street, Varney following close behind.

"I don't suppose you know any way of blocking a binding spell," I said to Devona.

"None whatsoever. I figured we'd just do what we always do: stick our noses in where they don't belong and see what happens."

I grinned. "I thought I was the improviser and you were the planner."

She shrugged. "What can I say? You've rubbed off on me."

We continued walking toward the two groups, and while I did my best to project an air of casual calm – letting anyone in Nekropolis see how scared you really are isn't conducive to your long-term survival prospects – I frantically tried to think of some way to diffuse the situation Devona and I were about to insert ourselves into. I'd restocked my weaponry before leaving the Midnight Watch, and I now carried a few of my more interesting toys in my pockets, but I couldn't see how any of them would prove useful against an angry mob of combined Arcane and Demonkin.

As we neared the two groups, I noticed a small shop

a couple doors down from Overhexed called The Tea-house of the Gibbous Moon. It had a large front window, and sitting at a table, keeping an eye on the incipient mayhem in the street, was a figure garbed in a voluminous crimson cloak with a large hood. At first I didn't think she saw me, but then she lifted her teacup in greeting, and I gave a slight nod in return.

Devona had picked up on the exchange, either tele-pathically or through old-fashioned observation. "Who is it?"

"The cavalry," I said. "I hope."

As we drew nearer to the mob, I could see that the binding spell was coming along nicely. Most of the De-monkin lay curled in fetal positions on the ground, rocking back and forth as they let loose blistering streams of curses or, just as often, loud wails and streams of tears. I wasn't sure how much longer it would take before the spell was complete, but I doubted we had more than a few moments at this point. No time left for subtlety.

I reached into my jacket pocket and brought out what appeared to be an empty glass vial sealed with a black rubber stopper. "Cover your ears," I warned De-vona and Varney, and then I hurled the vial toward the mass of magic-users. It struck the ground at the feet of an Arcane woman who appeared to be wearing a gown made of shifting multicolored mist. She held her hands raised above her head and was chanting along with rest of the Arcane, but the moment the vial burst her voice – along with the voices of her fellow magikers –

was drowned out by a high-pitched shrieking. The sound rapidly grew in volume until it seemed to fill the entire world, and the Arcane broke off their chanting and clapped their hands over their ears to block the deafening noise. It didn't bother me – no nerve-endings, remember? – but Devona pressed her palms tight against her ears to muffle the sound. Given her sensitive vampire hearing, the noise must've been incredibly painful for her, but the only reaction she showed was a slight tightening of her lips. A tough gal, my Devona.

Varney didn't bother to protect his ears. Maybe he was even tougher than Devona, or maybe his ears also had cyber implants and he was able to mentally turn down the volume on them. Either way, he simply watched and recorded the action unfolding before him.

The shrieking only lasted a few seconds, and when it was over, the Arcane slowly removed their hands from their ears and turned to look at us, confused.

"That was a gift from a friend of mine named Scream Queen," I said, shouting so that they could hear me over the ringing in their ears. "She was nice enough to bottle a bit of her voice for me. It probably didn't do too much permanent damage to your hearing, but it did manage to shut you all up long enough for us to get your attention."

Scream Queen was a banshee and lead singer of Kakaphonie, one of Nekropolis' hottest pop bands. Devona and I, along with the rest of the Midnight Watch, had helped her out once, and she'd been so grateful that – after paying Devona her fee – she gave me a few of her screams. How the banshee had managed to store them in a glass vial was beyond me, but I was grateful that it had worked. Up until the vial had shattered, I hadn't been a hundred percent sure that it would.

A middle-aged Arcane man – dressed as an Elizabethan nobleman in doublet and breeches, complete with a broad ruffled collar – stepped forward and scowled at me.

"This is none of your business, Richter," he said, speaking with an accent that sounded more Brooklyn than English. "This is between us and the hellrats."

The demons, who had begun recovering from the effects of the binding spell the moment the Arcane stopped chanting, had risen to their feet. They snarled upon hearing the derogatory term and fixed baleful gazes on the Arcane man, many of which were literally smoldering with hate.

I was mildly surprised he knew who I was, but I suppose I shouldn't have been. Even for Nekropolis, I'm a one-of-a-kind monster. And I had garnered a certain amount of fame over the last few months.

A demon spokesperson stepped forward then. The creature appeared to be formed from lumpy mounds of yellowish fat, making its gender impossible to determine, but when an orifice opened in its rough approximation of a head, the voice that came out was distinctly female, if a bit liquidy.

"You don't speak for us, wand-waver," she snarled.

"Now, now, children," I said. "Name-calling isn't going to get us anywhere."

"They started it!" the Elizabethan warlock said. "We were minding our business in the club when a group of them came in and told us that we were no longer welcome in the Sprawl."

"No, your people started it!" the lumpy demon said. "Several of you materialized inside our club and enchanted the music system so that instead of disco it began playing chamber music!" She shuddered at the thought, and a number of her fellow demons did likewise. I thought both types of music sounded equally horrid, but then there's no accounting for taste, especially when it comes to demons.

I glanced back at Shamika and Scorch. The demoness had shaken off the effects of the binding spell, but she remained standing on the sidewalk next to the girl. It wasn't like Scorch to hang back when there was trouble, and I guessed she was suppressing her more violent urges because she didn't want to leave Shamika unprotected. When it comes down to it, Scorch is a pretty decent sort for a demon, not that I'd ever tell her that. She'd probably set me on fire for insulting her.

"All right, so you guys don't like each other," I said. "Now that we've established that, why don't you return to your respective clubs and get back to boogieing down or whatever the hell it is you people do for fun that doesn't involve trying to kill each other."

Lumpy looked at me. At least, I think she did. It was hard to tell since she had a complete absence of facial features. "Don't you keep up with current events, zombie? Their people destroyed both of the Sprawl's bridges!"

The warlock sneered at her. "Only because your people have been kidnapping magic-users!"

"I know you Darkfolk are only too happy to have an excuse to tear into one another, but are you really this stupid?" I asked. "The Weyward Sisters destroyed the bridges. I ought to know: I was on one of them when they did it. And as for the disappearances, so far there's no proof who's behind them. But I can tell you this much: whoever's behind this, *all* Demonkin didn't abduct the magic-users, and *all* Arcane didn't destroy the bridges. So why fight with each other?"

Lumpy and the Elizabethan warlock looked at me for a moment and then looked at each other.

"He makes a lot of sense, doesn't he?" the warlock said.

"That he does," Lumpy agreed.

They fell silent for a moment.

"I hate people who make sense," Lumpy said.

"Me too." The warlock pointed a finger at me, and a beam of white energy shot forth and struck me on the chest. At the same instant the warlock spoke a single word: "*Discerpo!*"

I didn't feel anything, but I suddenly found myself unable to support my own weight. My legs fell out from under me, and I tumbled to the ground. My head hit the asphalt and bounced a couple times before coming to a stop. My face was pointed toward the rest of my body, which lay in a haphazard pile, but I could see that my hands and feet were no longer connected to their corresponding limbs.

Both the Arcane and Demonkin laughed at my predicament, and I supposed I should be grateful that I'd managed to unify them, if only for a moment and not exactly in the way that I'd hoped to.

Devona knelt by my head. "Are you OK, darling?"

"I'm fine." I gave her what I hoped was a reassuring smile. "After all, it's not like this is the first time I've lost my head."

The warlock grinned in delight. "Did you like that? It's a spell of my own devising, one designed to split a person apart. While it's nothing more than an inconvenience for you, it's usually fatal – not to mention a hell of a lot messier – for living folks." His grin took on a nasty edge. "Allow me to demonstrate." He pointed his finger at Devona and shouted, "*Discerpo!*"

As before, a beam of light lanced forth from his finger, and even if I hadn't fallen to pieces, I knew I wouldn't have been fast enough to get Devona out of the way in time. But just as he had at the Bridge of Nine Sorrows, Varney moved with incredible speed, grabbed hold of Devona's shoulders, and snatched her out of the beam's path before it could strike her. With nothing to stop it, the beam of mystic power continued streaking through the air toward the section of sidewalk where Scorch and Shamika stood. Scorch tried to get the girl out of the way, but the beam was moving too fast and it struck Shamika. She was momentarily wreathed in sparkling light, and then she fell in upon herself, collapsing onto the ground in what appeared to be hundreds of small pieces.

I didn't have time to wonder why the spell had affected her differently than it had me. Scorch howled with a mixture of fury and sorrow, and she spun to face the warlock. She began running toward him, her teenage girl guise fading as she assumed her true fire demon form, her clothes vanishing as her body outgrew them. The warlock looked momentarily taken aback – the sight of a fully grown and enraged fire demon coming at you tends to do that – but then he pointed his finger (which was only shaking a little) at Scorch, readying to use his separation magic on her.

Varney still had hold of Devona, and though she struggled to free herself of his grip – no doubt so she could attack the warlock too – he held her tight. As fast as Scorch was, there was no way she could reach the warlock before he unleashed another blast of magic at her, and if Devona couldn't get away from Varney to stop the warlock, Scorch was a goner. And as a severed head lying on the street, all I could do was watch.

"Well, now, what are you children up to?"

The voice – an elderly woman's – was gentle and kind, but there was something about it that caught the attention of everyone in the street, and all heads turned to look at her. Scorch stopped running, and the warlock lowered his hand without releasing another bolt of magic. They, like everyone else, focused their gazes on the newcomer. Her crimson cape came within an inch of brushing the ground, and it was trimmed with silvery fur, as was her hood which she wore up, cloaking her features in shadow. She wore a tunic and leggings, both of forest green, and brown boots. In her thin, age-spotted hands she carried a pair of silver daggers that, despite the gloomy half-illumination provided by Umbriel, somehow still seemed to glimmer and glint in the light.

No one spoke. No one moved. No one dared breathe. Most of them probably hadn't seen her in the flesh before, but they all knew who she was, and they were all terrified of her.

She stopped when she reached me – or my head, anyway – and looked down. Within the shadows of her hood, her thin lips stretched into a smile.

"Hello, Matthew. It's good to see you. Sorry I didn't get here sooner, but I had to finish my tea."

"No problem, Granny. A woman has to have her priorities."

Her smile widened. "I'm so glad you understand." She turned to look at the Elizabethan warlock and the lumpy fat demon. "You've had your fun. Now why don't you all head on home like good little dears, hmm?"

Several of the demons and magic-users in the crowd began to slowly move away, but the Elizabethan warlock, though shaken, held his ground. "You don't scare us, Granny Red. You might be something of a legend, but so what? Nekropolis is chock-full of beings just as famous as you, and most of the time they don't live up to the hype."

I looked at the warlock. "Some friendly advice: if you want to live, you will turn around and haul ass in the opposite direction as fast your little Shakespearean shoes will carry you."

The warlock sneered down at me. "I'm Arcane! I'm not afraid of some old wo–"

That's as far as he got. Granny Red stepped forward almost nonchalantly, her knives flashed in the air, and then she stepped back. The warlock stood for a moment, eyes wide with shock, blood gushing from a dozen wounds, and then he toppled to the ground, dead.

Granny turned to the crowd, the warlock's blood dripping from her silver knives.

"Anyone else like to show Granny how tough they are?" she asked sweetly.

Demonkin and Arcane alike decided that discretion was the more sensible part of valor, and they turned and fled *en masse*. When they were gone, Granny walked over to the warlock's corpse, cleaned her blades on his clothes, and then tucked them into sheaths on her leather belt. Varney had kept hold of Devona the entire time, but he let go of her now, and she came over to me and picked my head up. Her mind reached out to me.

Is that really her? she thought.

Yes. Granny Red, the most feared monster killer in history. A myth made flesh, a bedtime story told to so many children over the centuries that she came to life, birthed from the collective unconscious of the human race. She was a young girl when she started out, of course, just like in the story, and she began by hunting werewolves. But she branched out as she got older, and when the Darkfolk moved to Nekropolis, she followed. Everyone fears her, including, I suspect, the Darklords themselves.

I'd first met Granny when I was trying to track down a murderous cyborg lyke who called himself the Megawolf. She'd been on his trail too, and we'd ended up working together to take him down. I have to admit that Granny scares me too. As much as I don't like to think about it, I *am* a monster, and slaying monsters is her one and only purpose in life. In many ways, she's as single-minded in her motivations as a great white shark – and ten times as deadly. And because she's literally a living legend, she's intimidating as hell, truly larger than life – or maybe in her case, larger than death.

Granny turned to Devona and smiled. "I'd heard Matthew had found himself a nice girl. I'm so pleased to meet you, my dear."

Granny held out her hand, and Devona tucked me under one arm while she reached out and shook Granny's hand. I was impressed to see that my love trembled only a little as she clasped hands with Granny. Granny gave her hand a gentle shake and then released it. Devona kept a smile fixed firmly on her face, but I could feel her tension through our telepathic link. Granny has killed more than her fair share of vampires over the centuries.

Granny lowered her gaze to me. "It looks like you're quite literally in good hands, Matthew, so I think I'll go back and have another cup of tea. It was lovely to see you again. And remember–"

"Don't talk to strangers," I finished for her.

She grinned, nodded, and walked casually back to The Teahouse of the Gibbous Moon. Only when she was inside and the door closed did we relax.

"So that was Granny Red. How interesting."

Devona turned – which was good, since I wasn't at the moment capable of doing so – and I saw Shamika had joined us in the street.

"Don't take this the wrong way," I said, "and I'm very glad you're OK, but I thought you were blasted into pieces by the warlock's spell."

She laughed. "You call that a spell? A reasonably competent Arcane child can cast spells stronger than that! It was simple enough to reverse."

I reached out to Devona through our link, and I could sense my love's skepticism. Devona isn't Arcane, but she specializes in security, both mundane and mystical, and is therefore quite knowledgeable about magic. I could sense that Shamika's words didn't ring true with Devona. It was something that needed to be looked into – later. Right now we, or at least I, had more pressing problems.

"If you wouldn't mind," I said to Devona, "I'd appreciate it if you could try to put this Humpty together again."

NINE

We were only a couple of blocks from Varvara's stronghold when Scorch announced that she had to use the little demons' room. When I just looked at her, she said, "What? My natural form may be big, but when I'm in this shape, my bladder isn't much larger than a pea."

I wanted to ask her why demons needed to urinate at all, but I decided there are some things which, despite my naturally inquisitive nature, I'm better off not knowing. We stopped at at a Sawney B's, and Scorch entered the faux cave exterior in order to use the restaurant's restroom. Considering that the place is named after the infamous Scottish cannibal and serves fast-food items like lady fingers, marrow shakes, and homunculus nuggets, I hate to think what the restroom conditions are like. Darkfolk or human, one thing that unites both species is that females for some unknown reason seem compelled to visit restrooms in packs. Once we'd stopped, Devona decided she needed to go too, and she asked Shamika if she wanted to come along. The girl looked confused for a moment, as if she was unsure how to respond, but then she nodded and followed Devona inside the restaurant, leaving Varney and me to wait outside.

I leaned back against Sawney B's plastic cave wall and crossed my arms over my chest. Thanks to Papa Chatha's spell, I was managing to keep my various body parts holding together, but it took constant concentration. If I allowed my mind to wander too far, I would feel myself start to lose cohesion, and I had to be careful if I didn't want to go all to pieces again. The warlock's spell had severed my head, arms, hands, legs, and feet from my body. I felt more like a scarecrow than I did a zombie, with joints that could bend in any direction, and movements so loosey-goosey I felt like a comical marionette whose strings were being pulled by a half-drunken puppeteer. Papa had told me that the enchantment that allowed me to keep a severed piece of myself attached to my body would remain effective for about twenty-four hours. But he hadn't said anything about trying to keep multiple severed body parts attached. I wondered how long I would be able to keep up my scarecrow act before I fell apart and stayed that way. I didn't think I was in any danger of being a permanent collection of undead puzzle pieces, not as long as I could find a magic-user to fix me up – or I could always pay a visit on Victor Baron. He once reattached my head, and he could easily do the same for the rest of me. But I didn't want to take time out for repairs. I wanted to find Papa and the rest of the magic-users and stop the conflict between Talaith and Varvara before it erupted into all-out war.

I was grateful for the women's need to take a pit stop, though, for it gave me a chance to be alone with Varney. I had a few questions I wanted to ask my vampiric shadow.

Varney stood next to me, his head swiveling slowly back and forth as his gaze scanned the street.

"Filming?" I asked.

"Just some background footage," he said. "Never know when it'll come in handy. Not much going on here, though. The streets are practically deserted."

"We're close to Demon's Roost. If Varvara really is preparing for war, she's probably had her people cordon off the blocks around her stronghold."

"If that's so, then how will we get through?"

I smiled. "The same way I get through anything else. Boyish charm and rugged good looks."

Varney gave me a skeptical glance but didn't say anything.

"You were filming when we broke up the riot between the Arcane and the Demonkin, right? I mean, you're always filming, but I assume you were paying special attention then."

"Sure thing. I got some great stuff!"

"I bet you did. Did you happen to get any footage of Shamika being blasted by the warlock's spell?"

He frowned. "I think so. I can't review the footage mentally. I need a Mind's Eye set to transmit it to, but yeah, I think I shot that. Why?"

"Just curious. Curiosity is one of the prime qualities of a good private detective, you know. For example, I'm curious about you, Varney."

"Me?"

"You saved Devona from falling when the rest of the Bridge of Nine Sorrows collapsed. And you pulled her out of the way when the warlock tried to blast her. Don't get me wrong: I'm very thankful that you did, but I find it awfully convenient that you should just happen to be in the right place at the right time... twice."

He shrugged. "Just lucky, I guess."

"Maybe. Except I don't really believe in luck, Varney. You know what I do believe in? People with hidden agendas who pretend to be something they aren't."

Varney looked at me for a long moment. "Dude, you are *way* cynical. You need to cultivate a more positive outlook. I know a guy who teaches meditation to Bloodborn to help them control their thirst-rage. Maybe you should give him a call sometime."

"Or maybe you should just come clean and tell me what your game is."

Varney looked at me, and his organic eye narrowed in cold appraisal. For a moment I thought he might break down and tell me what I wanted to know, but then the women came out of the restaurant and re-joined us.

Devona held two cups with straws in them, and she handed one to Varney. "It's just aqua sanguis, but it should take the edge off your thirst."

Aqua sanguis is a synthetic blood substitute produced
in the Sprawl. It tastes like blood but doesn't provide
any nourishment. For the Darkfolk, it's like the equivalent of diet soda. From what I've been told, it tastes
rather weak, hence the slang term for it: redwater. Devona's not against drinking real blood per se. Officially,
humans aren't considered prey by law in Nekropolis,
and any real blood served in bars and restaurants either
comes from willing donors or from specially cloned do-
nator bodies produced by Victor Baron. But that doesn't
stop some of the more unscrupulous blood suppliers
from snatching a human or two off the street now and
again, and – like humans on Earth who boycott tuna
because of fishing practices that ensnare dolphins –
some of the more socially conscious Darkfolk choose to
drink aqua sanguis instead of blood whenever possible.

Varney thanked Devona, took the drink, and sipped.
He didn't look at me, and it was like our conversation
hadn't happened. But it had, and I intended to continue it later. I was certain now that Varney was more
than he appeared to be. The question was what, and
whether he was any kind of a danger. So far he'd saved
Devona twice, and that meant I was willing to give him
the benefit of the doubt for the time being, but that
wasn't the same as trusting him. Not by a long shot.

I desperately wanted a chance to talk with Devona
alone for a few minutes. I had yet to tell her about my
visit from Dis at Papa Chatha's, and I wanted to share
my suspicions about Varney with her, as well as my un-
easy feelings about Shamika. I could've done so

telepathically, I suppose, but I've found that our link works best for sharing emotions. It's harder to communicate complex concepts, and short back-and-forth communication works better than longer, more detailed exchanges. I decided it would be better to wait until we had a few moments of privacy so we could speak aloud to one another. But if the opportunity didn't arise soon, I'd settle for a telepathic exchange rather than wait too much longer.

Instead of a drink, Scorch had bought a ten-pack of testicles marinated in gastric juices, and she popped one of the horrid slimy things in her mouth.

"Things are likely to get more military from here on out," she said as she chewed, "so you'd better let me do the talking."

"Maybe you should finish eating first," I said, and despite the fact that I no longer possessed a functioning sense of smell or working taste buds, I couldn't help sounding queasy.

"Good idea."

Scorch assumed her fire demon form, opened her now large maw, and tossed the rest of the testicles into her mouth, package and all, and swallowed. Then she grinned at me.

"I'm ready."

Scorch took the lead, Devona, Shamika and I walked in the middle, and Varney brought up the rear, the better to film us, no doubt. I noticed he kept closer to Devona than the rest of us, and given his track record at protecting her, I wasn't about to protest.

By this point we could see Demon's Roost off in the distance. Varvara's stronghold resembled a sleek, gleaming, metal-and-glass high-rise that would be right at home in one of Earth's more modern cities. It rose a dozen stories into the sky, its bright lights standing out sharply against the starless black expanse that stretches above the city like a vast blanket of Nothing. Cold and stark, utterly lacking charm or grace, Demon's Roost is a monstrous monument to power and excess – and thus a perfect home for the Demon Queen.

When we reached the next block, I saw that my supposition had been correct: the streets were blocked off by wicked-looking barriers made from large steel spikes with razor wire stretched between. Demons larger, more muscular, and way uglier than Scorch patrolled the barriers, armed to the teeth with weapons both modern and ancient. Some carried automatic pistols, rifles, and flamethrowers, while others gripped broadswords and heavy battleaxes. A few carried futuristic high-tech weapons that wouldn't have been out of place on the set of a sci-fi movie. Varvara believes in being on the cutting edge of everything, and that includes technology. She has the means and the money to import any Earth weaponry she wishes, and there are any number of mad scientists living in the city who are only too happy to provide some seriously deadly upgrades to the toys she acquires – for a price. And if they don't already work for the Demon Queen, she has them on retainer. And since Darkfolk are tougher than humans, safety features like radiation shielding aren't necessary, and if a weapon should blow up in a demon's hands, what of it? They'll more than likely shrug it off, and if the explosion does manage to kill them, there are a hundred more waiting in line to serve, and more are being bred in Varvara's hatcheries every day. Back on Earth, some people say life is cheap, but they've never been to Nekropolis.

The guard demons fixed wary gazes on us as we approached, but they didn't raise their weapons. I guess we looked like a harmless enough bunch – and we did have our very own demon escort.

Scorch walked up to the barrier and addressed one of the demons, a mammoth creature ten feet tall that looked like a giant ape covered in snakeskin.

"Hey, Magilla. What's up?"

The ape-thing carried a weapon that resembled a giant blow dryer combined with a food processor. It looked ridiculous, which most likely meant it was exceptionally lethal.

Magilla tightened his grip on the weapon and raised it a few inches, but he still didn't level it at us, something for which I was profoundly grateful.

"Guard duty," the demon said in a low rumbling voice that sounded like a small avalanche. "The general's ordered all access points to Demon's Roost blocked off and guarded."

"General who?" I asked.

Magilla looked at me as if he was considering gutting me and using my eviscerated corpse for a field latrine. But he said, "General Klamm. Varvara put him in charge."

"She's already gathering an army?" Devona asked.

Magilla shrugged. "You know Varvara. Once she decides to do something, it's fast forward all the way."

"The bridges weren't destroyed by ground troops," I pointed out.

In response, Magilla hooked a thumb skyward. I looked up and saw a dozen winged demons flying above us. Some had bat wings, some had insect wings, and some just levitated, but, like their ground-based counterparts, they were all armed and ready for trouble.

"Looks like Klamm's thought of everything," I said.

"He's a pretty smart guy," Magilla agreed affably enough, though from our conversation so far, I figured he wasn't the greatest judge of intelligence levels. He went on. "What are you doing here, Scorch? You come to enlist?"

Scorch said, "Naw. You know me. I'm a lover, not a fighter."

Scorch's assertion was a bit hard to take considering that she now looked like something Hieronymus Bosch would've hesitated to paint, but it made Magilla laugh, and whenever a soldier is laughing instead of blasting you with his futuristic super-weapon, that's a good thing.

Scorch went on. "I've got some people here that need to talk to Varvara. This is Matthew Richter, the zombie PI. He has some information that might prove useful to the queen."

I was coming to ask questions of Varvara, not deliver information, but I didn't see the need to correct Scorch, not if her ruse would get us past the guard.

"I heard you've been hanging around him lately." Magilla gave me an appraising look with his simian eyes. "You can't mistake the smell, can you? Nothing reeks quite like a deader."

I frowned, but I held my tongue. I was tempted to draw my 9mm and put a couple bullets in the big scaly ape just to show him that I don't take shit from anyone, but I told myself that, satisfying as it might be, it wouldn't help matters – especially when Magilla decided to retaliate with a deadly blast from his Buck Rogers gun.

Magilla thought for a moment, and from the way his brow crinkled and the little grunts of effort he made, I knew it wasn't an easy task for him.

"I guess it's OK if you take the deader on to Demon's Roost," he said at last. "Everyone knows Varvara finds him amusing, and she could probably use a good laugh right now."

"Looks like my reputation has preceded me," I muttered.

Magilla's scaly lips drew back in a grin, exposing a mouthful of large yellowed fangs. "And if she's not in the mood to see you, she'll probably just blast you to atoms."

"Always a risk when you seek an audience with the Demon Queen," I agreed.

Magilla's grin fell away, and I had the impression he was disappointed that I hadn't found him intimidating. Monsters are like that. They're so used to being terrifying that when you don't automatically pee your pants at the sight of them, they're at a loss for what to do next. Usually they just try to kill you. And failing that, they try to scare anyone else in the vicinity. Magilla was no different. He turned away from me and focused his attention on Devona, Shamika, and Varney. He grinned again, wider this time.

"What about these three, Scorch?" he asked. "Who are they and why should I let them through?"

"They're friends," Scorch said, "and they also have information that might be of interest to Varvara."

Magilla looked them up and down for a moment. "I don't see that it takes five of you to talk to the queen, but I'll tell you what. You give me the girl to play with, and I'll let the rest of you pass." Magilla's grin widened into a full-fledged leer.

Shamika's eyes widened in shock, and Devona stepped closer to her and put a protective arm around her shoulders.

"We will do no such thing! I can't believe you'd even make such a suggestion!" Devona's eyes flashed dangerously.

Magilla laughed. "What part of 'I'm a demon' don't you understand?"

"No deal," I said.

Magilla shrugged. "Then none of you pass. It's as simple as that. Now go on and get out of here before I decide to use you all for target practice."

I fixed Magilla with the sort of unblinking stare that only dead people like me are capable of.

"I pick up a lot of nifty toys in my line of work," I said in what I hoped was a low, dangerous tone. "One of the nastier ones I've got is called a Judas bomb. Ever heard of it?"

Magilla shook his head. He didn't look especially scared, but he was paying attention.

"It's a magical device that when activated causes half the cells in your body to become cannibalistic. They immediately turn on the unaffected cells and begin devouring them. In a sense, your body betrays itself, hence the device's name. It's an extremely messy and unbelievably painful way to die."

Magilla smiled, but it was forced. "And what? If I say anything more about wanting to play with the little girlie you'll use the bomb on me? Just kill me in cold blood? I thought you hero types were better than that."

I kicked myself mentally for trying to bluff Magilla. It's almost impossible to out-nasty a demon. Of course, it would've helped if I'd actually had a Judas bomb on me. I'd heard of the devices but never actually saw one. If I'd had one, I'd have probably used it then, just to wipe the smug smile off Magilla's face and to hell with my heroic reputation.

Shamika stepped up next to me. "Thank you for trying to defend my honor, Matt, but I can take care of myself."

Magilla leered at her and a thick ropey strand of saliva dripped out of the corner of his mouth. "The question is, can *you* take care of *me*?"

The other guard demons had kept their distance so far, but they'd been watching our conversation with

interest, and they burst out with laughter upon hearing
the simian demon's less-than-subtle innuendo.

Shamika wasn't amused, however.

"Yes," she said softly. "I can."

She spoke no magic words, made no mystic gestures.
She did nothing more than stand and stare at Magilla.

We heard the sounds first – a soft scritch-scratch of
tiny claws on pavement coming from both sides of the
street. We sensed movement next, shadows roiling and
surging within the alleys between buildings. And then
the shadows broke free and flooded into the street.
Packs of small creatures ran out of the alleys and scam-
pered on tiny legs toward Magilla, and the other guard
demons shrieked when they saw the creatures. For
they belonged to a species so savage, so remorseless
that even monsters feared them, and with damn
good reason.

They were chiranha.

No one knows where they came from, whether
they're the result of some unnatural twist of evolution
or the unexpected outcome of some bizarre magical or
scientific experiment. No one believes they were
created on purpose, though. There isn't a sorcerer or
scientist insane enough to even contemplate such a
thing, let alone actually do it. Chiranha are a cross
between piranha and Chihuahua, and as silly as that
might sound, no one in Nekropolis laughs at them.
They're the city's ultimate predator-scavengers, and
the only good thing about them is that they keep the
carrion imp population under control.

They're the size of Chihuahuas, but scaled instead of furred, with beady black fish eyes and blunt piranha faces with a prominent lower jaw. Their teeth are tiny but razor sharp, and a pack of the little bastards can strip the flesh off your bones and start digesting it before your last scream has time to fade away.

Magilla shrieked at the sight of two packs of chiranha converging on him, sounding more like a young girl than Shamika. He aimed his futuristic blow dryer at the oncoming horde of miniature yapping death and unleashed a sizzling blast of glowing blue-white energy. The discharge disintegrated a huge chunk of the street, but the chiranha were too fast. They darted out of the beam's path just in time, without getting so much as a single fishy scale on their hides singed. The other guard demons let loose with their weapons, both mundane and esoteric, but with the same lack of success. The savage little bastards were just too small, fast, and agile. Fortunately for the other demons, they were only interested in Magilla. The chiranha were on him before he could fire his weapon a second time, and they swiftly covered the shrieking demon from head to toe. He fell to the ground, rolling and thrashing as he tried to fend off the chiranha, but no matter what he did, he couldn't dislodge the creatures.

All we could do was watch and wait for the inevitable to be over – or so I thought.

"Stop fussing," Shamika said. "They won't eat you unless I tell them to."

She had to repeat this several more times at increasingly louder volume, but eventually Magilla heard her and ceased his exertions. He lay motionless on the ground, the chiranha still covering his body, glaring at him with those tiny black eyes and growling softly. Shamika didn't say anything, but the chiranha covering Magilla's face moved away so he could see her.

The other guards, seeing that Magilla was, surprisingly enough, still alive, edged toward us, slowly raising their weapons.

I looked at them. "If she can summon chiranha to attack Magilla, what else do you think she might summon to attack you?"

The guards looked at me uncertainly, then at each other. Finally they shrugged and lowered their weapons. Demonkin aren't exactly a sentimental lot, and the others' concern for Magilla's fate didn't override their own survival instincts.

Shamika looked through the barrier at Magilla. "It's not nice to threaten people. Don't do it again."

Magilla looked at her as if she'd suddenly started speaking Urdu. Threatening people was one of the things demons like him did best.

"Um… OK. I'm… sorry?"

Before Shamika could respond, Devona gently nudged me. "We've got problems upstairs, Matt."

I directed my gaze skyward and saw a score of flying demons descending toward us. They'd doubtless witnessed what Shamika had done to Magilla, and while I doubted they gave anything remotely resembling a

damn for him, they'd been assigned to guard the envi-
rons around Demon's Roost, and they weren't about
to allow our aggression to go unchallenged. Now I really wished I had a Judas bomb – better yet, a few
dozen. I was desperately trying to figure out what we
could do to keep from being reduced to bloody gobs of
shredded and sizzling flesh, when an image appeared
in the air just above the barrier.

Varvara might be queen of all the Demonkin, but she
looks human – with the exception of her emerald eyes
which seem a bit too large and a bit too green to be
real. But her humanity is an almost cartoonish repre-
sentation of femininity. She's more gorgeous than any
supermodel, more sexy than any *Penthouse* centerfold,
with a body whose proportions would make a Barbie
doll so sick with envy that she'd develop an eating disorder. She's statuesque in every sense of the word,
with long full-bodied red hair that seems to glow with
an inner fire. She usually dresses in the highest of high
fashion, but today she was garbed in a military com-
mander's outfit that looked vaguely Nazi-ish. Black
fabric, black gloves, black boots, and a riding crop
clasped in one hand held at her side. Her red hair was
pulled back in a severe bun, and there was a stylized
flame insignia over one of her extremely large breasts.

I knew we were looking at a magically projected
image instead of the real thing because she was slightly
transparent. Nevertheless, her image exuded the same
psychic impression of Darklord power as her physical
presence did, and it took an effort of will on my part not

to take a step or two backward. No one else in our group did either – we were all a hardy bunch – but Scorch went down on one knee and bowed before her queen.

The flying demons that had been diving rapidly toward us stopped and hovered in mid attack, heads bowed, and Magilla's fellow guards did as Scorch had and knelt. Magilla, still covered by chiranha – who, I noticed, seemed oblivious to Varvara's presence – lay still, but the exaggerated relief on his face at seeing his mistress appear was almost comical.

"My queen!" he said, his voice more than a bit whiny. "These five attempted to breach the barrier and they've used Arcane magic to attack and insult me! I pray, Mistress, that you'll use your unholy powers to smite them for their transgression against your Infernal Majesty!"

I looked at Varvara. "He's laying it on a bit thick, don't you think?"

"More than a little, I'd say." Varvara scowled down at Magilla. "Get up. You look ridiculous lying there covered in carnivorous lapdogs. I swear, if I didn't need every able body to fight right now, I'd transform you into a school of catfish and let the chiranha have at you."

Magilla, far more terrified of his queen than he was of being devoured alive, leaped to his feet, scattering chiranha off him. The small creatures gave him a few last growls for good measure before turning away and padding back to the alleys from which they'd been summoned.

Varvara's image turned around to face the demon guards.

"Allow them through and escort them to Demon's Roost." She then turned her attention to Magilla once more. "And if any of them so much as stubs a toe on the way, I'll hold *you* personally responsible."

Magilla's scaly hide lightened a shade as he went pale. He tried unsuccessfully to speak, swallowed twice, and finally settled on a brisk nod. Varvara's image then turned back to us.

"So, Matt. I suppose you're coming to make my life even more hideously complicated than it already is."

"What else?" I said.

She smiled, said, "Sounds delicious," and then disappeared.

Varvara's parting words didn't exactly reassure me. When the Demon Queen says something sounds delicious, she might be speaking literally.

TEN

I've visited Demon's Roost on a number of occasions, almost all connected to a case in one way or another, and every time I've been there, a bacchanalia of epic proportions was taking place. But while there was still plenty of excitement in the air today, the atmosphere was military rather than celebratory. The Atrium was packed full of bodies as usual, but instead of a cross-section of partying Darkfolk, only Demonkin were in attendance. All subspecies were represented – reptilian, insectile, mammalian, piscine, elemental, conglomerate, humanoid, and conceptual. And while they still wore their civilian clothes, if they wore anything at all, they stood at attention in rows or conducted precise drills at the shouted commands of demons garbed in black uniforms similar to what Varvara had been wearing. Most of the demons were armed, though there was no standardization in the types of weapons they carried. I had the impression that they'd been summoned to Demon's Roost on a moment's notice and had been commanded to bring whatever weapons they could get their claws on. While a number had top-of-the-line Earth guns, bladed weapons, or futuristic hardware, quite a few carried baseball bats, lengths of metal pipe, or that old standby, a two-by-four with nails driven through it.

The makeshift army might've looked ridiculous if it wasn't for two things. One was the sheer number of them. A couple hundred demons were jammed into the Atrium, and there were at least twice that many outside drilling on the grounds surrounding Varvara's stronghold. The other thing that kept them from seeming ridiculous was the fact that they *were* demons – fierce, heartless, amoral, and savage creatures whose only reason for existing was to sate their appetites, especially if they could do so at someone else's expense. No blank expressions of military discipline on their faces. Their eyes blazed with battle lust, and their mouths were twisted into cruel smiles, no doubt as they imagined what they intended to do to anyone foolish enough to get in their way.

I thought of the total destructive force contained within this building and the horror that would result if it was released into the streets of Nekropolis. As important as finding Papa Chatha was to me, I knew it was even more vital that I find a way to stop the war between Varvara and Talaith before it spilled over onto the rest of the city. I thought of Devona's and my trip to the alternate Nekropolis. That world's Hyde plague would seem nothing but a minor inconvenience compared to the devastation an all-out war would cause in our world.

Magilla himself had escorted us to Demon's Roost, and he marched us across the Atrium, growling for demons to get out of our way in the name of the queen. No one challenged him or accused him of lying about acting under Varvara's authority. No demon was suicidal enough to use the name of their queen under false pretenses.

Magilla took us to the elevator that led straight to Varvara's penthouse quarters. And then, his duty done, he turned and departed without saying a word. None of us was sorry to see him go.

I was familiar with the demon guarding the elevator. Usually, he doesn't wear clothing, but since Jambha was one of the stronghold's staff, he'd been issued a black military uniform. Or at least, it *appeared* that way. Rakshasas are masters of illusion, so perhaps we only *thought* he was wearing clothes, which, if you think about, probably saves him a lot on dry-cleaning bills. Whenever I visit, he's wearing, or seems to be wearing, a necklace made of tiny decapitated heads – usually miniature versions of mine – but today all the heads were tiny copies of Talaith, their eyes rolled white, flesh pale; little beads of blood dripped from their ragged neck stumps. What else would a patriotic demon be wearing with an Arcane-Demonkin war in the offing?

Jambha's job is preventing anyone from trying to bother Varvara by using any or all means necessary, the more bloody and violent, the better. Considering that rakshasas are Hindu cannibal demons, there's usually a certain amount of biting, chewing, and swallowing involved. Jambha always gives me grief whenever I need to go up to Varvara's penthouse – though so far I've managed avoid ending up in his stomach – and since he'd dressed the part of a good little soldier that day, I expected him to demand that we present our papers to him or something similar as we approached. But all he did was give us a brisk nod, tap the elevator's up button with a claw, then returned to standing to attention and staring off into space as if we weren't there.

"Aren't you going to say something annoying?" I asked him. "It wouldn't be a visit to Demon's Roost without you threatening to eat me or one of my friends for having the temerity to even think of bothering your queen."

Jambha shrugged, though he continued looking straight ahead. "The queen knows you're coming, and she wants to see you. Why should I waste any time bantering with you? There's a war on, you know."

"You demons aren't much fun at the best of times, but you're downright dull when you get all militaristic," I said.

Jambha merely shrugged again, as if to say, *That's war for you*. The elevator arrived, the door slid open, and we entered. It was a bit of a tight fit for the five of us – it was Varvara's private elevator, after all, and not exactly designed for crowds – but we managed. The door slid shut and the elevator started to rise to the ac-companiment of a Muzak version of the *1812 Overture*.

"I've never met a Darklord before," Shamika said as we ascended. "How should I act?" She didn't sound particularly nervous, just curious – which was strange. Anyone else would've peed themselves at the thought of being in the same building as a Darklord, let alone in the same room. I've encountered all five Darklords on one occasion or another, but I know Varvara best, and I'm still intimidated by her, though I'd never give her the satisfaction of showing it. Anyone with half a mind should've been scared to death to meet the Demon Queen, and anyone with a whole mind should have been terrified right out of it. But not Shamika. She'd demon-strated that she could take care of herself against Magilla, but handling a single demon of middling rank was nowhere near the same as being able to defend yourself against the queen of the Demonkin herself. I wondered if Shamika was overconfident, naïve, or a combination of the two. Though she'd supposedly been born and raised in Nekropolis, she didn't always act like it.

"Let Matt do the talking," Devona said. "Varvara finds him amusing."

Shamika frowned. "And that's a good thing?"

"It's an irritating thing," I said, "but useful. As long as Varvara is entertained, there's a decent chance she won't destroy us for bothering her."

Varney grinned uncertainly. "You're joking, right?"

I looked at him. "You've met Galm. You tell me if I'm joking."

His grin fell away as he considered my comment.

The elevator came to a stop as it reached Varvara's penthouse. The door slid open, and we stepped out and into a place I didn't recognize. Normally, Varvara's private quarters look like a parody of a romance writer's ideal bedroom: silk and satin everywhere, a huge canopied bed covered with overstuffed pillows, perfume-scented air... All of that was gone now, replaced by a war room with dim fluorescent lighting and gray walls. Computer stations lined the room, manned by furiously typing demons wearing communications headsets. A black flag with a crimson flame emblazoned in the middle hung on the wall, along with a number of motivational posters that showed fierce-faced demons and featured slogans like SUFFER NOT A WITCH TO LIVE and PUT THE FLAME TO THE ARCANE! In the middle of the room sat a large gleaming metal table displaying a detailed three-dimensional hologram of the entire city. A keyboard lay flush with the tabletop, along with several monitor screens and rows of buttons and dials – the setup would've done a cheesy spy movie's evil mastermind proud. Standing before the projection dressed in her stylish black uniform was Varvara, and next to her, wearing a similar uniform, was a male demon I didn't recognize.

Like her, he appeared human – tall and handsome in a lean, wolfish way, clean-shaven, but with thick black hair hanging down to his shoulders. Not exactly a military haircut, I thought, but then again, he did serve in a *demon* army, and their regulations were no doubt somewhat more broad than an Earthly army. The golden stars on his shoulders, along with the fact he stood at the map with Varvara, told me who he was.

"General Klamm, I presume?" I said.

He looked up at me, and I saw that his eyes were as black as his hair, and they shone in the light as if made of polished stone. It was an eerie effect, and I was surprised to discover it creeped me out a little.

"And you must be Matthew Richter. I'd say it was a pleasure to meet you, but I don't see any point in lying." His voice was rich and cultured, with the weary, snotty edge of a food or theatre critic who'd long ago gotten used to the world constantly disappointing him.

"That's funny. I thought lying came as naturally as breathing to demons." I looked him up and down. "You know, given your name, I expected you to look somewhat more mollusk-y."

Klamm's dark eyes glittered. "And I expected you to be a loudmouth who thinks he's cleverer than he really is. At least one of us isn't disappointed."

As desperately as I wanted to hit him with a devastatingly witty comeback, nothing came to mind, so I settled for simply glaring at him.

Varvara's emerald eyes sparkled with delight at our interplay. "I'd tell you boys to behave yourselves, but where would be the fun in that?" She left the table and came walking toward us. Perhaps *sauntered* might be a better word. Even when she's all business, Varvara moves like a jungle cat in heat.

I expected her to ask me what information I had for her, but instead of approaching me, she walked up to Devona, bent down – Varvara's quite tall and Devona's petite – and gave her a big hug. "Congratulations, sweetie! I'm so thrilled that you and Matt are expecting!"

"Thank you," Devona said. "We're both quite excited."

"Well, of course you are!" Varvara said. "It's not every day that a zombie and a half-vampire have a child, let alone twins."

Devona and I just gaped at her.

Varvara frowned. "Did I say something wrong?"

"I'm only having one baby," Devona said. "The doctors at the Fever House–"

Varvara interrupted Devona with an imperious wave of her riding crop. "Don't know their fangs from a can opener. While I, on the other hand, am a dread and mighty Darklord." She grinned. "If I say you're going to have twins, you can count on it."

I was struggling to accept the bombshell the queen of demons had just dropped on us. Devona was right; during all our doctors' visits, no one had ever mentioned that she was carrying two babies. I had no reason to doubt Varvara. Despite what I'd said to Klamm about demons, I'd never known her to lie to me. When you're as powerful as Varvara, you don't need to resort to lying to get what you want. But I couldn't see how the Bloodborn doctors at the Fever House could've made such a mistake.

"The doctors performed ultrasounds…" I began.

"Which only picked up one heartbeat," Varvara said. "And that's because only one of your children *has* a beating heart. The other is… well, I'm not sure *what* she is, to be honest. She's alive… in a sense anyway." Varvara flashed Devona a smile. "She's moving around in there pretty good. Her brother, on the other hand, is a bit more sedate, but they're both healthy enough. I can't tell too much about them. The magic that surrounds them is too strong and too different from anything I've ever encountered before. But they're going to be very special children, that I can promise you."

Every demon in Varvara's war room broke off what they were doing and turned to look at Devona, expressions of curiosity and in some cases outright wonderment on their faces. Klamm looked at Devona too, but his gaze was focused on her mildly swollen belly, and the look on his face was one I couldn't read, but which made me uncomfortable for some reason.

"My father visited me recently," Devona said. "Why didn't he say anything?"

"He might not have sensed the truth," Varvara said. "We Darklords, while more or less equally matched in power, possess different skills. Talaith and I are both more versatile when it comes to working magic than the boys are." She paused. "Then again, Galm might've had his own reasons for not telling you. But I assure you, it's true. You are carrying twins."

I looked at Devona and she looked at me, and we both smiled. We'd once been trapped in a virtual reality in which we were a human couple living on Earth.

In that dream scenario, we'd have two children, fraternal twins, a boy and a girl. Though they hadn't been real, we'd believed they were, and when we'd realized we were living in an illusion, we'd fought to free ourselves. But in doing so, the virtual reality vanished – including our two children. Even though they'd been nothing more than dreams, losing them had still hurt like hell. There was no way the babies Devona was carrying were those two dreams made flesh, I knew that. And yet... Nekropolis is a damned strange place, and the impossible happens here with almost monotonous regularity.

I decided to go back to being a loudmouth, since it's something I seem to have particular talent for. "I'm surprised to see you so happy for us, Varvara. I didn't know you were the maternal type."

The Demon Queen gave me a look I couldn't read. What is it with me and interpreting demonic facial expressions today? I thought.

"The Creche of the Demonkin lies in the caverns beneath Demon's Roost." Her voice was even and without emotion, and I thought that I'd never heard her sound so dangerous before. "I may not personally lay every egg incubated there, but I make damn sure they receive the very best care. And if a single egg fails to hatch due to the negligence of a caregiver, the penalty for that failure is dire indeed. Do you understand?"

Since I'm dead, I don't need to swallow, but I did so at that moment anyway. "I do."

She looked at me for a long moment, and then frowned. "Is something wrong with your head? It looks a little lopsided."

I'd been so concerned with not angering Varvara further that I'd momentarily allowed my concentration to lapse, and my neck's hold on my severed head had slackened. Luckily Varvara had said something before my head had slipped off and fallen to the floor. That would've been embarrassing, and I didn't want to think about what cutting remark Klamm might've made if it had happened. I concentrated, and my head and neck gripped each other tightly again.

"I'm all right," I said, trying to sound casual.

Varvara looked me up and down, and though I didn't feel anything, I had the impression that she was mystically scanning me. When she was finished, her grin returned.

"Just try to keep it together, Matt." She then turned to look at Varney, Shamika, and Scorch. "The demoness I know, for am I not ultimately mother to all the Demonkin?"

She walked over to Scorch and gently touched her cheek. "There's a war on, dear. Go downstairs and join the rest of your fellow soldiers."

Scorch bowed her head. "Yes, my queen." She gave Devona and me an apologetic look before heading back to the elevator and getting on. As the door slid shut, she gave a thumbs-up to wish us luck. I didn't blame Scorch for leaving. She had no choice but to obey Varvara's command – not if she wanted to continue breathing, that is.

Varvara then turned to Varney and Shamika. "And who are these two charming people?"

I introduced them, and Varvara gave Shamika a long look, scowling as if she were puzzled. But then she shook her head as if to clear it and focused her attention on Varney.

"I'm glad you're here," she told him. "You have my permission to film and broadcast anything you see. When this war is over, history will vindicate the Demonkin, and I want the citizens of Nekropolis to see what we do here this day."

"My queen," Klamm began, "Do you really think that's wise? If the Arcane should somehow tap into the Bloodborn's signal…" He gave Varney a sideways look. "Assuming he isn't an Arcane spy, that is."

Varvara turned to Klamm and this time when she smiled, her mouth was full of shark's teeth. "I'm not afraid of anyone, General. Least of all the Arcane. Please do your best to remember that."

I had to give Klamm this: he was one cool customer. Anyone else would've fainted dead away to have Varvara talk to him like that, but he not only held steady, he replied in a calm voice. "Of course, my queen. I meant no disrespect. But you made me a general because of my skill at intelligence-gathering. I would be remiss if I didn't point out the potential pitfalls of allowing a cameraman with cybernetic implants access to our war room." He paused. "Especially right now."

Varvara looked at Klamm for a moment, shark teeth still bared, but then she sighed and nodded. She closed her mouth, and when she opened it again, her teeth had returned to normal.

"I suppose you're right." She looked at Varney. "If you're not a spy, I apologize for this."

She waved her riding crop, and Varney yelped as his cybernetic eye exploded in a shower of sparks. The flesh around the eye blackened as it burned, but Varney was Bloodborn, and the injury began repairing itself almost immediately. Too bad his camera eye couldn't be fixed as easily. He looked as if he wanted to protest, but he wisely kept his mouth shut. He was lucky that Varvara hadn't decided to completely incinerate him on the spot, and he doubtless knew it.

Devona stood next to Shamika, a comforting arm around the girl's shoulders. Shamika didn't seem all that intimidated by Varvara, even though the Demon Queen had just used her magic to burn out Varney's camera eye and could use her powers to do worse to us at any moment. Instead, Shamika's attention was focused on General Klamm. The girl stared at him, her gaze intense, but I couldn't tell if she was afraid of him or fascinated with him. Or both.

There was a lot about Shamika I hadn't been able to get a handle on, and it was really starting to bug me.

Klamm was aware of the girl's interest in him, and he returned her look with a knowing smirk that made her avert her gaze.

Varvara turned to me then. "You know I always enjoy catching up with you, Matt, but as you might imagine, I'm a wee bit busy at the moment, what with planning a retaliatory strike on Talaith and all. So why don't you tell me why you came to see me, and then we can both get on with the rest of our day."

I tried to decide how to begin. I couldn't tell her that Dis had asked me to investigate the disappearances of the magic-users in the hope that I might learn something that would stop this war. Dis needed to maintain the appearance of neutrality in the dispute between Varvara and Talaith, and I was determined to keep his involvement in the case quiet, more for my sake than his. The last thing I wanted to do was to make a god mad at me.

"Papa Chatha is missing," I said. I quickly filled her in on what little we knew. "That's why Shamika is with us," I finished. "She's helping us search for her uncle."

"Her uncle?" Klamm said. "Do you have any proof that she's related to Papa Chatha? Had any of you met her before today or even so much as heard Papa mention her?"

"Are you implying that Shamika's a spy?" Devona said, flashing Klamm a little fang to show what she thought of him.

"She *is* Arcane," Klamm said. "And by appealing to your sympathies, she's managed not only to worm her way into Demon's Roost, but into Varvara's war room."

I started to protest, but then I thought about what Klamm said. He had a point – one that I didn't want to examine too closely lest I become as paranoid as him.

"What do you want from me, Matt?" Varvara asked. "And make it fast: I'm busy planning a war, you know."

With Varvara, I've found that the direct approach works best, and the bold-as-hell approach works even better.

"I want you to release Papa – and the other magic-users while you're at it. Then you and Talaith can make nice, and the rest of us can get on with our lives, such as they are."

Varvara's green eyes blazed with baleful light, and her expression became one of cold fury. I could feel power building around her, and I knew I was a hair's breadth away from being turned into zombie fricassee.

I gave her a lopsided grin. "Come on – you *knew* I was going to ask."

Klamm fixed me with a disdainful glare. "My queen! You can't possibly tolerate such insolence!"

"Insolence is my middle name," I told Klamm. "Well, actually it's Stephen, but you get the idea."

The queen of the Demonkin looked at me for a moment, then she smiled and the power that had been building around her disappeared.

"Of course you were going to ask, Matt," she said, almost fondly. "It's what you do, isn't it? Ask the questions others are afraid to, go places they won't or can't, all in pursuit of an ideal called Truth that in the end may not even exist."

"I usually find answers," I said, trying not to sound defensive.

"Perhaps," Varvara said, "but they aren't always the answers you hope to find, are they?"

I didn't reply.

Varvara regarded me for a moment more before turning and walking back to the map table. Klamm joined her, but since no one had extended an invitation to me, I stayed where I was, standing with Devona, Shamika, and Varney. I figured I'd already pushed my luck with Varvara enough for the time being.

"I had nothing to do with the disappearances of the Arcane," Varvara said. "Nor did any of my subjects." She glanced sideways at Klamm. "At least, not as far as we know. Investigations are ongoing."

Klamm smiled coldly at that, and I could imagine the excruciatingly agonizing nature of those "investigations."

Varvara continued. "For whatever reason, Talaith has chosen to blame me for the disappearances, and I've been unable to convince her otherwise."

"Not that you tried very hard," I guessed. "After all, a war with Talaith would be too much fun to pass up."

Varvara's smile held more than a hint of slyness. "It *has* been a long time since we've had a decent war," she admitted. "The last full-scale conflict between the Dominions was the Blood Wars, and they happened over two centuries ago. We're long overdue for another."

"And it doesn't bother you that people will die while you and Talaith play soldiers?" I asked.

Varvara gave me a look. "What part of *Demon* Queen don't you understand?"

Klamm chose that moment to jump in again. "Have you considered the possibility that Talaith kidnapped the missing magic-users herself and then blamed Varvara for the crime in order to create an excuse to attack the Sprawl? In fact, the disappearances may have only been a ruse. The magic-users may have hidden themselves at Varvara's command."

"Papa Chatha would never do that," I said. "He may be Arcane, but he's his own man."

Klamm shrugged. "Perhaps. Then again, you may not know him as well as you think."

Despite myself, I couldn't help considering Klamm's words. Before that day, I hadn't known Papa had a niece. What else didn't I know about him?

I glanced at Shamika. She continued to stare at Klamm oddly, but she didn't say anything in defense of her uncle. I wondered if it was because she was too intimidated at being in Varvara's presence or if it was because she had no defense to make.

I told myself to stop heading down that path. Demons are notorious for getting inside your head – sometimes literally – and messing with your mind any number of ways.

"Do you have any proof to back up your suspicions?" I asked Klamm.

"Not yet," he admitted. "But as my queen told you–"

"Investigations are ongoing," I said.

Klamm smiled. "Indeed."

"Talaith claims to have proof of Demonkin involvement in the disappearances," I said. "Have you seen it?"

Varvara shook her head. "But even if she did show it to me, I wouldn't trust it. Talaith isn't above manufacturing evidence when it suits her purpose."

"Neither are you," I countered.

Klamm shot me a dark look, but Varvara let out a loud earthy laugh.

"True enough! But you know how scheming and vindictive Talaith can be. She makes the rest of us Darklords seem reasonable and even-tempered."

"I don't know if I'd go that far, but your point is a good one."

I figured I'd learned as much as I was going to from Varvara, but I wasn't ready to leave yet. I doubted the Demon Queen could be swayed from retaliating against Talaith, but I figured I should at least make the effort. I wasn't going to attempt to appeal to her better nature, since I was fairly certain she didn't have one. Instead, I decided to appeal to her mercenary side. With the best shops, clubs, restaurants, and attractions in Nekropolis, the Sprawl is the city's center of business – both legitimate and otherwise – and a lot of darkgems exchanged hands here. War wouldn't exactly be conducive to the orderly flow of commerce.

"Do you really think attacking Glamere is a good idea? I'm sure it would be emotionally satisfying, but it won't be good for business. With both bridges destroyed, the Sprawl is already cut off from the other Dominions, and that's going to put a dent in profits. And all-out war would be even worse. If the Sprawl becomes a battle zone…"

Klamm answered for Varvara. "Engineering crews have already been dispatched to rebuild the bridges, along with soldiers to guard them once they're finished." He smiled smugly. "If Talaith sends the

Weyward Sisters to destroy the bridges again, the witches will find us waiting and ready for them."

"Talaith won't bother attacking the bridges again," Varvara said. "She'll go for a bigger, bolder strike the next time. It's what I would do." She thought for a moment. "It's true that a war might adversely affect business in the Sprawl, and I've already met with several nervous representatives of the Merchants' Guild about that very matter. And I'm not unsympathetic to their concerns. I've worked hard to make the Sprawl the most interesting and exciting Dominion in the city, and I have no intention of throwing that away lightly. But there's a lot to be said for a good war, you know. Like a forest fire, it can be a cleansing force, burning away old, tired wood and making room for invigorating new growth." She flashed a smile. "Besides, it's *fun*!"

"So your main reason for going to war – aside from getting back at Talaith – is that it will give you a chance to remodel?" I shook my head in disgust. "You know, sometimes you Darklords are more like kids with Attention Deficit Disorder than immortal monsters."

In response, Varvara's smile only grew wider.

"The queen's forest fire analogy is particularly apt at the moment," Klamm said. He bent over the map table, typed a command on the keyboard, and then moved his index finger over the mouse pad. The hologram of Nekropolis blurred and reformed into a detailed image of Glamere, the Dominion Talaith ruled. I haven't spent much time there, considering how much Talaith despises me, but I recognized the more prominent features: the Valley of Silence, the Interstitial Maze, Re-version River, and the Greensward. In the middle of the latter stood Woodhome, Talaith's stronghold, a gigantic tree which contained dozens of interior chambers that had formed organically as it grew.

I had a bad feeling about this. "You're not going to attack Woodhome, are you?" If Varvara made a direct strike on Talaith's stronghold, the Witch Queen would be so furious that not even Father Dis would be able to stop the war then. Worse, it might drag the other three Darklords into the conflict. Galm, Amon, and Edrigu would sit back and watch Varvara and Talaith fight it out as long as their dispute didn't spill over into the other Dominions. But it would be a different story if either of the women attacked the other's stronghold. While the Darklords had fought against one another in ways large and small over the centuries, by unspoken agreement they had never attacked another Lord's stronghold. If Varvara broke that custom now, the other Darklords might decide she'd gone too far and join forces against her. If that happened, the destruction Devona and I had witnessed in the alternate Nekropolis would pale in comparison to the devastation a five-way battle between Darklords would wreak on the city.

"It's tempting, I'll admit," Varvara said, "but no, we're not going to attack Woodhome." She smiled darkly. "Just the next best thing." She nodded to Klamm, and he pressed a button on the map table's console. The Demon Queen then waved her hand and the walls of her penthouse became transparent. I'd always assumed

Varvara's quarters didn't have windows because she didn't want to be vulnerable to a possible attack by another Darklord – and because she didn't want anyone spying on the more lascivious activities she indulged in with playmates of either sex – but now I understood that the walls *were* windows... when she wanted them to be, anyway.

Vibrations juddered through the floor, and the entire building shook around us, as if in the grip of an earthquake. The vibrations ceased as a dozen fiery streaks shot up from the ground and arced up into the night-black sky above the Sprawl. The streaks flew northward and were rapidly lost to view.

Varney moaned. "My producer is going to kill me for not being able to film this!"

"Look at the map," Devona said in a tone that held equal parts of awe and fear.

We all did as she said and saw a dozen miniature recreations of the flame trails heading toward Glamere from the south.

"Are those missiles?" I asked.

"Yes," Klamm answered without taking his eyes off the holo-display. "Fired from silos surrounding Demon's Roost. Each contains a payload of a dozen salamanders." The light from the holographic recreation of the missiles bathed his face in bright orange, and it made his glossy black eyes gleam. "My own special design."

None of us could take our gazes away from the holographic scene playing out before us. We all watched silently as the missiles arced downward and impacted on the forest floor of the Greensward in a circle around Woodhome. I had no doubt that the salamanders Klamm referred to weren't the tiny amphibious creatures of Earth but rather mythological salamanders, magical fire lizards capable of igniting vast conflagrations. The recreation wasn't detailed enough for us to see exactly what happened once the missiles hit, but I imagined panels in the sides of the missiles popping open and hordes of small red-hided salamanders pouring forth. An instant later, a wall of flame sprang up around Woodhome and immediately began moving away from Talaith's stronghold, devouring the Greensward as it went. I imagined the salamanders scuttling forward in a circle, obeying a preprogrammed geis to keep their flames away from Woodhome. It seemed Varvara had been telling the truth when she said she wouldn't attack Talaith's stronghold.

Talaith didn't waste any time in striking back. Three small dots of light emerged from the holographic recreation of Woodhome, and flew up and over the rapidly expanding circle of fire.

"The Weyward Sisters," Varvara said. "Talaith's dispatched them to put out the fire." The Demon Queen spoke with barely contained excitement, sounding like an overeager sports fan watching a particularly tense moment in the game.

Thread-thin beams of light emerged from the dots representing the Weyward Sisters and lanced downward into the circle of flame. The salamanders' fire flickered and slowed down, but it continued spreading.

Klamm smiled. "Those aren't ordinary salamanders. They've been both mystically and genetically augmented to withstand any attack. The Sisters might be able to extinguish the flames the salamanders have already created, but they won't be able to stop them from making more."

"Another of your 'special designs'?" I asked.

Klamm looked up from the holo-display long enough to give me a smug smile before returning his attention to the action.

We continued to watch as the Weyward Sisters unleashed one mystic bolt after another in an attempt to stop the salamanders' fiery march across the Greensward, but while they were able to douse the flames the creatures created, they couldn't stop the salamanders themselves. Finally the Sisters broke off their attack and flew up to a point above Woodhome where they gathered together.

"What are they doing?" Varvara asked.

Shamika had been silent since we'd entered Varvara's penthouse, but she spoke now. "Since they can't destroy the salamanders, they're going to prevent them from spreading their fires throughout all of Glamere. And there's only one way to do that."

Devona's eyes widened in sudden comprehension. "Destroy the rest of the Greensward. That way, they won't have anything to burn."

Shamika nodded, and we watched as the three dots representing the Weyward Sisters began to blaze with light so intense that it was hard to look at them directly. The light then pulsed outward in a wave that rolled over the rest of the Greensward, and an instant later, the forest was gone. I wasn't sure what sort of spell the Weyward Sisters had used, but it was damned powerful, disintegrating the surviving trees instantly. The salamanders' flames continued to burn for a few seconds longer after that, but denied fuel, their flames died out. The Weyward Sisters then parted, each of them flying down into the burned-out plain where the Greensward had been and flying low over the ground.

"What are they doing?" Varney asked. "Capturing the salamanders?"

Varvara nodded. "Since they no longer have to worry about saving the Greensward, their magic can protect them from the salamanders' flames. They can just pick them up off the ground now. But it doesn't matter. My little pets have done their work."

I thought she was going to say something more, but before she could speak again, the image of a woman's head appeared above the holographic recreation of Woodhome. It was Talaith.

She appeared to be in her late sixties, with short gray hair, baggy eyes, and sagging skin. Her expression was normally fixed in a permanent tight-lipped scowl, but now her features were twisted with rage.

"How *dare* you!" she said in a low voice.

Varvara smiled sweetly at Talaith. "You made the first move, love."

"You kidnapped my people!"

"I've told you, I had nothing to do with that. And even if I had, do you really think the abduction of a few witches and warlocks rates the destruction of *both* bridges to my Dominion? It's hardly what I would call a reasonable response, dear."

"I'll show you a *reasonable response*, you demonic slut! I'll–" Talaith broke off, frowning. The image of her head slowly rotated until she was looking at me.

"Richter!" She said my name like it was a particularly nasty venereal disease. "I should've known you would be involved in this!"

"Actually, one of his friends is among the missing magic-users," Varvara said. "Matt came here to find out if I knew anything about his disappearance. Technically, I suppose that means he's on your side."

"Don't insult me," I muttered.

Talaith's eyes burned with such hatred that I was glad I was only looking at a mystic projection of her and not the real thing. If she had been here, she'd have likely hit me with a spell so powerful it would've reduced me to an undead smear on the floor.

"You've been a thorn in my side for far too long, Richter," she said. "First I'm going to deal with Varvara, and when I'm finished with her, I'm coming for you."

"Don't write checks your ass can't cash, dear," Varvara said.

Talaith whirled back to face her, snarled, and then the image of her head faded as she broke contact.

Varvara grinned. "That went well, didn't it?" She grinned at Klamm. "Excellent work, General."

Klamm bowed his head. "It's my pleasure to serve you, my queen. I'll have my people begin assessing the damage and running simulations to determine what Talaith's next move might be." He glanced sideways at us. "About our visitors… They've seen far too much, my queen. While I understand that you find the zombie amusing, he and his companions should be placed in holding cells where we can keep an eye on them until the current situation with the Arcane is resolved. It would be the…" he paused, searching for the right word. "*prudent* thing to do."

Varvara smiled at him. "In case you hadn't noticed, General, I'm not one for making the *prudent* choice. Where's the fun in that? Matt is far more interesting when he's allowed to roam free, causing his own unique brand of chaos."

I frowned. "I'm not sure if that's a compliment or an insult."

Varvara grinned. "Works either way."

I couldn't help but smile back. "Guess so." But then I grew serious. "You know Talaith will take the destruction of the Greensward as seriously as if you had attacked Woodhome. Unlike you, Talaith doesn't embrace technology, and she forces her people to live in harmony with nature – whether they like it or not. To her, destroying a forest is the same as destroying a city full of people. Actually, she probably considers it to be worse. And the Greensward isn't just a simple collection of trees, it's her personal forest, the one surrounding her home. Whatever she does next, it'll make the destruction of the bridges pale in comparison."

Varvara's grin took on a dark edge. "I'm counting on it."

ELEVEN

We left Demon's Roost without Scorch. We looked for her among the ranks of demons drilling in the Atrium, but there were too many, and we didn't spot her. Not that she could've come with us even if we had found her. Varvara had ordered her to join the ranks of her demonic army, and Scorch had had no choice but to obey if she didn't wish to incur the Demon Queen's wrath.

"I hope she'll be all right," Devona said when we were out on the street. Demons patrolled the area, but none of them challenged us. Varvara had likely sent word ahead that we were to be allowed to leave, and while her soldiers might not like it, none of them would dare disobey their queen.

"She's more than tough enough to take care of herself," I said. Still, if the war between Talaith and Varvara intensified to the point where ground troops were called in, Scorch might find herself in more trouble than she could handle. I didn't say this to Devona, though. I didn't need to. I was sure she was thinking along the same lines.

"That was a useless trip," Varney said, fingering his ruined cyber-eye. "You didn't learn anything, and I lost my camera. I can't believe I was present when Varvara struck back against Talaith, and I didn't get a single moment of footage!"

"It wasn't totally wasted," Devona said. "We learned that Varvara had nothing to do with the disappearance of the magic-users."

"We did?" Shamika said.

Devona nodded. "Of all the Darklords, Varvara is the most… I suppose honest isn't exactly the right word. Upfront, I guess is what I'm trying to say. She's a lot like a wild animal. She is what she is and does what she does and makes no effort to pretend to be something she's not. If she had kidnapped the magic-users, she wouldn't have denied it. In fact, she'd have gloated about it."

"And she loves an audience," I added. "As far as she's concerned, there'd be no point in striking against a fellow Darklord if there was no one around to appreciate the brilliance of her plan."

"But you don't have proof Varvara *didn't* order the abductions," Varney said.

"True," I admitted, "but Devona and I know her well enough that I'm willing to bet she didn't. But you're right: since we don't have any evidence that clears her, we can't completely rule her out as a suspect."

Shamika chimed in then. "That other demon – Klamm – said that maybe Talaith is only pretending magic-users were kidnapped as an excuse to attack Varvara. Do you think he might be right?"

I shrugged. "Talaith is devious as hell, and she has a history of attempting to attack the other Darklords." That was how I'd originally come to Nekropolis from Earth. Talaith had sent one of her servants to Earth to kidnap humans with strong psychic potential in order to harvest their brains and use them to create a device called the Overmind, which she planned to use against Lord Edrigu. My partner and I had tracked the kidnapper to a portal that led to Nekropolis, and we went through. Eventually we reached Glamere and confronted the kidnapper and Talaith in Woodhome. We destroyed the Overmind, and my partner lost his life in the process, but somehow the release of magical and psychic energies resulted in my being resurrected as a self-willed zombie. I still miss Dale. He was a good man and a good friend – rare qualities, no matter what dimension you're from.

"If Talaith is responsible, maybe Bogdan will uncover some evidence of it from his contacts," Devona said.

"Maybe," I allowed, "but Talaith plays things pretty close to the vest. There's a good chance no one but she would know the truth. But who knows? Maybe Bogdan will get lucky."

I didn't particularly like Bogdan, but he was smart. If anyone in the Sprawl's Arcane community had information relating to the magic-users' kidnapping, I was confident he'd find out – not that I'd ever admit it to him.

"We did learn one other item of interest," Devona said, reaching out to take my hand. She gave it a squeeze, and I could feel the seam between my hand and wrist weaken, then give way. "Oops!" Devona said. "Sorry about that. Way to spoil a tender moment, huh?"

My detached hand continued to grip hers, and we stopped walking long enough for her to place my hand against the stump of my wrist. I concentrated, and my hand reattached to my body. Devona let go, and I flexed my fingers to test out the connection. I wasn't sure, but it felt a bit weaker than before. If we didn't find Papa Chatha before too much longer, I'd eventually be unable to hold myself together and I'd end up a pile of disconnected parts, which would make it a wee bit harder for me to stop the war building between Varvara and Talaith.

I clasped Devona's hand once more. "Now where were we?"

"We're going to have twins," she said, grinning.

"Hard to believe, isn't it? Matt Junior and Devona Junior."

"Maybe we should try to come up with some better names."

"Maybe we should think about getting married," I said. The words popped out of my mouth before I was aware of it, but once I said them, they felt right. But then something occurred to me and I frowned. "Uh, Darkfolk do get married, right?"

Devona pulled me down toward her, then stood on her tiptoes and kissed me. When she pulled away, she beamed at me and said, "We can make plans later. Right now we should concentrate on finding Papa Chatha, OK?"

"All right."

Varney moaned. "Great! You propose to Devona, and I couldn't film it! My producer is going to put a stake in my heart for sure over this!"

Shamika smiled at us. "Can I come to your wedding?"

"Of course, honey," Devona said. "In fact, you can help us plan it if you–"

We were nearing one of the barriers around Demon's Roost, this one made of a row of vehicles parked end to end across the street, with armed demons standing on the roofs. The air rippled around us, as if distorted by waves of heat rising from the asphalt, and at first I feared that Talaith was already retaliating for the salamanders' fiery destruction of the Greensward. The distortion effect increased, accompanied by a strange disorientation, as if the entire world was slowly tilting to the left. Ghostly images began to appear around us – people thronging the sidewalks, vehicles clogging the street, tall modern office buildings rising into the sky... The people were all human, the vehicles normal cars, trucks, vans and the like, and the buildings lacked any hint of the bizarre that typified the Sprawl's architectural style.

"What's happening?" Devona shouted. Her voice had a strange hollow quality, as if she was shouting from the other side of a thick wall.

"I don't know!" I shouted back. The ghost images reminded me of Bonetown, the Dominion of Edrigu,

Lord of the Dead. But unlike Bonetown, these phan-
tasms all appeared to be from the same modern time,
and none of them possessed any sign of having died in
violent ways – their bodies were unmarked, and aside
from their transparent quality, they appeared whole
and healthy. It was as if we were gazing upon a faint
image of an Earth city, an American one, like New York
or Chicago.

Or Cleveland, I thought. My old hometown. Varvara
has a mirror in her penthouse – though it hadn't been
visible during our latest visit – and it opens onto a park
in Cleveland. It was through this mirror that Dale and
I had first traveled to Nekropolis. The more I looked at
the people and buildings around us, the more con-
vinced I became that I was looking at Cleveland. And
what was more, some of the people had begun staring
in our direction and pointing, as if they could see us
too. Others were looking around them, and I wondered if they were seeing ghostly images of the Sprawl
superimposed upon their city.

And then, just like that, the apparition of Cleveland
disappeared, and the world righted itself once more,
taking the strange sensation of disorientation with it.

"What in the Nine Hells just happened?" Devona
said, her voice sounding normal once more.

"Whatever it was, we weren't the only ones who experienced it." I nodded to the demons standing on top
of the barrier stretched across the street. They were
gazing about in terror, and a couple fired off shots into
the air, as if trying to fend off some unseen foe.

"Let me call my producer," Varney said in a shaken voice. He pulled a hand vox out of his pants pocket and made a call. "Murdock?" he said. "It's Varney. What—" He broke off and listened for a couple moments. "Yes... yes... All right. I'll get right on it." He disconnected and tucked the vox back in his pocket. "My producer said they experienced the same thing at the Eidolon Building, and reporters all over the city are calling in, saying it happened in the other Dominions as well." Varney looked at me. "Murdock wants me to forget about shooting footage of you for now and go find people to interview about what just happened." He sighed. "I didn't want to tell him Varvara destroyed my camera."

"So you're going to just keep hanging out with us since you can't do what your boss wants?" I asked.

"I guess so. He's got plenty of other reporters out in the streets to talk to witnesses, and as long as I stay with you, I can still observe what you do. It's better than nothing, you know?"

It sounded like a lame excuse to me. I had no idea how long it would take to repair or replace Varney's cyber-eye, but as strong as vampires are and as swiftly as they heal, surgery can be performed on them rapidly. Switching out Varney's cyber-eye might well prove no more difficult than changing the spark plugs in a car. So why wasn't he hauling ass back to the Eidolon Building for a repair job right now?

I was about to confront Varney about it, but Shamika said, "We were on Earth. Just for a few moments, but we were there."

The enormity of what she said stunned us into silence. When the Darkfolk decided to leave Earth four hundred years ago, they traveled to another dimension where they built the city of Nekropolis. But if what Shamika had said was true, the entire city had been transported to Earth's dimension, if only briefly.

"Is that even possible?" Varney said.

"The amount of power it would take is staggering," Devona said. "I'm not sure even a being as powerful as Talaith could do it."

"Why would she?" I said. "Why would anybody? It's not like the Darkfolk are completely cut off from Earth and dying to get back. They import goods and materials whenever they want, and they can apply for travel visas at each of the Darklords' strongholds."

"Maybe it was her retaliatory strike against Varvara," Devona suggested. "Perhaps she was trying to exile Varvara by transporting the Sprawl to Earth."

I thought about this for a moment. "Maybe, but Varney's producer said the entire city was affected, all five Dominions, Glamere included."

Devona shrugged. "Maybe Talaith screwed up. She wanted to transport only the Sprawl, but the spell accidentally affected the rest of the city."

"I guess it's possible. But if Talaith was in possession of a spell or magical device that powerful, why didn't she use it in the first place? Why bother with destroying the bridges?"

"Maybe she didn't want to risk using it until she felt pushed to strike out at Varvara in a big way," Devona said. "And the spell must be an unstable one and not very reliable. After all, it failed, didn't it?" She turned to Shamika. "What do you think?"

"That seems… logical," the girl said. I had the sense that she might have said more, that she wanted to, but for some reason she remained silent.

Devona continued. "And the other Darklords – including Father Dis – are probably going nuts right now. Using such a powerful spell was bound to get their attention, and Talaith wouldn't want to drag them into her war with Varvara unless she had to. But the destruction of the Greensward angered her so much that she no longer cared whether she upset the other Lords, so she tried the spell, but it got away from her and failed, thankfully."

"Maybe." Devona's theorizing sounded good, but like Varney had mentioned earlier, we didn't have any evidence. "If Talaith was responsible for what happened, let's hope she doesn't try it again. Next time she might get it right."

"That would be awful!" Shamika said.

"That's putting it mildly," I said. "It would be bad enough if the Darkfolk suddenly found themselves back on Earth. Especially the vampires, if they appeared outside during the daytime. The humans would panic, of course, and there would undoubtedly be fighting and casualties on both sides, but that wouldn't be the worst of it. If people and buildings suddenly occupied the same space… well, I'm not sure what would happen, but I bet the laws of physics would be mighty unhappy with the situation and the end result wouldn't be pretty."

We reached the car barrier, and the demons on top waved us past without a word. In the middle of the street on the other side of the barrier, people were starting to gather, and they were clearly upset about the ghostly images of Earth that had briefly appeared. Some were talking loudly about what they'd seen and demanding someone in authority do something, while others simply cried or just stared blankly into space, traumatized. The crowd continued to grow as we did our best to make our way through, and while most of them ignored us, a few recognized me and begged me to investigate the strange occurrence and prevent it from happening again. It was a weird feeling knowing that people were looking to me for help – and frustrating too. You save the damn city a couple times, and suddenly everyone expects miracles from you.

A middle-aged harpy grabbed hold of my left arm with one of her foot claws and held tight to me, while she attempted to explain in tearful detail how awful the vision of Earth had been. I made a few placating noises and tried to pull away, but her grip was so strong that I was afraid I'd tear my arm off if I pulled too hard. My vox rang then, and I told the harpy that I needed to take the call as it might be important information relating to the case. She let me go, and I answered my vox as Devona, Shamika, Varney, and I continued to push our way through the crowd.

"Matt? It's Tavi."

From the sound of his gruff voice and the rapid way he spoke, I knew he was still in his wildform, and I asked him to speak more slowly. Which he did, if only a little.

"I've been having a devil of a time following Papa Chatha's scent trail. It zigzags all over the Sprawl, and I've been tracking it for hours. I almost lost it when that weird distortion hit, whatever that was. I didn't just see a phantom city – I *smelled* it, too. Anyway, once the ghost city vanished, I picked up the scent trail again and followed it to the Grotesquerie. That's where I am right now. The trail dead-ends here, Matt. I've had a quick look around, and I can't put my finger on it, but something doesn't feel right here. I–"

Tavi's voice was cut off by a loud roar, which was immediately followed by an agonized scream, and then silence.

"Tavi!" I shouted into the vox. "TAVI!"

No response. The line was dead, and I hoped the same couldn't be said for Tavi.

"What's wrong?" Devona said.

I started to tell her, but before I could get more than a couple words out, the crowd around us shrieked and moved rapidly away as Lazlo's cab raced toward us.

I smiled grimly. It's good to have friends you can depend on, even when they look like mutated tarantula-bats. The cab's new tires screeched as the vehicle swerved to a stop in front of us.

Lazlo stuck his head out the window and favored us with a toothy grin.

"Going my way?"

The Grotesquerie is located on Sybarite Street, not far from the House of Mysterious Secrets. It covers several square miles and is surrounded by a hundred-foot-high wall made of a polished black substance that looks like solidified shadow, atop which sits a complex array of metal and crystal that continuously glows with a gentle, pulsing red light. The force field the wall generates is invisible to the naked eye, but it encloses the Grotesquerie in an unimaginably powerful energy dome that's a synthesis of the highest of high-tech science and the most potent of ancient magics – all in order to keep what the Grotesquerie houses from getting out. But this wasn't a prison. Nekropolis' prison is called Tenebrus, and it's located underground beneath the Nightspire, and I'd once had the dubious pleasure of being a guest there for a short time. What the Grotesquerie holds is far more dangerous and terrifying than anything a mere prison might contain, for the Grotesquerie is a zoo. But not just *any* zoo – it's a Darkfolk zoo.

When the Darkfolk decided to emigrate from Earth, they gathered up every wild monster they could find, like a twisted version of Noah and the Ark, and brought them along to live in the Grotesquerie. But new ones occasionally surface, due to natural or unnatural evolution or scientific experiments gone hideously wrong, and the Grotesquerie's hunters make periodic expeditions to Earth to search out these monsters and bring em back alive, as the saying goes. They do it for the sake of preservation – many of the Grotesquerie's monsters are rare species or literally one of a kind – but a side benefit is that humans don't have worry about getting stomped on by gigantic radioactive lizards, so it's a win-win all the way around.

Lazlo dropped us off at the main entrance, and brilliant detective that I am, I immediately suspected something was wrong when I saw all the people running screaming into the street. I turned to Devona and almost asked her to stay outside and watch Shamika, but given how the girl had handled herself with Magilla, I figured she was probably be in less danger going in than I was.

The three of us pushed through the mass of fleeing zoogoers, Varney right there alongside us. With his camera-eye inoperative he should've had no reason to follow us into what was undoubtedly a hazardous situation, but I wasn't surprised that he'd decided to accompany us. He might've been a reporter, but it had become clear to me that he had a hidden agenda for sticking so closely to us, and right then wasn't the time to try and figure out what it was. There'd be an opportunity to question him later – assuming the four of us survived our visit to the Grotesquerie.

Once we made it past the crowd and through the main gate, we moved off to the side to get out of the way, but we needn't have bothered. The majority of the Grotesquerie's visitors had managed to make it out, and only a handful of stragglers remained.

Inside, the Grotesquerie resembles an Earth zoo, with paved walkways winding between habitats set up for the creatures on display. The major difference is the landscaping. Instead of the pleasant trees and shrubs of an Earthly zoo, the Grotesquerie's paths are lined with deadly leech vine, tanglethorn, and rotweed. Visitors are always careful to give the plants a wide berth, and the plants usually leave them alone. But then they weren't put there to attack visitors. They were an additional deterrent should any of the Grotesquerie's attractions manage to escape their enclosures.

Huge Frankenstein monsters were employed as keepers, and a half dozen of them clomped past us in their gray coveralls and overlarge work boots, each of them clutching long metallic rods with glowing red tips at one end. The keepers' expressions were grim, but since Frankenstein monsters aren't known for their cheerful, sunny dispositions, it was hard to tell if they were upset over whatever was happening or if it was just another day on the job for them. Given the panicking visitors fleeing for their lives, I opted for the former. Told you I was a brilliant detective.

"Follow the keepers!" I said, and we did so, setting off at a run.

Given my undead state, I'm not that well coordinated at the best of times, even if I've just had a fresh application of preservative spells. But considering that I was currently a jigsaw puzzle of a zombie holding himself together through sheer concentration, I was even less coordinated than usual. With every galumphing shuffle-step I took, I felt my body literally threatening to come apart at the seams, and it took an extra effort of will to keep myself intact.

We followed the keepers past several enclosures, and though it had been a while since my last visit to the Grotesquerie, I remembered the creatures we passed well: the Beast with a Million Eyes, the Killer Shrews, the Monster That Challenged the World, the Crawling Eye, Q the Winged Serpent, and my personal favorite, the original Hound of the Baskervilles. Each of their enclosures had been specially designed to contain the beasts, using a combination of high-tech science, powerful sorcery, and good old-fashioned titanium steel. And if by some impossibly remote chance any of them somehow escaped, the Grotesquerie's deadly flora would stop them – or at least slow them down long enough for visitors to flee for the exit. The creatures glared, snarled, snapped, roared, and raged at us as we ran by their cages, but that was all they could do, and we were damned thankful for it.

When we caught up with the keepers, we found them, along with a dozen others, battling a large dinosaur that, despite all the Grotesquerie's safety precautions, had escaped its enclosure. I recognized the beast as Titanus, an oversized version of a T.Rex that had been captured in a hidden valley on Earth, and from his less than placid demeanor, it was apparent that his time in captivity hadn't mellowed him. The dinosaur stood on the path, roaring in fury, bleeding legs wrapped in tanglethorn, while Frankensteinian keepers jabbed him with their energy lances. The keepers were tall and their lances long enough to reach Titanus' abdomen and sides, and every time a lance struck the dinosaur's leathery hide, there was a bright discharge of crimson energy accompanied by a sizzling sound. Titanus thrashed and tried to get away from his tormentors, but the tanglethorn lining the path was doing its job, holding him in place while the keepers fought to subdue him.

As impressive as the sight of a dinosaur in full battle fury was, our attention was immediately drawn to a large chunk of meat caught in Titanus' dagger-like teeth – a chunk that looked disturbingly like the upper half of Tavi's body. Like most Darkfolk, lykes can take a lot of damage and survive, but getting bitten in half is a damned serious injury no matter what species you are, and though it was difficult to tell with Titanus shaking his head back and forth and roaring in pain and anger, Tavi appeared to show no signs of life.

"We have to get Tavi out of there!" Devona said. "As long as his brain's intact, there's a chance he'll be able to regenerate the rest of his body. But if Titanus swallows the rest of him…"

Devona didn't complete the thought. She didn't need to. Once Tavi's brain had been dissolved by the digestive juices in the dinosaur's stomach, neither magic nor science would be able to bring him back. We had to rescue Tavi – or what was left of him – but the question was how? We couldn't exactly walk up to Titanus, give him a stern look, and say, "Bad dinosaur! You spit that out now!"

"I think those keepers could make better use of their lances," Devona said, and without waiting for a reply, she dashed toward the closest of the Frankenstein monsters.

"What's she going to do?" Shamika asked.

"Something ridiculously brave and incredibly foolish," I said with admiration. I turned to Varney. "Well, what are you waiting for?"

He gave me a look that said he should be trying to come up with some excuse to act, but then he obviously decided to hell with it. His expression changed, and I watched as Varney the slightly airheaded hippy cameraman once more became a cool, determined man of action. He raced after Devona, and I followed at the best speed I was capable of. Shamika kept pace with me, but I didn't worry about her. Maybe she would summon a few hundred chiranha to show Titanus what it was like to be someone's dinner.

Devona reached a keeper and snatched the energy lance out of his hand. The Frankenstein monster might've towered over my love, but she's a hell of lot stronger than she looks, and she'd had the additional advantage of taking the keeper by surprise. She flipped the lance into a throwing position, aimed, and hurled it at Titanus' open mouth. The metal rod streaked toward the dinosaur, its tip glowing a baleful red, and struck the roof of his mouth with a crackling blast of released energy. Titanus, unsurprisingly, was less than thrilled with this development, and he opened his mouth wide and let out an ear-splitting cry that was half roar, half scream.

The moment the lance struck Titanus, Varney leaped into the air and transformed into a whirling black vortex of shadow that flew toward the dinosaur like a miniature dark tornado. I'd never seen Varney assume his travel form before, and I was impressed as he flew swiftly up to Titanus' mouth, wrapped his shadowy substance around Tavi, pulled him free of the dinosaur's teeth, and carried him back down to us, keeping the lyke aloft by spinning beneath him to create a cushion of air. Once Varney deposited Tavi gently on the ground, the vampire reassumed his normal shape, and Devona and I grabbed hold of Tavi under his arms and together carried him a dozen yards to get him out of further harm's way. Varney and Shamika followed, and we laid him down gently once again and examined him.

It wasn't pretty. The lower half of his body from mid-abdomen down was gone, and bits of viscera dangled from his open body cavity, though there was little blood. His shapeshifter healing ability had already cut off most of the bleeding, and it was struggling to grow new skin to close off the huge gaping wound where his abdomen had been. It was slow going, though. Tavi's injuries were incredibly extensive, even for a lyke, and repairing them was pushing his system to its limits.

Devona placed a pair of fingers against the artery in Tavi's neck. "His pulse is faint and erratic, but at least his heart's still beating."

As if her words had roused him, Tavi's eyes flickered open and a long sigh escaped his lips. He began speaking then, pausing now and then to catch his breath. As he spoke, his wildform slowly gave way to his human guise.

"I... tracked Papa Chatha's scent to the... dinosaur's enclosure, and–" He broke off coughing, and bloody spittle flecked his mouth. "– the trail dead-ended there. I... called you, Matt, and as I was talking, somehow... the enclosure's force field deactivated, and... the dinosaur got free. I was... so shocked that I just stood there." He looked down at what remained of his body and gave us a weak smile. "And as you can see, the beast was... rather hungry."

Devona gently touched Tavi's cheek. "Don't try to talk anymore. We need to get you to the Fever House."

Given enough time, Tavi might have been able to regenerate the lower half of his body on his own, but the doctors at the Fever House could speed up that process considerably, and help make him a damn sight more comfortable while he healed.

"Lazlo's still waiting for us outside," I said.

"I'll carry him." Varney stepped forward and bent down to pick up Tavi, but as he did I caught a glimpse of movement out of the corner of my eye. It wasn't the keepers and Titanus. The tanglethorn held the dinosaur fast and the keepers kept harrying him with their energy lances, and though the dinosaur still roared his fury to the world, his exertions were beginning to lessen as the fight left him. It was only a matter of time before the keepers managed to subdue him and force him back into his enclosure. The movement I saw was much smaller and low to the ground. I had the sense of small black shapes moving silently along the paths around us, though when I turned my head to look at them, I saw nothing.

I knew it wasn't my imagination, though, for Shamika was turning her head back and forth, as if her eyes were tracking something that mine couldn't quite catch, and in a soft, frightened voice she said, "This is bad. This is very bad."

I started to ask her what was wrong, but I was cut off by the sound of alarms going off throughout the Grotesquerie.

Tavi drew in a wheezing breath, and then said, "That's exactly what it sounded like... when the dinosaur got free."

The keepers broke off their battle with Titanus and looked around, startled and – I was more than a little disturbed to see – scared. The keepers had been produced by Victor Baron in his Foundry, and while he endows his creations with free will so they aren't merely the equivalent of organic machines, they do share certain qualities: strength, a strong constitution, and an almost complete lack of fear. So if the keepers were frightened by the sound of alarms going off throughout the Grotesquerie, I knew we were in some truly deep shit.

We felt it first – vibrations beneath our feet as if an earthquake was happening, followed by assorted roars, bellows, growls, and shrieks, a horrifying symphony of rage, malice and bloodlust. All around us gigantic creatures shambled forth from their enclosures, freed from their captivity to once again run rampant and wreak destruction on whatever was unfortunate enough to be in their path. Which in this case was us.

"We need to leave," Devona said in a small voice. "Now."

I wasn't about to argue with her, but we also needed to get Tavi to the Fever House, and I feared that carrying him would only slow us down. And since we couldn't leave him, that meant we needed to make him easier to carry. I reached into one of my pockets and pulled out a shrunken head. I held the withered thing up to my face and gave it a hard shake.

Its eyes sprang open and it glared at me. "This better be important. I was dreaming that I was trapped on a tropical island with the head of a supermodel." Its lips were stitched together with black thread, but the loops were loose enough so it could speak. I'd picked up the head when I stopped the Goremeister from killing the Wizard of Odd, and this was the first time I'd had the chance to put his talents to use.

"I don't have time to banter with you, Livingstone," I said. "We're in trouble, and I need to you do that voodoo you do so well."

Livingstone sighed, which was rather impressive considering he didn't have any lungs. "A guy gets carried around in a pocket all day, then is rudely yanked out of a great dream, and it's straight to work without so much as a 'Hi, nice to see you, how are you doing?'" He sighed again. "All right, just point me in the right direction."

Varney hadn't picked up Tavi yet, so I turned Livingstone around to face the injured lyke. Twin beams of dark light shot out of the head's eyes and struck Tavi on the chest. The lyke shuddered and then rapidly began dwindling in size. You see, Livingstone isn't just a shrunken head: he's a *shrinking* head, too. Within seconds, Tavi had been reduced to the size of an action figure – or in his current condition, half an action figure – and I knelt down and scooped him up with my free hand.

"Sorry about this," I said. "It may not be the most dignified ride you've ever taken." I didn't need to apologize, though, for Tavi had lapsed back into unconsciousness. I tucked him in a pocket, did the same with Livingstone, who grumbled that he'd received better treatment at the hands of the witch doctor who'd shrunken him in the first place, and then I stood.

"Ready to run?" Devona asked me, as giant monsters of all sorts lumbered toward us.

"Like the wind," I answered, and the four of us turned and began running toward the exit.

TWELVE

We had a couple things going in our favor. Compared to most of the escaped creatures, we were small, which meant we didn't easily draw their attention, and they were more interested in attacking each other than they were in going after the tiny things scampering past them. Plus, the keepers began fanning out through the facility, attempting to subdue the monsters with their energy lances, further distracting them, although considering that the keepers usually ended up getting stomped, chomped, or zapped with radioactive energy blasts of one sort or another, it would've been better for them if they'd had the sense to flee with us.

We maneuvered through a forest of segmented legs as a giant spider and a praying mantis fought to turn each other into dinner. Too bad I didn't have a few thousands cans of Raid stashed in my pockets.

"Is this another attack by Talaith?" Varney asked as we ran.

"Maybe," I replied. "If the monsters break out of the

Grotesquerie and rampage through the Sprawl, they'll cause more destruction than a hundred armies." Good thing Varvara had gathered her demon soldiers. If the Grotesquerie's perimeter security failed, she was going to need every warrior she could muster to try to contain the giant monsters.

Next we encountered a giant Gila monster easily the size of Titanus blocking the path. The lizard's forked tongue flicked the air, and its beady black eyes fixed on us as we approached. The creature was slower than many of its gigantic brethren, and Devona and Varney had no trouble avoiding its snapping jaws as they ran past. But Shamika slowed as she drew near the lizard, almost as if she wished to give it a closer look, and the creature opened its maw and lunged toward her. Gila monsters are venomous, and if this beast managed to bite Shamika, it could well prove fatal to her.

I was behind Shamika, so I put my hand between her shoulder blades and shoved. She stumbled forward just as the lizard's jaws snapped shut on the space where her head had been only an instant before. Angered at losing its prey, the Gila monster hissed and thrashed its head, unfortunately slamming into me. I felt no pain from the impact, but the force sent me flying backward, and I lost concentration and along with it, cohesion. My body parts became disconnected, and while my clothing kept most of them more or less together, when I hit the ground my head and hands popped off.

The Gila monster gazed down at me, and its leathery dragon-like tongue flicked the air once more. I had no

idea if the beast was a carrion-eater, but the last thing I
wanted was to end up sharing the same fate as the lower
half of Tavi's body. I concentrated, and my two hands
flipped over and began scuttling toward my head. They
backed up to the stump of my neck, and tendrils of skin
reached out from all three parts to fasten them together,
and an instant later, I was an ambulatory head resting
atop a pair of hands. Feeling absurdly like a zombie spider, I crawled toward my body and rummaged around
in one of my jacket pockets as best I could.

The Gila monster lumbered forward and lowered its
head toward me as I searched for something that might
allow me to fend the beast off. I wasn't just worried
about myself. Tavi was in one of my pockets, and if the
Gila monster devoured my body, the lyke – what was
left of him, anyway – would get eaten too. As it approached, the lizard opened its maw and dripped thick
saliva onto the ground, and carrion-eater or not, it
looked like the beast was going to have itself a zombie
snack. I was fairly confident my head and hands could
scuttle out of the way in time, but there was nothing I
could do for the rest of me. I hoped my undead body
would give the damned thing heartburn.

Devona leaped on top of the Gila monster's back and
crawled along its pebbly neck with inhuman speed and
grace until she reached its head. She leaned down over
its left eye, gripped its pebbly hide with one hand to
steady herself, made a fist with the other hand, and
rammed it into the beast's shiny black orb. The eye
popped like a liquid-filled balloon, and the Gila monster

threw back its head and cried out in pain. It thrashed back and forth, trying to dislodge Devona, but she held on with superhuman strength and tenacity.

"That's my husband you're trying to eat!" she said through gritted teeth, and jammed her arm into the lizard's eye socket all the way to her shoulder and groped around inside, trying to get hold of the beast's tiny brain.

I reached out psychically to her. *Have I told you lately that you're magnificent?*

Tell me a few months from now, when I'm big as a house and feeling like I swallowed a couple bowling balls.

I'll make a mental note.

An instant later, Varney jumped onto the Gila monster's head – an impressive feat considering that the creature was still thrashing and bucking. Varney reached into his own eye, the cybernetic one that Varvara had ruined, and drew forth a thin cable. He continued pulling until he'd exposed several feet, and then he bit the rubber coating off the end and plunged the exposed wires into the Gila monster's other eye. Crackling electricity discharged, and the beast's cries of agony became shrill. Devona continued rooting around in the lizard's skull, and she finally found what she'd been searching for. She smiled grimly, yanked her arm free of the socket in a spray of dark blood, and threw a handful of giant lizard brain onto the path. The Gila monster shuddered, stiffened, and then collapsed to the ground, even deader than I was.

Devona jumped off the Gila monster's carcass and rubbed her hand and arm along its rough hide to scrape off the worst of the goo coating her. Varney also climbed off and fed his cable back into its eye socket.

"We need to keep moving," I said. "The lizard's body is going to attract hungry monsters before long, and it would be a good idea for us to be somewhere else when they get here. We don't have time to put me back together, so if you three wouldn't mind…"

Varney grabbed the bulk of my body. Since my clothing held most of my pieces together, he cradled the bundle against his chest and wrapped his arms around it.

"Don't forget Tavi's in my pocket," I said, and Varney nodded.

Devona picked up my head-and-hands combo and perched me on her shoulder as if she were a vampirate and I her zombie parrot. The four of us then continued toward the exit, trying to ignore the loud footfalls of giant predators eagerly approaching the Gila monster's corpse.

We had more to worry about than the Grotesquerie's escaped creatures, though. The zoo's defensive flora was going crazy – perhaps goaded into action by the sound of alarms – and was reaching out to grab anything that came near. The leech vine couldn't harm me since I had no blood for it to drain, but the same wasn't true for Devona, Varney, and Shamika. Even though the former were vampires, they still had plenty of the red stuff pumping through their veins, and leech vine actually prefers blood aged and refined in a vampire's body. All tanglethorn would do to me was create puncture wounds I'd need to have repaired later, but rotweed was a different story. It causes accelerated decay in anything it touches, and since I already struggled with decomposition, rotweed can reduce me to dust in short order, so I make sure to stay well clear of it.

As we ran, we did our best to avoid the guard plants, and while we took a few hits, none of us were seriously injured, and it began to look like we would make it out. But when we reached the main gate, I was once again reminded why I'm not an optimist. Two behemoths the size of office buildings blocked the entrance, one a giant ape, the other a huge sinuous dragon-like creature. I expected to see Kongar and Reptilikan fighting each other, but the monsters stood side by side facing the entrance, roaring with fury as they slammed their bodies against an invisible force field. Energy crackled and flared bright with each blow the monsters struck, but the force field held strong.

"The Grotesquerie's security system initiated a total lockdown when all the creatures escaped," Devona said. "The whole place has been sealed off – nothing can get in or out."

"Maybe the force field isn't covering the entrance," I said. "We were able to get inside without any trouble."

"Every way in and out of the Grotesquerie is blocked, no matter how small," Devona said. "Including the entrance we came through. Remember, not all of the monsters in here are giants. Hopefully, the keepers will be able to get things under control soon. The Grotesquerie's security system is designed to release powerful knock-out gas throughout the zoo in the event of a mass escape." We looked at her and she shrugged. "What? Security's my business, remember?"

It's true. Other people come to a zoo to look at the animals. My love prefers to spend her time examining the traps and alarms.

Still perched on Devona's shoulder and feeling absurd, I frowned. "If that's true, then the gas should've been released as soon as the monsters were freed. Something's wrong."

"I should think it's obvious," Varney said, sounding even less like the airheaded cameraman than ever. "Whoever freed the monsters also disabled the knockout gas to prevent them from being recaptured."

Shamika had been quiet while we ran, but now she spoke. "We should put Matt back together... while we can." She glanced around nervously, which given that we were trapped inside the Grotesquerie with any number of deadly behemoths was only natural. But instead of directing her gaze skyward, she kept looking toward the ground, as if she were worried about a threat of much smaller stature. I remembered thinking that I'd seen something out of the corner of my eye just before the monsters were released: many small somethings, as a matter of fact, moving so swiftly I hadn't been sure that I'd seen them at all.

"Good idea," Devona said, and she took me off her shoulder, and with Varney's help, managed to reassemble me without too much trouble.

I stood. Everything stayed where it belonged, but I felt even more like a scarecrow than I had before. It seemed the more often the connections between my parts were broken, the harder it was to keep myself together again afterward. I'd have to be more careful.

Once I was a whole man again – or at least a reasonable facsimile of one – I reached into my pocket and removed Tavi to check on him. The miniaturized lyke was still unconscious, but at least he was breathing. I tucked him away again

Kongar and Reptilikan were still too busy trying to beat the hell out of the force field to pay any attention to us, but I knew we wouldn't be safe for much longer. One or both of the monsters would eventually notice us, or worse – more of the behemoths running loose in the Grotesquerie would arrive to try to break through the force field, likely stomping us into jelly as they went by. So far the force field was holding, but only two giant monsters were battering it right now. How long could it hold up under the onslaught of five gargantuan beasts? Or a dozen?

And that thought led to another. "If the saboteur responsible for releasing the monsters also disabled the knock-out gas, why didn't he, she, or they also deactivate the force field? If Talaith is behind this, she'd *want* the monsters to escape and flood the streets of the Sprawl. So why aren't the monsters out there right now, doing what they do best – performing urban renewal on a macro scale?"

"The force field won't hold up forever," Devona said. "Right now emergency power is being fed to the field to strengthen it, but the power boost is designed to be temporary. It's only supposed to last long enough for the knock-out gas to be deployed."

"And since the gas isn't working—" I said.

"The force-field generators will eventually burn out," Devona said, "the force field will collapse, and the monsters will break free."

I told myself not to worry about that right now. Tavi needed medical attention, and as long as the force field was in emergency mode, we were trapped inside. Time to call for help. I grabbed my vox, selected one of my contacts, and pressed call. Varvara had probably already been informed of what was happening at the Grotesquerie, but in case she hadn't…

"It won't work," Varney said. "You won't be able to get a signal through the force field."

He was right. The vox's mouth said, "I'm sorry, but your call cannot be completed at this time. Please try again later." And then it gave me a loud raspberry to taunt me. I flipped the cover closed with a bit more force than was absolutely necessary and put the vox away. So much for that idea.

Varney looked at the entrance, and a thoughtful expression came over his face. "If we could reach the gate, I might be able to use the energy from my cybernetic systems to disrupt the force field long enough for us to get through." He frowned. "There's only one problem."

"You mean two problems," I said. "Both of them about the size of a small mountain."

Varney nodded. "We're going to have to find a way to get past them."

"I suppose we'll just have to be extra sneaky," Shamika said.

We looked at her, and Devona and I couldn't help smiling. For the first time since we'd met her, she'd sounded her age.

"Good plan," Devona said.

"Works for me," I added.

Varney just rolled his eyes.

The four of us started toward the gate, doing our best to heed Shamika's advice. Getting past Kongar didn't worry me too much. The giant ape had his feet planted firmly on the ground for leverage as he pounded away on the force field with his fists. I doubted he was going to suddenly lift a foot as we drew near and accidentally stomp on us. Reptilikan was another matter. The dragon-beast was long and thin, something like a monstrous snake with bat wings and tiny feet. Its preferred method for attacking the force field was to rear back on its hind legs and slam its body forward, and each time it did so, it bounced back and slid a few dozen feet. It then scrabbled forward for another go at the force field. Since Reptilikan' s movements were more erratic, we made sure to stay well clear of the beast as we approached the gate. Unfortunately, this meant that we had to pass so close to Kongar's right leg that we could've reached out and ruffled his coarse fur if we'd wanted to.

I'm not sure what happened, whether one of us did something to catch Kongar's eye or whether the oversized ape just happened to pick that exact moment to look down. Whichever the case, he saw us and snarled.

He stopped pounding his fists against the force field and bent down, reaching out to grab hold of us with one of his gigantic paws.

"Keep heading for the gate!" I shouted. "I'll distract him!"

Devona looked as if she wanted to protest, but she said nothing. We've worked together long enough for us to trust one another in tight situations, though it's never easy to watch someone you love put himself or herself in harm's way. It's not like I'm a hero or anything, though. Facing impending doom is a lot easier when you're already dead.

I darted off in the opposite direction, ran a dozen yards, then turned to face Kongar. I waved my hands in the air to attract the ape's attention and shouted so he could hear me.

"What's wrong with you? Are you *completely* stupid?"

Kongar glared and showed me his teeth. He moved damn fast for something so huge, and he snatched me up in his hand before I even had the chance to try and dodge out of the way. He straightened and lifted me up to his face to examine me more closely. The giant ape had a hell of a strong grip, and he could've squeezed me to zombie pâté if he'd wanted to. But though he held me tight, none of my bones had yet broken and I could still take in enough air to talk. Maybe Kongar's curiosity had gotten the better of him and he didn't want to squish me before he figured out what my problem was. Whatever the reason, I decided to speak fast before the titanic ape changed his mind.

"If you manage to break out of here, you'll have the fun of knocking down a bunch of buildings and scaring the crap out of a lot of people, but when the fun's over and you realize you've worked up a monster-sized appetite, what are you going to eat? A big boy like you needs a lot of food to keep going, and in the Grotesquerie you get super-sized meals delivered to you every day. Once you're out on the streets foraging for yourself, you're going to find it pretty slim pickings."

I had no idea how intelligent Kongar was or if anything I'd said had gotten through to him, but the ape no longer looked angry. He frowned, as if he were thinking hard.

I glanced down to check on the others' progress. Devona, Varney, and Shamika stood at the main entrance, right at the edge of the force field. Varney was once again in the process of pulling cable out of his eye, and Devona and Shamika stood back several feet to give him room to work. While you couldn't exactly see the field, its energy had a tendency to ripple like heated air rising off hot asphalt, allowing them to pinpoint its precise location. I needed to keep Kongar busy for a few more moments.

Up to this point, Reptilikan had continued slamming its scaly coiled bulk against the force field, but now the giant dragon-thing broke off its assault on the field and turned to look at Kongar, as if to ask the monster-ape why he was slacking off.

Varney held his eye's cable up to the force field. As soon as the exposed wires touched the energy of the

containment field, sparks shot off in all directions. I
don't know how Varney controlled the power output
of his cybernetic parts, but he must've done something,
because the sparks increased in number and intensity
until the energy discharge was so bright I could no
longer see Varney.

Kongar and Reptilikan noticed it too, and as they
turned to look at the light, I started talking again, almost shouting at the top of my lungs this time to keep
them from being distracted by the crackling energy
bouncing off the section of the force field blocking
the entrance.

"And Nekropolis isn't like a city back on Earth – it's
a city full of monsters. Sure, they may be smaller than
you, but they're mean and there's a hell of a lot of
them. At first they might flee in terror when they see
you coming, but they'll eventually band together
against you. They'll fight back, and some of them will
want to do more than just fight you. One of the most
popular restaurants in town is called Kaijushi. You
know what's on the menu? Fresh sushi made from raw
giant monster meat."

Kongar turned to Reptilikan and gave his fellow behemoth a doubtful look, as if he were reconsidering his
plan to escape.

I looked down again. The energy discharge had
ended, and the entrance was free from distortion. Devona grabbed hold of Shamika's hand and pulled the
girl along with her as she hurried through the opening
Varney had made in the force field. Shamika looked

back at me and pointed. I could see that she was saying something to Devona, but I was too far away to hear.

Reptilikan was clearly irritated at Kongar, and the dragon-beast horked up a mass of nasty greenish gunk and spewed it at the giant ape. Kongar tried to dodge, but Reptilikan was too good a shot, and the goo struck the massive simian on the chest. Immediately fur and flesh began to smoke and sizzle as the acidic substance began its work. Kongar roared in pain and fury as Reptilikan's corrosive venom continued eating away at his skin. I didn't escape unscathed. Several large droplets had splattered on me and were eating holes in my forehead and right shoulder. The wounds didn't hurt, of course, but I was glad I couldn't smell. I've been told the stench of burning zombie is more than a bit stomach-churning.

I knew the time for distraction had passed. Devona and Shamika had made it to the other side of the force field, and Kongar and Reptilikan were going to start beating the hell out of each other any second – and I didn't want to be caught between the two behemoths when the fists, claws, teeth, and corrosive vomit started flying in earnest.

Even though I was clasped in Kongar's hand, I could still move my arm, and I reached into one of my pockets and withdrew Livingstone again. As soon as the head got a good look at the two giant monsters, he said, "You can't be serious!"

"Unfortunately, I am. I don't know if you're strong enough to do this, but focus an eye on each one of them and make with the magic. Oh, and try to avoid shrinking me while you're at it."

Livingstone grumbled something about how I'd need to take him to see an ophthalmologist after this, but he did as I asked. Beams of light shot forth from his eyes, one for each monster, and struck them both right between their own eyes. I gave Livingstone bonus points for good aim and style.

Kongar and Reptilikan stiffened as Livingstone's magic suffused their bodies. At first, nothing more happened and I feared Livingstone simply didn't have enough mystic energy for the job. But then both Kongar and Reptilikan began to shrink. Slowly at first, but with increasing speed. Livingstone didn't let up; he continued blasting both monsters with his eyebeams, but the strain took a toll on him. I could feel him trembling in my hand, and I wondered how much longer he could keep it up.

Kongar held on to me while he shrank, more because he'd forgotten he was holding me than for any other reason, I think. When he was down to about fifteen feet, he could no longer keep hold of me and let go. I hit the ground and felt my body parts threaten to lose cohesion, but I'd anticipated the impact and managed to maintain enough concentration to keep myself together. I also managed not to drop Livingstone. He'd ceased blasting the two monsters with optical rays by this point, but it didn't matter. The job was done. Kongar dwindled in size until he was no larger than a chimpanzee, and Reptilikan shrank down to the size of a juvenile alligator.

I got to my feet, gave the diminished monsters a stern look, and said, "Shoo!"

They yelped, turned, and fled.

I looked down at Livingstone, intending to thank him, but I realized that the shrunken head was, in fact, beginning to shrink even further.

"I used too much power, and some of it backfired on me," he said. "I managed to keep any of it from spilling on you, though."

As he shrank, his voice rose in pitch, and he soon sounded like a bodiless chipmunk.

"I'm sorry," I said. "If I'd known this would happen…"

Livingstone was now the size of a raisin in my palm, and still shrinking. "It's all right. To God there is no zero. I still exist!"

And with that, he was gone.

"Hurry it up, Matt! I can't keep the hole in the force field open much longer!"

I felt bad for Livingstone, but I didn't have time to mourn his loss. I turned to see Varney standing at the main entrance, holding his eye-cable out before him. No longer did bright energy flashes erupt in midair. Only a faint shower of sparks, like a Fourth of July sparkler on the verge of sputtering out. Opening a hole in the force field hadn't done Varney any good. White smoke curled forth from his eye socket and blood trickled from his nostrils and ears.

I hurried through the main gate, feeling a slight resistance for a moment as if I were moving through water. Devona and Shamika were waiting for me on the other side, and my love gave me a big hug before pulling back and wrinkling her nose.

"Nothing personal, but you reek! Reptilikan vomit is strong stuff!"

I smiled. "I'll shower after the war is over." Then I turned back to Varney. He remained standing there, smoking and bleeding as the sparks from his eye-cable grew weaker.

"What are you waiting for?" I said. "Come on!"

Varney grimaced as the blood trickles became gushes.

"I can't. In order to keep the portal open, I have to stay on this side of it. You three go on without me!"

I turned to Shamika. "Can you use your magic to get him across before the portal snaps shut?"

She looked uncomfortable. "I, uh… I don't know. I've never done anything like that before."

Devona stepped past us without a word, went through the gate, grabbed hold of the waistband of Varney's pants, and leaped backward, pulling the cyber-vampire with her. There was a final flash of light and then the two of them landed in a heap before Shamika and me. I reached down to help Devona stand.

"Sometimes simple solutions are best," she said, grinning.

Shamika helped Varney to his feet. The vampire looked quite a bit the worse for wear. He was pale from blood-loss and the socket of his cyber-eye was a melted, blackened ruin. He snapped off the eye-cable and dropped it to the ground. As we watched, the blood covering his shirt began to flow upwards, back into his nose and ears. It was an effective, if disgusting, way for vampires to heal themselves, and within moment's Varney's clothes were blood-free and he was no longer pale. Well, no paler than a normal vampire, that is.

"I'm impressed," I said. "I thought only truly powerful vampires could do stunts like that. I didn't realize you were so high up in the Bloodborn hierarchy."

Devona frowned. "He's right, Varney. Who and what are you, really?"

Varney looked at us without expression for a moment. Finally, he said, "Let's just say that I wasn't always a cameraman and leave it at that, all right? We still need to get out of here before—"

The Grotesquerie's alarms had continued to sound the entire time we were trying to escape, but now their tones rose in pitch and intensity.

"The force field fails entirely," Varney finished.

No more time for talk. We ran out into the street where Lazlo was still waiting for us in his cab. We were about to jump in when there was a *pop!* of displaced air and suddenly Varvara was standing on the sidewalk next to us. The Demon Queen gave me an irritated look.

"This is quite a bit of trouble – even for you," she said.

We could hear the sounds of giant monsters roaring and shrieking as they lumbered toward the main gate. I pictured creatures throughout the Grotesquerie preparing to climb over or batter through the wall as soon as the force field finished collapsing.

"I tried calling," I said lamely, "but I couldn't get a signal."

"Good thing I don't have to rely on you for my intel," she said. She pointed skyward and I saw a half-dozen flying demons overhead. No doubt they'd spotted the trouble in the Grotesquerie and had reported it to their queen.

"Now if you don't mind," Varvara said, "Mommy's got some work to do."

She stepped closer to the main gate, planted her feet apart as if to steady herself, and raised her hands high. She began chanting in a language I'd never heard before. The words were rough and guttural, and they blistered the air with unholy power. Just hearing them felt like my spirit was being violated. Filaments of glowing green energy streamed forth from Varvara's fingers, lengthening and picking up speed as they went. They flowed over the walls, completely covering them, and continued upward, rising into the air and curving inward from all directions until they formed a green dome over the Grotesquerie. The process took several minutes, and Varvara had a grim look of determination on her face the entire time. But when she was finished, the entire Grotesquerie was sealed in a dome of mystic power. We could still hear monsters roaring inside and more than a few began pounding at the newly erected barrier, but their cries were muted now, their blows muffled.

Varvara stopped chanting and lowered her arms. She staggered backward, and I was so shocked to see a sign of weakness in her that for an instant I hesitated. Then I stepped forward and took hold of her elbow to steady her.

"Thanks," she whispered. "That took a bit more out of me than I expected. But it should do the trick until the keepers can repair the force-field generators."

I was about to ask her who was going to help the keepers – those who were still alive, that is – subdue the giant monsters running wild within the Grotesquerie. But just then a long red truck came roaring around the corner, sirens wailing and flames trailing behind it.

"Right on time," Varvara said.

The vehicle pulled up to the curb not far from Lazlo's cab, which growled beneath its hood and rolled back several feet to give it room. Considering that the entire truck was wreathed in flame, I didn't blame the cab one bit. Emblazoned on the side of the truck was a stylized SFD: Sprawl Fire Department. They aren't firefighters, though; they're fire *bringers*. The doors opened and a horde of fire demons armed with pitchforks poured out into the street.

Varvara pointed to the Grotesquerie's entrance. "Get in there and help the keepers put the monsters back in their enclosures. And try not to burn them too badly. They're one of our best tourist attractions."

The demons inclined their heads to acknowledge their queen's command, and then formed two ranks and began running toward the Grotesquerie's entrance, leaving a trail of black and smoldering footprints behind them as they went.

"How can they get inside?" I asked. "You just sealed the place off."

"Give me a little credit. The barrier is impassable to everything *but* demons," Varvara said. She waited until the fire demons were all inside and then said, "There. That should take care of that. Now, if you don't mind, I have a war to win." She made a mystic gesture then, but nothing happened. She scowled and tried again, with the same result. Finally, she furrowed her brow in concentration, made the gesture more slowly, and this time she vanished with a *whoosh* of inrushing air.

"She wasn't kidding when she said creating the dome took a lot out of her," Devona said. "I've never seen a Darklord have trouble performing a simple tele-portation spell before."

I was just as surprised as Devona by what we'd just witnessed, and more than a little disturbed, but we didn't have time to consider the implications right then. We needed to get Tavi medical attention, and we needed to do it fast. We hopped in Lazlo's cab, and he hit the gas and roared away from the curb.

As he drove, something hit me.

"Hey, Lazlo, why didn't you get out of your cab and kneel before Varvara? I mean, she *is* the queen of all the Demonkin, and that includes you."

Lazlo let out a raucous honk of a laugh. "You're funny, Matt! Why would I kneel to my own sister?"

THIRTEEN

During all the excitement in the Grotesquerie, I'd forgotten about the destruction of the Bridge of Nine
Sorrows. With the bridge out, we couldn't get from the
Sprawl to Gothtown, and that meant we couldn't get
to the Fever House. Klamm had said that crews had
been dispatched to repair the bridges, but Lazlo said
both of them were still a long way from being rebuilt.
I considered having Lazlo drive us to the broken bridge
and then asking Varney to assume his travel form and
fly Tavi over to Gothtown, but the vampire still looked
pretty wiped out, and the last thing I wanted was for
him to get halfway across and be unable to hold on to
his travel form. If that happened, he'd resume his humanoid shape and plunge into Phlegethon, taking Tavi
down with him. And to be honest, though Varney had
helped us out of a couple tight spots, I didn't entirely
trust him.

If Papa Chatha had been home, I'd have had Lazlo
take us there, but of course, Papa was missing. Instead,

I told Lazlo to take us to the Midnight Watch, and then I called Bogdan on my vox and told the warlock to meet us there.

When we arrived, I couldn't resist asking Lazlo if he'd been serious when he'd said Varvara was his sister. All he did was laugh, and give me a parting wave as he drove off.

Bogdan had beaten us back and was waiting inside for us. The Midnight Watch building is fairly large, and though all of the employees have their own homes, they each have a room there as well. We went into Tavi's quarters, which, aside from a couple paintings depicting jungle scenes, was decorated as sparsely as any hotel room. Devona pulled back the covers of his bed, and I removed him from my pocket and laid him gently on the mattress. Varney and Shamika stood off to the side, watching.

Bogdan took one look at our miniature friend and then turned to me. "I take it there's a story behind his condition," the warlock said.

"He got bit in half by a dinosaur and I shrank him to make him easier to carry," I said.

"Of course you did." Bogdan looked at Tavi once more. "How did you shrink him? Wait – you used that shrunken head of yours, right?"

"Yeah, but Livingstone didn't make it, so I can't use him to unshrink Tavi."

"So not only do you want me to try to heal Tavi, you need me to restore him to his normal size as well," Bogdan said.

"Not to make a joke, but that's about the size of it," I said.

Devona gave me a look that let me know I wasn't funny.

"Like anyone else, we Arcane have our individual talents and strengths," Bogdan said. "We're all born with the ability to generate, focus, and channel magical energy, but the specific form that magic takes can vary quite a bit from person to person. My own specialty is the conjuring of objects, not making alterations in another's body. Changing someone's size and healing injuries are both outside my realm of expertise."

"Tavi's a lyke, and his body stands a good chance of healing itself," Devona said. "We just need to give him a little help."

Bogdan smiled at Devona. "All right, boss. I'll give it my best shot."

I didn't particularly appreciate the way Bogdan smiled at Devona, but I decided now wasn't the time to act petty. There'd be plenty of time for that after Bogdan did what he could to help Tavi.

Bogdan's specialty wasn't just conjuring objects. In a way I didn't understand, his talent lies in conjuring *useful* objects, ones he needs at any given moment. Sometimes I wonder if Bogdan himself fully understands it. He kept his gaze fixed on Tavi's miniaturized form, gestured, and a magnifying glass appeared in his hand. He held it over Tavi and a beam of light shone through and down onto the lyke. As we watched, Tavi's body slowly grew until he was once again nor-

TIM WAGGONER 245

mal size. When Tavi was finished growing, the light from the magnifying glass winked out, and a second later the glass itself disappeared. It's too bad that Bogdan's objects never stick around long once they've fulfilled their purpose. He'd make a fortune if he could conjure up permanent magical items.

"That's step one," Bogdan said. "Now let's see if I can do anything to help him start healing."

I was used to the warlock sounding supremely confident, so the doubt in his voice took me by surprise. I felt Devona reach out to me through our psychic link.

Why are you surprised? she thought. *Tavi is Bogdan's friend, and he doesn't want to let him down.*

Nothing against Bogdan, but I didn't think he was especially fond of any of us – with the exception of you, that is.

Jealous: table for one, Devona thought, with more than a trace of amusement. *But seriously, you should take the time to get to know Bogdan better – and Scorch and Tavi too.*

This wasn't the first time that Devona had gently chided me for keeping to myself too much. I'd been something of a loner when I was human. Dale had been my only real friend back then, and after we came to Nekropolis and he died, I'd been on my own for the most part. Oh, I'd made a number of acquaintances, but I never got close to anyone. I didn't let myself. That changed when I met Devona. She's more than my lover; she's the best friend I've ever had. But she encourages me to "expand my emotional palette," as she puts it, and establish deeper friendships. I'm working on it. Slowly.

Once more Bogdan fixed his gaze on Tavi, concentrated, and gestured. This time nothing appeared in his
hand, and he frowned. He closed his eyes, took several
deep breaths, and allowed his features to relax. When
his expression was one of serene calm, he gestured
once again, and this time an old-fashioned glass thermometer appeared in his hand.

He opened his eyes and looked at it.

"Please tell me it's not a rectal thermometer," I said.
"Because if it is, I'm afraid Tavi's out of luck."

Devona gave me a look that said I was even less funny
than the last time she had given me the look. Bogdan
ignored me and gently placed the thermometer between
Tavi's lips. There were no obvious signs of any magic at
work – no glowing light, no strange sound – but the lyke
stirred and gently sighed. He settled back into the bed,
and a peaceful expression came over his face.

"I'd say that's a good sign," Devona said.

"I hope so," Bogdan said. "Like I told you, healing's
not my specialty."

"Once Tavi regains consciousness, he's going to be
ravenous," I said. "He lost a lot of mass, and he's going
to need help replacing it."

"You're right," Devona said. "We should lay in a supply of raw meat and blood."

That wouldn't be a problem. One of the nice things
about Nekropolis is that you never have any trouble
finding a butcher's.

A slight breeze ruffled my hair, and I knew Rover
was in the room with us.

"Keep watch over Tavi," I told the guardian spirit. "And let us know if there's any change in his condition."

Rover blew gently on my face one time, a signal for yes. We left Tavi's quarters and adjourned to the great room. Devona, Shamika, and Bogdan sat on the couch, I took up my usual position near the fireplace, and Varney stood on the opposite side of the room and leaned against the wall, arms crossed, an unreadable expression on his face. He'd been awfully quiet since we'd escaped the Grotesquerie, but at least he was no longer making any pretense of wanting to make a documentary about me. I still didn't know what his game was, and that needed to change. First things first, though. I told Bogdan what we'd been up to since we'd seen him last. When I was finished catching him up, I asked if he'd learned anything of interest from his Arcane contacts.

"I stopped by *Overhexed*, only to discover that you'd been there before me and broken up a street riot before it even got started," Bogdan said. "As you might imagine, not many of the patrons were inclined to chat with me after that, seeing as how I work with you. The Sea Hag was sharing a table with Dr Bombay, and they'd both had more enough than enough drinks to put them in a talkative mood, though. They told me they'd heard rumors that Talaith had solid evidence that Varvara was behind our people's disappearances, though neither could tell me what precisely that evidence might be. Dr Bombay is something of a gossip, and once he started talking, it was hard to shut him up. He told me the names of the Arcane who disappeared. A dozen in all, men and women who specialize in different facets of magic." Bogdan grimaced in distaste. "He also told me more about their vices and sexual proclivities than I wanted to know. Beyond the fact that they all happen to be Arcane, there doesn't seem to be any connection between them."

"Do you remember the names?" I asked.

Bogdan gave me an affronted look that seemed half put on, half genuine. "I'm a professional. I know better to rely on memory." He gestured and a leather-bound notebook appeared in his hand. He opened it and read off the names of the missing Arcane.

Papa Chatha was on the list, and while I wasn't familiar with every name, I knew most of them: the Bedazzler, Preston Digitator, Ms Mockery, the Uncanny Gaston, Alteria, Chang-Xi, and the Crystalline Dancer.

"They do have something in common," I said after a moment's thought. "They're all powerful and highly skilled in their particular specialty, but not necessarily well known to the public at large."

Varney had only listened up to this point, but now he said, "Why is that important?"

"Because their disappearances would go unnoticed, at least for a while," I answered. "If any of the town's famous Arcane vanished, it would be big news, and Talaith and the Adjudicators would immediately begin scouring the city for them. But if lower-profile magic-users vanished, the disappearances would have to mount up and a pattern would have to emerge before someone noticed and decided to do something about it."

Devona picked up on my train of thought. "And that would give the kidnapper – or kidnappers – time."

"Time to do what?" Bogdan asked.

"Maybe time to falsify evidence implicating Varvara in the disappearances," I said. "Time enough to start a war between two Darklords."

"Varvara could still be behind the disappearances," Bogdan said, but he sounded unsure.

I shook my head. "Since when does Varvara do anything halfway? If she wanted to kidnap Arcane she'd select the most famous and powerful of them. If for no other reason than as a personal affront to Talaith."

"You have a point," Bogdan conceded.

"Did you learn anything else at *Overhexed*?" I asked.

"No. After a while, Dr Bombay started telling some truly awful jokes, and I made my excuses and got the hell out of there. I stopped in at Nosferatomes and asked Orlock if he'd heard anything related to the disappearances. He's Bloodborn, but he carries a lot of magic books in his store, and he's pretty plugged in to what goes on the Arcane community. But he wasn't able to tell me anything."

Devona and I exchanged looks. We knew from first-hand experience that Orlock was more than he seemed, though we'd never shared this knowledge with anyone else. Orlock knew that Bogdan worked with us, and if he'd had any information about the disappearances, he'd have given it to the warlock to pass along to us – for a price to be named later, of course. I was more than a bit glad Orlock hadn't known anything, though. Devona and I had owed him a favor, and repaying him had nearly caused us to miss our only opportunity to conceive our child... make that our children. Because of this, I wasn't eager to get mixed up with the ancient vampire again.

"I decided to try *Magewrights' Manor* next," Bogdan said. "The club's quite exclusive, and I don't have a membership – though I've been on the waiting list for years," he hastened to add. "You know how much Talaith hates that some Arcane prefer the urban lifestyle of the Sprawl to the pastoral life in Glamere. Well, *Magewrights' Manor* is the most prominent symbol of that preference, and the magic-users that frequent the club have little love for Talaith. In order to belong, you have to be both powerful and well-connected socially, and having a certain amount of fame doesn't hurt either."

A metaphorical light bulb went off over my Reptilikan-vomit-scarred head. "Is that what attracted you to working for the Midnight Watch in the first place? Devona and I had just saved the city from being destroyed during the Renewal Ceremony, and if the Midnight Watch was successful, you hoped that some of our fame might rub off onto you."

I could feel Devona's anger through our link, but Bogdan didn't seem upset in the slightest by my words.

"That was one of the considerations," he admitted. "But there have been other benefits to working here."

Bogdan pointedly avoided looking at Devona. He thought for a moment, then lowered his gaze to the floor and then gave what I thought was an almost embarrassed smile. "To be honest, it's nice to use my talents for something productive. It's funny. My specialty is conjuring useful objects, but before I started working here, I myself wasn't very useful. I hired myself out to wealthy, prominent people when I needed money, but the rest of the time I frittered away my life, moving from club to club, trying to make connections and ingratiate myself with the 'right' people, whoever they happened to be at any given moment, all to increase my own status. It was a very empty way to live, and I didn't even know it until I came here."

I hate it when Bogdan gets sincere. It means I have to work twice as hard to dislike him.

"So did you manage to get in?" I asked.

He looked up and nodded. "On my way there, that strange reality distortion hit, where Nekropolis seemed to overlap with Earth for a short time. It was extremely disconcerting, more so for us Arcane I imagine, because we feel mystic energy in a way that most others do not. And that distortion felt deeply, profoundly wrong in a way I can't easily describe." He shuddered at the memory. "Anyway, when I arrived at the *Manor* and told the doorman why I'd come, I was immediately ushered in. The members had already been discussing the dispute between Talaith and Varvara when the reality distortion hit, and now they were furiously debating what and who had caused it and why.

When they learned I was assisting you in investigating the disappearances of our people, they invited me to take part in their discussion."

It was weird to think that my name had paved the way for Bogdan gaining admittance into a club he'd tried for so long to join. I know I've acquired a certain amount of fame over the years, but I don't take it seriously and try to ignore it. But I guess it can be a useful tool sometimes. If Bogdan resented the fact that it was my name that got him inside the *Manor*, he didn't show it.

"Some of the most well-known Arcane in the city were there: Dr Faustus, Circe, Baron Samedi, Baba Yaga, Chandu, Marie Leveau, Cagliostro, Rasputin, Calypso, the Blair Witch... A veritable who's who! I learned that they'd all performed their own investigations into the disappearances, and not one of them had been able to find so much as a trace of the missing Arcane. It was as if they'd vanished completely from Nekropolis."

Shamika had been silent since we'd returned to the Midnight Watch, but she now drew in a surprised breath. "I thought so!" she said.

We all looked at her.

"What do you mean?" I asked.

She looked extremely uncomfortable. "Just that since I couldn't find any trace of my uncle, I didn't think anyone else would either. That's all."

Her words didn't quite ring true, but as with Varney, I decided now wasn't the time to push it. Shamika didn't say anything more, and after a moment, Devona spoke.

"Tavi picked up Papa Chatha's scent trail and followed it, though. Surely magic-users as powerful as those in *Magewrights' Manor* wouldn't have failed to detect such a trace."

"It does seem highly unlikely," Bogdan said, "but none of them said anything about scent trails while I was there."

"Maybe the scent trail isn't important," Devona said. "It's possible Papa just happened to be visiting the Grotesquerie when he was abducted."

"And then Titanus just happened to escape when Tavi followed Papa's trail there?" I said. "And on top of that, when we arrived to save Tavi, all the creatures in the Grotesquerie just happened to escape as well?"

Devona smiled ruefully. "When you put it like that, it sounds like a trap."

"Talaith saw you in Demons' Roost," Varney said. "And she's not exactly your biggest fan. Maybe she set the trap to get rid of you and strike a blow at Varvara in the process."

"Maybe," I allowed. But that didn't feel right somehow. Talaith is more than devious enough to devise any number of traps, but somehow this just didn't seem like her style.

Bogdan spoke then. "If Varvara *didn't* abduct the Arcane, then who did? Talaith herself?"

"I doubt it," I said. "Like Varvara, she'd have struck a stronger opening blow if she wanted to start a war – a blow more fitting a Darklord."

"Maybe war wasn't the point," Devona said. "Maybe

abducting the magic-users was, and war was just a side-effect. Or–"

"A distraction!" I finished.

"From what?" Bogdan asked.

"From whatever the kidnappers *really* want to do," I said. "And whatever it is, they need magic-users to do it."

"Magic-users that for some reason they can't simply hire," Devona said, "and so they're forced to abduct them. I wonder…" She trailed off then, and her expression went blank. "I need to step outside for a moment."

She rose from the couch, her movements somewhat stiff, and started walking out of the great room. The rest of us exchanged puzzled glances, except Shamika. She looked worried.

"This isn't good," she whispered. Shamika sounded more than worried now; she sounded scared, and her tone prompted me to action.

"Devona, wait!" I followed after her, but Varney was already ahead of me, and he trailed Devona down the hall toward the front door.

"What's wrong?" he asked. "You're acting–"

That's as far as Varney got before Devona spun around and shoved her hand toward him. She didn't connect with him physically, but I could feel the psychic force pouring off her in waves. Telekinetic energy slammed into Varney and threw him back against the wall. The Midnight Watch building is old and made almost entirely from stone, and Varney's skull made a sickening scrunch as it connected with the wall. His eye

went wide as he hit, and he fell face-first when he re-
bounded, leaving a bloody smear where his head had
struck the stone. I wasn't worried about Varney. He'd
recover, but it would take him a few moments. In the
meantime, I had to stop Devona.

As soon as she saw Varney was no longer a problem,
she turned around and headed for the front door again,
not running, just walking with a slightly stiff-legged
gait, as if she weren't entirely in control of her actions.

Devona's psychic abilities had continued to grow in
strength since we met, but I'd never seen her wield
telekinesis to that degree. Whatever was happening
with her, it had given her a power boost, and I knew
I had to approach her cautiously. In my current condition, if she hit me with a blast of telekinesis as
strong as the one she'd directed at Varney, I'd fly apart
and this time I might not be able to put myself back
together.

I was tempted to try and reach out to Devona
through our link. If she was trying to fight whatever
was happening to her, she might still be herself inside
her mind, and we might be able to connect psychically.
On the other hand, if she *wasn't* still herself, she could
send a flood of mental energy through our link and
stun me – or worse, reduce my brain to tapioca. I decided to try another approach.

"Whatever's happening, my love, you have to fight
it – for the babies, if nothing else!"

She didn't say anything, didn't turn around, didn't
attack, but she didn't stop walking, either. I thought

she might have hesitated for a second or two, but it might've been my imagination.

We were almost to the door now, and while I had no idea what would happen when she went outside, I didn't think it was going to be good. I hated to do this, but I didn't see that I had any other choice.

"Rover!" I called.

An instant later a torrent of wind came rushing down the hallway toward us. Devona ignored it and reached out to take hold of the door knob.

"Something's wrong with Devona, Rover! You have to stop her from leaving!"

Rover is a living, sentient wardspell, but I wasn't sure exactly how intelligent he (or more accurately it) was. In the time since Devona had purchased the Midnight Watch building, we'd gotten to know Rover, and while I was certain he understood simple commands, I was afraid the complexity of the current situation would be beyond him. His mistress was simply trying to leave the building, and her partner was ordering Rover to prevent her from doing so. I wouldn't blame Rover for being confused – hell, *I* was confused, and I was right in the middle of the situation – and if it came down to a case of conflicting loyalties in Rover's mind, Devona versus Matt, I had no doubt who would win.

But Rover must've understood the situation, or perhaps being a creature composed entirely of magic he was able to detect that something was wrong with Devona, for either way, he blew past me, surrounded Devona with a mini cyclone, and pulled her away from the door.

For a moment I thought that would do it, and I began trying to think of a way to snap Devona out of the spell that was affecting her. But before I could come up with anything, she reached into one of her pockets and brought out a small metal charm. It was a simple thing, a coin-sized disk with a yin-yang symbol painted on it, but I'd seen her use it in her work, and I knew how potent it could be. A reverser is aptly named, for it reverses the effect of any magic it comes in contact with. A freeze spell can become a fire spell, a stasis spell can become a fast-motion spell, *et cetera*.

Devona flipped the reverser into the air, where Rover's cyclonic wind currents snatched it up and began spinning it around. It orbited Devona twice before it began to take effect. Rover's wind started to blow slower and with less force, and within seconds it dissipated to little more than a light breeze. Another second after that, and it was gone. The reverser plunked to the floor, and Devona left it where it lay, walking to the door once more, gripped the knob, turned it, pushed the door open, and stepped outside.

I didn't know if the reverser had merely negated Rover's wind or if it had nullified the creature entirely, essentially killing him, but I didn't have time to worry about that right then. I still had to try and stop Devona.

I followed her outside. She'd walked down the front steps and was standing motionless on the sidewalk, staring out into the street. I hurried down the steps toward her, doing my best not to lose control of my barely held together scarecrow body, when I saw something

small and black scuttle out of the gutter and head toward her feet. It looked something like an oversized
roach – thick carapace, six segmented legs, wiggling antennae – but I knew it was no Earthly insect. I'd seen it
before, or rather, ones like it, but I thought I'd never
see one again. But I had, hadn't I? And not that long
ago. I'd seen one in Devona's room at the Fever House,
and I'd seen others at the Grotesquerie, moving so
swiftly that I'd hadn't been certain I'd seen anything at
all. Those bugs belonged to only one being I knew of –
actually *were* that being, in fact, for each insect was
nothing but a tiny component of a single gigantic
group mind.

It was Gregor.

The insect scuttled onto Devona's right foot and
perched there. I was a bit surprised. I expected it to do
something a lot ickier, like crawl up her body, enter her
ear and dig its way into her brain. I'd seen Gregor's insects do it before. But this one seemed perfectly
content to sit there on her foot, as if it had no intention
more nefarious than hitching a ride.

I hurried up to Devona and stopped when I was
within an arm's length of her. I didn't know what to
do next. One of Gregor's insects wasn't much of a
threat, but there could be hundreds of them – maybe
thousands – hiding all around us, cloaked by shadow,
wedged into cracks in the buildings and sidewalk, waiting to attack. I feared that if I made a wrong move, I
might set them off. I thought about drawing my 9mm
and shooting the bug on her foot. Devona would get

injured in the process, but she was a vampire – albeit a half one – and she'd heal quickly enough. But once the bug was off her, I could haul her back into the Midnight Watch, and once we were inside, she would be safe. The security features of the building, both magical and technological, are so powerful that nothing would be able to harm her inside, including Gregor. His insects wouldn't be able to get in and…

I understood then. Gregor couldn't get in, so he'd needed to get Devona out.

I reached for her just as the insect clinging to her foot began to glow. I grabbed hold of her shoulder as her body became transparent, faded, and disappeared, bug and all. I frantically tried to connect to her through our psychic link, but I felt no echo of her presence. Wherever she'd gone, she was outside the range of telepathic contact.

Devona was gone. And as I looked down at the stump protruding from my right sleeve, I realized she'd taken my right hand with her.

I found Varney in the hallway, sitting up against the wall and massaging the back of his head. Shamika and Bogdan stood close by, but I ignored them.

"What happened?" Varney said when he saw me approaching. "Did you stop her?"

In response, I drew my gun with my left hand, only fumbling a bit in the process, crouched down and pressed the muzzle to Varney's temple. Shamika gasped, and Bogdan took hold of her by the shoulders and slowly edged her back. I regretted scaring her, but I needed answers from Varney, and I was determined to get them, no matter what it took.

"I'm not as good a shot with my left hand as I am with my right, but at this range, all I need to do is pull the trigger." I was struggling to control my emotions, knowing that if I was going to be any help to Devona I had to remain calm, but I was too scared and angry, and it came out in my voice. "You know the kind of ammo I carry – silver bullets dipped in holy water and garlic, and infused with so much magic that each bullet is practically an anti-Darkfolk bomb. So if you don't want me to finish the job Devona started and decorate the wall with the rest of your brains, you need to start talking and you need to do it fast."

"Please don't hurt him!" Shamika said, and she tried to come toward, but Bogdan held her back.

If Varney felt any fear, it didn't show on his face. "I'll tell you whatever you want to know, but first tell me where Devona is."

"I don't *know* where she is!" I said, almost shouting. "She vanished before my eyes!"

Part of my mind was already starting to wonder if the missing magic-users had all disappeared the same way, but right now I was too upset to worry about solving mysteries. I just wanted to get Devona – and our unborn children – back safely.

I pressed my weapon harder against Varney's head and I tightened my finger on the trigger.

"Who are you really?" I demanded.

"My name truly is Varney, but my job as a camera-man is just a cover. My real employer is Lord Galm, and he assigned me to watch over Devona during her pregnancy. It was my idea to do a documentary on you, so I'd have an excuse to stick close to her."

I thought back to Galm's visit to Devona in the Fever House. He'd tried so hard to convince her to move back to the Cathedral where she'd be safe for the rest of her pregnancy. While that was the first time he'd expressed his concern about her pregnancy to us, in typically de-vious Darklord fashion, Galm had put an agent in place to guard Devona well before that.

I thought about it for a moment, and then I removed my gun from Varney's head, though I didn't holster it. "That explains why you were so upset you couldn't ac-company us with Darius to the alternate Nekropolis. You were worried something might happen to Devona and you wouldn't be there to protect her, like you did when the Weyward Sisters destroyed the Bridge of Nine Sorrows and at the Grotesquerie."

I stood and reached out to help him up, but he just stared at my wrist stump.

"Sorry. I had hold of Devona's shoulder when she vanished, and my hand went with her." I wished the rest of me had gone along for the ride. Wherever she was right then, I might have been able to help her. If nothing else, at least we'd have been together.

I lowered my arm and Varney got to his feet on his own.

"Now that you know the truth, there's no need for me to pretend anymore," he said, and as I watched, the ruin of his cybernetic eye began to repair itself. "My systems are more sophisticated than they appear."

"And I bet that's more than just a camera too."

Varney smiled.

"You know," I said, "Devona's going to be very upset when she learns that you've been spying on her all this time." Assuming we ever find her, I thought, and then hated myself for it. We'd find her. Somehow. We had to. I couldn't imagine life – even my zombie version of it – without her.

"Not spying. Watching over her," Varney said. "It's not the same."

"Try telling that to her. All right, so now we know who you are." I turned to Shamika and Bogdan and pointed my 9mm at the girl. "How about you?"

Shamika's eyes widened at the sight of my weapon trained on her, but she said nothing.

Bogdan looked shocked. "You can't be serious, Matt!"

When I spoke, my voice was as cold as only the voice of a dead man can be. "The woman I love just vanished, and I suspect our most dangerous enemy is responsible. I'll do whatever is necessary to get her back, and if that means threatening a young girl, so be it. Both Varney and Shamika have been keeping secrets from me. Varney's spilled his guts, and now it's time for her to do the same."

Bogdan looked at me, shock in his eyes, along with something else. He was seeing a different side of me, one he hadn't known existed, and I could tell he was reappraising me.

"Matt," he said softly, speaking in the overly gentle way people talk to someone who's on the verge of losing it. "Don't do this. She's just a girl."

My gun hand didn't waver.

"This is Nekropolis," I said. "No one's ever *just* anything here."

Bogdan opened his mouth as if he intended to argue with me, but then he shut it. He knew the truth when he heard it.

I trained my best intimidating gaze on Shamika, one I'd honed during my years as a cop and enhanced by the fact that zombies don't need to blink.

"You're not really Papa Chatha's niece, are you?"

I was trying to look and sound scary – I figured the acid-vomit scars on my face had to help – but as upset as I was over Devona's disappearance, I didn't have to try very hard. I'd suspected for some time that neither Varney nor Shamika was telling the truth about who they were, but I'd let it go, telling myself that the time would come to confront them. Varney had turned out to be benign enough – assuming his story was true, and it meshed with what I'd observed, and it was exactly the sort of devious controlling move Devona's father would make. But if it turned out that Shamika was mixed up in this somehow, if she was responsible for Devona's disappearance in even the most tangential way, I'd never forgive myself for not confronting her earlier with my suspicions.

But despite my attempt to intimidate her, Shamika didn't seem scared in the slightest. Instead, she seemed sad. "I'm not his niece," she confirmed. "I've never even met him."

"Then who are you?" I demanded.

She paused, and then almost apologetically, she said, "I'm Gregor's sister."

I looked at her for a long moment, and even though I didn't need to blink, I blinked in surprise.

"Uh… what?"

FOURTEEN

"Who's Gregor?" Bogdan asked.

I ignored him and continued focusing on Shamika.

"Gregor can't have a sister. The Watchers are a group mind that share a single consciousness."

"Gregor is only one manifestation of that consciousness," Shamika said. "I'm another."

"But you don't look anything like Gregor." I kept my gaze – and my 9mm – on Shamika, but I spoke to Bogdan and Varney now. "Gregor was – *is* – some kind of insect thing. A giant roach with obsidian gems for eyes. And his component parts are miniature versions of him. He posed as an information broker located in the Boneyard. His insects traveled throughout Nekropolis, watching from the shadows, gathering information, eventually returning to Gregor to report what they'd learned. But Gregor had his own reasons for gathering as much knowledge as he could, and they had nothing to do with turning a profit. When Dis and the Darklords first traveled to this dimension to build Nekropolis, they discovered something was already living here. Millions, hell, maybe trillions of small insect-like creatures. The native life form didn't appear to be intelligent and showed no reaction to the Darklords' arrival. So the Darklords thought no more about them and began the work of creating their great city.

"Turns out the life forms *were* sentient, but their group intelligence was so different from that of any Earth creature, the Darkfolk included, that it didn't even recognize the newcomers as life forms, for it had no concept of Otherness. But as the centuries passed, the intelligence's insect components infiltrated the city and secretly watched the citizens of Nekropolis, eventually coming to understand Otherness – and to *hate* it.

"The Watchers' group mind created Gregor as a mask for itself, a way to interact with Darkfolk and study them more directly. It gathered all the knowledge it could, with the ultimate goal of finding a way to destroy the *Others* who'd invaded its home dimension. Once the Darkfolk were no more, things would return to the way they were, the way they were supposed to be, and the Watchers would be alone once more."

I paused and looked hard at Shamika. "How am I doing so far?"

"I'd argue some of the details, but your tale is essentially accurate."

"Good," I said, a sarcastic tone in my voice. "I wouldn't want to misrepresent you." I went on with my story. "Last Descension Day, Gregor stole a magical artifact called the Dawnstone from Lord Galm. The Dawnstone was the only object in Nekropolis capable of emitting actual sunlight, and Gregor planned to use it to disrupt the Renewal Ceremony. Umbriel does more than provide the shadowy half-light that illuminates the city. The Shadowsun's power keeps Phlegethon burning and maintains the city in this dimension. Gregor planned to use the Dawnstone to kill Father Dis, and without his power, the five Darklords wouldn't be able to recharge Umbriel on their own. The Shadowsun would fade away, Phlegethon would go out, and the deadly energies of this dimension would pour into the city, destroying everyone in it. And Gregor would've succeeded if Devona and I hadn't stopped him.

Afterward, Dis paid Gregor a visit and used his vast power to erase him from existence, along with every other Watcher in the city. Or so I thought."

"All true," Shamika said. A slight smile then moved across her lips. "But it's not the whole story."

I kept my gun trained on her. "Then why don't you tell us the rest of it?"

Before Shamika could go on, Bogdan interrupted. "Do we really need to keep standing here in the hallway like this, with you waving your gun around like some kind of zombie cowboy, ready to shoot first and ask questions later?"

"I am not *waving it around*," I said. "I'm holding it rock-steady. And in point of fact, I'm asking questions *now*, and I have yet to fire a single bullet." Still, I understood what the warlock was trying to get at. Shamika hadn't made a threatening move toward any

of us in the time I'd known her, and she *was* cooperat-
ing with my interrogation. And if she really was a
Watcher, even the special ammunition in my gun
probably wouldn't do much more than tickle her.
What finally broke the tension for me, though, was the
tiny breeze that blew through my hair. Rover was back
– small and weak, but he was still alive, if that word
can be applied to a creature made entirely from magic
– and he was recovering. I made a decision.

"I guess we're not going to find Devona standing
around like this." It was awkward using my left hand,
but I managed to holster my gun. Then I bent down
and picked up the spent reverser. The talisman would
be useless until Devona could get it recharged, but I
didn't want to leave it lying around. The damn things
were incredibly expensive, and Devona only owned a
couple. I vowed to hold onto this one and give it back
to her when I saw Devona again. And I would see her
again, even if I had to open a Kongar-sized can of
whup-ass on the entire city to make it happen.

"You can still call me Shamika if you like. It's a good
name, isn't it? I got it from a woman who works as a
chef at the Six-Legged Café. I figured that since she
cooks insects, and my people resemble insects…" She
grinned as if she was making a joke, but when none of
us reacted, her smile fell away. "I thought it was kind
of funny. I guess I don't fully understand humor yet."

We were back in the great room. I stood at my usual
place by the illusory fire, Varney once again leaned on

the wall opposite me, but this time only Shamika sat
on the couch. Bogdan was standing over next to me.
We'd taken a moment to check on Tavi. The lyke was
still unconscious, but the lower half of his body had
begun to regenerate. The healing was proceeding at a
glacial pace, and it might be days before he was whole
again, if not longer, but at least he *was* healing.

Varney's optic implant had completely repaired itself
by now, and his cybernetic eye glowed red. I had no
doubt it functioned as a weapon as well as a camera, and
though I'd chosen to holster my gun, I suspected Varney
was – not to make a pun – keeping his eye on Shamika.

"But you don't look like an insect," Varney said.
"You look human."

"I can look like whatever I want," Shamika said. "We
didn't have any form before the Darklords arrived. We
were one vast shadowy creature, stretching for hundreds of miles in all directions. But when the Darklords
saw us moving and rippling in the dark, one of them
thought we resembled a carpet of black insects, and so
we took that form."

"Insects with obsidian gems for eyes?" Bogdan said.

"It was Varvara, wasn't it?" I said. "She was the
Darklord who accidentally gave you form, and you
gained gem-like eyes because she thought of a demonic version of an insect."

"That's right," Shamika said. "We kept that form for
many years, even after we began to become aware of
the Darkfolk as Others. Insects can go anywhere in a
city. There are thousands of places to hide, and when

insects are spotted, no one pays them much attention. It was a perfect guise to wear while we conducted our observations. But we are not limited to that form."

I thought of murals I'd seen on the walls of the Nightspire depicting images of the Darkfolk's origins and evolution. The Darkfolk had begun as amorphous shadow creatures that were psycho-reactive, and as humans evolved, the Darkfolk took on shapes and attributes inspired by humanity's fears and nightmares. The Shadowings evolved naturally, but humans had turned them into the Darkfolk. From what Shamika was saying, it sounded like something similar had happened in this dimension. Only in this case, it was the Darkfolk who had unwittingly turned the native life form into the Watchers.

A couple more pieces of the puzzle fell into place for me then. "When you got blasted outside *Overhexed*, I saw you fall apart, just like I did. Except that you were separated into your component pieces, and all you had to do was reassemble them. And those chiranha you called upon to deal with Magilla. They weren't really chiranha at all, were they? They were more components of you that took on the form of chiranhas."

"Right on both counts," Shamika said. "Since I'm not really Arcane, I can't perform any magic. I know *lots* about magic," she hastened to add. "I know all kinds of things from my years observing the Darkfolk. I just can't work any spells. So I used my abilities to fake magic powers."

"Why masquerade as a human?" I asked. "And why pose as Papa Chatha's niece in particular?"

I remembered when we'd been in Papa's workroom, and Dis appeared and froze time for everyone but him and me. He'd given Shamika a look then, almost as if he'd known who and what she was, but he hadn't said anything to me about it. Maybe he'd just sensed something odd about her but hadn't been able to put his finger on it. Then again, he *was* Father Dis, the single most powerful creature among all the Darkfolk that had ever existed. I had a hard time believing he hadn't recognized Shamika as a Watcher. But if he had, why hadn't he done anything about it? Why hadn't he at least warned me?

"I told you that Gregor and I are different manifestations of the same consciousness. Gregor is the part of us that fears Otherness. I am the part that is intrigued by it. Where he observes in order to gain knowledge to destroy the Darkfolk, I observe simply because I wish to learn more about you. I take on humanoid form so that I can move freely among you and interact." She smiled playfully, looking like the teenage girl she resembled. "It's a lot more fun that way. As for why I posed as Papa Chatha's niece… well, that's more complicated." Her smile faded. "Dis did destroy every one of us in Nekropolis after Gregor's plot to stop the Renewal Ceremony failed. Dis killed us all – both those who were Gregor and those who were me. But even though Dis is a god by your standards, even his power has limits, and only those Watchers within the city were slain. So we waited a bit and then more of us simply moved in." A ghost of her smile returned. "Just like real insects, we're damn hard to get rid of."

"But if Dis destroyed you both, how do you still have your memories?" I asked.

"We're not the same as you. Our memories aren't stored within a single body or even a thousand bodies for that matter." She pointed to the stump of my right wrist. "It's more like your injury. You've lost a hand, but you haven't lost the essence of who you are. It was the same with us."

I was about to ask Shamika another question when I had the strangest sensation that my right hand was moving – except of course I had no right hand. It was with Devona, wherever she was. I chalked the sensation up to the phantom limb syndrome that amputees often experience and decided to leave it at that. But it was a really weird feeling.

Thinking of Devona made me realize something else, and I felt a surge of new hope.

"If you and Gregor are different aspects of the same mind, that means you know what he knows," I said, "which means you know what happened to Devona!"

"I'm sorry, Matt, but it doesn't work like that. I wish it did. Gregor and I might technically be the same mind, but our different... viewpoints, for lack of a better word, have caused us to become separated. Right now, we're more like one mind suffering from multiple personality disorder, and our separate personalities can't and won't communicate." She smiled sadly. "In fact, Gregor views me as the ultimate proof of the contaminating effects of Otherness. Where once we were one, now we're two. He blames the Darkfolk for this schism in our shared being, and it's only strengthened his determination to see you all destroyed."

"What's the point of being an unimaginably vast shadow creature if you don't have access to all your memories? It's a damned inefficient way to run a group mind, if you ask me." I sighed. "I should've known it wouldn't be that easy."

"I watched you and Devona stop Gregor from disrupting the Renewal Ceremony, and when I learned that Gregor was abducting Arcane, I knew he had come up with a new plan to destroy the Darkfolk. I like watching the Darkfolk. They're interesting, and I've learned so much from them. I won't let Gregor hurt them, and I'll do whatever it takes to stop him. I tried to discover what his plan is, but though I searched throughout the city, I couldn't find where he'd taken the Arcane, nor could I discover what he wanted them for. I knew I needed help, and I immediately thought of you and Devona. And once Papa Chatha was abducted, I knew how I could approach you. I was too afraid to come to you as myself. I feared you wouldn't trust me if you knew who and what I really was. But if I posed as Papa Chatha's niece... I kept watch on you, and when I learned you were going to see him, I got to his home before you, let myself in, and waited."

She smiled almost shyly at me. "I've watched you since you first came to Nekropolis, Matt. I've seen you help so many people, solve problems that seemed unsolvable, triumph against impossible odds... I knew if anyone could stop Gregor, it would be you."

"By Merlin's ingrown toenails!" Bogdan said, sounding half amused, half irritated. "She's one of your fans!"

I ignored the warlock's comment, mostly because I had no idea what to say in response. I wasn't sure how I felt about being entertainment for a Watcher, even a seemingly harmless one like Shamika.

"That was you I saw in Devona's room at the Fever House, wasn't it?" I said to her. "Or one of you, at any rate."

She nodded.

I frowned. "How did you manage to get into Papa's place? You said you can't work any magic, and the wardspells on it…" I stopped as the answer occurred to me. "At one time you secretly observed Papa deactivating the wardspells to enter his home, so you knew how to do it."

She smiled again, looking proud of herself. "Like I said, I know a lot of things."

"I wish you'd trusted me with the truth from the beginning," I said, "but I can understand why you didn't. I honestly don't know how I would've reacted if you had told us who you really were, so maybe it's best you didn't."

Another huge chunk of the mystery had made itself clear to me, but I didn't see how knowing Shamika's true identity made much difference. I'd already learned that Gregor was behind the Arcane abductions, and I could assume that he used the same technique to teleport his chosen targets as he'd used to snatch Devona. Shamika confirmed it for me when I asked a moment later.

"We can't perform magic, but that doesn't mean we can't make use of it," she said. "Each insect carries a small teleportation gem in place of one of its eyes.

"We can do more than change our shape," Shamika said. "We can change our scent as well. Gregor left the scent of Demonkin at the site of each abduction. Not strong evidence, but more than enough to convince Talaith, who has a highly suspicious and accusatory nature."

Yet another piece of the puzzle slid into place. "That's how Gregor lured us to the Grotesquerie. He imitated Papa Chatha's scent and laid a false trail for Tavi to find – a trail that ended at the Grotesquerie. And once Tavi was inside, Gregor's insects released Titanus, and then when we arrived, they released the rest of the monsters. Guess he wanted to stop us from finding out what he was up to." I frowned. "But why would he abduct Devona? She's not a magic-user. She deals with magic in her security work, but she doesn't actually cast spells."

"I understand why Gregor had to lure Devona outside to teleport her," Bogdan said. "The mystical defenses on the building prevent any of his insects from entering without one of us letting them in. What I don't understand is how he compelled Devona to go outside in the first place."

"I can answer that," Shamika said. "When Matt and Devona were investigating the theft of the Dawnstone, Devona agreed to carry one of Gregor's insects with her. At the time, they still believed Gregor was nothing more than an information broker, and that was the price he asked for his help. Unfortunately, she had to carry the insect inside her."

I shuddered at the memory of the insect burrowing its way into her ear. Devona's half-vampire physiology had allowed her to withstand the pain of the insect's entry into her body, but it had been far from pleasant for her.

"But that insect left her body after Gregor's plan to stop the Renewal Ceremony failed," I said.

"Yes, but it left some residue of itself behind," Shamika said. "Not enough to harm her, but enough to influence her mind should the need ever arise. Gregor wanted to abduct her, but he couldn't physically reach her in here, so he made her go outside using a post-hypnotic suggestion he telepathically implanted in her mind earlier, probably when we were at the Grotesquerie."

"But that brings us back to the question of *why* he wanted to abduct her," Bogdan said. "She isn't a magic-user, and it doesn't appear Gregor wants to hold her hostage. So why did her take her?"

I remembered then what Varvara had told Devona and I about our children during our visit to Demon's Roost.

I can't tell too much about them. The magic that surrounds them is too strong and too different from anything I've ever encountered before. But they're going to be very special children, that I can promise you.

A horrible realization occurred to me. "Devona might not possess magic, but our babies do – or at least they will. Strong magic. Varvara told us so. And when Galm visited us in the Fever House, he pretty much said the same thing, although at the time we all thought Devona was only going to have one child. Galm didn't know what kind of magic our children would have, but he said it would be powerful and he was determined to control it if he could."

"It's true," Varney said. "Lord Galm does believe your progeny will possess great power. But that's not the sole reason he charged me with protecting his daughter. He is truly concerned with her welfare."

"Forgive me for being skeptical," I said, "but I've never known a Darklord yet who wasn't concerned primarily with satisfying his or her own needs." Although Dis was different, I thought. He might be the darkest of dark gods, but I'd only known him to act in his people's best interest. Still, that didn't mean I trusted him fully.

"Believe what you wish," Varney said evenly. "It doesn't alter the truth."

I expected Varney to stand up for his lord and master, and I almost said so, but now wasn't the time to get sidetracked by petty bickering. We needed to stay focused so we could find Devona and stop Gregor from doing whatever nasty thing he was planning.

"Maybe Gregor plans to use the twins' magic somehow," I said. "Even if they aren't born yet." I felt a chill in my soul then, and I turned to Bogdan. "Will Gregor… I mean, in order to use the twins' magic, will he need to…" I couldn't bring myself to say it.

Bogdan put a hand on my shoulder. "If he intends to draw upon their power, he will need them alive and healthy. That means he won't harm them or their mother."

A wave of relief washed over me. Bogdan's words rang true. The Gregor I'd known was cold and calculating, not given to reacting emotionally. If it was in his best interests to keep Devona alive, he'd do so. I turned my attention back to the problem at hand. "But what does he need that power for?"

Before anyone else could speak, my vox let out with its obnoxious ring-ring-ring. Without thinking, I reached for it with my right hand, and though I no longer had a right hand, I once again felt the strange sensation of it moving. I used my left hand instead, pulled my vox out of my pocket, and opened it.

"Hello?" I said.

"Matt, I don't have a lot of time, so listen closely."

It was Scorch, and she was speaking softly, as if she didn't want to be overheard.

"Several squads of demons were deployed a few minutes ago, and the rumor going around Demon's Roost is that they're headed for the Midnight Watch. Supposedly Klamm's spies have come up with some kind of evidence linking you to the magic-users' abductions, and he wants you brought in for questioning. I've got to go before I'm caught talking to you. Good luck."

She disconnected before I could thank her. I tucked my vox back into my pocket, and told the others what she'd said.

"So since Gregor failed to kill you at the Grotesquerie, he's trying to frame you now," Bogdan said. "I wonder what evidence he created for Klamm's people to find."

It was the look on Shamika's face that made me realize the truth. I remembered the way she and Klamm had looked at one another in Demon's Roost, almost as if they'd recognized each other.

I looked at Shamika. "Klamm didn't need any evidence, did he? Because he's really Gregor in disguise."

She nodded. "I didn't know he'd taken another form until we were in Varvara's penthouse, and since you didn't know the truth about me then, I couldn't tell you about him. I'm sorry."

"It makes good tactical sense," Varney said. "It's a lot easier for him to use war as a distraction when he can take a direct hand in guiding Varvara's strategy."

"He's playing a dangerous game," I said. "He might be able to fool Varvara for a time, especially if her attention is focused on her war with Talaith, but she's a Darklord. He won't be able to fool her forever."

"Maybe he just needs to fool her long enough to accomplish whatever his ultimate goal is," Varney said.

"I hate to interrupt your theorizing," Bogdan said, "but have you forgotten what Scorch told you? Demons are on their way here to arrest you, Matt. You need to get out of here before—"

There was a loud pounding at the front door.

"—they arrive," he finished.

The portable Mind's Eye set that someone had brought into the great room to watch Varney's "improved" footage of me was still there. All the sets in the building were programmed to display images from the Midnight Watch's security cameras on command, so I activated this one and mentally commanded it to show us the view from the front-door camera. A squadron of demon soldiers had cordoned off the street and stood in ranks outside the Midnight Watch. They were all armed and had their weapons drawn and aimed at the front door. Which, I thought, was unfortunate for the poor sonofabitch who was currently knocking on it.

"That guy better hope his people don't have itchy trigger fingers," I said.

The demon resembled a satyr – horned, bearded, with hairy black goat legs – except his skin was turquoise and he had a mass of tentacles growing out of his back. He looked supremely unhappy at having been chosen for the dubious honor of knocking on my door, almost as if he feared it was booby-trapped and would explode in his face. Too bad it wasn't. Maybe I'd talk to Devona about adding that feature.

The demon might have been nervous, but when he spoke, his voice was deep and steady. "Matthew Richter! We know you're in there! In the name of the Darklord Varvara, we order you to exit the building and surrender to us for questioning!"

"Too bad Scorch didn't call a couple minutes earlier," I said. "We'd have had time to sneak out." I commanded the Mind's Eye to show us a view of the back entrance, and the scene was the same – a squad of armed demons stood outside, weapons aimed at the door. I checked the alley cameras and saw demons there as well. The roof camera showed several greasy black spots where flying demons had attempted to land, only to encounter the defenses in place there. A dozen more demons hovered twenty feet above the roof, weapons out and ready, unwilling to come any closer and risk sharing their comrades' fate, but still determined to catch anyone who might try to use the roof as an escape route.

I commanded the Mind's Eye to display the front view once more. The turquoise satyr was still talking, but he'd taken several steps back from the door, and a number of demons in the squad were hurriedly assembling some kind of large weapon in the street.

"If you refuse to turn yourself over to us voluntarily, we will be forced to come in and get you," the satyr said. "You have two minutes to decide."

Looking relieved to still be alive, the satyr turned away from the door and hurried to rejoin his fellow soldiers.

"What kind of weapon is that?" Bogdan asked.

I didn't have an answer for him, for I'd never seen anything quite like it before. There was an underlying metal framework that formed a pyramid shape, and into this framework demons slid metal panels with mouths attached to them. They were real mouths, not artificial constructs, surgically removed and affixed to the panels. It didn't take a genius to sense the maniacal hand of Victor Baron behind the device.

"It's a Blastphemer," Shamika said. "It's built from the bodies of dead sinners and focuses their negative energy for use as an offensive weapon."

We looked at her, and she smiled. "I know a lot of stuff, remember?"

Once the mouth panels were all in place, another demon came forward carrying a black sphere the size of an overinflated basketball, which he placed atop the point of the pyramid. Though there was no obvious parts to connect the sphere to the pyramid, it balanced on the point perfectly and remained there.

"That sphere contains distilled negative energy from the sinners' black hearts," Shamika said. "It's what gives the Blastphemer its power."

I turned to Bogdan. "Have you ever heard of such a thing?"

"No. It's Demonkin magic, not Arcane, and it looks to have been technologically augmented as well."

"Do you think they'll be able to breach the Midnight Watch's defenses with it?" I asked.

"I have no idea," Bogdan said. "The building is old, and its stonework was suffused with magic long before Devona bought the place, and she's improved the defenses since then. But if Klamm – I mean Gregor – is as smart as you say he is, I doubt he'd send the demons to fetch you unless he knew the Blastphemer would allow them to break through our defenses."

"We need to assume they'll be able to get in then," I said. "There's no point in trying to stop them."

"You can't give yourself up!" Shamika said.

"But if Matt goes along with them, maybe he can reach Varvara and tell her who and what Klamm really is…" Bogdan began.

Varney shook his head. "Whatever Gregor does, he won't take Matt to Demon's Roost. He won't risk Varvara discovering the truth."

"I can use my magic to conceal us all," Bogdan said. "I'll conjure an object that will make us invisible, then as long as we remain very still, the demons won't be able to find us once they break in."

"They'll have devices both magical and technological to help them search the place," I said. "If we're here, they'll find us."

"So we need to leave," Shamika said.

"Right. But we can't take Tavi with us. He's not up to traveling yet, and frankly, he'd just slow us down." I turned to Bogdan. "Go to Tavi's room and use your magic to conceal both of you. I'll draw the demons away from the Midnight Watch, and with any luck, they won't even come inside. After all, it's me they want. If I'm not here, they should have no reason to come in."

Bogdan looked as if he wanted to protest, but I added, "Tavi's our friend. We have to take care of him."

Bogdan didn't look happy about it, but he nodded. "Good luck, Matt." He then hurried off to Tavi's room.

I didn't know how much time remained before the demons would start firing the Blastphemer, but I figured we didn't have long.

I turned to Varney. "Devona and I added a secret passage to the building not too long ago. It leads to…" I was under a geis not to speak directly about the Underwalk, and so I said, "– an alternate travel route that few people in Nekropolis know about. Shamika should, though." I looked at her and she nodded. "Good. Shamika, I want you to take Varney and–"

The video feed from the front security camera was still playing on the Mind's Eye set, and I saw a figure step out of the alley across the street. A figure that looked remarkably like me.

He waved the stump of his right wrist and called out cheerfully to the demons, "You guys looking for me?"

The demons all turned to look in "my" direction, and one standing next to the Blastphemer spoke a command and pointed at "me." The devices' mouths began speaking words that were so unholy that the Mind's Eye refused to transmit them as anything other than harsh static. The black sphere atop the Blastphemer began to pulse with dark energy, and then a beam of power shot forth, streaked across the street toward the alley, and struck my doppelgänger in the chest. He stiffened, let out an agonized cry as if his very soul was in pain, and then collapsed into a puddle of black goo.

The Blastphemer's beam winked out, and for a moment the demons simply stood and stared. Then one of the braver ones stepped forward and examined the ebon puddle that my doppelgänger had been reduced to. He leaned down, sniffed the goo several times, then stood, turned back to his fellow soldiers, and gave them a thumbs-up. The squad then broke into cheers, and their work done, they set about dismantling the Blastphemer.

"Did I overdo it?" Shamika asked. "I was afraid the death-cry was a bit much, but I couldn't resist."

I remembered what Shamika had told us about how she could make herself look like whatever she wished. She'd created a decoy resembling me and had sacrificed it to throw the demons off my trail.

"I thought your component pieces had to touch each other to communicate," I said.

"That's the easiest way, but we can communicate by low-level telepathy if we're close enough," she said. "Good thing I did that. The Blastphemer packs quite a punch. That stung like hell!"

I couldn't help smiling at her choice of words. "I think that's the general idea."

Devona and I had built the entrance to the Underwalk in one of the storage rooms, so after checking on Tavi one last time and saying goodbye to Bogdan, then Shamika, Varney, and I went into the storage room, through the trapdoor, and down the ladder into the Underwalk. An electric cart was parked by the ladder, a ramshackle device cobbled together from cast-off odds and ends, some mechanical, some organic, and some indeterminate.

Varney eyed the cart skeptically, but once he saw it held together when Shamika and I got on, he climbed in after us and took a seat in the back. I started the cart, turned on the headlights, and we headed down the tunnel. It wasn't very wide or tall, but there was room enough for two carts to pass by one another, if only just.

"The cart may not look like much, but it works just fine," I said. "Its makers abhor waste, and they recycle everything. Their tech may not be pretty – and its smell may leave something to be desired – but it's always functional."

"What makers?" Varney asked. "And what is this place?"

"I can't tell you," I said. "I've been magically sworn to secrecy. If I even try to tell you, my tongue will explode and take my head with it – quite literally."

"But I can tell you," Shamika said. "These tunnels are called the Underwalk, and they were created by the Dominari so that they could move throughout the city undetected. The Underwalk exists in all five Dominions, but you can't use it to cross from one Dominion to the other because Phlegethon blocks the way. You still have to use the bridges for that. The Dominari tried to dig under Phlegethon, but its fire extends downward for so many miles that eventually they gave up."

Varney's eyebrows rose. "The Dominari? I didn't know you associated with criminals, Matt. Then again, you *were* imprisoned in Tenebrus for a time." His tone clearly indicated his disapproval.

"I was imprisoned on a false charge, and I received a full pardon," I said. "But don't worry that Galm is going to be upset that his future son-in-law has ties to the Dominari. All the Darklords know about them. Dis too. They couldn't do business in the city without the Lords' approval, tacit though it might be. The Dominari operate a literal underground economy, and whatever you or I might think about their activities, they're necessary for the city's survival."

Most people know the Dominari as Nekropolis' version of the mob, and that's true enough as it goes, but there's more to it than that. Nekropolis is as self-sustaining as a city can be, producing its own goods and services for the most part, and importing anything else it might need from Earth. But the Dominari fill in the cracks in the city's economy, and without them, Nekropolis couldn't go on. As a former cop, I'm uncomfortable with the situation, to say the least, but as a pragmatist, I understand it.

"And your connection to them is..." Varney asked.

"Something I can't talk about. The tongue thing again, remember? But I'm no criminal, if that's what you're asking."

He thought about this for a moment and finally nodded. "Very well. I've observed you long enough to believe you're a trustworthy man. I'll accept your word on that matter."

"What about you?" I said. "How did you get to be a secret agent for Lord Galm?"

He shrugged. "There's little to tell. As you might imagine, Galm has many servants, and he uses us as he sees fit. I have a talent for pretending to be someone I'm not. Centuries ago, when I was human, I dreamed about being an actor, and in a way, I suppose I've become one."

"I'm no theatre critic, but as far as I'm concerned, you played the part of an annoying airheaded cameraman to perfection."

He smiled, showing a hint of fang. "Thank you."

"Where are we going?" Shamika said, sounding more like a kid eager to get on with the next fun activity than an ancient alien entity struggling to defeat the darker half of her personality. Maybe in a way this *was* fun for her. I wondered what it was like, observing the Dark-folk for four hundred years, getting to know them in intimate detail, but never actually being part of their lives. Never actually living. I couldn't imagine how lonely it must've been.

"I've been thinking about that," I said. "If we're going to find Devona, we need to confront Gregor. And since he's masquerading as General Klamm right now, that means we need to get into Demon's Roost. But we have to do so on our terms, not his."

"And there's the little matter of a demon army standing between us and him," Varney pointed out.

"Correct. Which means that we're going to need help. The kind of help that specializes in dealing with Darkfolk in general, and demons in particular."

Varney's organic eye widened in surprise. "You can't mean…"

I smiled. "Yep. We're going to pay a visit on the Hidden Light."

FIFTEEN

But first we had a stop to make.

We drove through tunnels for the better part of twenty minutes, taking turns as necessary, and passing other carts as we traveled. The other carts were usually laden with cargo of one sort or another, almost always packed away in anonymous brown cardboard boxes. The carts were driven by vermen – human-sized bipedal rats – though they were patchwork Frankenstein versions of the creatures, dead who'd been returned to life so they could keep on working. Like I said, the Dominari loathe waste.

The "repurposed dead" ignored us as we passed. I had no idea if they recognized me or if they simply assumed that anyone traveling the Underwalk belonged there because the Dominari were so careful about whom they revealed their subterranean tunnel system to. All I know is that ever since I accepted the geis that makes it impossible for me to talk about the Underwalk, I can travel it without anyone challenging me.

As I steered the cart with my one remaining hand, I tried not to worry about Devona. I reminded myself that she was more than capable of taking care of herself. She was intelligent, strong, emotionally resilient, and she had her psychic abilities to draw on. Gregor might be a powerful adversary, but he wouldn't harm Devona if he needed her, and the longer she remained alive, the more chance she'd have to find a way to escape or, at the very least, contact me. It helped that several times during the trip I felt the weird phantom sensation of my missing right hand moving. I knew the sensations were just my imagination, but since my hand was with Devona, feeling them was like sharing a connection with her and it was a comfort, strange though it might be.

Eventually we came to a ladder, and I stopped the cart and turned it off. A light in the ceiling came on to illuminate the ladder for us, and we climbed up and opened the trapdoor. The door opened easily for me, though the security spells on it would've stopped Shamika and Varney, and probably reduced them to ashes in the process. We entered a basement filled with crates and barrels, and shelves containing bottles of wine and various other types of alcohol.

"Where are we?" Varney asked.

Shamika answered for me. "This is *Skully's* basement," she said.

Varney thought for a moment. "Isn't *Skully's* a dive bar on the western edge of the Sprawl? I've never been there, of course," he added, as if it was important to make that point. A lot of the older Bloodborn tend to put on aristocratic airs, and I found myself actually missing Varney's hippy cameraman persona. That Varney might have been irritating, but at least he wasn't a snob.

"Well, you won't be able to say that after today," I told him. I turned to Shamika. "Do you know if Gregor is aware of what we're doing?" I wasn't sure how the split personality thing worked with Shamika and Gregor, but I gathered that one side of their group mind didn't know what the other side was thinking. So while that meant Shamika couldn't tell us what Gregor's ultimate plan was, it also meant he couldn't read Shamika's thoughts and automatically know what we were up to. But that didn't mean he couldn't simply observe us, and I knew from experience that Gregor had eyes and ears everywhere in Nekropolis.

"Gregor has trouble getting his insects into the Underwalk," Shamika said. "As do I. The Dominari work very hard to keep us out. We always manage to get a few in, but I didn't sense Gregor's presence in any of the carts we passed." She paused and looked around *Skully's* basement. "He's not down here, either." She looked up at the ceiling. "Nor is he upstairs. I'm doing my best to keep him busy throughout the city by creating other copies of you for him to follow. Right now, there are several dozen Matts running around the Sprawl, and they all have Shamikas and Varneys with them." She grinned. "I made them right after the first duplicate was destroyed by the Blastphemer. I knew Gregor was watching, and he wouldn't be fooled by my duplicate. He could sense what I'd done. So I decided to distract him with even *more* duplicates." She paused. "Is that OK? Should I have asked first?"

Maybe there was a reason she'd chosen the form of a young girl beyond trying to pose as Papa Chatha's niece, I thought. The more I got to know Shamika, the more childlike she seemed. Maybe in a sense she *was* a child. The Watchers might be ancient as a race, but the personality that called itself Shamika had only recently emerged. And like a child, she was eager for an adult's approval.

"You did great," I said, and she beamed.

We headed upstairs and entered the bar proper.

Skully doesn't believe in wasting money on décor. The nine-foot-high front door is solid iron, and there are no windows for customers to break – not because Skully cares about his patrons' safety, but because it's a pain in the ass to keep replacing glass all the time. The walls are brick and the floor concrete, which makes mopping up bloodstains less of a chore. The solid oak tables are bolted to the floor, and the wooden chairs are cheap and easy to replace. Darkfolk tend to get more than a little rowdy when they overindulge, and Skully has learned from experience that the best way to protect his place is to make it hard to destroy.

Beyond beating the shit out of your fellow bar-goers, the only entertainment at *Skully's* comes from a jukebox sitting in the corner. As we entered, the three heads bolted to the top of the machine saw me and started singing a rendition of Oingo Boingo's "Dead

Man's Party." The scars, fresh cuts, and bruises on the singing heads showed that *Skully's* customers enjoyed their potential as targets more than they appreciated their musical offerings.

Skully's clientele glanced our way as we entered, either out of curiosity or to size us up as possible threats. I recognized a few of them – Suicide King, Patchwork the Living Voodoo Doll, and Sally O'Sorrows – and nodded a curt greeting, but I didn't head over to anyone's table to chat. I was looking for someone who might be able to tell me what I needed to know, and I found him sitting at the bar, talking with a young woman I also knew.

Before we could start toward them, the front door opened and a teenage boy with mussed hair and a pouty expression walked in. He had the elongated canines of the Bloodborn, but his skin gave off a glimmering sheen.

A couple of bald, overly muscled, heavily tattooed vampires clad in scuffed leather snarled at the sight of the luminous teen. They rose from their chairs, stalked toward him, flanked him on either side, grabbed hold of his arms, lifted him off the floor, and started escorting him back toward the door.

"Hey, take it easy, guys!" the teen whined. "It's not my fault I sparkle!"

The biker vampires laughed as they left the bar, and the iron door slammed shut ominously behind them.

The three of us then headed over to the bar, and I took the empty seat next to Carl, leaving Varney and

Shamika to stand. The seat on the other side of me was occupied by a gill man wearing a diving helmet with rubber hoses attached to a humming machine he wore like a backpack. The helmet was filled with murkish, vaguely luminescent water, and I knew the gill man's H2O was laced with tangleglow, a Darkfolk-created drug too strong for human consumption. The gill man looked a little wobbly on his chair, and I knew if he didn't dial back the amount of tangleglow his device was pumping out, he'd end up in a coma before the night was over.

I ignored the gill man and turned to the older man sitting on the other side of me. His thinning reddish hair was covered by a straw porkpie hat, and he wore an ancient wrinkled seersucker suit that he claimed was white but was really more on the yellowish side.

"Hey, Carl. How are things?"

Carl didn't look from his beer. Instead, he reached into his jacket pocket, removed a small folded newspaper, and tossed it down on the counter in front of me. I unfolded and smoothed it out. It was the latest edition of the *Night Stalker News*, the alternative paper of which Carl is the sole owner, reporter, photographer, printer, and distributor. Today's headline read: RICHTER AND KANTI STOP HYDE PLAGUE. Accompanying the story were photos of Devona, Darius, and me battling Hydes as we fought to reach the *House of Dark Delights*.

I turned to Carl, impressed despite myself. "How did you get these? We *were* in a another dimension, you know."

The young woman seated on the opposite side of Carl laughed. "You should know better than to expect Carl to reveal his sources!"

Fade is a petite woman in her early twenties with long brunette hair that hangs past her waist. She usually dresses in dance-club chic, and tonight she was wearing a ripped Sisters of Mercy T-shirt, thigh-high black boots, and a skirt so mini it was barely there. Her earrings were shaped like silver cobras, and they swayed back and forth from her earlobes, tiny tongues flicking the air, serpent eyes narrowed as they gazed upon the world with cold disinterest.

Varney looked over my shoulder at Carl's paper.

"Dude, when my producer sees those photos, he's going to be even madder at me for not getting to go along on that trip!"

Now that we were in public, it seemed Varney had assumed his cover persona again.

Carl looked at Varney with more than a little disdain. "You Mind's Eye reporters are too used to letting your technology do the work for you. You need to rely less on cybernetic implants and more on good old-fashioned journalistic know-how."

There was something about the way he said this, though, an almost mocking tone that made me wonder if Carl knew Varney's hippy cameraman act was a lie. I wouldn't have been surprised. Back on Earth, Carl had been an investigative reporter who'd uncovered the existence of the Darkfolk and worked to expose them. His stories were ridiculed by the mainstream media, though, and eventually he found his way to Nekropolis, and he's lived here ever since, producing his own newspaper and exposing truths that more than a few rich and powerful citizens wish he would keep his damn mouth shut about.

Carl turned to Fade. "And you, my dear, should quit wasting your time with that silly gossip column of yours and start reporting some real news for a change." He finished the last swallow of his beer and slammed the mug down on the counter as if to emphasize his point.

Fade didn't seem the least bothered by Carl's criticism. "Not all of us are cut out to be crusaders, you know. Gossip sells papers, love, and in my case, the more readers I have, the happier I am."

Fade isn't a shallow fame-seeker. For her, having a large readership – and being a well-known personality about town – is literally a matter of life and death. She's reality-challenged. For reasons she's never shared, her existence is so uncertain that if she doesn't constantly reinforce her own reality, she's in danger of vanishing. Hence her name. That's why she spends so much of her time club-hopping, and why she writes the gossip column for the *Daily Atrocity*, Nekropolis' sleaziest and therefore best-read tabloid. I myself rarely read it, and when I do, it's only in the interest of professional research – I swear.

I introduced Varney in case Fade didn't know him, and then I introduced Shamika as Papa Chatha's niece. I saw no reason to tell Carl and Fade the truth about who Shamika was, partly because we were in a hurry and the truth was too complicated to easily explain, but also because if they knew who Shamika was, they'd learn that Gregor was back. And it was safer for Carl and Fade not to know about Gregor. If they knew, Gregor might decide they were a threat to him, and if that happened, he might get it in his head to do something painful and permanent to get rid of them. Sometimes ignorance isn't just bliss, it's also necessary to one's long-term survival, especially in this town.

"So what are you two fine members of Nekropolis' journalistic establishment doing hanging out in a bar?" I asked. "Don't you know there's a war going on?"

Fade frowned. "Tell me about it. Half the clubs in the Sprawl are empty. People don't feel safe to go out. Personally, I feel that wartime is the perfect opportunity for partying. The chance that the club you're in might become a bombed-out crater any second adds a little zing to the festivities, don't you think?"

That was bad news for Fade. The more people she interacted with on a daily basis, the firmer reality's grip on her was. I hadn't noticed, but her colors seemed muted, a bit less intense and washed-out, as if she wasn't as *there* as she should be. If the war continued and escalated, fewer and fewer people would go out and the Sprawl's clubs, bars, and restaurants would become deserted. And if that happened, Fade wouldn't be able to find enough people to talk to, and there was a good chance she'd live up to her name.

I saw Fade's glass was empty, and since Carl had finished off his beer, I offered to buy the two of them another round. Skully was at the other end of the bar talking to the Jade Enigma, and I motioned to catch his attention. He looked at me, and I pointed to Fade and Carl and held up two fingers. He nodded, made them another pair of drinks, and brought them over. Carl got another mug of beer, and Fade got a bubbling blue concoction called a Miasmic Overload whose chief ingredient was poison: tree frog toxin. It should have been deadly to humans, but Fade sipped it without ill effect. Who knows? Maybe the attention she received from ordering such a deadly drink shored up her reality and neutralized the poison. At any rate, she didn't instantly keel over dead, and her color did seem sharper and brighter.

"Hey, Matt," Skully said. "I'm surprised to see you here. Word on the street is that Varvara's put out a warrant for your arrest."

"You know what I always say: it's nice to be wanted."

Skully laughed which, given the ways he looks, is an unsettling sight. From the neck down, Skully resembles a stocky, broad-shouldered man. But from the neck up, he's a skull. No hair, no skin, nothing but bone. Skully usually wears a white shirt with the cuffs rolled up, and a black leather apron designed to protect his clothes from being eaten away in case he gets a little sloppy with any of the more dangerous chemicals he uses to mix his customers' drinks. Despite his appearance, Skull comes across as a good-humored barkeep, but the enchanted silver broad axe he keeps behind the bar in case of trouble tells a different story, as does the fact that his place is a Dominari-owned establishment. For years I'd been unaware of Skully's ties to the Dominari, and when I learned about them, it put a strain on our friendship. I'm still not entirely comfortable with Skully's business dealings with the Dominari, but I try not to think about them too much. Skully's helped me with a lot of cases over the years, and in Nekropolis, a friend is defined as someone you can trust not to devour you when your back is turned or steal your soul when you're not looking. By that standard, Skully is my friend, and as for the rest, I figure in the end it'll all come out in the wash.

Carl narrowed his eyes as he peered at my acid-scarred face. "A little mortician's wax would fix that right up."

I said, "Reptilikan hocked a loogie at me."

"And you look a little loose in the joints," Carl added. "If you were a Frankenstein monster, I'd advise you to get your bolts tightened."

"That sounds vaguely naughty," Fade said, grinning. She then nodded at my wrist stump. "Looks like you lost a hand somewhere along the way too."

"Occupational hazard," I said.

Fade raised an eyebrow. "You don't really expect Carl and I to let it go at that, do you? We're reporters. Do tell us the all the details, the gorier the better."

"*I'm* a reporter," Carl said. "What you write is entertainment." He sipped his beer. "Not that either of us is getting to do much writing at the moment."

"Why's that?" I asked.

"Demon's Roost has instituted a complete informa-tion blackout," Carl answered. Then he made a sour face. "Or rather, the great General Klamm has. None of the Demonkin are allowed to talk to the media, and we're forbidden from writing or broadcasting any in-formation related to the war. Why else do you think my charming companion and I are sitting around this dump drinking?" He looked at Skully. "No offense."

"None taken," Skully said, but the tiny pinpricks of light that momentarily glowed within his empty sock-ets told a different story. If Carl noticed Skully's reaction, he ignored it.

"You know it's sad when reporters are reduced to in-terviewing each other," Fade added. "That's why we're so glad to see you, Matt. You're usually in the thick of things. Why don't you let me pump you for informa-tion? Who knows? You might even enjoy it."

I didn't take Fade's flirting seriously. It was just an-other way for her to draw attention to herself.

"I don't have time to chat," I said, with more of an edge in my voice than I wanted. "I have a problem, and I need help."

"Something's happened to Devona," Carl said. Be-fore I could ask, he added, "I don't know anything. I'm merely making an educated guess based on your obvi-ously agitated state."

"And there's the fact that Devona's not here," Fade put in.

"That too," Carl agreed.

"Look, I promise that I'll sit down with both of you for an exclusive joint interview once the current situation is resolved." Varney gave me an offended look. "Oh, don't bother pretending to be upset," I snapped. I didn't care about helping Varney maintain his cover just then. "But right now I need to get in touch with the Hidden Light, and I don't have time to go through the usual channels."

Carl raised an eyebrow. "What makes you think any of us know how to get hold of them? The location of their headquarters is the most carefully guarded secret in the city. I ought to know. I've tried for years to get an interview with their leadership."

"Me too," Fade said wistfully. "Can you imagine how many hits my blog would get if I could? It'd be enough attention to keep me solid for an entire month!"

At the mention of the Hidden Light, the drugged-out gill man seated next to me got up and staggered away at a good clip, wobbling as he headed for the door and made his exit. Just speaking the Hidden Light's name can be enough to clear a room in Nekropolis, if you say it loudly enough.

Carl wasn't joking about the Hidden Light's location being secret. When I'd first decided I needed the Hidden Light's help, I asked Shamika if she knew where their HQ was. But she had no idea, and she assured me that Gregor didn't either. How the Hidden Light managed to hide themselves from the Watchers, I didn't know, but I wasn't surprised. The Hidden Light is one of the most powerful organizations in the city, and the only way

they survive among the Darkfolk is to keep their iden-
tities and location, like their name says, hidden.

I knew how to get hold of Magdalene Holstrom, my
contact in the Hidden Light, but the process took some
time. First I leave a message for her taped beneath a
specific table at the Ghost of Meals Past, a restaurant
that serves ectoplasmic recreations of the best meals
you've ever enjoyed. The food's emotionally satisfying,
though not very filling. After dropping off the note, I
wait, anywhere from a couple days to as much as a
week, before I get a call on my vox. The caller is always
someone different, and I never recognize the voice. I'm
given instructions on where and when to meet Maggie,
and if I'm so much as a minute late, she's gone when
I get there. She always comes in disguise, wearing a
different body each time – or at least appearing to. I'm
not sure if she cloaks herself in some kind of illusion
spell, if she's a shapechanger of some kind, or if she's
a bodyswitcher. But her voice is always the same,
which is how I recognize Maggie. She never spends
longer than ten minutes with me, we conduct our
business – which usually consists of her giving me a
few items I can't get anywhere else, such as holy water
and blessed religious tokens. After that, she leaves, and
that's the last I hear from her until the next time I need
to get in touch with her.

I tapped Carl's paper with my left index finger. "You
knew about my extra-dimensional exploits," I told
him. "Is it such a stretch to think you might know
where the Hidden Light is located?"

"Getting information from other dimensions is easy if you know how," Carl said, a bit smugly. "But finding out anything to do with the Hidden Light? Well, that's damn near impossible."

"Rumor has it that even the Darklords don't know how to find them," Fade said.

Skully had been quiet since I'd first mentioned the Hidden Light, but now he said, "You think the Hidden Light will be able to help you get Devona back?"

"That's what I'm hoping," I said.

"She's a good woman," Skully said. Then his flesh-less mouth seemed to stretch wider, as if he were grinning. "Better than you deserve."

I smiled back. "Don't I know it."

He thought for a moment more before, finally coming to a decision. "I can tell you what you need to know." Before Carl or Fade could say anything, Skully looked at the two reporters. "And no, I'm not going to tell you two, and if either of you ask me a single question about it, I'm going to bring out Silverado and lop both your heads off." He said this as calmly as if he were making a comment on the weather, but I knew he wasn't joking.

Carl and Fade kept their mouths shut, but they were clearly unhappy about it.

I'd come here hoping that Skully could give me a lead on someone who could help me track down Maggie. I hadn't expected Skully himself to have the knowledge I needed. This had turned out better than I'd hoped.

Before he could say anything more, though, the bar's iron door opened and the two biker vampires walked back inside. The sparkly kid wasn't with them, and they were covered in copious amounts of blood – far more than one skinny teenager should've been able to contain.

One of the vampires looked at me, and his upper lip curled in a disdainful snarl.

"Now that we cleared that punk out, let's do Skully another favor and get rid of that stinking deader."

The second vampire grinned in agreement.

I looked at Skully and he shrugged in apology. "Sorry, Matt. They're new here."

"Don't worry about it," I said.

I rose from my seat as the biker vampires stomped across the floor over to me. One of them gave Varney a disgusted look.

"What are you doin' hanging out with a goddamn zombie?" the vampire said. "You're Bloodborn. You're better than that."

Varney pursed his lips and the light in his cyber-eye turned an angry red, but otherwise he didn't react.

"This goddamn zombie has a name, you know," I said evenly.

The first vampire grinned at me, displaying his fangs. "Look, Marlon, it talks!"

Marlon said, "What do you know, Brando? I thought all deaders could do was walk around moaning while they look for somebody's brain to munch on."

"This one must be like some kind of genius of the living dead!" Brando said, and laughed.

I looked at them. "Marlon and Brando? Seriously?"

They scowled, and now both bared their fangs at me.

"You say you got a name, deader," Marlon asked. "What is it?"

Using my left hand, I drew my 9mm, aimed, and squeezed off two shots. The vampires' mouths exploded in twin showers of blood and broken teeth. They staggered backward, then fell to their knees and doubled over, blood streaming out of their ruined mouths and splattering onto the concrete floor.

"Fuck You's my name," I said. "But you can call me *Mister* Fuck You."

"The way you took care of those two loud-mouthed vampires was totally awesome!" Shamika said.

"Totally stupid, you mean," I muttered. "Given my current condition, the recoil from my gun nearly tore my hand off." As it was, I was having trouble keeping my left hand attached, no matter how hard I concentrated, and my loose limbs made me look more like a drunken scarecrow than ever. I was glad Varney had turned out not to be a real reporter, because I really would've hated for him to shoot any video of me the way I looked right then.

We'd left *Skully's* via the basement trapdoor, climbed back into the hodgepodge cart, and were heading through the Underwalk once more, headlights on, electric engine humming. As near as I could tell, the tunnel we were traveling down paralleled Sybarite Street, and I wished the vermen carts came equipped with GPS so I'd know for sure. I was impatient to reach our destination, and I really didn't want to take any wrong turns and be delayed, or worse, end up lost. The longer I was separated from Devona, the more worried about her I became and the harder it was for me to control my emotions. But she needed me to keep cool if I was going to be of any help to her, so I shoved my feelings down, put a tight lid on them, and concentrated on doing what I had to do.

As we drove, I wondered if I was going about this all wrong. Maybe asking the Hidden Light for help wasn't the way to go. Back at Papa Chatha's, Dis had told me that he couldn't interfere in a dispute between two Darklords, but surely the current situation had progressed beyond that. If Gregor was involved, it was no longer just a clash between Talaith and Varvara, and if that was the case, then perhaps Dis *would* step in and do something. I had no idea how powerful Dis was, but he'd dealt with the Watchers the last time they'd infested the city, and there was no reason to think he couldn't handle them again. And if Dis was still reluctant to help, I could try the other Darklords. Amon had no particular dislike for me, but then again the king of the shapeshifters also had no love for me, either. I'd helped Edrigu recover a mystic object that had been stolen from him – though he had rewarded me by making it possible for me to return to mortal life for twenty-four hours, giving me the chance to have children with Devona. Edrigu might figure our accounts were balanced and be disinclined to help me. Galm would wish to help, if for no other reason than to protect his future grandchildren. But I wasn't sure I could trust him. What if we found Devona only to have Galm try to take her and lock her away in the Cathedral, where she'd be safe until she delivered our babies? And once they were born, what if Galm chose to keep them so that he could exploit their magic, whatever that might be?

The more I thought of it, the more the idea of going to any of the Darklords for help seemed like a bad idea. The more of them that got involved in this mess, the worse it would get, and the war between Talaith and Varvara could easily become a war between all five Darklords. And besides, it wasn't as if Gregor wasn't keeping all the Darklords, Dis included, under observation. Gregor might not be powerful enough to defeat the Darklords in a direct confrontation, else he would've done so long before now, but if I sought out any of their help, I'd expose myself and Gregor would have no trouble taking *me* out.

No, if I wanted to rescue Devona, free the abducted magic-users, and stop Gregor, I was going to have to do it myself. And that meant I needed the Hidden Light's help.

I glanced at Shamika and Varney. Make that *we* needed their help. I was grateful that the two of them had chosen to accompany me. Having a highly trained spy and a powerful alien entity along for the ride would no doubt come in handy. Plus, though I hated to admit it, I'd gotten used to working with partners over the last few months, and having them with me was a comfort. Despite myself, somewhere along the line, I'd become Matt Richter, the Not-So-Lone Ranger. And you know something? All things considered, it wasn't so bad.

The air in front of the cart's headlights began to ripple in a way I found disturbingly familiar. A ghostly image superimposed itself on the tunnel – another tunnel, higher and wider, with metal rails on the ground. We passed the phantom figures of men and women standing on a raised platform. They gawked at us as we drove by, and I had to resist a crazy impulse to wave hello. The images became more solid, and suddenly I found myself having to steer around and between the ground rails in order to keep the cart from overturning. It was happening again, the crossover to Earth, only this time it was more than just a ghostly overlapping. This time we were really co-existing in the same dimensional space. Which was unfortunate for us, because the bright headlights of a subway train glowed in the distance, growing ever larger as they drew near. If the train was as solid as the railings beneath our cart, our quest to find the Hidden Light's HQ was about to come to an abrupt and very dramatic end.

We felt the deep juddery vibrations of the train's approach, heard the rattle-whoosh of its metal wheels rolling over the rails. There was no way to avoid a collision. There wasn't enough room in the tunnel for me to pull the cart out of the train's path, and we certainly couldn't turn around and outrun the damned thing, not with our tiny electric engine.

I wondered where we were. Not Cleveland, not if we were in a subway tunnel. New York, probably. Or perhaps the Tube in London, the Métro in Paris, maybe even the Tokyo Metro. But it didn't really matter what Earth city we were occupying space with. All that mattered was when that train hit us, we would be in for two worlds' worth of hurt.

"Varney!" I had to shout to be heard above the din of the approaching train. "Can you get both of us out of here using your travel form?"

"I can only carry one of you at a time!" he said.

I started to tell him to take Shamika, but she said, "Take Matt! I'll be OK!"

Before I could protest, Shamika stood and leaped off the cart. In mid-air she separated into dozens of roach-like insects – except these sprouted tiny black wings and buzzed away. Varney's form melted into a shadowy whirlwind which grabbed hold of me, and carried me away from the cart, spinning around like an undead top. I wasn't able to see through the dark substance of Varney's travel form, not that I'd have been able to focus clearly, given the way I was spinning around, but I heard the train hit the cart with a violent crash and rending of metal. Varney kept me spinning in the air for a few moments, until the sound of the train began to diminish, then he lowered me to the ground, deposited me on my feet, and resumed his normal form beside me.

I wasn't dizzy. Being dead, as I've said before, has some advantages. I looked around for Shamika – or rather the cloud of insects she'd transformed into – but

I didn't see her. Varney and I both called her name, and when she didn't respond, I feared that she'd gotten herself splattered on the train's front, like a bug on windshield. But a moment later, the flying black bugs buzzed our way, gathered together, and flowed back into Shamika's shape.

"I didn't know you could fly," I said. "Gregor never did that."

She smiled. "My brother lacks imagination. I don't."

I smiled back. "Good for you."

"What do we do now?" Varney asked. "If Nekropolis and Earth remain merged…"

Before he could continue, the air shimmered once more, and the tunnel resumed its previous size and the subway rails disappeared. The Underwalk had returned to normal.

"Never mind," Varney said.

"That was worse than last time," I said. "It lasted longer and was more solid. The next time it might be permanent."

"I'm just glad we were in a subway tunnel," Varney said. "If we'd appeared outside during the day…" He shuddered.

"You might think about buying some imported sunblock, just in case," I told him.

In reply, he just frowned at me. Some people just don't know a good joke when they hear it.

"Do you think Talaith did that?" Shamika asked.

"Maybe. But like I've said before, I don't think she'd cast any spell that would affect the entire city. It's the

Sprawl she wants to attack. I've been thinking... maybe Gregor's behind the dimensional crossovers with Earth. It could be why he's abducted the magic-users. He'd need a lot of mystical power and know-how to pull off something that big."

Shamika frowned. "But why would he do such a thing? Gregor *hates* Others! And from what I under-stand, there are *billions* of humans on Earth. I can't imagine my brother wanting to expose himself to that many people."

I had to admit, it didn't seem in character, but I just couldn't see how Talaith could be responsible for the crossovers. I decided we'd just have to ask Gregor once we found him.

Right before I squashed the sonofabitch like the bug he was for abducting my wife.

SIXTEEN

We passed a number of ladders leading to the surface – and the remains of several carts and their vermen drivers who had been unlucky enough to encounter the subway train – until we finally came to the ladder we wanted. That is, if I hadn't screwed up the directions Skully had given me. The ceiling light above us activated as I parked the cart, and we climbed the ladder. Just as I had at *Skully's*, I opened the trapdoor to protect Varney and Shamika from any defensive spells there might be, and we stepped into a basement. Like *Skully's*, this basement was used for storage. The big difference was *what* was stored here.

Shamika looked around, frowning. "What are these things?"

Varney and I exchanged uncomfortable glances. We both knew that Shamika only looked like a young girl, that in truth she was far older than either of us, maybe older than any being in Nekropolis – with the exception of Gregor, of course. But I still couldn't help feeling more than a little awkward at having to explain all the sex toys and S&M equipment lining the shelves around us.

"They're, ah, recreational devices," I said lamely.

She looked at me with too-innocent eyes. "What, you mean, like for kinky sex? Do you and Devona ever use stuff like this?"

Varney looked as if he was trying really hard not to laugh. I ignored Shamika's question and said, "Let's go."

We headed up the basement stairs. The door at the top of the stairs wasn't locked – with the defensive spells on the trapdoor, it didn't need to be – and we opened it easily and stepped out into a small parlor. The room was done entirely in crimson: ceiling and walls, carpeted floor, chairs, couch... all were a deep, rich red. The parlor wasn't empty, though. A naked two-headed man was on the couch servicing an equally naked woman whose mottled skin resembled a snake's. The man had a trim athlete's physique, and when I say he had two heads, I'm not referring to what sat atop his neck. His name was Richard... Richard Deux, and he was one of the most popular men on Bennie's staff for two very obvious and prominent reasons.

The woman was too busy moaning and gyrating to notice us, but Richard looked in our direction, startled at first, but then he smiled.

"Hey, Matt! What's up?"

I resisted making the obvious joke. "Hey, Rich. Sorry to, uh, disturb you at work."

As he talked, Richard continued performing his duties with energetic enthusiasm, seemingly unbothered to have an audience, even one that contained a being who appeared to be a young girl. But then, this was the *House of Dark Delights*. They got all kinds here.

"Not a problem. I can multitask." He grinned.

There was a soft whirr as Varney's cybernetic eye focused on the salient portions of Richard's augmented anatomy. "I can see that," he said, sounding impressed despite himself.

Richard's grin only grew wider.

I myself made sure to keep my gaze fixed firmly on Richard's face. "We need to talk to Bennie, Rich. It's kind of an emergency."

"Last time I saw them, they were holding court in the lounge. I'd look there first."

The woman's moans suddenly increased in volume and pitch.

"Now if you don't mind, I really need to concentrate for this next part," Richard said.

"No problem. Uh, good luck," I said, and we left through the parlor's other door. I closed the door as the woman's moans became screams of pleasure.

Shamika looked thoughtful. "You know, I've never tried that sort of thing before. I wonder–"

"Maybe you should wait until you grow up a little more," I said without thinking.

She looked at me with a surprised expression for a moment, and then she smiled. "Yeah, maybe you're right."

We headed through the *House of Dark Delights* until we came to the lounge. It was very strange to be here again, considering that my last visit had been to an alternate version of the lounge that existed in a different dimension. That lounge had been crawling with Hydes, and while this one was no less crowded, at least things were normal here. Or as normal as they ever got, I guess I should say. Clients sat at tables drinking, talking, and laughing as they impatiently waited for their appointments to begin, tried to recover from an especially vigorous session, or – for those with stronger sexual appetites and an abundance of stamina – paused for a rest between assignations. Every type of Darkfolk was represented in the crowd, along with more than a few humans. If there was one thing that Darkfolk and humans had in common, it was they both loved sex. And as we stepped into the lounge, I couldn't help thinking, who would've thought that the city's most famous brothel was also a cover for the Hidden Light?

We found Bennie at his/her usual table, surrounded by some of the city's most famous and infamous citizens. Arvel the ghoul was there, sitting atop a titanium chair designed to hold his incredible – and grotesquely naked – bulk. The banshee pop singer Scream Queen sat next to him, occasionally fanning the air near her nose in a vain attempt to dissipate Arvel's stench. Victor Baron sat on the other side of Scream Queen, dressed casually in a long-sleeved white shirt and gray slacks, looking like the platonic ideal of a male supermodel. Overkill sat next to him; the petite mercenary smiled and gave me a nod of greeting. And next to her sat Acantha the gorgon. She pointedly avoided looking at me – at least I think so; it was hard to tell considering the wraparound sunglasses she wore – but her camera-eye head serpents hissed to let me know she was considerably less pleased than Overkill to see me. And sitting between Acantha and Bennie was a woman who called herself the Psychovore. I knew her only by reputation, and while she looked normal enough, supposedly she had no need to eat or drink. Instead, she subsisted off the psychic emanations of those around her. If that was true, being in the *House of Dark Delights* must've have been like an all-you-can-eat buffet for her.

Bennie was currently female as we approached, and she gave me a grin when she saw me coming.

"Well, if it isn't the savior of my fine establishment! Well, one version of it, at any rate. I trust my other-dimensional counterpart was suitably grateful for your assistance?"

"You helped too," I said. "It was your antidote that did the trick. All I did was deliver it."

I introduced Varney and Shamika, once again saying that she was Papa Chatha's niece. And then a sudden thought struck me. "Have any of you have seen Darius lately?"

"Funny you should ask," Arvel said in his wet, bubbling voice. "We were just wondering the same thing."

"Indeed," Victor Baron said in his mellow tenor. "We thought if anyone could shed light on the strange dimensional disturbances the city has experienced of late, it would be the Sideways Man."

Which was what I'd realized. Great minds think alike – even if one of them was transplanted by a mad scientist and the other belonged to a walking dead man.

"But no one's seen any sign of him since you re-turned from the other Nekropolis," Bennie – now a man – said. "You and Devona left abruptly for the Fever House, and in the confusion, I lost track of him. By the way, how is Devona?"

I gave Shamika and Varney a warning glance. "Bet-ter now. Thanks for asking."

My companions gave me looks that said they weren't clear on why I wanted to keep the truth to my-self, but they went along and said nothing. It wasn't that I didn't trust Bennie and his/her tablemates. Well, I trusted Bennie, Baron, and Overkill. I didn't trust Arvel as far as I could hurl his immense bulk, and Acantha would gleefully tear me to shreds with her own hands if she got the chance. I didn't know the Psy-chovore, but I've always found psychic vampires to be manipulative sociopaths, and she was supposed to be the strongest psychic vampire of all. But the real reason I didn't want to tell them the truth was I wanted to avoid drawing Gregor's attention to them. I had no doubt that a number of Gregor's bugs were present in the *House of Dark Delights*, and while it was tempting to ask Bennie for help – not to mention Baron and Overkill – I didn't want to draw bullseyes on their backs. Bad enough Gregor was out to get me, Shamika, and Varney. I didn't want to add any more names to his hit list.

"We were here when the last dimensional fluctua-tion occurred," Acantha said. "It was most dreadful!"

Scream Queen nodded. "We found ourselves sharing space with a group of humans working in tiny areas separated by flimsy partitions. More nightmarish than anything you can find in Nekropolis, if you ask me, darling!"

I couldn't help smiling. "Sounds like the lounge overlapped an office building. What you saw is something humans call a cube farm."

"Whatever it was, I hope to Perdition I never see it again!" Scream Queen said. Her companions agreed and everyone toasted to it.

"Why don't you and your friends sit down and join us?' Bennie – female again – asked. "You look like you can use a rest. Nothing personal. I know your job can be a bit rough on you sometimes."

"Rough?" Acantha said. "He looks like he's been through a rusty meatgrinder!"

"If you drop on by the Foundry later, I'll fix you up," Baron offered.

Before I could acknowledge his offer, Overkill said, "You get caught up in the war between Varvara and Talaith?"

"I'm surprised you're not out there fighting for one side or the other," I said.

She grinned. "No one's made me an offer yet. This girl doesn't fight for free, you know."

"Not even if the cause is right?" I asked.

She laughed. "Righting wrongs is your department. Mine's kicking ass and cashing a fat paycheck for it."

"Do you have any news of the war?" Arvel asked.

He gestured to the Mind's Eye screens around the lounge, all of which were displaying music videos or reruns of razorball games. "Since General Klamm ordered an information blackout, news is harder to come by than a virgin around here."

The frustration in the ghoul's voice was palpable. Arvel owns a restaurant in the Sprawl, the *Krimson Kiss*, but in addition to being a glutton for fresh raw meat and blood, he also has an insatiable appetite for information. I've found him to be a useful source in the past, and I knew the media blackout had to be driving him nuts.

"Sorry," I lied. "I don't know any more than the average citizen."

Arvel scowled. "As if I believe that!" But he didn't press me further.

I wish I could've told him. He'd have been indebted to me then, and I could cash in the favor later. Instead, I turned to Bennie. "I see the war hasn't hurt your business any."

"And why should it?" she said. "The threat of imminent death is one of the greatest aphrodisiacs of all! Other businesses in the Sprawl might be empty right now, but my boys and girls are busier than ever." She took a sip of her drink – some bubbling concoction of her own mad design, I'm sure – then said, "What can I do for you? I know you're not here for pleasure, so it must be for business."

"Just tying up a loose end," I said. "Like you said, Devona and I left in a hurry once we returned from the other Nekropolis. I had some Hyde plague antidote left over, but in the rush I forgot to leave it with you. I know you told me the chemicals can turn volatile over time if they're not stored properly, so I figured I'd better return the extra to you."

I'd thought of the cover story on the way over. In fact, we'd used up all the antidote Bennie had given us. And I'd made up the part about the chemicals becoming unstable. But before Bennie could contradict me, I used the code phrase Skully had given me.

"By your good graces," I added.

Bennie's eyes widened, and a look of surprise crossed his now-male face. But he recovered quickly, took another sip of his bubbling drink, then smoothly rose from the table.

"Please excuse me," Bennie said to his companions. "It won't take more than a few moments to get the chemical stored away properly. After all, we wouldn't want it suddenly exploding and destroying our poor Matthew, would we?"

"Speak for yourself," Acantha muttered.

Bennie came over and escorted us across the lounge, smiling and nodding at people as he went, but not pausing to chat with anyone. As the Madam/Master of the *House of Dark Delights*, Bennie isn't only the host of the endless party that takes place in the establishment, he/she is also the most sought-after sexual companion in the place, and there's never any end of people trying to catch his/her eye. But Bennie is most particular about who he/she spends time with, and the fortunate few who receive his/her favors are in a very exclusive – and satisfied – club. However, Bennie took no time to flirt now, and we made it across the lounge within a few moments.

By then she was a woman again, and she led us down a hallway to a plain wooden door.

"Are we going to get to see someone else having sex?" Shamika said eagerly.

Bennie looked at me and cocked a curious eyebrow. I sighed.

"We came in through an… alternative entrance and accidentally ran into Richard Deux at work," I explained.

"You know about the Underwalk too?" Bennie said. "I have to say I'm impressed, Matt. I knew you were a good detective, but I didn't know you were aware of *that* particular secret. Or this one."

She opened the door and gestured for us to precede her. We entered and found ourselves standing in… the laundry room.

Several dozen washers and dryers were hard at work, and the noise was quite loud. Four of Bennie's staff were present, tossing dirty linen into washers, or removing clean sheets from dryers and folding them.

"As you might imagine, we go through a lot of bed linen around here," Bennie said. She smiled with more than a hint of lasciviousness. "Not to mention underwear."

"I really didn't need to hear that," I said.

Bennie clapped her hands to get the workers' attention.

"Take a ten-minute break everyone." She paused, then added, "*Now*."

The workers didn't speak. They merely stopped what they were doing, left their laundry lying where it was, and quietly filed out of the room. When the last one had departed, Bennie locked the door, then turned to face us.

"I don't know how you found out, and I don't want you to tell me. The less I know the better. But I must warn you: a code phrase won't be enough to get you in. They'll decide whether to admit you or not. And if they decide against it... well, let me just say that it's been a pleasure knowing you, Matt."

Before any of us could reply, Bennie walked down the row of front-loading dryers until she came to the very last one – which wasn't in use. We followed. She removed a key ring from her pocket, aimed a small re-mote control at the door, and pressed a button. There was a soft click, and the dryer's door swung open. Then she stepped back.

"You crawl through this one at a time. There's an entrance to an elevator on the other side. Once you're all in, the entrance will close. After that, what happens will be up to them. Good luck."

Bennie was in the process of changing into a man when she leaned forward and gave me a quick kiss on the cheek. It felt disturbingly like a goodbye kiss.

He started to go, but before he got far, I asked, "I un-derstand why the Hidden Light would locate its headquarters here. Who'd ever suspect it? But why do you allow it? It doesn't quite seem to fit with the, ah, *tone* of the rest of your establishment."

Bennie turned around and gave me a smile. "As you might recall, my ancestor was obsessed with discovering chemical means to isolate the good and evil natures of human beings. My light and dark sides might express themselves slightly differently than my predecessor, but I have my dichotomies too. As I said, good luck."

Bennie turned and left the room. A second later there was a soft snick as he locked the door.

I gazed at the open dryer door. "It's not exactly through the looking glass, but shall we see what's on the other side?"

"You bet!" Shamika said and started toward the circular opening, but Varney put a hand on her shoulder to stop her.

"I'm not so certain it's a good idea that I accompany you," he said.

Shamika frowned. "Why not? It'll be interesting!"

"Undoubtedly," Varney said wryly. "But the Hidden Light is an organization of humans who represent Earth's major religions. Throughout history, those religions fought against the Darkfolk, driving us out of their towns and villages into the wilderness and doing their best to exterminate us. Such persecution was one of the major reasons we left Earth and founded Nekropolis. But our leaving wasn't enough. The humans followed us to our new home, and continued their persecution of us in the guise of the Hidden Light, harassing us at every opportunity!" His expression

grew dark. "They may paint themselves as representatives of the Light, but the truth is they're nothing more
than terrorists."

I didn't want to argue with him. It's true the Darkfolk left Earth, but they still had means of getting back
and coming and going as they pleased. And while Dis
and the Darklords forbid preying on humans, it still
happened in Nekropolis all too often, and something
had to be done about it. Despite having been resurrected from the dead, I'm not a particularly religious
man, and I might not always agree with the Hidden
Light's tactics, but that didn't mean I was going to write
them off as terrorists. And the religious artifacts Maggie
provided me had helped me and my clients out on
more than one occasion. But I sensed Varney had
something other than philosophical and political objections for not wanting to visit the Hidden Light.

"You're scared, aren't you?" I said gently.

At first I thought he might deny it, but then he
sighed and cast his gaze downward as if ashamed. "Yes.
I'm middle-aged as Bloodborn go, but that means I've
lived many centuries, and I remember life on Earth:
the vampire hunters with their holy symbols always
chasing us, searching for our sleeping places by day-
light, and once they found us, loudly chanting prayers
as they hammered sharpened stakes into our hearts…
" He looked up then. "How do you know they won't
simply kill us the moment they set eyes on us?"

Shamika walked over and took Varney's hand and
smiled. "Don't worry. I'll protect you."

Varney looked into the face of the being who only appeared to be a teenage girl, and he couldn't help but return her smile.

"Very well." He turned to me again. "And I suppose it *is* my duty, after all. Lord Galm charged me with protecting his daughter, and I must do everything in my power to fulfill that charge." He sighed again. "Even if I don't like it."

And then he climbed through the open dryer door and was gone.

"Me next!" Shamika said, and then climbed after him, giggling.

I've done a lot of strange things during my time in Nekropolis, but I have to say that climbing into a dryer that housed a secret entrance to a clandestine religious organization ranks right up there with the strangest. But in I went, and just as Bennie said, there was an opening on the other side. Once through, I was able to stand, and I joined Varney and Shamika in a closed elevator. A panel slid shut over the opening we'd just come through, sealing us in. But the elevator showed no sign of moving.

There was no control panel, so there were no buttons to push, and no intercom to speak into. There was no floor display atop the elevator door to indicate which level the elevator was stopped at or might go to. There was nothing but a door, three walls, a ceiling, a floor, and us.

"Now what?" Varney said.

In response, a woman's voice issued from a hidden speaker somewhere in the elevator.

"Now you have thirty seconds to tell us why we shouldn't flood the elevator with toxic gas and melt the flesh from your bones."

Varney gave me a look as if to say, *I told you so.* Shamika's only reaction was to look around to see if she could determine the speaker's location. I guess when you're part of a group mind, you don't really worry about losing part of your body any more than humans worry about sloughing off a few skin cells.

"My wife has been kidnapped, there's an extremely stupid and unnecessary war going on, and Nekropolis and Earth are in danger of merging permanently," I said. "Basically, a lot of shit is broken and I intend to fix it. So let me in or let me go, but don't waste my time."

For a moment nothing happened, but then with a slight jolt the elevator began to descend. It took a while for us to reach our destination. I half-expected the elevator to play a Muzak version of the "Hallelujah" chorus on our way down, but the ride was quiet. The *House of Dark Delights* has a number of subterranean levels, and I doubted the Hidden Light would have their headquarters located in any of them. Some religions have a more liberal attitude toward sex than others, but not *that* liberal, and I figured the Hidden Light was located on an even deeper level still. Eventually, we got where we were going, the elevator stopped, and a moment later the door slid slowly open.

Bright light flooded the elevator, making it impossible to see, and Maggie – the woman who'd spoken to us in the elevator – shouted, "Keep your hands where we can see them!"

I held up the stump of my right hand. "I've only got the one at the moment."

Varney hissed as the light poured over us and he averted his face and held up his arm to block his eyes. Shamika stared directly into the light, eyes wide open, as if the intense illumination didn't bother her a bit. The light didn't hurt my dead eyes either, but it was annoying not to be able to see our welcoming committee.

Another voice, this one male and slightly nervous, said, "We've got three nonhumans. One Bloodborn, one corporeal revenant, and one unknown. Our scanners can't read her, but whatever she is, she's definitely not human."

"Corporeal revenant?" I said. "Is that what the cool kids are calling zombies these days?"

A third voice, this one male but deeper and rougher, almost animalistic. "A word of warning: we've got you covered with weapons that will destroy any kind of Darkfolk. Make one move without our express instructions, and we'll fire."

I get ornery when people try to tell me what to do. You can imagine how much fun I was for supervisors to deal with back when I was a cop.

"Your nervous friend just admitted you don't know what Shamika is, so how can you be so confident your weapons will have any effect on her?" I asked.

Maggie answered, "We could always start firing and see what happens."

"I retract the question," I said.

Maggie chuckled. "We're going to turn off the illuminaries, but I want you to remain inside the elevator until we tell you, OK?"

"All right," I said, and a second later the light cut out.

My zombie eyes don't need time to recover from exposure to bright light, and I was able to instantly see the three people standing outside the elevator: a middle-aged woman, a thin bespectacled man in his thirties, and a large armored creature who resembled a bipedal armadillo. They were all armed, and the woman and armadillo lowered devices that looked like high-tech guns whose barrels were covered with glass. I assumed those were the illuminaries, the weapons that had blasted us with light, and I wondered how I might be able to get hold of one for myself. There are a lot of Darkfolk who aren't especially fond of light, and a device like that would come in handy in my line of work.

The man held some sort of scanning device in his other hand, while Maggie and the armadillo both held offensive weapons. The armadillo held a small crossbow armed with silver-tipped bolts, while Maggie held a gun that looked to be covered in snakeskin.

"Is that a serpent's tooth?" I asked her. I'd heard of the weapon, but never actually seen one.

She smiled. "Nothing sharper, and the venom the teeth carry is deadly to any form of life, natural or supernatural."

"I'm surprised to see a member of the Hidden Light carrying a weapon so nasty," I said.

She shrugged. "God filled the Omniverse with tools for his servants to use. This is but one of them." Then she smiled. "But I have to admit, this one kicks particular ass."

The devices weren't the only weapons the three had. Maggie wore a golden cross around her neck, as did the man, who also wore a Star of David, an ankh, a yin-yang symbol, a Native American dreamcatcher, a Celtic knot, a triple moon, and several other symbols I didn't recognize. It looked like he believed in being prepared. The armadillo wore nothing – I mean that literally; he was naked. It appeared he was content to rely on his illuminary and crossbow. Then again, since he was obviously Darkfolk of some kind, perhaps wearing holy symbols was too uncomfortable for him.

These three weren't the only ones come to greet us, however. A half-dozen men and women stood behind them, armed with everything from automatic machine guns to gleaming broadswords, and from the grim looks of determination on their faces, they were more than ready and willing to use their weapons if necessary.

Maggie looked us over for a moment more before lowering her serpent's tooth. Then she looked over her shoulder.

"Stand down. I'll take responsibility for these three."

One by one, the men and women lowered their weapons and moved off.

The armadillo kept his crossbow trained on us a moment longer, but in the end he lowered it as well. The man with the scanner continued pointing it at Shamika and fussing with the controls, as if he were determined to wring some kind of reading out of it.

Maggie tucked her serpent's tooth into a leather holster on her belt, then came forward and shook my left hand. She showed no distaste upon touching my undead flesh, and my estimation of her went up a notch. Many people say they don't have a prejudice against zombies, but ask them to touch one, and you'll find out differently. Not Maggie, though.

"So this is what you really look like, I take it."

She was in her sixties and shorter than me, though not by much. Her silver hair was cut short, and she wore jeans and a white T-shirt displaying a cartoon image of Christ holding a razor, his beard covered with white foam, below it the words JESUS SHAVES!

"In the flesh," she said. "No need for disguises here." Maggie turned toward her two companions. "The big guy in the leathery shell is Houston. He's a weremadillo."

"I never would've guessed," I said.

Houston gave me a hard look. "Don't mess with Texas," he growled.

"Duly noted," I said.

"And this trim fellow here is Arthur Van Helsing. He's one of our best researchers."

Arthur wore wire frame glasses that made his eyes look larger than they really were. His unruly brown hair was badly in need of trimming, and from the pallor of his skin, it looked like he could use a few days in a tanning bed. He wore a white lab coat that was marred by several stains and scorch marks. His T-shirt

said VAMPIRES SUCK! Varney's lip curled in a silent
snarl when he saw it, but the Bloodborn said nothing.

"I take it you've decided not to destroy us," I said.

"For the moment," Maggie said. "Come on in, and try
not to look around too much. This *is* supposed to be a
secret headquarters, you know." She turned and walked
away. Arthur followed her, casting backward glances at
Shamika as if he was still trying to figure out what she
was. Houston waited for us to follow, the big lyke clearly
intending to bring up the rear and keep an eye on us. I
was certain his crossbow bolts weren't merely silver-
tipped; they were probably dipped in all kinds of nasty
poisons and blessed seven ways to Sunday. They'd prove
deadly to Varney, probably to me, and maybe even to
Shamika – or at least this particular component of the
Watchers' group mind calling itself Shamika. It was a
strong incentive to remain on our best behavior.

The Hidden Light's HQ was located in a hollowed-
out cavern, fluorescent lights hanging from the ceiling
and power cables stretching along the floor near the
walls. Workstations were set up throughout the cavern, and while some contained books, scrolls, and
parchments, just as many held high-tech computers
and shimmering holo displays. Most of the men and
women at the workstations were human, but there
was a fair number of Darkfolk scattered among them.
Maggie must've noticed me looking at them, for she
said, "Just because someone's a monster doesn't mean
they don't have spiritual needs." She paused, then
added, "Sometimes they need the Light even more."

"Traitors," Varney muttered.

Arthur turned around to look at him as if he intended to comment, but when Varney saw the holy objects around the man's neck, he hissed and averted his gaze.

"Sorry about that," Arthur said, sounding embarrassed. Arthur tucked the scanner he'd been holding into a pocket of his lab coat, rummaged around in there, then brought out a pair of dark glasses which he held out to Varney. "Put these on. They won't take away the pain entirely, but they should make it bearable."

Varney hesitated, but he took the glasses from Arthur and donned them. He looked at Arthur, then at Maggie, then back to Arthur.

"It *is* better," Varney said. "Thank you." He sounded as if it took some effort for him to express his gratitude, and Arthur seemed equally uncomfortable accepting it.

"You're, ah, welcome. We call them diffusers. They're made from solidified shadow caught in a highly focused time-dilation field." He became more enthusiastic as he went on. "We have more call for them than you might think. We actually have Bloodborn in our organization, some of them quite high up in your people's hierarchy, and–"

Maggie cut in. "The less we tell them the better, Arthur."

He looked chastened. "You're right, of course. Sorry."

The men and women around us represented a number of different ethnicities and religions, and while many were dressed in normal street clothes, more than a few wore clothing that indicated their religious tradition. I saw Catholic priests and nuns, Moslem clerics, Hasidic Jews, Buddhist monks, Shinto monks, and Hindu swamis. They worked side by side in apparent harmony, without any obvious conflict due to their different backgrounds and philosophies.

Well, *harmony* might be overstating the case. Right then the men and women of the Hidden Light were more than a bit agitated, moving quickly from one workstation to another, consulting with each other in front of computer monitors and holo displays, or talking loudly into voxes and microphone headsets. The atmosphere reminded me of Varvara's war room, and I assumed it was for the same reasons.

"I assume it's not always this lively down here," I said to Maggie.

She said, "Hardly. Right now, we have a Situation with a capital S to deal with – as you well know."

"You mean the war?" Shamika asked.

Maggie laughed. "Goodness, no, child! What do we care if the Darkfolk want to go around slaughtering each other? More than usual, that is. Nekropolis is their city, and if they want to war with each other, that's their business, regrettable though it may be."

"That attitude seems a little more 'eye for an eye' than 'turn the other cheek,'" I said.

Maggie led us through the maze of workstations and people, and stopped before a rectangular glass structure that resembled a coffin – probably because sealed inside was the perfectly preserved body of a man wearing brown robes, a rope belt, and sandals. His hair was cut in a tonsure, making him look like a slimmed-down version of Robin Hood's Friar Tuck.

Maggie turned to look at me. "The Hidden Light has a clearly defined mission, Matthew, and keeping peace between the Darklords isn't part of it."

"What *is* your purpose?" Varney said. "Besides harassing us Darkfolk, that is."

Houston prodded Varney in the back with his crossbow. "Watch it, Fangboy! No one speaks to Sister Holstrom like that! If you knew who she *really* was…"

Maggie shut the weremadillo up with a stern glare. "All they need to know is that I speak for the Hidden Light. That's enough."

Houston lowered his gaze. "I'm sorry, Sister."

Maggie accepted his apology with a nod and then gestured to the monk under glass. "This is Saint Bartelmeu the Recondite. He's been deceased for a millennium, but like you, Matthew, he doesn't let a little thing like death slow him down."

As soon as Varney heard the word *Saint*, he stepped back from the glass coffin. The diffusers might help him gaze upon holy objects, but it seemed there was only so much they could do when it came to an honest-to-God saint.

Tendrils of ectoplasm curled up from the coffin to coalesce into a ghostly image of the monk hovering in the air. The ghost was typical of its kind, looking as if it were formed of shaped white mist, and when it was complete, Bartelmeu opened his eyes and smiled at us.

"Visitors?" he said in a cheery voice. "I *love* visitors! Who are they, Joan?"

Maggie sighed. "I go by Magdalene these days, Bartelmeu. Remember?"

The monk made a dismissive gesture. "Yes, yes. A rose by any other name. Now tell me who these fine people are."

Maggie introduced the three of us, and Bartelmeu grinned at each of us in turn, not seeming put off in the slightest by the fact we weren't human.

"It's a pleasure to meet you all!" he said. "Nothing against my fellow champions of the Light, but it gets somewhat dull having the same people to talk to day in, day out." He lowered his voice. "And just between you and me, our people can be a bit on the stuffy side."

Arthur seemed a bit offended by this last comment, but Maggie took it in her stride.

"Bartelmeu is better than a dozen computers," she said. "Not only is his knowledge encyclopedic and his recall perfect, his clairvoyant and precognitive abilities are legendary."

Bartelmeu grinned. "If my cheeks weren't formed of ectoplasm, they'd be blushing right now."

Arthur picked up the conversation's thread then. "It was Bartlemeu that first informed us of what was happening – and who told us you three would be arriving soon."

Bartelmeu looked startled. "You mean *these* three are *those* three? Why didn't you tell me?" He turned to us and grinned even wider than he had before. "It's even more of a pleasure to meet you then!"

I looked at Maggie. "Perfect recall?"

She shrugged. "Cut him some slack. He *is* over a thousand years old, you know."

I looked at the ghostly saint and felt a surge of hope. "So you know what's going on? You can tell me where my wife is?" I wasn't really sure when I'd begun thinking of Devona as my wife, but I was aware I'd been doing it for a while now. It didn't matter that we weren't officially married. We were married in our hearts, and that was what counted the most.

Bartelmeu looked a bit chagrined. "Not as such, no."

Maggie explained. "It's not that he doesn't know. He has to be careful of how much he tells us."

"He has to avoid temporal paradox," Arthur said. "By giving us information about the future, he risks changing that future, thereby rendering the information he gives us useless."

"And perhaps making things even worse in the process," Maggie added.

Despite his lack of physical lungs, Bartelmeu sighed. "It's true. Sometimes I think God has a warped sense of humor."

I struggled to contain the frustration I felt. This man – well, this *ghost* – knew everything I needed to know in order to stop Gregor and save Devona. Only he couldn't tell me.

As if reading my mind, and perhaps he did, Bartelmeu hurriedly added, "But that doesn't mean I can't help!

You came here to obtain weapons that will help you get through Varvara's army and reach Demon's Roost. That was your own idea, and I won't be interfering with the natural course of events by telling you that we plan to supply you with such weapons."

"You'll have to go on your own, though," Maggie said. "Just the three of you, the way you'd planned to before coming here."

Arthur gave us an excited smile. "Since we knew you were coming, I had time to prepare some real good ones for you!" As quickly as it had come, his smile faded. "I just wish I could go along and watch you use them. One of the problems with being a techie is that I hardly ever get out into the field."

Maggie gave him a consolatory pat on the back. "Maybe next time."

Behind his diffusers, Varney frowned. "But *why* will you loan us weapons? Why help us at all, for that matter? You said you don't care about the war."

"Because helping you supports our mission," Maggie said. "Bartelmeu has confirmed that someone is attempting to move Nekropolis to Earth. Not just part of it, not just a single Dominion, but the entire city. The Hidden Light has been around in one form or another since the Darkfolk first appeared, trying to protect humanity from being preyed on by the monsters that dwelled in the dark. As you might imagine, we were quite happy to see the Darkfolk leave Earth for Nekropolis. In fact, you might say that we helped you move. As powerful as Dis and the Darklords are, opening a portal to another dimension, building a city there, and transporting an entire race of people to live in it was a task they couldn't quite accomplish on their own. They needed our aid, and we were glad to provide it. But once they settled in Nekropolis, not every member of the Darkfolk was thrilled to be cut off from the pleasures Earth had to offer, and some attempted to return. The Darklords tried to stop them, but some got through."

"And that's where we came in," Arthur said. "We set up shop here in Nekropolis to make sure the Darkfolk *stay* here. We don't want to hurt you, especially, but we want to make certain that you never return to Earth and begin preying on humanity again."

"We intend to stop whoever and whatever is attempting to transport Nekropolis to Earth," Maggie said. She glanced at Bartelmeu. "And according to our resident psychic saint, arming you three is our best shot at doing so."

Bartelmeu smiled. "And I predict a solid fifty-fifty chance of success! You can't ask for better odds than that!" He frowned. "Well, I suppose you could, but you're not going to get them."

"So either we'll win or we won't." I sighed. "How comforting."

You know something? Sometimes I really hate my job.

SEVENTEEN

Arthur was giving Varney and Shamika some last-minute instructions on how their weapons worked, and since he'd already checked me out on mine, I pulled Maggie aside to talk with her.

"Thanks for the assist," I told her. "We'll try to bring your toys back unbroken if we can."

She smiled. "Don't make promises you can't keep. Besides, it'll be worth the loss of our equipment if you manage to prevent Nekropolis from being transported to Earth."

"Bartelmeu called you Joan at one point," I said. "If you're who I think you are, you're looking awfully good for a woman who died over five hundred years ago."

"This is Nekropolis, Matt. You above all people should know that death doesn't mean the same thing here as it does on Earth." Her smile edged toward a grin. "Besides, haven't you ever heard of the eternal flame?"

She raised an index finger and fire suddenly wreathed the flesh. She then lifted the finger to her mouth and, with a wink, blew out the flames.

When we were ready to say our goodbyes, Saint Bartelmeu's ghostly form began to fade.

"Good luck to you all," he said. "And Matt, no matter what happens, don't despair. Devona will give you a hand if she's able."

I didn't know what he meant exactly, but his cryptic words implied that Devona was still alive, and I found that immensely reassuring.

Then Bartelmeu was gone, and Maggie, Arthur, and Houston the weremadillo walked us back to the elevator.

"Aren't you going to try to wipe our memories or something?" I asked Maggie. "You've worked so hard to keep the location of your headquarters secret, I'm surprised you're simply going to let us walk out of here."

"We don't get many visitors," Maggie said, "but we have chemical means of removing all memory of their stay with us, thanks to our benefactor upstairs."

"You mean Bennie-factor," I said, and Maggie smiled.

"Indeed. But we can't afford to tinker with your memories, not if we want you to recall how to properly use the weapons we provided you. We'll just have to trust you not to reveal our location to anyone. And if you're ever tempted... Do you remember the verse in the Bible about how God notes the fall of every sparrow?"

"It sounds familiar," I said.

Maggie gave us an intense look. "Well, He's not the only one with His eye on you. Don't forget that."

• • • •

We took the Underwalk to a club only a couple blocks from Demon's Roost. I would've liked to have gotten closer if we could, but this was the closest exit to Varvara's stronghold, and it was the best we could do.

As we walked up the ladder and entered through a trapdoor in the club's storeroom, Shamika said, "I know the situation is serious, and you're worried about Devona, Matt – and please don't take this the wrong way – but it's nice to actually be taking part in events instead of just watching them happen around me. I spent so many years hiding in the shadows, just observing, never taking part... Whatever happens, however this turns out, at least I *did* something for once, you know?"

I tried to imagine what it must've been like for Shamika, spending centuries being a fly on the wall, always watching, always alone. What did it say about such an existence that she found being in the middle of a war preferable? I guess it said everything.

The club was deserted and when we went outside, we saw the street was empty as well – no traffic, no pedestrians. Given how insanely busy the Sprawl is twenty-four hours a day, I found the lack of activity and the silence that came with it profoundly eerie.

We walked into the street and headed in the direction of Demon's Roost, Varney on my right, Shamika on my left. We'd emerged from the Underwalk within the cordoned-off area around Demon's Roost, but it seemed the Demonkin soldiers had all drawn closer to their queen's fortress, perhaps in anticipation of

Talaith's next attack. Whatever the reason, we didn't encounter any resistance until we were within sight of Demon's Roost.

A squad of demons sat in the middle of the street, smoking, drinking, drugging, gambling, and generally showing a complete lack of military discipline. Hey, no commanders were around to chastise them, and they *were* demons.

The first to notice us was a she-demon with a cat's head, and a giant python for a tail.

She spoke in a slightly slurred voice. "Hey guys, either the hallucinogens I took just kicked in, or someone's gotten through our perimeter."

The other demons turned to look at us, and while a few grinned in anticipation of the fun they were going to have slaughtering us, several noted how we were armed with looks of confusion and mounting concern.

A heavily muscled blue-skinned demon, whose facial features were embedded in his chest, stood up and shouldered what looked like a bazooka made out of a half-dozen spinal columns.

"Time for some target practice!" he said in a booming voice.

The rest of the squad rose to their feet and readied their weapons, but not all of them did so with equal enthusiasm. I assumed the hesitant ones sensed the power in the objects we carried, but weren't yet quite sure what to make of them, or us.

"Stay close to me," I whispered to Varney and Shamika, and they both nodded. Then pitching my voice louder so the demons could hear, I said, "One warning: run now and you get to live!"

The face-chest demon laughed. "Some threat, zombie! You look like you're about to fall apart any second. We won't even have to waste any ammo on you. All one of us will have to do is walk up and tap you on the shoulder, and you'll collapse like a house of cards!"

Several of his fellow soldiers laughed, though some did so uncomfortably. The closer Varney, Shamika, and I got, the more they could sense the power we carried with us, and the more worried they became. I couldn't blame Face-Chest for laughing at me, though. By this point, it took all the concentration I had to keep my component pieces together, and I moved like a drunken puppet suffering from constant seizures. Hardly the most intimidating sight.

Face-Chest went on. "Still, I think shooting you will be more fun." He pulled the trigger on his weapon, there was a loud *ka-chunk* as it fired, and a screaming severed demon head shot forth from its barrel and came flying through the air toward me, fangs gnashing in anticipation of taking a big bite out of me when it hit.

I didn't do anything to protect myself. I just kept walking. If what Arthur had told me was correct, my coat would take care of the rest.

The coat I wore was long-sleeved and stretched down past my knees, almost making it look like a robe. It was striped with different colors, but which colors precisely was hard to say, for the longer you looked at them, the more they seemed to change. I recalled what Arthur had told me.

The Coat of Every Color is just what its name implies. Every color of every spectrum of Light is represented – and not just the basic Roy G. Biv colors that everyone knows about. The Shades of Reverse Enlightenment, the Hues of Spiritual Transmigration, the Seventeen Ur-colors of the First Moment After Creation… they're all here.

As the shrieking demon head drew near, light exploded forth from my coat, and when it vanished, the head was gone.

I turned to look at Varney. "You OK?"

The vampire was encased in a black hazmat suit made from pure curseweave, a fabric so evil that it was supposed to be proof against the power of any holy object. I couldn't see Varney's face behind the black glass of the suit's faceplate, but his muffled voice came through clearly enough.

"That stung more than a little, but I'm all right."

I turned to Shamika and saw she was smiling.

"That tickled!" she said.

The light hadn't exactly tickled the demons, however. Despite the fact they were still a dozen yards away from us, most of them had suffered flash burns, and several appeared to have been blinded. Half cried out in fear and despair, dropped their weapons, and fled. The rest – including Face-Chest – remained behind, looking grimly determined, if more than a little afraid.

I'd used holy objects against Darkfolk before, but I'd never given much thought as to where the source of their power came from. I know that primitive forms of the Darkfolk evolved before humans, and that the more sophisticated forms they eventually took were influenced by humanity's fears and imagination. I'd always assumed that religious objects were effective against certain types of Darkfolk because humanity imagined them that way. But there was no denying that the Coat of Every Color had power all its own, but as to what exactly the ultimate source of that power was, I couldn't tell you. But I was damn thankful to be wearing it.

"I don't know what the hell that was," Python-Tail said, "but do you really think one magic coat is going to be enough to get you past us?"

"It might be," I said. "But luckily for us, we've got more. Shamika, Varney, why don't you show them?"

Varney fired first. He carried a wooden tube and he aimed it at the demons and pressed a hidden switch. A trio of soft pops sounded as tiny rolls of paper shot out of the tube and sailed toward the squad of demons. The paper rolls expanded in size as they drew closer to the demons and unfurled, revealing characters written in Japanese kanji. The paper grew large enough to wrap around demons like blankets, and when they did so, the demons caught in their embrace screamed in agony. The papers were *osame-fuda*, Buddhist prayer slips, and when they touched demon flesh, they burst into flame, rapidly burning themselves – and the demons caught in their grip – to ash.

Shamika carried a pair of sterling silver hand bells, and she rang them with vigorous enthusiasm. The pure

tones of the Herald Bells rang through the air with
crystal clarity, each note containing more beauty than
a dozen symphonies, and as they rang Shamika
chanted a phrase she'd heard Arthur say.

"'Every time a bell rings an angel gets its wings!'"

Demons screamed and clapped their hands to their
ears to shut out the sound, but the music was as much
of the spirit as physical sound, and their efforts were
futile. Blood streamed from their ears and eyes, and
some fled, hands still held fast to their ears. Of those
who didn't flee, more than a few had their heads explode in bursts of blood, bone, and brain matter.

Of the original squad, only five demons remained,
Face-Chest and Python-Tail among them. All of them
were bleeding from their eyes and ears, but they
were tough enough to withstand the power of the
Herald Bells, though the effort had obviously taken
a lot out of them. They began firing their weapons,
and automatic gunfire strafed us along with high-
tech energy beams and mystic power blasts. But the
Coat of Every Color blazed with Light in response to
the demons' attack, neutralizing everything they
threw at us. After several moments, they realized
their efforts were useless and they stopped firing, and
the coat stopped shining.

"I gave you the chance to run," I told them, and I
swung the weapon Arthur had given to me. It looked
like a Native American dreamcatcher attached to a handle, and I swung it back and forth through the air as if
it were a small handheld net. But this wasn't for *catching*

dreams. It was a Dream*thrower*, a device that disgorged the nightmares that a dreamcatcher collected.

Every time I swung the Dreamthrower, a tiny shadow-creature leaped forth from the device and began growing as it landed on the ground and ran swiftly toward the remaining demons. The Nightmares swelled in size as they went, becoming large as elephants, all ebon teeth and claws, and though the last few demons finally had the good sense to turn and attempt to flee, it was too late. The Nightmares fell upon them and within seconds tore them apart. When there were no more demons to kill, the Nightmares simply faded as if they'd never existed.

Shamika, Varney, and I stood alone in the street, completely unharmed by our encounter with the demons.

"I'd call that a successful field test," I said. "Now that we've had a chance to practice with our new toys, I think it's time to pay General Klamm-slash-Gregor a visit."

We continued toward Demon's Roost, mowing down every demon that didn't have enough sense to get the hell out of our way.

Reaching Varvara's penthouse turned out to be easier than I thought. Because demons are so self-centered, once they realize they can't win a fight, they immediately focus on doing whatever is necessary to save their asses, and to blazes with whatever cause they were fighting for. Word must've spread quickly among the Demonkin's ranks, because by the time we were actually inside Demon's Roost, few of Varvara's people remained to give us any trouble. I'd been keeping an eye out for Scorch the whole time – I wanted to make sure we didn't accidentally hurt her on our way to Varvara's stronghold – but I saw no sign of the demoness. Either she was stationed elsewhere in the Sprawl or she'd taken off when she heard we were coming. I was glad. Scorch is tough, but I knew she couldn't stand against the holy weapons the Hidden Light had loaned us.

The elevator to Varvara's penthouse was unguarded, and while I wasn't thrilled at the idea of taking it, I was even less thrilled at the prospect of walking up a dozen flights of stairs.

"Are you sure it's safe?" Varney said through his hazmat hood.

Before I could answer, Shamika said, "It is. Gregor has eyes everywhere. He's known we were coming since we engaged that first squad of demons. If he didn't want us to use the elevator, he'd have disabled it."

"Maybe he booby-trapped it," Varney pointed out. "Wouldn't Gregor love it if we fought all this way to reach Demon's Roost only to get crushed in a falling elevator?"

Shamika shook her head. "I know how my brother thinks. He'll want to see me, if for no other reason than to tell me that he's right and I'm wrong." She looked at me. "And he'll want to have words with you too, Matt."

I said, "That's good, because I have a few things to say to him myself."

I pressed the elevator's up button.

No Muzak played as we ascended, which was just as well. I hate Muzak.

Varvara's penthouse-cum-war-room was empty, with the exception of the Demon Queen herself and General Klamm. The computer stations around the room were vacant and their monitors were black. The holo table in the middle of the room was still active, though, and it currently displayed an image of Demon's Roost. Klamm stood at the table, Varvara beside him.

Klamm smiled when he saw us.

"Welcome! You made it just in time for the closing act in our little drama. Matthew, Varney…" He gave both of us nods of greeting before turning his attention to Shamika. "*Sister*," he said, his false bonhomie giving way to derision. "Ready to see the error of your ways?"

I examined Varvara more closely. Her expression was blank, and she stared off into space as if she wasn't aware of our presence.

"Let me guess," I said. "Once Varvara was weakened by using her power to create a new force field over the Grotesquerie, you were able to implant one of your bugs inside her and control her."

Klamm – Gregor – smiled. "That was my real reason for releasing the creatures and disabling the Grotesquerie's force-field generators. Of course, if you'd gotten squashed in the process, I wouldn't have cried about it. But I suppose you can't have everything, can you? Taking control of Varvara was the main thing. As General Klamm, I could only do so much to manipulate her – and through her, her demons – but once she was under my complete control, all the Demonkin were under my power. It made things so much easier."

"I'm surprised you were able to gain her trust with your General Klamm persona," I said. "Varvara knows all of her people. She must've been quite puzzled when a new demon suddenly appeared in town."

"Which was why I killed the real Klamm and assumed his form," Gregor said. "He was a mid-level functionary in Varvara's service, but once I 'became' him, I was able to use my abilities to refashion Klamm as a highly effective intelligence-gatherer. After that, it was just a matter of time until I made myself invaluable to Varvara, and when Talaith attacked, I stepped forward to help and she made me her second in command." He turned to Varvara and smiled. "The fool. She allows her passions to rule her far more than any Other I've ever met. Manipulating her was far easier than I'd ever imagined."

Seeing Varvara like this, I knew my original plan wasn't going to work. I'd hoped that if we could reach her, we could tell her the truth about who and what Klamm really was, and she'd deal with him. Now it looked like we were on our own. We were well armed, thanks to Maggie Holstrom, but as Gregor wasn't actually a demon, I wasn't certain any of our holy weapons would work against him. And even if they did, this one body wasn't really Gregor – not all of him, at any rate. It was just one manifestation of a much larger consciousness. Besides, I didn't want to kill him just yet. He had information I needed.

"Where's Devona?" I demanded. "If you've harmed her…"

"You'll what?" Gregor said. "Continue talking at me in a threatening tone of voice?" He smirked. "No need to fear, Matthew. Your paramour is fine. She's with me elsewhere, helping me complete my ultimate objective."

"Along with the magic-users you abducted," I said.

Gregor nodded. "And Darius. It's not as if you haven't worked that much out for yourself. But do you know what I'm doing?"

"You've set up a war to distract the Darklords from your real plan, which is transporting Nekropolis to Earth," I said. "But why? I thought you wanted to destroy the Darkfolk, not relocate them."

"I think I understand," Shamika said. "Gregor's real motive is to be alone once again. He doesn't really care how that happens. Sure, it would be better if the Darkfolk were all dead. Then he would be assured of being alone. But there are so many of them, and as a group they're too powerful to easily destroy. But if he can return them all to Earth–"

"The hated Others would be gone, and life could return to the way it was before they came here," Gregor said. "You remember what it was like, sister. We were One then. It was so peaceful, so… perfect."

"Maybe so," Shamika admitted. "But it was boring, too. I didn't know how boring until the Darkfolk arrived."

Gregor's face clouded over. "We didn't invite them to come here, and they didn't ask our permission to build a city in our world! They were nothing more than invaders!"

As much as I hated to admit it, I could see Gregor's point. The Darkfolk – whether through ignorance or because they just didn't care enough to check – had chosen a new home that was already inhabited. And while I couldn't blame him for being less than pleased with the situation, I couldn't condone how he was going about trying to remedy it.

"Has it never occurred to you that maybe you should try to accept the way things are, whether you like it or not, and attempt to make peace with the Darkfolk?" I asked.

Gregor answered as if he were explaining a simple fact to a particularly slow child. "Otherness is an aberration, Matthew. An infection. The only way to deal with it effectively is to cast it out – which is precisely what I intend to do."

Varney had been silent up to this point, but now he removed the hood of his curseweave protective suit. He said nothing, but his cyber-eye glowed red and a thin beam of energy lanced out and bored through Gregor's head, right between the eyes. Gregor just stood there, smiling, and when Varney's beam winked out, the blackened hole in Gregor's flesh quickly repaired itself.

Varney shrugged. "I didn't think it would work, but it was worth a try."

"Nice shooting anyway," I said.

Varney looked at Gregor. "Seeing as how you didn't have the good grace to die when I zapped you, tell me this: even if you succeed in transporting Nekropolis to

Earth, what makes you think the Darkfolk won't simply return? And when they come back, your existence will no longer be a secret. All the Darkfolk will be aware of you, and they'll all be prepared to fight you. You may be powerful, and you may be able to destroy many of us, but you can never kill all of us."

"All true," Gregor conceded. "Which is why I intend to transport Nekropolis to an Earth city. I'm not sure what the ultimate effect will be. It's possible Nekropolis and the Earth city will merge into an entirely new metropolis. It's equally possible the two won't be able to coexist in the same dimensional space, resulting in a truly spectacular explosion. Either way, the Darkfolk will become known to humanity, and once the humans realize the monsters from their legends and folklore truly exist, they will hunt you down and slaughter you with a ruthlessness that I couldn't hope to match. And these aren't the same humans the Darkfolk left behind four hundred years ago. They've had centuries to develop new ways of killing, far more deadly and efficient than simple wooden stakes and silver bullets. They may create a genetically engineered virus that targets only Darkfolk. They may find a way to 'cure' you and make you just like them. Or they may simply use nuclear weapons to reduce you to radioactive dust. Whatever they choose, there are far more of them than there are of you, and in many ways they're worse monsters than you could ever hope to be." Gregor's mouth stretched into a slow, satisfied smile. "The Darkfolk won't have a chance."

I'd lived on Earth most of my life, and I feared Gregor was right – which made it even more vital that we stop him.

I started to speak, but I once again experienced the strange sensation of my missing right hand moving. But this time it was accompanied by a strange feeling of pressure, as if my hand were being gripped tight and something sharp pressed into my palm. I did my best to ignore it. When you've got a bad guy speechifying about his ultimate plan, the best thing to do is keep him talking as long as possible. If nothing else, it buys you time to think of ways to kick his ass and maybe, if you're lucky, save your own skin in the process.

"You're bluffing," I said. "If you could transport Nekropolis to Earth, you'd have done it by now. You've already tried a couple times and failed."

"Those weren't serious attempts at transport," Gregor said. "They were calibration runs to help me set the dimensional coordinates and determine the final power levels needed. Everything is now ready. Darius is the key to opening the dimensional gateway, and the magic-users will power the device that allows me to direct his abilities. Only one thing remains: I need to gather the raw energy to initiate Nekropolis' transport."

"And where do you intend to find it?" I asked.

Gregor gestured at the holo image of Demon's Roost on the table before him. Four red dots appeared in the air above the image, followed by several dozen smaller ones.

Gregor looked at me and grinned. "It's true the war

made a useful distraction as I went about my work, but it wasn't *only* a distraction."

Thin beams of light emerged from the four larger red dots and streaked down toward the holographic version of Demon's Roost.

"Get down!" I shouted. I threw myself to the floor, grabbing hold of Shamika's arm on the way and pulling her with me. Varney joined us just as a huge explosion rocked the penthouse. For several moments all I knew was light and noise, and it felt as if the building was shaking itself apart beneath me. But then the rumbling died away and the smoke began to clear, and I became cautiously optimistic that I hadn't been blasted into several trillion atoms.

I opened my eyes. Shamika lay next to me, covered with a fine layer of dust.

I shook her gently. "Are you OK?"

She opened her eyes. "I think so." Then she smiled. "That was exciting! Do you think it'll happen again? Do you think it'll be even louder next time?"

"Let's hope not." I stood and helped Shamika to her feet. I turned to check on Varney. The vampire appeared unscathed, and he rose to his feet easily. Gregor and Varvara seemed unharmed as well, and both continued standing by the holo-display table. Gregor was looking up into the sky – for the penthouse no longer had a roof – and he was grinning from ear to ear.

Hovering above us were the three Weyward Sisters, along with several dozen Arcane men and woman riding various flying devices – brooms and flying carpets being particular favorites. But in front of all them, standing in mid-air as if on solid ground, was Talaith. Unlike Varvara, she hadn't donned a faux military uniform. The queen of the Arcane wore her usually austere Puritan dress, but she was wreathed in crackling mystic energy, and power rolled off her in almost seismic waves. Behind her the sky was filled with black clouds and lightning lanced forth from them as she spoke, her voice echoing like thunder.

"Varvara! For the transgressions you have committed against me and my people, I demand that you surrender your Dominion to me at once! If you refuse, I will destroy you and burn your stronghold to the ground! And afterward I shall begin the systematic slaughter of all the Demonkin! When I am through, not a single stinking demon will be left in this city, and I will see your name purged from the history of the Darkfolk! It will be as if you never existed, hell-bitch! So what is it to be? Dishonor or death? Choose swiftly, or I shall choose for you!"

Gregor didn't take his eyes off Talaith, but he whispered something to Varvara out of the side of his mouth. The Demon Queen had shown not so much as the slightest reaction to the destruction of her penthouse, no reaction to anything. Under Gregor's control she'd been more of a zombie than I'd ever been. But now she smiled serenely.

"Go suck a wand, you spell-slinging cunt."

I didn't think it was possible for Talaith to look any angrier than she already did, but somehow she managed.

She let out an inarticulate cry of rage and stabbed a hand toward Varvara. A torrent of energy streamed forth from the Witch Queen's fingers like water released from a high-pressure hose, but Varvara made no move to defend herself. I started forward, hoping the Coat of Every Color might be able to repel Talaith's mystic blast, but knowing that even if it could, I'd never be able to reach Varvara in time. But as it turned out, I didn't have to.

Gregor swiftly removed a metal device from his uniform pocket. It looked something like a miniature lightning rod, and he held it out in front of Varvara. The rod absorbed every bit of Talaith's blast, and when it was finished, Varvara continued to stand there, blank-faced but unharmed.

Talaith looked more puzzled than upset.

"What was that?" she asked softly, almost as if speaking to herself.

"A little something I stole from Victor Baron when he wasn't looking," Gregor said. "Now, if you'll all excuse me for a moment, I need to transfer this." He pointed the rod skyward and then released the energy the device had collected. It streaked off into the sky, missing all the hovering Arcane and disappearing off into the darkness.

Gregor smiled and let out a satisfied sigh. "That turned out to be easier than I thought." He looked at me then. "Well, Matthew, this is farewell. I have work to do, and I no longer need this particular body. I hope you enjoy your trip back to Earth." Then he turned to Shamika. "Why don't you go with them, sister? There's no place for you here anymore."

Then without another word, he dropped the lightning rod and his General Klamm body broke apart into dozens of black insects which skittered away in all directions.

Talaith and her Arcane soldiers gazed down at us with perplexed expressions, unsure what had just happened and what, if anything, they should do about it. I took the opportunity to go to Varvara. I'd hoped that Gregor's leave-taking would free her from his control, but she continued staring off into space, oblivious of what was happening.

I grabbed her shoulder with my left hand and shook her hard.

"Snap out of it, Varvara!" I yelled. "Things are not looking good, and I could really use a Darklord's help right now!"

A voice whispered in my mind then, one that felt almost like Devona's.

Will I do?

A flock of black bats flew in through the open roof, swirled together, and coalesced into the form of...

"Lord Galm!" I said.

The Vampire King bowed.

"At your service," he said.

I looked at Varney, and he smiled.

"I thought we might need some backup, so I sent a message to Lord Galm when we were on our way to Demon's Roost. My cybernetics are good for more than just shooting film, you know. I can send e-mails, text messages, you name it."

I turned to Galm, more than a little surprised at how relieved I was to see the Vampire King. "Varvara's mind is being controlled. Can you free her?"

Galm walked briskly over to Varvara and touched his ivory-white fingers to her forehead. Then he turned back to us. "Her own mind is working to throw off the mental shackles that constrain it. If I use my powers to hasten the process, I risk damaging her psyche. She should be free of her own accord soon enough."

I pointed toward Talaith. "Maybe not soon enough to deal with *her*."

The Witch Queen had managed to shake off her confusion, and now glared down at us.

"So you're in this with her, are you, Galm? Our two Dominions have been at peace for years, but I suppose you got tired of being a good neighbor, eh? No matter. I claim this Dominion by right of conquest, and you stand in my way at your peril!"

Galm bared his fangs at Talaith, and I could feel the psychic pressure as his power began to build in response to her threat.

"Choose your words carefully, witch! I do not claim to fully understand what is going on here, but it's clear there's more to this affair than meets the eye." He gestured to Varney. "This man is my servant, and from what he has told me, this war is nothing but a ruse. Both you and Varvara have been tricked. Call off your people and come down here so we can talk and sort this mess out before things get any worse."

Talaith looked uncertain, and for a moment I thought she might do as Galm suggested. But then a sly expression came over her face.

"What does it matter to me how and why this war began? All that's important is how it ends. And I intend for it to end with my being the ruler of two dominions! So step aside, Galm, while I finish off Varvara and claim what is rightfully mine!"

"I can't do that, Talaith." Galm's icy calm was a terrible thing to behold. "We Darklords have one Dominion apiece. That's the agreement we made when we founded Nekropolis, and that's how it's going to stay."

Talaith sneered. "And who's going to stop me? You? You're powerful enough, I admit, but you're alone, while I have several dozen of my strongest people with me." She gestured at the Arcane assembled behind her. "You cannot possibly hope to stand against us all!"

Galm's smile was cold as ice. "Who said I was alone?"

Shadows gathered on the walls of the penthouse, and out of them stepped a host of Bloodborn, some of the most powerful vampires in the city: Waldemar the Librarian, Orlock the Collector, the Scarlet Orchid, Baron Lamprey, the Exsanguinator Supreme, Countess Carpathia, Incizor, the Dalai Lamia and more. Dread and terrible beings all, they gazed upward at Talaith and her soldiers with cold dead eyes and smiles like Death itself.

Varney looked insufferably pleased with himself. "I told Galm it might not be a bad idea to bring along some backup."

"Good thinking," I said.

Galm gave no command, but the Bloodborn hissed a battle cry and leaped skyward, their bodies melting into shadowy forms as they streaked toward the hovering Arcane. Witches and warlocks began loosing bolts of magic energy, but the vampires dodged them easily, and the fight was well and truly on.

Galm turned to us.

"I'll have to confront Talaith directly," he said. "You're on your own from here on out. Find my daughter, Richter. Make certain she and my grandchildren are safe, and then see to it that the creature who abducted them pays for his crime. Varney, you're with us."

Galm then burst apart into a flock of shadow bats and headed toward Talaith. The Witch Queen let out a cry of frustrated fury and started slinging energy bolts as the king of the Bloodborn came for her.

"I'm sorry," Varney said. "But I must do as my lord commands. Good luck to you both."

He assumed his whirlwind form and flew off to join the fight, and his curseweave hazmat suit, now empty, collapsed to floor next to us.

As tempting as it was to watch a battle between Bloodborn and Arcane, not to mention two Darklords, I tore my gaze away from the action above us. Shamika and I still had work to do.

I looked at Varvara. The Demon Queen's gaze

remained glassy, her face expressionless. Galm had said she was fighting to throw off Gregor's mental control, but there was no outward sign of her efforts. I had no idea how long it would take, but I doubted we could count on Varvara to regain control of her body in time to help us.

I forgot about Varvara and turned to Shamika. "Where's Gregor at?" I asked her. "He has to be using some kind of machine to transport Nekropolis to Earth. Where is it?"

"I don't know!" she said. "I told you, I searched throughout the city for the missing Arcane, but I wasn't able to find a single trace of them, and I didn't find any dimension-shifting machinery during my search either."

"Maybe he's hidden the machine using magic," I said. "Or maybe he's located it underground some-where." But neither of those possibilities felt right to me. A thought was nagging at the back of my mind, one that I couldn't quite catch hold of. I pictured the way Gregor had stood after he'd absorbed Talaith's magic strike. He'd pointed the lightning rod toward the sky and unleashed the bolt into the darkness. I remembered what he'd said just before doing it.

Now, if you'll all excuse me for a moment, I need to transfer this.

He'd sent Talaith's energy to the machine, wherever that was. And I was certain he had another body there to run the show from that end. How long would it take for him to put Talaith's power to work and begin transporting the city to Earth, this time permanently? Not long, I feared, and we had no idea where he was. If only I could think…

Once more I felt the sensation of my missing hand moving, only it felt different this time, kind of tingly. I looked down at the stump protruding from my right arm, and I was surprised to see my hand reappear right where it belonged, attached more or less firmly to my body. My fingers were clenched into a fist, and when I opened them I saw that I was clutching a small metal disk. I grinned. It was a reverser! Somehow Devona had gotten hold of my hand and used one of the magic disks to reverse Gregor's teleportation spell, sending my hand back to where it was taken from: my wrist. But why hadn't she used the reverser to send herself back too? Why just my hand?

And then I saw that my palm was marred by thin lines, and I remembered feeling a sensation of pressure on my hand a while ago, almost as if someone were cutting into it. I pulled away the reverser with my other hand and held up my palm so I could examine it more closely. There, cut into the flesh – with Devona's teeth, I guessed – was a single word.

Ulterion.

I grinned from ear to ear.

"I love that woman."

EIGHTEEN

"I've never flown this high before. It's fun!"

"Not exactly the first word that leaps to my mind," I said. "Terrifying, maybe. Hazardous, certainly. But fun? I don't think so."

Shamika had reshaped herself into something that resembled a large black moth, and I sat on her back, clutching two fleshy handles she'd created at the base of her head for me to grip. Her fan-like wings beat the air with forceful strokes as we soared through the darkness above Nekropolis, the city spread out below us like a child's toy. A dark, twisted child, that is. While the Sprawl, Gothtown, and the Boneyard are the most urban Dominions, only the first two had enough lights burning to cut through the darkness. The Boneyard is the realm of the Dead, and they have no need of street-lights to illuminate their way. Glamere and the Wyldwood are both pastoral for the most part, but even they had fires dotting the landscape here and there. The most light, of course, came from the mystic energies released in the continuing battle between the Bloodborn and Arcane in the air over Demon's Roost. I wondered how the fight would turn out. If Galm and his vampire soldiers could keep Talaith and her people busy long enough for Varvara to regain control of herself, then the Demon Queen could join in and repel Talaith. Otherwise, there was a chance that when – if – I returned home to the Sprawl, I might find it under new management. That is, assuming Gregor didn't succeed in relocating the whole damn city to Earth.

Umbriel the Shadowsun hung in the air off to our left, and we were almost even with it. Umbriel is an artificial construct, created by Dis and the Darklords to help maintain Nekropolis in this dimension, as well as provide the city's atmosphere and the power for Phlegethon. As such, it's not located off in space, as is the case with Earth's sun, and it's much smaller than Sol. But as for where Ulterion was located, I had no idea. There was a reason it was called the Hidden Moon, after all. We'd started out in the general direction in which we'd seen Gregor release the mystic power he'd gathered from Talaith, and Shamika had told me that if we got close enough, she should be able to sense her brother's presence. But so far we'd had no luck. I'd hoped that if we drew near Ulterion we might be able to spot it visually, but the sky above Nekropolis is totally and completely black, with no stars to provide illumination. Umbriel is a sort of grayish color that makes it easy enough to see against the darkness, and I'd hoped Ulterion might look similar, but if it did, I couldn't see it.

As we flew, I thought of what Ichorus had told me
in the Fever House, how he'd been searching for Ulterion and been blasted with some kind of energy ray. I
wished I'd questioned him then, for it was obvious
now that he'd come close to stumbling across Gregor's
operation and triggered some kind of defense system.
Ichorus had been lucky to survive with only a few
scorched feathers. If Shamika was unable to sense Gregor, and we couldn't spot Ulterion visually, my last
hope was that we might repeat Ichorus' mistake and–

Light flared in the darkness ahead, and a beam of energy lanced toward us. I tried to warn Shamika to brace
herself, but I wasn't able to get the words out in time.
I closed my eyes and gritted my teeth as energy crackled around us and then dissipated harmlessly. I opened
my eyes, only mildly surprised that Shamika and I
hadn't been burned to a crisp. It seemed the Coat of
Every Color had once again done its job and shielded
us from Gregor's energy blast.

"I see it now!" Shamika said, and she banked right,
her wings beating faster, and we surged forward at increased speed.

I didn't see anything, but then my zombie eyes
aren't any better than the ones I had when I was alive.
Shamika was an alien creature, and I had no idea exactly how her senses worked, but if she said she saw
Ulterion, I believed her. A moment later I was finally
able to make out a dark shape of an orb, black against
the black sky behind it. I couldn't tell how large it was,
for there was nothing nearby to lend perspective, but

I guessed that while it was a far smaller version of the satellite that orbited Earth, it was at least big enough for Gregor's dimension-shifting machine.

Gregor didn't bother firing his energy ray at us again. He learned fast – information was his stock in trade, after all – and he probably needed all the power he could get to make his machine work. Why waste it on us if the Coat of Every Color would just repel his attacks? So Shamika and I were able to approach Ulterion without any more trouble, and she descended to the surface of the Hidden Moon and landed with surprising gentleness for someone who'd just completed her first flight.

I climbed off and stood on wobbly legs. My physical condition had little to do with how nervous I'd been during our flight and everything to do with how difficult it was for me to keep my various body parts together. The cohesion spell that Papa Chatha had cast on me was close to wearing off, and when it finally failed, I'd collapse into a pile of useless pieces. If we were going to stop Gregor, we had to do it fast.

I looked around, but it was like standing in the middle of a deep cave without any light source. I could sense the solid weight of Ulterion beneath my feet and feel its rocky surface under my shoes, but I couldn't see a damn thing.

"It's OK," Shamika said. "I'll lead you."

Ulterion, like Umbriel, lay within the atmospheric bubble that encloses Nekropolis, so even though we were technically standing on the surface of a moon, there was air to transmit our voices, even if neither of us needed it to breathe.

Shamika took my hand with human-seeming fingers, and I knew she'd once more taken the form of a teenage girl. She started walking, and I went with her, moving with the spastic jerky motions that were all I was capable of. Shamika surely noticed my awkward movements, but she said nothing about them.

"There's a dome a few hundred feet in front of us," Shamika said. "It looks like Gregor created it from Ulterion's substance."

I imagined hundreds of insects scuttling over the moon's dark surface, tearing chunks out of the ground and refashioning them bit by bit into a dome to hide Gregor's machinery. "Can you see anything that looks like an entrance?"

"I doubt there is one," she said. "Gregor used teleportation magic to bring the magic-users here, remember? It's probably how he moved his equipment in as well. But don't worry. I'll be able to get us inside."

With every step we took, I anticipated an attack by a horde of insects, but none came. I still wore the Coat of Every Color and carried the Dreamthrower, and I had the Herald Bells and the *osame-fuda* gun tucked into my pockets. Maybe Gregor knew his insects couldn't stand against the holy weapons. Or maybe he had another reason for not attacking us. Whatever it was, I knew I wouldn't like it. Gregor always stacked the deck in his favor.

I sensed the dome ahead of us rather than seeing it, but I still would've bumped into it if Shamika hadn't

stopped me. Before either of us could say or do anything, a tiny pinprick of light appeared in the surface
of the dome before us. It quickly widened as a semicir-
cular door formed, spilling greenish light onto the
moon's dark surface.

I could see Shamika's face now, and she was frowning.

"I was wrong," she said. "Gregor didn't make the dome
out of Ulterion's substance. He made it out of his own."

I looked at Shamika. "Welcome to my parlor, said
the spider to the fly."

She gave me a confused look, and I said, "Means
we're expected. Shall we?"

We stepped inside, and I didn't bother to check if the
entrance sealed shut behind us. I knew it would.

Greenfire torches were set in sconces around the inside of the dome, providing illumination. The mystic
flames were set to burn at a low level, and I remembered how Gregor had once told me that since the
Watchers were native to this dark dimension, intense
light could hurt them. Too bad I hadn't asked Maggie
to loan me one of the Hidden Light's illuminaries.

The inside of the dome was fashioned from the same
dark substance as the outside, and it creeped me out to
think that in a sense I was standing inside Gregor. In
the middle of the dome stood a circle of men and
women, all of them mired in black goo that stretched
from the floor and covered them up to their waists.
Their hands and arms had been left free, but since each
of them stared blankly into space, their facial features
slack, I knew they were under Gregor's control. They

were the missing magic-users, and I was relieved to see
Papa Chatha among them, though I hated seeing my
old friend held in this trance-like state. The magic-users
faced inward, gazing sightlessly at each other, connected by black wires attached to metal bands around
their heads.

In the middle of the circle lay Darius. He was covered
by a cocoon of black goo up to his neck, and he was
clearly in a trance as well. Like the magic-users, his
arms were free, and they lay folded over his chest.
Clutched in his hands was another metal lightning rod,
a twin to the one Gregor's General Klamm body had
used to transmit Talaith's captured power. The rod
pulsed with yellowish light, and there was a feeling of
barely restrained energy in the air, like a storm that
might erupt any moment. Darius also had a metal band
around his head with wires protruding from it, but instead of being connected to the circle of magic-users,
his wires stretched across the floor, out of the circle and
over to a bank of computer consoles set up near one
section of the wall. The equipment was extremely
high-tech and reminded me of the holographic display
table in Varvara's war room. This was a different con-
figuration of machinery, but there was no mistaking
how advanced it was.

Gregor stood outside the circle. The real Gregor, or
at least the giant insect guise familiar to me from years
of going to him for information: a human-sized roach
standing upright on a quartet of segmented legs, obsidian gems in place of eyes, antennae in constant

motion as they greedily drank in all sensory data in his vicinity. And standing next to Gregor, mired in the same black gunk that imprisoned the abducted magic-users, was Devona.

"It's about time you got here," she said, smiling.

The relief I felt upon seeing my love alive was so strong it nearly knocked me to my knees.

"Sorry it took so long," I said. "We ran into a few problems along the way."

"Don't you always?" Devona said.

I held up my right hand with the word *Ulterion* scratched into the palm. "Thanks for the message. But one thing puzzles me: how did you hide my hand from Gregor?"

"It hid itself," she said. "As soon as we arrived, it scuttled off behind the computer banks and stayed there until Gregor was busy, then it crawled back over to me. I had the idea to scratch a message into it with my teeth, and then I put a reverser in it and watched it teleport back to you." Devona turned to Gregor. "You really should've kept me in a trance, you know. Or at least searched me and taken the reverser away before I could use it."

Gregor shrugged, the motion looking awkward on his insectile body. "Once I brought you here, I knew there was nothing you could do to stop me, so I didn't bother keeping you entranced or searching you. I admit the latter was a mistake." He paused. "But I found it oddly... gratifying to have someone conscious to bear witness as my plan unfolded."

Shamika's tone held a note of triumph. "Are you telling us you found it pleasing to have someone to talk with? That you actually took satisfaction in contact with an Other?"

Gregor whirled around to face his sister and let out an angry hiss. "Do not insult me! I have not been infected with the madness that plagues you!"

Shamika's satisfied smile said that she thought otherwise, but she didn't say anything.

"I'm confused," I said. "I thought you abducted Devona because you wanted to use the magic our children possess. But she's not hooked up to anything."

"That's because your surmise is incorrect," Gregor said. "It may well be true that your progeny possess significant potential to wield magic, but I have no use for it. I have all the magic power I need right here." Gregor pointed toward the ground with one of his insect arms. "Earth's dimension is rich in magical energy, but there's little in this realm, so Dis and the Darklords needed to create a source of mystic power for their people to draw upon once they moved to Nekropolis. Ulterion is the source of that power, and all of Nekropolis' magic-using Darkfolk use it – including Dis and the Darklords – even if most Darkfolk are unaware of precisely where the power comes from. The Darklords prefer that no one knows where this power comes from, which is why the moon is hidden and its existence kept secret. They'd rather someone not attempt to use Ulterion's magic for his or her own purposes – such as transporting the city to Earth." Gregor's roach-like face didn't possess the physiognomy to smile, but I could hear the grin in his voice as he said this last part.

I looked down at the ground beneath my feet. "Ulterion is a gigantic magic generator?" I said. I understood then why no one in Nekropolis, including the Darklords, had been able to magically track the missing magic-users. Ulterion's energy field had hidden them from everyone's mystic perceptions. I looked at the circle of entranced witches and warlocks. "If the moon is your power source, what do you need them for?"

Devona answered. "To safely channel Talaith's power into Darius, which will allow him to draw on Ulterion's energy without being destroyed. Darius will then become capable of opening an immense dimensional portal and shifting all of Nekropolis to Earth."

"And the computer equipment?" I asked.

Gregor answered that one. "Is for dimensional targeting. Like the magic-users, I need to keep Darius in a trance in order to control him. One of my insects burrowed into his brain is sufficient for that task. Unfortunately, Darius isn't fully capable of precise targeting in his current state, and while the insect inside him *is* me, I do not have his instinct for interdimensional travel. So I need technology to help me guide Nekropolis' transference to Earth."

"So if the equipment was destroyed…" I began.

"It would make no difference ultimately," Gregor said. "I might not be able to shift Nekropolis to Earth, but I would still be able to send it out of this dimension, which is all that truly matters to me. I have no idea where the city would end up in that case, but I don't care, just as long as the hated Others are gone."

"So Darius is the key to your entire plan," I said. "Without him, you cannot use Ulterion to open a large enough portal to send Nekropolis away."

"Indeed," Gregor confirmed.

"And if you don't need the twins' magic, Devona is here for... what?" I asked.

"Insurance," Gregor said.

More of the black substance that formed the dome – *Gregor's* substance – flowed up Devona's body until she was covered all the way to the neck. The ebon gunk hardened around her throat and took on the shape of a mouth filled with sharp black teeth.

"All it will take is a single thought, and the mouth will snap shut, instantly decapitating Devona," Gregor said, sounding smug. "A full Bloodborn might be able to recover from such a severe injury, assuming someone quickly put their head back in place and gave them enough fresh blood to drink. But for a half-human/half-vampire, decapitation would prove fatal."

"And you'll kill her if I try to stop you," I said.

"Yes. Once I became aware you were searching for Papa Chatha – at the urging of my sister–" he added, shooting Shamika a glance, "–I knew there was a chance you might uncover my plan. I did my best to destroy you, but you have an irritating habit of finding ways to survive, and so I decided to abduct Devona to give me leverage in case you managed to reach Ulterion. And here we are. If you want Devona to live, you will stand by and do nothing while I shift Nekropolis to Earth."

"You know I can't do that, Gregor." I couldn't look at Devona as I said these words, even though I could feel through our psychic link that she agreed with me. "If Nekropolis materializes on Earth, the loss of life will be staggering, for both Darkfolk and humans."

"Perhaps," Gregor said. "I really don't care. Just as long as I am alone once more." The longing in his voice was profound. "Consider this: once the transference is complete, I will send you and Devona through to Earth as well. You'll at least have a fighting chance to survive there. And all you need to do is stand by and do nothing."

Devona looked at me. *Don't even think about it!*

But of course I did think about it. I loved Devona more than I'd ever loved anyone in my life. And our children… I wanted so much to see them born, to discover what I would be like as a father, to watch my kids grow into the amazing people I knew they would become. My son, my daughter… how could I sentence them to death before they were even born? But then I thought about all the people who'd die if I let Gregor complete his insane plan. How could I allow that to happen? Could I live with all these deaths on my conscience?

I turned to Shamika. "Think you're faster than Gregor?" I whispered.

"I don't know," she whispered back.

"You'd better be."

I drew my 9mm with my recently restored right hand, took aim at Darius' head, and fired.

Gregor cried out in surprise as a mixture of blood and brains sprayed from the top of Darius' head, leaving the Sideways Man very dead. In that same instant Shamika transformed into a cloud of flying black insects which streaked toward Devona. Once there she resumed her human shape, grabbed hold of the ebon mouth Gregor had formed and, with a strength that belied her guise as a teenage girl, she tore Gregor's black substance away from Devona's body, freeing her.

Gregor seemed not to pay attention. He was staring at Darius' messy corpse, and though his insect face wasn't capable of expression, his attitude was one of total bewilderment.

"You bad guys should never explain how your shit works," I said. "It just makes it easier for us good guys to fuck it up."

Gregor continued staring at Darius' body. "I can't believe you did that." He turned his gaze upon me then. "I never imagined you were that cold-blooded."

I smiled grimly. "I'm a zombie, remember? My blood's as cold as it gets."

Through our psychic link, I could feel that Devona was shaken by what I'd done, but she was trying her best not to let it get to her.

Enough talking, lover, she thought to me. *Let's tear Gregor apart!*

Fangs bared, she leaped for Gregor at the same instant I raised the Dreamthrower, intending to release a horde of Nightmares to attack him. But I'd forgotten that the dome we were in was made of Gregor's substance. Pseudopods extruded from the floor and ceiling and snatched us both. Devona was suspended in mid-leap, and my arm was yanked from its socket before I was able to release even a single Nightmare from the Dreamthrower. The arm had barely been attached anyway, and it came off as easily as the leg of a well-done roast turkey.

Black coils of Gregor-stuff wrapped around my neck, ankles, and the wrist of the hand that remained attached to my body. I didn't struggle. I could feel myself coming apart at the seams, and I knew if I resisted the tentacles' embrace too strongly, I'd collapse into a heap of useless body parts. Devona was caught in a nest of tentacles that hung down from the ceiling, and though she thrashed to free herself, even tried to bite through the tentacles with her fangs, she was unable to make a dent in the gooey shadowy substance that held her.

I still held my 9mm, but I knew mere bullets wouldn't kill Gregor. They wouldn't even slow him down.

"You haven't stopped me, you know," Gregor said. He spoke calmly, or rather like someone who was working very hard to sound calm. "I might not be able to shift Nekropolis to another dimension now, but I still have the power of Talaith stored in Victor Baron's lightning rod. Perhaps I'll use it to destroy Ulterion and deprive the Darkfolk of their magic. Or better yet, I'll use it to put the moon into motion and crash it into Umbriel. Without the Shadowsun, Nekropolis won't be able to survive in my dimension. And even if those plans fail, what does it matter? I'll just keep on trying until I *do* succeed! Nothing will stop me! Nothing!"

"You're wrong," I said.

Gregor scuttled over to me so rapidly that it seemed he teleported across the distance. Alarmed, Shamika assumed an insectile form like his and started toward him, obviously intending to protect me, but I shook my head. She stopped, hesitated a moment, and then returned to her human form.

Gregor leaned in close until his giant roach face was only inches from mine.

"What do you mean?" he asked softly.

"You can't succeed for one simple reason," I said. "You've already lost. You told us that after you teleported Devona here, you released her from her trance because you saw no need to keep her in it. But then you said you found it, and I quote, 'oddly gratifying' to have someone watch as you put your plan into action. You hate Otherness, Gregor. So why would you enjoy having someone else here with you while you worked?"

Gregor's gem-like eyes were impossible to read, so I went on.

"And what about my hand?" I said.

Gregor cocked his head, puzzled. "What about it?"

"My severed hand, the one you accidentally teleported along with Devona. Once it got here, it hid itself until you were distracted, and then Devona was able to use it to send me a message."

"So?"

I said, "So how was that possible? And I don't mean the animated severed-hand part. I admit that's weird, but I know I can exert some control over my body parts once they've been separated from me, and I guess they have a life of their own, at least in some small ways. What I'm talking about is how could anything take place inside this dome without your knowledge? This place is made from your body, right? It *is* you. So how could you not be aware my severed hand was skulking about?"

Gregor didn't say anything at first, but he shifted his weight back and forth several times, as if he were agitated and trying not to show it.

"I've been rather busy, you know." He sounded more than a little defensive. "You can't possibly imagine the magical and technological complexity of dimensional transference. The concentration required to get all the calculations just right..." He trailed off, sounding unconvinced by his own words.

"You're a group mind, Gregor," I reminded him. "You've got more mental capacity than all the Darkfolk combined. And yet you failed to notice my hand. Why?"

Gregor had no answer for that, so I answered for him.

"It's because your mind isn't clear. You're not thinking straight. I mean, why did you bother explaining your plan once Shamika and I got here? Why did you answer all the questions I asked you? I'll tell you why: because you wanted us to appreciate how smart you are. You've spent so much time observing Others, Gregor, that you've changed. Maybe you haven't changed

as much as Shamika, but like her, you've become infected by Otherness. You've begun to appreciate it, to
need it. And because of that, your emotions are beginning to override your intellect, interfering with it and
clouding your thinking. And there's no going back to
the way you were. Even if you got rid of the Darkfolk,
even if you somehow managed to get rid of Shamika,
some part of you would still long for Otherness. You
wouldn't just be alone. You'd be *lonely*. Forever."

Gregor continued to stare at me with his black gem-
like eyes for a long time. But eventually he turned away,
and when he did, the tentacles that were holding onto
Devona and me released us and slithered back into the
walls and floor. Gregor walked several feet away, sat
down heavily, and hung his head. Shamika looked at
him for a moment before going over and sitting down
next to him. She then put an arm around her brother
and leaned against his ebon carapace. Then, as we
watched, their two forms merged into one large amorphous black mass. The mass reformed, shrinking as it
did so, until it became Shamika. Only this version of
Shamika had Gregor's black gem-like eyes.

She smiled. "We're One again."

Devona came over to me then and put her arms
around me. I only had one arm at that moment – the
other lay on the floor where Gregor's tentacle had
tossed it – but I wrapped it around her and hugged her
as tight as I could.

A moment later there was a shimmering in the air
next to the circle of magic-users, all of whom were just

beginning to stir from their trance. Darius materialized and gazed down upon his dead body.

"I *thought* I felt someone shoot me," he said.

NINETEEN

I watched myself walk down the street, a black silhouette melting into the darkness around me.

And so it goes. Another case ended, and another waiting for me somewhere up the road. And though I was victorious, I felt nothing, for what had I really accomplished in the end? Sure, I'd tilted at a few windmills and saw to it that some very bad people got what was coming to them. But no matter how many cases I solve, no matter how many wrongs I right, at the end of the day I'm still a dead man playing at being alive – and that's all I'll ever be.

I'm Matt Richter, zombie PI. And my story continues... though sometimes I wish it didn't.

The Mind's Eye screen went blank, the orb closed its lid, and Devona clapped.

"I thought that was pretty good," she said.

I leaned back on the couch, looked up at the ceiling, and sighed. "I can't believe Varney finished that stupid film. This has to be the most embarrassing thing that's ever happened to me."

Devona scooted closer and put her arms around me. "More embarrassing than the time you accidentally switched bodies with Esperanza the Six-Breasted Stripper in the middle of one of her performances?"

"Much," I said. "I just pray Varney's producer doesn't get it in his head to do a sequel."

Once Devona learned who Varney really was, Galm ordered him to return to his job as a cameraman since his cover was blown and he could no longer guard Devona in secret. Devona hadn't been thrilled with the fact that her father had assigned a babysitter to watch over her, but she'd been impressed with Varney's skills and was considering asking him to leave Galm's employ and come to work for her at the Midnight Watch. One thing about my love: she doesn't hold a grudge, at least not where business is concerned. She still, however, wasn't happy that we'd had to return the holy objects the Hidden Light had loaned us. As powerful as the objects were, we could've made good use of them in our work, but I'd promised Maggie I'd return them, and a deal is a deal. Besides, I needed to stay on the Hidden Light's good side. Where else in this town am I going to get holy water and silver bullets? Plus, I can use all the good karma I can get.

Despite Devona's anger at Galm for sending one of his servants to guard her, she'd begun talking with him again, and while I doubted they'd ever be close – Galm wasn't exactly Father of the Year material – they were no longer quite as estranged as they'd been. I didn't trust him, and I knew Devona didn't either, but if she wanted to try to repair the rift between them, I would support her. He *had* come when Varney called, and without his help, we'd never have stopped Gregor. That counted for something. But I still planned to keep a close eye on the sonofabitch.

Devona hugged me tight, but there was no danger of my falling apart at the seams any more. My body was once again in good shape, thanks to Papa Chatha. After all the magic-users had been freed from Gregor's trance and the insects inside their heads removed, we'd all returned to the city. Once Papa was back in his place, he immediately saw to shoring up the cohesion spells that were keeping my body together, and he reattached my severed arm and fixed the acid-scarring on my face. All at no charge, which I thought was damn decent of him. I should rescue him more often.

Devona and I sat on the couch in our apartment, a number of cardboard boxes stacked against the wall behind us. Devona must've noticed me looking at them, for she said, "You going to miss this place? It's been your home since you first came to Nekropolis."

I looked around the living room, but the only memories of the apartment that came to my mind involved Devona.

I shook my head. "This place is just a few cramped rooms. It only became a home once you moved in."

She cuddled closer to me. "Good answer, Mr Richter."

Tomorrow Scorch, Bogdan, and a fully healed Tavi were going to show up and help us move our stuff into the Midnight Watch. I wasn't sure what it was going to be like living there, especially with the others around all the time. But if our children were going to be as magically gifted as Galm and Varvara thought they'd be, we needed a safe place to raise them, someplace where it would be harder for anyone who wanted to exploit their power to get at them. And since Devona still refused to accept her father's invitation to move into the Cathedral – a decision I wholeheartedly supported – the Midnight Watch seemed like our best alternative.

"I'm glad you approve, Mrs Richter."

Varvara had been so grateful for our part in exposing Klamm's true identity and ending the war between her and Talaith that, when she discovered Devona and I wanted to get officially married, she'd insisted on performing the ceremony herself – and more to the point, hosting the party afterward. Being a Darklord made Varvara one of the six highest authorities in this dimension, so she was as qualified to marry us as anyone else in the city. Besides, the true marriage between Devona and myself had taken place in our hearts. The ceremony was just an outward way to honor that commitment in front of friends and family. And I had to admit, Varvara threw one *hell* of a celebration for us afterward. It had been over a week, and I'd heard there were still people struggling to recover from their hangovers.

A small voice somewhere close by said, "I liked the movie too."

We turned and saw a roach-like insect clinging to the wall behind us. It quivered under our combined gaze as if frightened, but it didn't flee.

"Hi, Shamika," Devona said, speaking gently. "How are you doing?"

"Good," the insect said, still keeping its distance. "The two halves of my consciousness have finished merging mostly, but I'm still having trouble adjusting to my new personality. I'm sorry I haven't been around much. I mean, I've been *around*, of course. I just haven't been very... social. I hope you understand."

"Of course we do," Devona said. "We enjoy seeing you whenever you feel up to visiting. Isn't that right, Matt?"

"Yep." A zombie of few words, that's me.

After Shamika and Gregor merged on Ulterion, they'd returned to Nekropolis as one being, and eventually their change was passed on to every component of the Watchers throughout the city and beyond. Now all the Watchers were One, and that One was a combination of Gregor and Shamika. Gregor had hated and feared Otherness, and Shamika had been fascinated by it. The new personality that resulted from their merging liked Others well enough, but was shy around them, unsure how and when to interact. As such, Shamika – for the Watchers had chosen to be known by that name from now on – remained hidden in the shadows for the most part. But she no longer wanted to destroy Nekropolis and get rid of the Darkfolk, and with every passing day she seemed to – you'll pardon the expression – be coming out of her shell more. She'd even showed up in her teenage girl guise briefly at our wedding, just long enough to have a dance with me. She'd also taken to helping out around town. She'd already helped finish the reconstruction of the two bridges the Weyward Sisters had destroyed, and she was currently aiding in the reconstruction of the top level of Demon's Roost.

Darius – at least the version of him that appeared on Ulterion – bore me no ill will for shooting one of his selves. I'd known something that Gregor, for all his skills at gathering information, hadn't: one of the things that allows Darius to traverse dimensions is because, in a sense, he's a hive mind like Shamika, one consciousness spread across the entire Omniverse. Killing one aspect of him was akin to a human losing a toe. Painful and inconvenient, but not life-altering. Darius had offered to take Shamika to another dimension where the Darkfolk had never left Earth and where no other Watchers already existed, a place where she could be completely alone if she wished. He warned that it would take him a while to transport all of her, considering that her consciousness was contained in trillions of separate bodies, but he was willing to do it if she wanted. She'd considered his offer, but in the end she'd chosen to remain in Nekropolis. I was glad. A city of monsters just wouldn't seem complete without hordes of intelligent insects crawling around in the shadows. And, truth to tell, while I was glad Gregor's personality was no more, I'd grown more than a little fond of Shamika.

"Forgive me for snooping," Shamika said, "but I was in your bedroom a minute ago, and I saw you haven't packed up your computer yet."

Our laptop computer was a prime example of Victor Baron's flesh-tech: constructed from skin, bone, muscle, and specially designed organs, it lived, breathed, and moaned in complaint whenever asked to do even moderately complex tasks. Devona spoiled the damn thing rotten, which was why it wasn't packed up with our other belongings yet. She'd said she didn't want to hurt its feelings by sealing it away in a box and letting it sit there overnight. Me? I'd have been happy to leave it out on the curb with a sign that said FREE TO A GOOD HOME (OR EVEN A BAD ONE, JUST AS LONG AS YOU TAKE THE STUPID THING!).

Shamika continued. "Would you come into the bedroom with me? There's something I want to show you on the computer. I've been experimenting with uploading my consciousness to the Aethernet, and I think I've succeeded." She paused, and I could hear the girlish smile in her voice when she added, almost shyly, "I'm my own website!"

Devona looked at me and raised an eyebrow. In return, I shrugged. Shamika was an alien creature, and we didn't understand exactly how her hive-mind consciousness worked. Maybe she didn't have to confine herself to a strictly physical existence. But it did make me wonder. Nekropolis' Aethernet is connected to Earth's Internet via some kind of interdimensional connection, and if Shamika – or at least part of her – now existed on the virtual plane... well, the folks back home on Earth might be in for a surprise the next time they logged onto their computers.

"That sounds awesome!" Devona said. "Show me!" She held out her hand toward Shamika. The insect hesitated, then hopped onto the back of Devona's hand, skittered up her arm, and perched on her shoulder.

"Coming?" Devona asked me.

"I better not," I said. "Yesterday I tried to get the computer to open a new spreadsheet program I set up for client billing, and we, ah, had a disagreement." I held up my hand to show the scorch marks from where the computer had shocked me.

Devona laughed, and the insect on her shoulder giggled. Devona then stood and carried Shamika with her to the bedroom.

I settled back on the couch and mentally commanded our Mind's Eye set to tune into a razorball game between the Black Talons and the Intercity Manglers, but the set's eyelid remained stubbornly shut. I tried again, but the Mind's Eye still refused to cooperate. I was starting to wonder if the set was broken, when I heard a voice next to me.

"Don't bother. Not only will the Manglers continue their losing streak, it's going to be a dull game. Only three fatalities, none of them permanent."

I turned to see Father Dis sitting on the couch next to me.

"I know you're an ancient Roman god, so you might not know this, but there's a new concept these days called a 'spoiler.' It's generally considered good manners to avoid them."

Dis' lips stretched into a small, thin smile. "I'll try to remember that. I *did* see a very amusing program recently. It was a documentary about a tortured dead man trying to bring a tiny bit of justice to a city of unrelenting evil and darkness."

I groaned.

"Would you like me to tell you how many people watched it?" Dis asked.

"I don't want to know. I just hope everyone forgets about it – and me – eventually."

"There's little chance of that. You stopped a war between two Darklords and helped us make peace with the Watchers. If you thought you were well known before…"

I sighed. "At least Devona will be happy. The publicity will be good for business. And speaking of Devona…" I turned to look in the direction of the bedroom.

"Neither she nor Shamika can hear us talking," Dis said. "I've seen to that." He smiled. "Even if I hadn't, they're having too much fun playing with Shamika's website to pay any attention to us."

"So what's the situation with the Darklords?" I asked. "Talaith didn't show up at our wedding, even though Varvara invited her. Despite my objections, I might add."

"Most of the Darklords try not to hold grudges. Given how long we live and how often we come into conflict, we'd never get anything done if we stayed mad at one another. But not Talaith." He shook his head. "Sometimes I think she lives to hold grudges. But to answer your question, she's keeping to herself these days, overseeing the restoration of the Greensward and layering it with even stronger protective spells than it possessed before. She did lodge a formal complaint with me against Varvara and Galm, and while I'm sure she'll seek revenge on both of them at some point, I expect her to behave herself for the time being. So the balance of power in the city remains intact, and I have you to thank for that, Matt."

I said, "Gratitude is good, but unfortunately you can't spend it."

"My staff made a deposit into your bank account this morning, and I think you'll find the sum more than acceptable. Thank you once again for your service to the city, Matt."

Shadows began to coalesce around Dis, and I knew he was about to dematerialize.

"One moment," I said.

The shadows paused, then slowly flowed back to the corners of the room.

"Yes?" Dis said.

"You didn't tell me the full truth when you spoke with me at Papa Chatha's, did you? I saw the way you looked at Shamika. You knew who and what she was, but you didn't say anything to me about it."

"I was confident you'd figure it out on your own eventually."

I said, "That's not it. You wanted my help to avert a war, but it wasn't a war between Talaith and Varvara you were worried about, was it? It was a war between Gregor and Shamika – or maybe between the Darkfolk and the Watchers."

Dis looked at me with cold, impassive eyes, but he didn't contradict me.

"You didn't want Shamika to know you'd talked to me. That's the real reason you froze everyone at Papa Chatha's, and why you're concealing our conversation from Devona and Shamika now. You don't want her to feel manipulated – even though she was."

Dis looked at me a moment longer before letting out a soft sigh. It was a sigh full of weariness, long centuries of it, and hearing it made me feel for a moment as old as Time itself.

"The Darklords and I made a mistake when we chose this dimension as the location to build Nekropolis," Dis began. "It's ironic, but we were fleeing from the persecution by humanity, and by building our city here, we ended up doing the same thing humans have done so often throughout their long, sad history: colonizing a land already inhabited by others... a land where we were not welcome. As powerful as we Darkfolk are, I knew we could never win against the Watchers. There were simply too many of them. And abandoning the city and starting over in another dimension just wasn't practical. So when I became aware that not only was Gregor still alive, but he'd fragmented into two separate personalities, I decided that you were the city's best hope for dealing with the Watchers."

"Me? What did you think I could do?"

Dis smiled. "In case you hadn't noticed, you have a knack for finding unorthodox solutions to problems. More to the point, you've kept your humanity, despite having become one more monster in a city filled with them. I knew if anyone could help the Watchers discover the better part of their nature, it would be you."

"If I had a functioning circulatory system, I might blush," I said. After a moment's thought, I added, "And despite your insistence that you couldn't interfere, it strikes me as awfully convenient that my severed hand was able to operate so effectively on its own, and that Gregor should be completely oblivious to it. You didn't perhaps secretly use a little of your power to make that happen, did you?"

Dis' silence answered for him.

"You know, you might be the Lord of all the Darkfolk, the biggest, baddest horror in a city full of foul creatures and evil fiends, but deep down you're not so bad."

Dis' eyes clouded over with shadow until they were completely black, like a shark's, and when he spoke next, his voice was as cold as the grave.

"Don't be mistaken, Matt. I care only about my people's welfare, and I'll do whatever it takes to protect them. If I had to slaughter a million innocents to preserve the Darkfolk, I'd do it, and without a moment's hesitation. In this case, it just so happened that peace was the most logical and efficient solution."

I looked into the deep black eyes of a being so ancient and powerful that he could destroy me with a single thought.

"Bullshit," I said.

In reply Dis just smiled, gathered the shadows around him, and was gone.

I sat there a bit longer, trying to decide if it was worth watching the razorball game even though I knew how it was going to turn out, but in the end I decided to get up and go into the bedroom and check out Shamika's website.

But before I could stand, the Mind's Eye opened its lid of its own accord, and an image appeared in my mind. It was Lord Edrigu. He looked to the right and then the left, as if making sure we were alone. There was a nervous, almost desperate energy in his movements, and his eyes looked, appropriately enough, haunted.

"Is Dis gone? Good. Listen closely, Matt. I have to leave Nekropolis. Immediately. Until I return, I need you to fill in for me. As of this moment, you're Lord of the Dead."

Edrigu vanished, and the Mind's Eye closed its lid as the transmission ended.

I sat there for several moments, staring at the deactivated set, and then finally, I cleared my throat and called out in a strained voice.

"Devona? Honey? There's something I need to tell you."

ABOUT THE AUTHOR

Tim Waggoner is an American novelist and college professor. His original novels include *Cross County*, *Darkness Wakes*, *Pandora Drive*, and *Like Death*. His tie-in novels include *The Lady Ruin* series and the *Blade of the Flame* trilogy, both for Wizards of the Coast. He's also written fiction based on *Stargate: SG-1*, *Doctor Who*, *A Nightmare on Elm Street*, the videogame *Defender*, *Xena the Warrior Princess*, and others. He's published over one hundred short stories, some of which are collected in *Broken Shadows* and *All Too Surreal*. His articles on writing have appeared in *Writer's Digest*, *Writers' Journal* and other publications.

He teaches composition and creative writing at Sinclair Community College in Dayton, Ohio, and is a faculty mentor in Seton Hill Univerity's Master of Arts in Writing Popular Fiction program in Greensburg, Pennsylvania.

www.timwaggoner.com

TIM WAGGONER

Introducing
Matt Richter.

Private Eye.

Zombie.

Nekropolis

TIM WAGGONER

Dead Streets

Matt Richter. Private Eye. Zombie

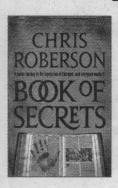

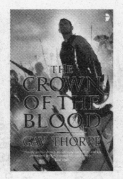